THE NAKED TRUTH

The Naked Truth

DONNA KAUFFMAN

BEVERLY BRANDT

ALESIA HOLLIDAY

ERIN McCARTHY

BERKLEY SENSATION, NEW YORK

THE BERKLEY PUBLISHING GROUP
Published by the Penguin Group
Penguin Group (USA) Inc.
375 Hudson Street, New York, New York 10014, USA
Penguin Group (Canada), 90 Eglinton Avenue East, Suite 700, Toronto, Ontario M4P 2Y3, Canada
(a division of Pearson Penguin Canada Inc.)
Penguin Books Ltd., 80 Strand, London WC2R 0RL, England
Penguin Group Ireland, 25 St. Stephen's Green, Dublin 2, Ireland (a division of Penguin Books Ltd.)
Penguin Group (Australia), 250 Camberwell Road, Camberwell, Victoria 3124, Australia
(a division of Pearson Australia Group Pty. Ltd.)
Penguin Books India Pvt. Ltd., 11 Community Centre, Panchsheel Park, New Delhi—110 017, India
Penguin Group (NZ), Cnr. Airborne and Rosedale Roads, Albany, Auckland 1310, New Zealand
(a division of Pearson New Zealand Ltd.)
Penguin Books (South Africa) (Pty.) Ltd., 24 Sturdee Avenue, Rosebank, Johannesburg 2196,
South Africa

Penguin Books Ltd., Registered Offices: 80 Strand, London WC2R 0RL, England

This book is an original publication of The Berkley Publishing Group.

Cover design by George Long.
Text design by Kristin del Rosario.

First edition: November 2005

Library of Congress Cataloging-in-Publication Data

The naked truth / Donna Kauffman . . . [et al.].— 1st ed.
p. cm.
ISBN 0-425-20614-9 (trade pbk.)
1. Love stories, American. 2. Truthfulness and falsehood—Fiction. I. Kauffman, Donna.

PS648.L6N35 2005
813'.0850806—dc22

2005020476

PRINTED IN THE UNITED STATES OF AMERICA

10 9 8 7 6 5 4 3 2 1

CONTENTS

The Winning Truth

ERIN McCARTHY

ONE

TANSEY Reynolds had sworn off men and embraced celibacy.

Okay, so maybe *embracing* was an exaggeration, because every time she saw a two-legged human male even remotely attractive and over the age of twenty, she started to drool and engage in a battle with her willpower. But she really had sworn off dating men.

And she was celibate. For now. For as long as she could stand it.

The problem was, she wasn't a virgin. And once you got the ball rolling, it was kind of hard to stop it. Her ball wanted to tumble down a long driveway at top speed with the first boy ball that bounced by, and she was trying to force it to stay still. It wasn't working, and she hadn't figured out how to deflate her ball yet.

"What are you staring at, Tansey? We're next in line." Her best friend, Emily Baker, gave her a little nudge.

Forcing herself to stop salivating over a construction worker's tight butt in line ahead of her, Tansey clutched the contest flyer in her now sweaty hand and pondered a life without car payments. She frowned at Emily and tried to hold on to the dream. "How long have we been standing in this line? It feels like an hour."

Taking another king-size bite of her pretzel and a slurp of her cherry slushie, she added, "And I'm starving, Em. I wanted to eat a real lunch today for a change. The clock is ticking on my break."

"Eewww," Emily said, curling her lip in horror. "Close your mouth, Tansey. It looks like open heart surgery in there."

Carefully chewing the soft pretzel remnants, Tansey swallowed. "Sorry."

But there was nothing better to do than eat carbs and fat standing in line at the mall, waiting for a chance to win a free car. Eat or talk to the guy behind her, which she had done for a minute or two. And although he was cute, in an eager, much-younger-than-her sort of way, Tansey needed to concentrate her energies on the F word. *Focus.*

No more men. Not until she figured out what to do with the rest of her life. Not until she figured out how to stop herself from being attracted to gorgeous, sexy, lying male sluts.

"I can't even see the car because the fountain's blocking it," she said, feeling grumpy.

This wasn't exactly where she had pictured herself being at age twenty-eight: single and spending ninety percent of her waking hours at the mall between work and shopping, with fatty food as her only consolation. And as unexciting and low-paying as her job was, she was going to get fired from the department store if she didn't get back to work in about two minutes. "This is a total waste of time. I'm getting out of line."

Emily looked aghast. "But Tansey, if you get out of line, you can't win the car."

"The chances of me winning that car are about the same as the balance on my credit card being zero." A long time ago, in a galaxy far, far away, her credit card balance had been nothing. These days it heaved and bubbled and popped, threatening to overflow with a life force all its own.

"Well, you won't win if you don't enter," Emily said, the eternal optimist in a sunny yellow sweater. Emily was chronically cheerful. She thought everyone was sweet and adorable and oh-so-sincere, and she doled out trust like Tic Tacs. Somehow it seemed to be working for Emily.

Emily was happy. Tansey just felt crappy.

There was a life lesson there. Like maybe what goes around comes around. You receive what you give. Don't sweat the small stuff.

Or maybe just stop being an ungrateful bitch.

The thought made her feel better. "You're right, Em." *She* controlled her destiny. She could stand back and react when things happened to her, or she could make them happen. "I'm in charge of my life."

Like swearing off men. That was taking action. See, she had taken charge already.

Her eyes strayed back to the construction worker's fine behind. It was very . . . firm in those worn jeans. Her mouth went dry.

Tansey didn't need a man. But she sure wanted one.

Just like that, please. One gorgeous, tool-belt-wearing guy to go.

Order up.

Tansey watched the hunk with blond hair step out of the line in front of her and take the clipboard handed to him. He wore faded jeans that hugged his thighs, scuffed work boots, and a tool belt that hung down around his waist, dragging those jeans even lower. A white T-shirt strained across a multitude of male muscle, and on top of that was a red flannel shirt.

Tansey fought the urge to lick her lips. She'd always had a thing for men who worked with their hands. All those calluses and tanned skin in the summer. Rippling muscle and dirty jeans. The total lack of modesty they displayed as they slung hammers around, bare-chested in ninety-degree weather. Even though it was February right now, she could visualize it.

Whew.

Yeah, she could visualize it.

As he turned, he saw her. Though he was a little too far away to be sure, she would guess his eyes were blue, given his light hair with blond streaks.

She would not do anything. She would not. She couldn't . . . She smiled, did the hair flip. Damn. She was addicted to flirting. After nearly fifteen years of mating behavior, she couldn't just drop it as easily as she wanted.

Sexy's mouth turned up in a return smile. Then he moved on, heading over to the camera to be interviewed, and she knew she should be grateful.

Stability. Respect. A new job. Those were all things she wanted, needed. She was tired of folding sweaters and suffering sensory tag injuries in the name of a puny paycheck, and no man in a muscle shirt was going to dissuade her from her course. It was all about focus.

Yet somehow she kept finding herself drawn to men who only concentrated on a different F word. The one that rhymed with *duck, luck,* and *truck*.

Like that guy, whose fine behind she could not peel her eyes off.

Emily smiled and pulled Tansey by the arm. "Look, it's already our turn."

They approached the big table draped in black as the line moved forward, and Tansey's view cleared. Various people were scurrying around busily, with cameras and video equipment.

A couple, who she guessed were Joey and Amber—DJs from the radio station that was sponsoring the contest—were sitting on bar stools talking with microphones in their hands. And behind them was parked a big red Ford Expedition.

Something shifted inside Tansey. She had sudden and painful SUV envy. Her dinky two-door Cavalier she'd been driving since the beginning of time reminded her of an elderly Chihuahua napping next to a sleek young Great Dane.

"I-yi," she said eloquently. Then she searched around for the entry forms, more than willing to forget the potentially wasted lunch hour and Mr. Tight Butt. "Where's the little scrap of paper to fill out?"

A perky guy in a turtleneck sweater noticed her attacking the table and smiled. "Did you want to enter?"

"Yes." She wiped her hands on her black wool skirt and struggled for composure. It was just a car. No biggie. She wasn't going to win, after all. But what a cool car.

"Do you understand the way the contest works?" He handed her a clipboard with a form on it.

"No." She took the clipboard and pen and studied the first question. Name. Okay, easy enough.

"You have to live in the car to win it."

She blanked out after writing T-a. "What? Live in it?"

"Yes. Four chosen contestants will live in the car in assigned seats. The last person left in the vehicle wins it."

Emily gasped. Tansey stared at the guy. Was he serious?

His earring swung back and forth as he nodded. "I'm serious. It's a blast. We're going to have a live webcam set up to monitor what's going on in the car twenty-four hours a day. You get disqualified if you move from your seat."

Tansey started to hand him back the clipboard. There was no way she was going to live in a car, having a webcam recording her snoring.

"If you don't want the car, you can take twenty-five grand instead."

Hel-lo. Tansey yanked the clipboard back. Okay, for that kind of money, she could live in a car for a day or whatever. Hadn't she driven to Florida with her parents and brothers every year when she was a kid? If she could endure her brother Josh's gross jokes and Eric's car sickness for sixteen hours, she could handle this.

"When you're finished with the questionnaire, just step up to the cameraman there, and they'll ask you a few questions." He handed Emily a clipboard as well and gave another inflated smile.

Emily grinned. "This is so wild. God, I hope they pick me. I need a car really bad. I'm getting sick of taking the bus."

"If I win, Em, I'll give you my old car." No, wait, she was taking the cash. That would go further. That would send her back to college, to finish the teaching degree she'd abandoned when her mother had suddenly died of an aneurysm. That money could give her the brand-new start, the elusive focus she'd been searching for.

This was a sign, on a mall flyer, that it was time for her to start phase two of adulthood—securing a job with eight to five hours and purchasing furniture that hadn't fallen off the back of a truck.

Tansey finished filling in the basic information and scooted herself over into the line in front of the camera. A minute later a woman gestured for Tansey to move closer. "Hi, we're going to point the camera at you and ask you a few questions. Just act natural."

Natural. She could do that. And this woman didn't look Hollywood. She was wearing high-waisted jeans and had Jennifer Aniston's haircut from six years ago. Tansey relaxed.

"What's your name?"

"Tansey Reynolds."

"What do you do for a living?"

"I'm an assistant manager in women's retail sales at Dillard's."

"Are you able to get time off from work to live in the car for an unknown amount of time?"

"Yes." If she begged, pleaded, did some major schedule shifting, and promised weird favors for the next two months.

"What would you do with the money if you chose the cash option?"

This could be a trick question. They probably wanted someone fun and upbeat. "Go on vacation," she answered, thinking it wasn't a bad idea. Anyplace above forty degrees had to be better than snow-slogged Cleveland in February.

But twenty-five thousand dollars was a lot of money. She studied the red blinking light on the camera in front of her. She could just see herself reflected in the lens, her burgundy sweater shifting at the neck. Her face serious, eyes wide. This money could be her chance to make a real change in her life. Focus. The dream that had been pricking into her subconscious for the last month or two suddenly became vividly clear, and she couldn't pretend she would just dash off to Cancun for *Girls Gone Wild Seven*.

"And I would go back to college, finish my degree, and become a teacher in an urban area like I always wanted, to really make a difference."

"Okay, thank you. Next."

Whoops. Dismissed. Tansey turned around as the woman wrote notes on her entry form.

Emily patted her arm. "That's very Oprah of you, Tansey. I'm proud of you."

It had been an honest answer, something that had been a dream, a far-off, if-I-wasn't-a-lazy-chickenshit kind of dream. When her mom had died her junior year in college and she had dropped out, she had thought she'd go back to school after she'd gotten over her grief.

Instead, she'd effectively stuffed that grief down deep, had gone into retail, and had never dealt. With any of it. And now she was drawing it all out right here in the mall on a Tuesday to analyze.

Obviously the people at Z103 were not impressed with her desire to change the lives of America's youth, nor her ache to be useful for something other than fetching a different size for a customer. Plus she'd wasted her entire lunch hour and was facing an afternoon of starvation.

A soft pretzel didn't go far when you were playing fetch and carry for demanding customers.

But at least she had resisted temptation in the form of one very gorgeous construction worker who was currently standing in front of camera two, big hands in his front jean pockets.

Score a point for her maturity.

"Tansey Reynolds? Can you head over to camera two for another shot?"

Oh, damn. Tansey's maturity went the way of the dodo. It no longer existed.

TWO

J. T. Kowalski looked around for the woman who had told him to stand by camera two and wait. What was taking her so long? If he didn't need the money so badly he would have walked right on past this circus and gone back to the electrical rewiring he had been doing before lunch.

But the thought of twenty-five grand made him break out into a sweat. That kind of money could save his dad's floundering construction business, which had been touch-and-go since his father's divorce settlement.

"You already made it through the first cut, which is better than me." J.T.'s friend Steve looked a little put out by that fact.

J.T. was a little embarrassed by the fact himself. "Listen, these media people are weird. Who knows what they're looking for?"

"Good, you're still here." The woman in the jeans came back and smiled at him, a headset bobbing on her curly brown hair.

He wondered exactly where she thought he was going to go, since he was just about roped in by equipment, a table, and the SUV to his right.

"I've got another potential contestant here, and I'm going to ask you both some more questions. I want to see how you interact with each other, okay?" Another smile blinded him.

J.T. was feeling less and less sure about this. Now he was supposed to do small talk with some total stranger?

Then he saw her.

She was coming around behind the woman. She stopped short, her eyes round. It was the woman who had been staring at him when he had been in line a few minutes earlier, with a needy and openly hot gaze that had gone straight below his belt.

But J.T. had dismissed her then as high maintenance. Expensive clothes, dark hair, with funny little streaks of red in it. Jewelry. Definitely not his type. He was looking for someone to settle down with and raise a couple of little Kowalskis, not burn up the sheets with.

Miss Makeup here probably didn't know the first thing about kids—though he imagined she might know a sheet-burning trick or two.

She gave a little gasp of surprise that went straight to J.T.'s . . . ear.

But he could handle his hormones. Call it a benefit of being thirty.

"Hi," she said. "I . . . are you? Well . . ."

Her voice was low, a wonderful husky, rich, full voice that soothed and stroked.

And all benefits of being thirty flew out the damn window. The unmistakable feeling of an erection swelling sent him digging his hand in his pocket. He nodded to her, pissed off that his body had reacted like a fifteen-year-old in coed gym class. "Hi."

Undeterred, she smiled at him. She had perfect suburban teeth, white and straight, the result, no doubt, of her parents' hard-earned money.

The radio lady said with interest, "Do you know each other?"

Miss Makeup shook her head.

J.T. shrugged. "No." Then some inner demon, the one who controlled him below the waist and who hadn't seen any action in a dog's year, said, "I'm looking forward to it, though."

That smile froze, suggesting she was startled, but her brown eyes connected with his, encouraged him, crinkled at the edges with amusement.

"The feeling's mutual."

The radio lady raised her eyebrows in urgent interest. "Roll cameras!" She brushed Steve out of range, who walked off in irritation.

Miss Makeup twirled her hair around her finger and cast him curious side glances, her mouth opening to say something, then clamping shut as she thought better of it.

J.T. ignored her full, pouty lips and called up a visual of Janie, the woman he'd been considering asking out, who worked in the mall Hallmark store. Quiet, a little plain, with straight brown hair and a shy smile. Sensible clothes, nothing flashy about her. Maternal.

The opposite of this woman in front of him.

"So where's your boyfriend?" J.T. asked her.

"My boyfriend?" She dropped her hair and looked at him in confusion.

J.T. was way too aware of the woman—and the fact that Janie had never caused him to go hard at one in the afternoon with half a dozen people around. Miss Makeup was standing really close, because the radio lady kept gesturing for her to shift in to get them both on camera. He would have expected her to smell artificial, like heavy perfume, but she didn't. She smelled like freshly washed sheets, and it was driving him to distraction.

He didn't want to think about sheets when he was standing next to her. Sheets went on the bed, sheets that rumpled when you had sex on them. Sex meant naked; sex meant this woman beneath him, her long hair falling across those same rumpled sheets . . .

Great. The camera was now recording a world-class boner that all his tugging around in his pocket could not camouflage.

"Yeah, your boyfriend. The guy standing behind you in line."

The confusion cleared, and she shrugged. "Not my boyfriend. Not my anything. He happened to be standing in line behind me, and we chatted for a minute." She leaned against the SUV, and he appreciated the gesture.

He had the complete and unabridged version of her from top to toe. She was wearing a knee-length skirt and black boots that were tight against her calves and went all the way to just under the knee, showing him a sliver of thigh covered in black tights, or whatever women called them. Her sweater hugged a couple delicious curves without being showy, and her hair fell just past her shoulders, true black in color.

Her skin was the opposite of his. He was what one ex-girlfriend had termed "robust." Even in the frigid sunless month of February, his summer tan still clung to him, and he was rough and scratchy everywhere, like that alligator on that lotion commercial.

This woman was smooth, pale, soft, so alabaster and shiny that no tan would ever stick and no blemish would dare to land on her face.

For some inexplicable, or maybe obvious, reason, he couldn't take his eyes off her. It didn't seem a damn bit fair. At thirty, he shouldn't be susceptible to this kind of boy-meets-girl crap.

Yet that didn't stop him from saying, "That kid did look kind of young for you. I don't think he'd know what to do with you."

It sounded a little sexist, he realized, too late to take the words back.

Her fists clenched, and he waited for her to ream him, which he would deserve. He had gone stupid—too much blood flowing south.

Instead of yelling at him, she tilted her head a little, pulling herself off the car. "Oh, and you would? Know what to do with me?"

It would have been better if she had reamed him. Because now he had a full mental videotape rolling through everything he could do with her. Twice.

He shouldn't answer. He should let it drop, go back to his normal life, where he didn't flirt like George Clooney without the good clothes or the money.

"I most certainly would know what to do with you. Starting with dinner and ending with whatever."

What in the hell was he doing? Hadn't he just thought to himself five minutes ago he was not going to talk to this woman? That she wasn't his type? That she was high maintenance?

Think Janie; think future mother of his children; think boring, dull, monotonous sex for the rest of his life . . .

Maybe it was the stress of his dad's money problems, which had become his, and the constant worry that Kowalski Construction might go belly-up at any minute. He hadn't been on a date in months, and now standing here with a woman who was all wrong for him, he was busting loose a little.

Much more, and he'd be busting through his jeans.

A soft sigh came out of her mouth as her glossy lips spilled open. "Hmmm."

She either didn't know what to say, she thought he was insane and might be dangerous, or she was drowning in the same pool of precoital lust he was.

Possibly a combination of all three.

Her hair slid over her shoulder, and J.T. ached to touch it. Instead, he stuck his hand so deep in his pocket he about ripped through to the other side. "My name's J.T. And I'm thirty."

Not that he was acting it.

"Tansey," she said in a breathless voice. "Twenty-eight."

"It's a pleasure to meet you, Tansey." He smiled at her, utterly unable to resist.

"Nice to meet you, too." Her eyes dropped to his waist, and she licked her lips.

Heat rushed through him. Did she know she was doing that? That she kept wetting those already-slick lips over and over again?

"You're in construction? Are you working on the Dillard's remodeling project? I work in the women's department."

Was he? For a minute he couldn't even remember who he was. "Yes."

She gave a little smirk as she lifted her hand and casually gestured to his waist. "Nice tools."

A short jerk of laughter came from him before he could stop himself. J.T. didn't think she was talking about his Stanley socket wrench. And he had the feeling that he wasn't going to convince his energetic lower half that Tansey was all wrong for him and the goals that he'd clearly defined for the future. Nope.

His body was just wondering if she'd like a demonstration of his drill.

Tansey listened to J.T.'s laughter roll over her and wondered if he would catch her if she fainted from pure admiration right now. He was incredible, with a firm jaw and blue eyes that just reached out and arrested you.

Standing this close to him was seriously dangerous. It was only a matter of time before her control snapped and she humiliated herself by reaching out and scraping her fingernails across his chest.

It had been six months since that torrid scene involving Bill, another woman, and zero clothing. The horror of realizing that she was a lousy judge of men. Since college, two for two she'd picked men high on sexy, low on commitment. Both had found it necessary to drink from another fountain while still sipping off hers.

That latest humiliation was still fresh.

Yet one hundred eighty days was a long time without any nookie.

The mall was hot, the air thick and stale from the heat blasting to combat the February frigidity, and she was flushed inside her sweater.

It didn't help when he smiled. "Thanks. I only use the best tools."

Tansey didn't think either one of them was talking about a wrench or hammer, and she suddenly felt that maybe she was over her head here, given her lack of understanding about casual sex and the men who seek it.

Despite her apparent bad taste and enthusiastic carnal urges, she had never been one to have casual sex. She had always thought she was in a monogamous relationship, silly her, only to find that her partners hadn't made that same assumption. She was coming to realize that the majority of men thought "monogamy" meant stitching your initial on a towel.

If she wasn't careful here, she was going to find her vow of celibacy shattered and her name nothing more than a notch on his leather belt.

Besides, she wasn't really his type. J.T. probably had women throwing themselves at him all the time. Women who had blond hair and big breasts, and were tan all year round. Women who were up on professional sports and who went Jet-Skiing in bikinis.

Her brain told her to abort this conversation. To blink with wide-eyed innocence and not give in to the hussy half of her self who was urging her to take his tools and see what she could build.

"They look like they're in great condition." Ugh, the hussy half reigned supreme. She mentally grounded the hussy, instructing her to not come out of her room until further notice.

He was taking a step closer, the flannel on his shirt brushing her hand in scratchy awareness as he leaned, leaned.

"Excellent condition," he whispered.

Ay, carumba. Was he going to kiss her? Right here in the . . . of course not.

But she really, really wanted him to. No, she didn't. Well, she did, but she couldn't. It didn't matter that he looked like a man who was good with his hands.

Hands that were rough as they brushed across her bottom lip, while those baby blue eyes studied her with intrigue and longing. She leaned into his touch, heart pounding, silently urging him to take that kiss, and to hell with celibacy and dignity. To have him grab her, rush his lips over hers, to bend her back, to lay her down, pull her skirt up and . . .

"Okay, camera off."

Tansey blinked.

J.T. yanked his thumb from her mouth. "You had a piece of salt on your lip." He held it up for her to see.

It was then she remembered why she was here instead of back at work like she should be, straightening turtlenecks. This was a screen test of sorts. They were being recorded to see what their chemistry was like together. So far she thought it ranged somewhere in the area of a nuclear explosion. They were freaking Chernobyl.

Given another five minutes, she was sure there would have been a kiss. It was quite possible groping might have been involved, too. And it would have all been recorded on tape for posterity—or humiliation, however you wanted to look at it.

So why was she so damn disappointed?

J.T. took a step back while Tansey tried to ignore the throbbing between her thighs. Salt. He'd been picking salt off her lip. Then why did she feel like, given another minute, they would have gone right to the good stuff, and she would have made her first porno movie?

She would have had to change her name to Tansey Tawny Hotsie and moved to a seedy apartment in Hollywood. It was much better that nothing had happened.

Her burning body disagreed.

God, what was the matter with her? She was focusing all right, but on the wrong F word.

"J.T., head over to camera six. Tansey, you stay here."

J.T., who looked as foggy as she felt, gave a nod. With a last look of longing toward her, he swaggered off in the direction the woman had pointed. Tansey grabbed the SUV for support.

Emily rushed over to her. "What was that? Holy macaroni."

"That was every woman's dream come true." Tansey tried to drag her eyes from the seat of his jeans as he walked away and found she couldn't. It was just too good of a view. The butt that broke Tansey Reynolds.

"Actually, I think that was you flirting with a total stranger on camera."

"I don't know what's wrong with me," she said with absolute and utter horror. "I was throwing myself at him. I'm not supposed to be dating at all, and I was flirting shamelessly."

"I don't think he minded." Emily grinned.

Emily was then shooed backward again as Headphone Woman returned with a guy about Tansey's age wearing an expensive sweater and black pants. He had a stylish haircut and was carrying an assortment of shopping bags.

Tansey thought he looked soft and artificial, like breast implants.

Where was the mystery, the strength, the raw masculinity?

Walking away, that's where.

"Camera roll," said the lady.

"Hi, I'm Jason," her new companion said as he set his bags down in front of him. "I love your sweater."

It was a perfectly polite thing to say, and was accompanied by no sexist ogling. So why did that suddenly seem so boring? She forced a smile and told herself to behave and make an effort. Here was the type of man she should be looking for, if celibacy was an unnatural and unrealistic state for her—which it clearly was. Here was a man who would take her to the ballet and gladly accompany her shopping, and if she couldn't resist flirting, now was the time to do it.

"Thanks, I'm Tansey."

"I can't believe I'm doing this," he confided. "I have a new car so I don't really need one, but hey, who can't use a little extra money?"

"Absolutely," she said and tried to inject enthusiasm into her voice. Jason should be sending her into rapturous purring, but all she could think was that she would be just as excited by a Diet Coke as she was from talking to Jason.

She was losing him, she could tell. His smile was becoming polite and strained. *Say something,* she commanded herself.

"Ahh," she muttered incoherently. Nothing came to mind.

"Camera off."

She'd blown it.

"Let's try one more alternative," Headphone Woman told her, gesturing Tansey impatiently toward camera four.

"Me?" Tansey asked stupidly, thinking by now she had definitely outstayed her welcome on the Z103 tour of desperate people at the West Park Mall.

"Yes, Tansey Reynolds, right? See how you get along with this guy over here."

Tansey finally figured out what they were doing. When they shut four humans together in a car for a couple days, they wanted it to be entertaining. Maybe she appeared to be so ridiculous they were certain she'd be worth a laugh or two on camera.

The guy waiting at camera four was the sweet, much, much younger than her guy who had been standing behind her in line.

"Hi again," she said, dredging up a smile.

"What did you say your name was?" Cute, very young guy named Logan asked.

"Tansey." He must not have been able to understand her earlier with all the pretzel guts in her mouth.

Logan scratched his head. "How do you spell that?"

Tansey did a spelling bee imitation, wishing she could feel an ounce of enthusiasm that he seemed interested in her. He was really cute, polite, and hadn't even once checked out her chest or another woman while talking to her. She could flirt like crazy with him and get it out of her system.

Yet he was *so* cute and young, when she looked at him, all she could think was that he might as well be on *Barney and Friends*.

Logan tilted his head a little, a lock of unruly hair falling across his adorable, cheek-squeezable face. "That's a pretty name, I guess, but kind of weird."

Pretty weird. Maybe that summed her up.

"So, are you busy this weekend?"

"What?"

"If you're not busy, maybe we could go out. You and me," he clarified, rubbing his hand on his black wool jacket.

She should have gotten out of this obnoxious line for another cherry slushie and given up on the car contest. Her chances of winning anything were about as likely as her getting a raise in the near future, and that was about as likely as her running a twenty-five-K marathon.

Not freaking likely.

Now she was going to have to say no and embarrass herself and Logan by turning him down. She hadn't gotten desperate enough to resort to combing the high schools for dates, tempting the boys with candy and rides in her car. Maybe she would be in another six months of celibacy, but right now she was hanging tough.

No. More. Men. Besides, while Logan deserved points for asking her out on camera, she just couldn't bring herself to date a guy who hadn't been born yet when she was buying her first bra.

"How old are you, Logan?" Maybe she was wrong and he just had a baby face and she was using age as a lame mental excuse to justify turning down a nice guy.

"Twenty-one."

"No way," she blurted out without thinking. Geez, he was twenty-one? She had thought eighteen was being generous, and she was suddenly very aware of her own age. If twenty-one years old looked young to her, then she was just flat out old.

Old and unfocused. Fabulous. Like eyes with cataracts. And there was no surgery to fix this.

Logan reminded her of a fuzzy new chick, ready to leap from the nest, except that Tansey was thinking chickens didn't live in nests. Anyway, she suddenly felt like a cranky old hen. Logan was fresh, eager, cheerful.

She was . . . not. She was the unsettled hen who always fell for the wrong cock.

She could have baby-sat Logan once upon a time. His hair was doing that weird, floppy-eye thing that she would never understand, and he wore gym shoes that looked large enough to float a family from Cuba to Florida.

"No, I'm not lying about my age." He pulled out his wallet and flipped it open. "See?" He shoved his driver's license in her hand.

He sported a choirboy smile in the picture, and if her math was correct, he was telling the truth.

"I'm twenty-eight," she told him, waiting for the look of horror to cover his face. It was certainly horrifying her lately. Twenty-eight meant it had been seven years since she'd dropped out of college, which meant she'd spent a hell of a lot of time doing nothing.

Except date men who cheated.

God, she needed an IV transfusion of Emily's optimism. She was depressing herself.

He stared at her blankly. "So?"

Why were kids today so slow? "That makes me older than you. A lot older."

"It's just a date," he said, taking back his wallet. "I'm not talking about marriage or anything."

Gak! Neither was she. She wasn't even interested in dating. All she was interested in was sex.

Wait. That didn't sound right.

No, she didn't need a man. Tansey had a very fulfilling life all on her own . . . well, no she didn't, but she could if she ever got her act together.

This wasn't even about men. This was about *her life*.

"Of course not! I wasn't talking about marriage either. Please. I doubt I will ever get married."

Tansey wished she hadn't pitched her slushie. She was hot and thirsty and needed to get back to the store before her manager docked her for being six seconds late.

She turned to the woman with the headset, ready to shout "Off camera!" herself, knowing she was never going to have a chance to win a free car and she needed to get back to her real life.

Reality wasn't about hot-burning affairs with tool-toting men or futile dates with barely legal boys. Reality was about going back to college, getting her act together on her own, without the interference of men at all.

But reality was something of an uncooperative bitch. Like her boss.

The woman's back was to her. She spoke to her assistant as she scratched notes on her clipboard. "Okay, pull J.T. back over here. I'm putting both him and Tansey in the car. I want them in the backseat together, got it?"

Tansey thought she must have heard wrong. Because if she hadn't, she was in deep you-know-what. They wanted her to live in a car, with J.T. next to her in the backseat.

All nice and cozy. Touching.

Twenty-four hours a day. Live on the Internet.

For as long as it took.

Oh, yeah. She was in trouble. If she couldn't control herself in the mall for five minutes, how could she control herself tucked in next to J.T. every minute of every day?

She sure hoped porn stars had health insurance.

THREE

"HAVE you read all these rules?" Emily lay sprawled across her bed, flipping through the packet Tansey had received from the contest coordinator.

"No, I haven't had time." Tansey threw another sweater on the bed. "This is hopeless. I don't know what to pack. I've never lived in the backseat of an SUV with an orgasm-inspiring carpenter before."

"Not many people have," Emily said, turning another page. "I think you need to read this."

"Later." After she was done having a wardrobe anxiety attack. "I need to make sure I'm sending the right message to J.T."

Emily propped her head up with her hand, her fingers entangling in her blond curls. "Then I guess you should go naked."

An image of herself strolling through the mall nude sent Tansey's blood pressure shooting up. It didn't even make her laugh, not under these circumstances. She picked up a black sweater and studied it.

Too last year. She flung it back into her closet where it landed in a heap with the other discards.

"I want to send the message that I'm not interested." She grabbed a rust turtleneck. Turtlenecks were studious, very Velma from *Scooby Doo*. Maybe she could wear that and her glasses with the fake lenses. "What about this? Very unsexual."

"It makes your boobs look huge."

Tansey dropped it like a hot potato and looked at Emily in frustration. "What should I wear, Em? Sweat pants?"

Emily glanced up from her reading. "Why do you want him to think you're not interested when you so obviously are? I don't get it."

"Because, he is wrong for me. J.T. is a construction worker with probably less money than me." Well, probably no one had less money than she did, but it was likely he came close. "I have to think about the future, finishing my degree. Then after that I can consider settling down with a nice guy with a good job who will take me to the theater and nice restaurants. Preferably with a low sex drive so he won't be tempted to cheat."

Funny, that sounded like Jason, the guy who had evoked nothing in her except a yawn that afternoon. Well, it sounded like him except for the sex drive part. She couldn't claim to know that about Jason after three minutes. But strangely enough, she was fairly certain she had J.T.'s sex drive pegged after just a few minutes. And *low* wasn't the word she'd use to describe it.

"But if he has a low sex drive, won't *you* be tempted to cheat then? With J.T.?" Emily smiled in all her blonde logic.

Maybe just once. "No! Because he's all wrong for me. J.T. would probably want to take me out for a beer and darts." Then back to his place for wild, rip-roaring, cosmic, mind-blowing sex.

Which she didn't dare think about.

This was her chance. This was fate grabbing her by the SUV and slinging her into the future. It was time to Change, with a capital C.

She was going to win that money. She was going to go back to college. She was going to find a man who could go six months without cheating on her.

Her father would be so proud.

She turned back to the closet, moving each hanger rapidly, trying to find anything that made her look disinterested yet not like a total slob.

"So what if you don't have the same interests? You're attracted to him." Emily rolled onto her stomach and got caught up in her denim skirt.

As Emily tugged her waistband back around to face front, Tansey said, "You can't build a relationship on biceps."

Emily snorted. "I can."

She thought of J.T.'s chest and felt drool pooling in the corner of her mouth. Swallowing hard, she forced superiority into her voice. "That's because I have evolved. I'm ready to think lifetime, not one-night-time."

Which didn't explain why she'd spent the entire damn day trying to justify having sex with J.T. Just once. To get it out of her system.

"Yeah, well, while you're evolving in the backseat of a car with J.T., I'm going out with Tim, who's twenty-two and very eager to please." Emily sat up and closed the packet. "Should we see who has more fun?"

No. Tansey threw herself down on the bed and buried her face in a pillow. Emily nearly toppled off onto the floor from the force of her hitting the mattress in a dramatic flop.

"There's something wrong with me. I need to find the right guy, but all I can think about is the wrong guy."

"What you should be thinking about are these rules." Emily picked up the packet again.

Tansey was starting to worry about that dumb packet. She was starting to worry about everything. Was twenty-five grand worth all this?

Stupid question. Twenty-five grand was worth anything.

Well, not walking naked through the mall, but it was worth shutting herself up in a closed environment with a man gorgeous enough to tempt a nun.

And even if she wanted to give in to temptation, two other people were going to be in the front seat of the car. Not to mention a live webcam. Not exactly private.

"Okay, what do these rules say?"

Emily cleared her throat and flipped open the packet. "Number one. Contestant may not leave the vehicle at any time other than scheduled breaks. Failure to comply will result in disqualification."

Pft. That was no big deal. That was the whole point of the contest, to stay in the car.

"Number two. Contestant must remain in their assigned seat in the vehicle. At no time may they move to another seat. They may stretch and shift to the adjoining seat, but portions of their body must remain in their assigned seat at all times."

Tansey blinked. "What does that mean?"

"I think it means you have to keep your butt in your seat."

That sounded . . . uncomfortable. Tansey got off the bed and wandered over to the mirror hanging over her dresser. "What else?" She checked her face for zits.

"Contestant must consent to being videotaped and viewed via a web camera on the Z103 website with a twenty-four-hour feed."

Damn, she had a zit on her chin. Did those show up on web cameras?

"Contestant will receive a ten-minute bio break every three hours. All personal hygiene must be conducted at this time. Contestant will be allowed additional breaks under emergency circumstances but may not request more than two emergency breaks per twenty-four-hour period or they will be disqualified."

Well, that was gross.

Tansey paced her small bedroom in horror. "They're scheduling our bathroom breaks for us? And if I'm understanding this right, that means no shower, and we'll have to brush our teeth in the mall's public restroom."

An involuntary shudder coursed through her. The mall's restroom was about as clean as the bottom of her shoe. Normally she mummified her hands in toilet paper so she wouldn't touch anything with bare skin. It was going to be hard to brush her teeth with TP wrapped around her fingers.

Emily shrugged. "I guess so. But look on the bright side. You won't have to worry about turning J.T. on. The smell of you without a shower will discourage him from making any moves."

"That's not comforting!" Tansey didn't want the guy to think she had body odor, for crying out loud, despite her vow to stay away from him.

"I'm hopeless," she concluded. "There is something wrong with me that compels me to make bad choices."

"I think you're overreacting."

Tansey snorted and started sifting through her closet again. "That's because you don't have the same goals I do. You're perfectly happy dating a twenty-two-year-old."

"Well, you said it yourself. Happy. That's what I am, and you are obviously not."

Emily did look content. She liked her job as co-manager of the shoe department, and she didn't mind living in a poky little apartment. She dated who she wanted, when she wanted, and wore clothes that pleased her.

Tansey was bored with her job and loathed her apartment, which was really one and a half rooms squeezed into the attic of a ninety-year-old house. She hadn't dated since she'd walked in on Bill, and she had become lost in a sea of black clothing in an effort to look urbane and hide tummy flab.

And she didn't even want to think about her car.

"So what do you suggest I do?"

"Jump J.T.'s bones."

With Emily, everything was so simple.

Tansey had struck the word from her vocabulary the day she had turned thirteen and discovered the opposite sex.

"No," she said firmly, struggling to ignore the memory of J.T.'s finger on her lips. It didn't matter that he had called to her inner femininity with his powerful maleness in some kind of bizarre nature show mating call.

"I don't have any room in my life for screwing around with carpenters. I'm going to sit in that car, behave myself, collect the twenty-five grand, and go back to college." She punched the air with an empty plastic hanger. "I'm going to have a job I love, a great apartment, a new car, and a man in my life who knows the word *dossier* is not a French bra."

Emily shook her head in wonder. "Then you'd better wear the sweat pants."

"SHOULDN'T you be heading over to the car?" Steve was giving J.T. a worried look.

J.T. stepped over a pile of drywall bits and shook his head, reaching for his measuring tape. "No, because I'm not going."

Steve gawked at him, his nail gun dangling from his hand. "Are you crazy?"

"No. That's why I'm not doing it." He had been nuts to even consider it. After reading that thick stack of papers that asked him to basically sign away all dignity for an unspecified amount of time, he had rethought this car contest.

There were too many hassles. He would have to leave this job for a day or so, he would have to share airspace with the mysteriously alluring Tansey, and he would have to go to the bathroom on cue. None of which sounded appealing.

Well, Tansey sounded appealing. Tansey *was* appealing.

But he knew he shouldn't get involved with her, despite that flirtatious push and pull they had shared. He knew her type. She would demand constant attention and pout incessantly. After a few dates she would be picking out new clothes for him and suggesting a hair salon for him to use. She would call his cell phone twelve times a day and complain to her friends that he was a selfish lover.

Yep, he knew her type. Had dated a few just like her.

And he had never, ever been a selfish lover.

He could show Tansey how selfless he could be. Given the hot reaction between them the day before, it wouldn't take much to make her beg and squirm . . .

"I would kill to have that chance, and you're just walking away from it." Steve pulled off his baseball hat and rubbed his forehead with his sleeve.

"What's my son walking away from?"

J.T. swore under his breath as his father walked up to them, his flannel shirt hanging a little loose since he had lost some weight in recent months.

It had been a hell of a year for his dad. First J.T.'s stepmother had left his father after fifteen years of marriage, then his father had taken a huge lump of the construction company's assets to pay Naomi a divorce settlement. J.T. couldn't figure out why, if she left, she should get all that money, but his father had told him it was none of his damn business.

Even when that decision had nearly cost them both the construction business.

J.T. shrugged. "Nothing, Dad. Just that car contest the radio station is running."

"You're not doing it?" His father looked at him curiously. "But Steve said it was big money—twenty-five grand."

J.T. slipped his measuring tape back into his pocket and felt the urge to strangle Steve. "Yeah, well, maybe twenty-five grand isn't worth being made a fool of."

His father's eyes narrowed. "You aren't afraid to leave this job, are you? Think I can't handle a little store remodel for a couple days? I may be old, but I'm not out to pasture yet."

Damn. J.T. felt a headache coming on as well as the urge to just ram his head into the glass window. "Dad, you're not even old—you're forty-seven. And that's not why I decided not to do it."

He rubbed his jaw. "I've only got a one in four chance of winning, and they want me to jump through some pretty big hoops. I don't feel like it, that's all."

That was the end of it as far as he was concerned. He rubbed his dusty hands on the seat of his jeans and turned toward the wall. What the hell had he been doing when Steve had interrupted him?

His father frowned. "Are you sure that's all there is to it? Because if I find out you're hanging around to baby-sit me, I'll take you over my knee. I don't care how old you are. I was in construction before you could walk."

Though the thought of his father, who had never once raised a hand to him, taking him over his knee made him smirk for a second, J.T. wasn't amused for long. If he didn't go to the contest, his father was going to assume it was because of him. Since Naomi had left, his dad had been quiet, tentative, not himself at all.

"You never hit me when I was a kid."

"I could start." His dad grinned, though it didn't reach his eyes.

His father wasn't old, not by a long shot, but he'd been looking tired and, well, sad since Naomi had left. Not even when J.T. was a little kid and his mom had died had he seen his father look quite so defeated. So ready to give up.

J.T. was going to have to go do this stupid contest so he wouldn't upset his dad. And if he was going to go, he might as well try to win.

The glass window in front of him shook as someone tapped on it. He looked up and there she was.

Tansey.

She was wearing a black velvet warm-up outfit. It should have been baggy and unexciting. But it wasn't. The pants were sliding down on her hips, revealing a strip of pale, smooth skin, and the little hooded top was tight and short, marking her delicious curves.

He wondered how she got those two funny little streaks of red in her dark hair on either side of her face. They weren't natural red, but more like Corvette red. It should have made her look weird, but instead she looked interesting and exotic.

Her cheekbones were long and dramatic, and her lips were a natural vivid cherry that coordinated with her hair. She gave him a little smile and spoke on the other side of the glass. He couldn't hear her, but he could read her lips.

"Are you coming?" she asked.

J.T. broke out in a sweat. The minute he was around her, he became a total pervert. He knew what she meant, but his adolescent mind had leapt to a much better conclusion. Those sheets were in his head again.

She pointed in the direction of the mall's atrium where the SUV was parked, waiting for them. They were supposed to be in the car at three o'clock, in time for the start of rush-hour traffic. The radio DJs wanted to interview them on the air after they had been in the car about an hour.

Tansey's fingers played with the zipper on her sweatshirt. She didn't seem to be aware she was doing it, and it went a little low, giving him an eye-popping shot of creamy white cleavage.

He clenched his teeth.

The zipper went back up, and he remembered to breathe.

Father or not, he couldn't resist getting in that car with Tansey.

"I'll be there in a minute," he said, nodding so she could understand him.

She smiled and mouthed, "I'll wait."

He was already regretting his decision. If she smiled like that one more time, he was going to embarrass himself.

When he turned and started to unhook his tool belt, his father and Steve were grinning like demented hyenas.

"So that's all I had to do to get you to go?" Steve asked. "Smile at you and show you my chest?"

The image jumped out at him like a closet monster. "Ahh, you're a sick man, Steve."

They laughed at him as he turned his back and went out the front of the store.

Tansey smiled and gave a little wave, her other hand clutching a messenger bag. "Hi, J.T."

"Hey." He smiled back, then decided he needed to clear the air right away. Falling in beside her, he said, "Look, I wanted to apologize for yesterday. That was really . . ." Damn, what was the word for leaning over a woman you just met and eyeballing her breasts, all while tossing off bad nightclub pickup lines?

Nasty. Perverted. Rude.

"It was inappropriate, some of the things I said."

She raised an eyebrow like she had one of those other words in mind instead. "Don't worry about it. It was a moment, I think. You know, where you're just caught up in something, an instant attraction, and then you can't imagine what you were thinking, and given the same set of circumstances you wouldn't react like that a second time."

No, that's not what he meant. He would do the same thing over and over again, he was sure, and take it farther still. He just meant he should have dragged her off behind a wall or something first instead of embarrassing her on camera.

"Right. A moment." If he had been worried about her coming on to him, he clearly didn't have to now. He was a bad impulse that she was over and didn't plan on repeating.

Which was good, he figured, as he walked beside her to the central atrium of the mall, past the ice-cream shop. She wasn't his type any more today than she had been yesterday.

"Where's your bag?" Tansey asked.

He shrugged. "I didn't bring one."

"You didn't bring a CD player? Or a book? Or a crossword puzzle, or a deck of cards, or anything? What are you going to do the whole time we're in the car?" She grabbed her bag as if to confirm she still had it and all its entertainment within with her.

"I wasn't sure I was even going to go through with it." He still could bail. "I'm having second thoughts."

Tansey grabbed his arm. "You can't do that! How many people get a chance to win this kind of money?"

There was that point. But more important, her breast was brushing his arm as she leaned. It felt firm, yet soft against him, her velvet zip-up smooth across her curves. He no longer cared how undignified this contest might be. The breast talked him into it.

"Oh, I'm going to do it, you know, because of the money." And because of her, a couple of creamy curves, and killer cherry lips. "But I don't have a bag or anything."

"I'll share with you," she offered, with clearly no idea the lustful vein his thoughts were running on.

"Thanks."

"I brought snacks, like pretzels and peanuts and a couple Snickers bars." She moved away from his arm and readjusted her bag on her shoulder.

"You'd share your Snickers with me?" He meant it to be a light comment, but instead his voice was husky, and her eyes went wide.

"Sure, I'd share my Snickers with you. You look like you'd enjoy it."

She was either talking about caramel and he was a total pervert, or she had changed her mind about not repeating yesterday's flirtation.

He was going with him being a pervert.

Fortunately, no answer was required. Susie, the woman in charge of this whole sideshow, saw them approaching and flagged them over with broad, flapping arms.

"Are we late, or is she just tense?"

"I think both," Tansey said.

Susie was standing with two other people, a man and a woman, and as they approached she said, "Thank God you're both here! Jesus, we should have been in the car already. Okay, okay, you know your seats. J.T. you're behind the passenger, Tansey is behind the driver, Brenda is in the driver's seat, and Jay has the passenger seat."

Susie stopped for air. "On the count of three, you'll all get in the car and the contest begins."

J.T. felt one last moment of hesitation, but then shoved it aside. *Think of the money, man,* he told himself. That was a lot of money. Chances were good that none of the other contestants would last longer than a day.

Working his job over the years, both in and outdoors, he had been in a lot of uncomfortable spots. He could handle boredom and cramped calves.

It was Tansey he wasn't sure he could handle.

FOUR

AS Susie hit three, Tansey climbed into the backseat of the SUV and closed her door. Dropping her bag on the floor, she threw herself back against the seat and sighed.

Her plan wasn't working.

She was supposed to be avoiding J.T., not knocking on the glass of the store he was in to get his attention and offering to share chocolate with him. Chocolate. Could there be a bigger turn-on than picturing eating chocolate off J.T.'s lips? She didn't even want to get started on sticky caramel and where she could eat that off.

Tansey flapped her hand in front of her face like a fan.

J.T. was on the passenger side, and he took up more than his half of the backseat. He absorbed the space, inhaled her air, his elbow brushing against her, his knee bent toward hers in his dusty jeans. She hit the down button on the window, hoping for fresh mall air. Nothing happened because the car wasn't turned on.

Help.

He smelled like a construction site, a blend of drywall dust, caulk, and coffee. Tansey took long, gasping breaths, wondering if she'd suddenly become claustrophobic.

Shifting in the seat so she was clinging to her door, as far from him as possible, she glanced around at the black leather seats and little TV mounted above them. "Nice interior."

"Yeah, it's nice except for the camera staring at us." He pointed to the camera mounted on the front driver's side ceiling.

Tansey gasped. "Why is it on my side?" Squished against the door avoiding J.T., her face was probably less than twelve inches from the camera.

Lurching away, she carefully kept her butt in her seat and pressed as close to J.T. as she could without touching him. Great. She was stuck between irresistible temptation and utter mortification.

"I think it's a conspiracy," Brenda in the driver's seat said. "The camera is on the female side of the car. How f'd up is that?"

Tansey could clearly see Brenda now, because she was leaning to the right as well, hanging precariously over the gearshift. Brenda was a few years older than Tansey, with immovable blond hair and very red lipstick.

"They can still see us," Jay said, and proceeded to blow the camera a kiss. "That's for all the lovely ladies out there. The name is Jay, and I'm available."

"With good reason," Brenda said, rearing back away from him. "And they said there's no audio, you dork."

Brenda realized immediately she'd put herself in view of the camera again, and lurched back toward Jay, screeching to a halt over the gearshift again, her lip curled in disgust. "Stop looking at me," she told him.

Tansey envied women who had the guts to say out loud exactly what they were thinking. Though Jay wasn't an unattractive guy, even if he was a little skinny, he made poor fashion choices. Like the black shirt he was wearing against his pale skin that said *Will Dance for Food*.

Fashion disasters she understood. Hadn't she gone through a legging phase herself?

Jay shrugged. "Where the fuck am I supposed to look if I don't look at you? You're three inches from my face."

"Look out the window," Brenda ordered. "Look in your lap, look at yourself in the little flip-down mirror, I don't care. Just don't look at me."

"Screw me, bitch."

Brenda sputtered, her eyes narrowing. "You wish."

J.T. sighed next to her. Tansey glanced at him.

He wiggled his eyebrows. "Having fun yet?"

"A blast." Time for a Snickers. Digging in her bag, she tried to distract Brenda and Jay. "So what do you do for a living, Jay?"

"I work for the sanitation department in Lakewood."

There was a pause while they all absorbed this. Tansey wasn't sure exactly what that meant, and she was about to ask for clarity when Brenda snorted.

"You're a garbage man? Figures."

Jay, who had been chewing on his fingernail, spat a piece out at the window. Tansey dug in her bag for her antibacterial gel and squirted a drop in her hand, rubbing vigorously.

"You got a problem with that? You don't exactly look like a rocket scientist, you know."

Apparently Susie had a really warped sense of humor to stick Brenda and Jay in the front seat together. Of course, that had probably been the whole point; that way the DJs would have plenty to discuss about the contest on air. Which meant make fun of Brenda and Jay. They were predetermined to piss each other off for listeners' entertainment. And she and J.T. were probably supposed to "hook up."

If the idea weren't so appealing, she would be annoyed.

With great dignity Brenda said, "I'm a hair stylist."

Jay laughed, slapping his hand on his knee. "Told you. You look dumb as a fence post. Hair spray kills brain cells, you know."

Tansey found her Snickers and tore it open enthusiastically.

Brenda bristled. "It takes hard work to become a stylist. I had to pass an eight-hour board exam! I know all the muscles in the head, thank you very much."

Jay leaned forward and whispered something to Brenda. All the color drained from her face. She turned to face forward again, hitting her chest against the steering wheel. Giving a little yelp, she settled back against the leather upholstery and turned left toward the camera, lips pursed.

Jay looked supremely satisfied.

Tansey said around a mouthful of chocolate, "You want this other one, J.T.?"

He took the proffered candy bar. "I think I'm going to regret not having any headphones."

Waving her now-empty wrapper, Tansey nodded. "I'm going to regret not bringing a twelve-pack of these."

Brenda and Jay's scuffle had a positive effect though; she felt much more relaxed sitting next to J.T. Her inner thighs were hardly burning at all.

After a quick swipe of her tongue across her top teeth, she asked, "Do I have chocolate on my teeth?"

She peeled her lips back and bared her teeth for him.

"A little bit." His finger came up and touched her lip. "Right here."

The pressure was faint, but it set her heart thumping. When he took the little fleck of chocolate up to his own mouth and sucked it off with a sly smile, she forgot all about being comfortable.

She forgot all about her determination to postpone dating and sex until after she had her college degree.

She even forgot about the camera.

There was nothing but baby-blue eyes, a rugged chin, and soft worn jeans hugging in all the right places. Chocolate, black leather interior, and a naughty, naughty smile that had her breath permanently lodged in her throat like a peppermint gone the wrong way.

"So what do you do, Tansey?" Brenda tapped her on the shoulder, sending Tansey jerking back into her seat.

She'd been leaning toward J.T., her right butt cheek sliding across the stitching that indicated which seat was hers. Five minutes into this gig and she was already forgetting the rules. Butt in seat, hands to herself. It wasn't all that hard.

Swallowing, she turned to Brenda, trying to ignore J.T.

"Um, I'm a manager in the women's department at Dillard's and a college student." Well, soon to be anyway. It was just a matter of filling out the paperwork. Signing up for classes. Throwing herself into massive debt. Beyond what she already had, that is.

Brenda fiddled with her earring, a gigantic gold circle Tansey thought could double as a hula hoop for most average-size children. "Is your discount any good?"

"Thirty percent, including sale items."

"Oooh, not bad. What about you, J.T.? You smell like sawdust, so I'm guessing construction."

J.T. nodded. "You got it."

Brenda cocked her head to the right, the tips of her aggressively sprayed bangs touching the rearview mirror. "Just a little hint if you're in the market for a woman. Caramel highlights. It would make all the difference in the world. Jazz you up a bit."

Tansey and Jay laughed while J.T. looked skeptical. "Thanks, but I'm not dying my hair."

"Not everyone wants to look like they dipped their head in gold paint," Jay remarked, flicking his finger across Brenda's hair.

Brenda swatted his finger. "Don't touch me. And my hair is naturally blond."

Tansey swallowed a hefty lump of disbelief, and even J.T. looked doubtful. Brenda's hair was an aggressive mix of the yellow from the McDonald's arches and a suspiciously darker undercoat—a blend of colors clearly not found in nature.

"No, it's not." Jay snorted.

"Is, too."

Tansey glanced at her watch. They had been in the car for exactly seven minutes, and for once in her life, she actually missed folding turtlenecks. Being at work had to be more relaxing than this. It was like baby-sitting without getting paid.

"If that's your natural hair color, prove it to me," Jay said.

"How?"

"Lift your skirt." Jay grinned.

Hello. Tansey clapped her hand over her mouth, appalled. J.T. winced. Brenda gasped and then cracked Jay right across the face with the palm of her hand.

"Asshole." Brenda settled back in her seat, looking out the driver-side window, shoulders tense.

Jay rubbed his face and looked back at Tansey. "You see that? She hit me. I think she should be kicked out of the car for that, don't you?"

And Jay should get removed just for being a schmuck.

"What's it say in the rules?" Tansey asked, wishing they'd both get kicked out so she could fantasize about J.T.'s chest in private.

"I don't think there was a section on assault," J.T. said.

"I'm not leaving this car," Brenda said, turning to glare at Jay. "Ever. Until it's mine."

Tansey felt the force of her anger even though she could only see the right side of Brenda's face. That was one determined hair stylist.

"Yeah, well, I've got nothing but time, honey babe." Jay relaxed back in his seat. "I don't get bored, and I don't give a shit if I get fired. I can wait you out for as long as it takes. This car is mine."

Tansey started to think maybe she wouldn't be home in time for *CSI* like she'd originally planned. She turned to J.T. "What about you?"

He shrugged. "I'm comfortable."

Trying to read J.T. wasn't easy. His expressions were subtle, arms closed, movements still and casual. Tansey fidgeted twenty times to every one of his slight shifts, and his eyes focused on her, steady and unwavering. The only thing she seemed to be able to ascertain about him was that he was interested in her, and maybe that was pure hope on her part.

J.T.'s gaze dropped ever so briefly down to her chest. "I'm in no hurry to leave."

That was interested, yep. But his words were also determined, and given J.T.'s ability to sit completely motionless, he was serious competition for this contest. But at least with J.T. around she wouldn't be alone with Double Trouble up front.

She glanced at her watch again. Twelve minutes. They'd been locked in here as prisoners of entertainment for only seven hundred twenty seconds. It felt like at least a thousand.

When was her first bio break? As luck would have it, she needed it.

FIVE

J.T. was lying, of course.

He wasn't the least bit comfortable at all. Listening to Brenda and Jay fight was as much fun as watching birds peck each other's eyes out.

Then there was Tansey. He was aware of every single jiggle and jerk her body made, which were plentiful, given that she kept bending over to dig in her bag and adjust and readjust her feet beneath her legs.

It was causing him to do an elevator imitation in his pants. Going up, going down, going up, up, up again.

He'd wanted to kiss that chocolate off her lip, to shove his tongue into her mouth and lick and suck all around, and that was just damned annoying.

Tansey pulled out a magazine and started flipping through it. It was one of those chick magazines, with a half-naked tanned anorexic on the front and bold headlines that screamed *How to Find His Hot Spot* and *The Hottest Colors for Spring*. Every other word was *hot*, *guy*, or *orgasm*.

It confirmed that he couldn't pursue his massive erection . . . attraction . . . toward Tansey. Women ready to settle down and start shopping for maternity clothes did not read magazines like that. He needed a woman reading *Martha Stewart Living*, *Cooking Light*, or *Good Housekeeping*, and he'd bet Kowalski Construction none of those were tucked in Tansey's messenger bag.

She glanced over at him. "Do guys really like women like this?" she said, flipping her finger over the cover model. "You can't seem to keep your eyes off her."

"I was thinking that her skin color looks fake. It's the shade of a corn dog." And the model was shiny, which brought to mind a greasy corn dog—definitely not the way he liked a woman.

Tansey laughed. "A corn dog? I was thinking she was shaped like a lollipop, but hey, I think you're right, too."

"A corn-dog-colored lollipop. Maybe some guys are into that, but not me." He was starting to think he'd like to be in a pale woman with dark hair with red streaks.

Up, up, up went his jeans.

Dammit. He shifted. Both Jay and Brenda had slapped headphones on, and Jay was eating from a bag of potato chips.

The soft hum of their music blended together with Jay's chewing and made a garbled backdrop to Tansey's low, throaty laughter. The air smelled like salt and chocolate and Tansey's sweet-sheet smell, and he was starting to think he'd *pay* twenty-five grand to get out of there and away from temptation.

Instead, he touched the red streak in her hair, letting the silky strands fall over his rough fingers. "What are these for? Are you in a band on the weekends or something? The Redheads?"

She rolled her eyes but still laughed at his lame joke. "It's just for fun. I'm clinging to the illusion that I'm hip and fashionable and not approaching thirty with very little to show for my life so far."

Her words were lighthearted, but he heard some truth behind them. There was a thin layer of disappointment in her dark, luminous eyes.

"And here I just thought you were a part-time punk rocker with hidden body piercings."

She laughed. "I'm not hiding anything under my clothes, I promise."

Would she slap him like Brenda had if he repeated Jay's request? *Lift your skirt and prove it?*

J.T. couldn't think of anything to say that wasn't perverted, so he drummed his fingers on his knee. Tansey went back to flipping through her magazine, and the minutes ticked painfully by, while he stared out the window at the pretzel stand. The employees rolled out the dough, tossed the middle of the snakelike strand up in the air, and slapped it down onto the counter into a pretzel shape. Roll, toss, slap.

Over and over.

He was going to go insane if he had to watch this for a day or more.

"Do you want to read my magazine? I'm done with it." Tansey held out the glossy pile of makeup ads and orgasm articles, and for some inexplicable reason he took it.

She smiled and opened the *Time* magazine now in her lap. That wasn't fair. He got *Cosmo* and she got *Time*? He flipped to a spring hairstyles page. Boring.

As was the ten ways to wear a denim skirt.

Followed by a sex quiz. All right. Now this could be interesting.

Are you a spontaneous lover or suffering from sameness?

Well, he wasn't anyone's lover at the moment, but he supposed he could base his answers on past experience. And while he wasn't going to be in demand as a gigolo any time soon, no girlfriend had ever complained. He was spontaneous, creative, romantic.

Hell, yeah.

Question 1: What do you do on a Friday night?

a) Watch a video at home

That sounded pretty standard for him.

b) Hit the clubs for hot Latin dancing

Who was he? Ricky Martin?

c) Dash off to New York for a romantic weekend and catch a Broadway show

That would require money, which, generally speaking, he didn't have.

d) Burn your pesto chicken when your dinner at home turns into sex on the table

Hey, he ate on his table, and he didn't even know what pesto chicken was. J.T. mentally checked "a" and flipped to the next page to check the score. A four meant you had chosen the spontaneous answer, a one meant you were boring. Which he was apparently. He had scored a one.

Annoyed, he looked at question two.

Question 2: Where is the most exciting place you've had sex?

a) A hot tub

J.T. snorted. Again, the assumption here was that he had access to a hot tub. The only amenity available in his apartment was the plastic mini-blinds.

b) Outside

He had done that, more than once. An old girlfriend had been into camping. And they had been standing up a couple times. That certainly qualified for spontaneous.

c) At work

Like that would ever be possible. *Here honey, lie down on this plywood, and let's hope you don't get a splinter in your ass.*

d) The bedroom

J.T. figured he had improved with this answer. Having sex outside was way more exciting than the bedroom and had a certain element of risk to it. He checked the answer guide.

"Two points? What the hell?" he said out loud, thoroughly pissed. Why did doing it at work get a four? That wasn't spontaneous. That was out of control.

"What are you doing?" Tansey asked.

J.T. looked over at her, closing the magazine so she couldn't see the quiz. "Nothing."

She grinned. "Do you need a pen? That way you can just add up all your answers at the end."

"I wasn't really doing the quiz. I was just looking at the answers."

"Uh-huh." She stared at him from under those long, mink-colored lashes and turned a little so her warm-up jacket buckled and revealed the top of her breast. "So what's the question you were just reading?"

"What is the most exciting place you've ever had sex."

Tansey's eyes widened just slightly. "What are the choices?"

He read them to her, trying to sound casual.

"I think I score a one on that," she said.

"You've never been daring enough to do it in a hot tub?" It wasn't his personal fantasy, but the thought of Tansey naked with steam rising around her had him fogging up the windows.

"No." She shook her head, and damned if she didn't look disappointed. "I've never done any of those."

"Not even in the bedroom?" he asked, suddenly terrified that he had been thinking lusty thoughts about a virgin-by-choice.

She laughed. "Well, okay, yes, that one."

Relief had him relaxing his grip on the magazine. Thank God. "Not that it's any of my business," he added, realizing that since the very second he'd met Tansey, he'd been acting like a complete and utter ass.

That twenty-year-old she'd been talking to in line had probably displayed more maturity than he was currently.

Tansey grinned like she knew exactly what his thoughts were. "What's the next question?"

He glanced down, but a knock on the window had him starting and guiltily shoving the magazine toward Tansey.

"Keep it," she whispered. "We'll answer the questions together later, okay?"

For such a bad idea, it sounded so really, really good. "Sure."

Fortunately, it was just Steve at the window, so J.T. wasn't too humiliated. He opened the door. "What's up?"

"I'm taking a break. You need anything?"

He needed to get out of the damn car. "Yeah, get me something to eat, will you?"

"Chocolate doesn't fill you up?" Tansey asked, her expression coy when he glanced over at her.

"Nah. I'm a growing boy." J.T. lifted his legs off the seat and dug in his pocket for his wallet.

Suddenly Tansey's hands were about on his crotch, splayed out and pushing down. He froze. "What?" He couldn't even get any more than that past his lips.

"Part of you has to stay in your seat! You'll get kicked out." Tansey was leaning over him, still shoving, so he dropped his legs back down until he was touching leather.

"Thanks." He studied her, curious as to why she'd be helping him compete against her.

She must have realized the same thing, because she blushed a little, her pale skin staining a rosy pink, and J.T. thought he could like Tansey for a whole lot more than her exotic looks.

He shoved a twenty at Steve. "Get me a gyro, would you? And a book. Not that true crime stuff you read, but something off the fiction best-seller list. Thanks, man."

"Got it." Steve took the money and headed for the food court.

"You read?" Tansey asked, her voice incredulous.

Obviously she had construction workers lumped in a category with gorillas—hairy with opposable thumbs, but not ready for chess.

"Yep. Since first grade."

Her blush deepened. "No, I just meant . . . I don't know. I'm sorry, that sounded rude."

"Never judge a book by its cover," he said with a grin.

She laughed. "I guess. So what do you like to read?"

"I like thrillers like Grisham, and I like Tom Clancy, but I also like literary fiction and the classics. Hawthorne, Hemingway, Fitzgerald . . . I guess I focus on the American authors."

"Did you go to college?" Tansey was leaning back in her seat, playing with the zipper on her sweatshirt, turned toward him.

"No. I just like the library. Makes me a geek, huh?" He had judged Tansey, too, based on her appearance. She looked like her main concern in life was whether she was over the credit limit on her credit cards or not, and clearly, there was much more to her than that.

"No, not at all. I love to read, too. Before I dropped out of school, I discovered the Russians. Tolstoy, Doestoevsky, Tergenev. Those are some of my favorite books, because the characters are so grounded, so moody, so eccentric."

"I've never read any of them. What do you recommend?"

"Not *Anna Karenina*, that's for sure. The writing is gorgeous, but I couldn't root for the heroine at all."

"Isn't that supposed to be a romance?"

"Yes, but she falls for a man who wants her because he can't have her. Then when she cheats on her husband with him, he eventually doesn't want her anymore and she throws herself in front of a train. End of story." Tansey curled her lip. "Not very romantic to me."

"Me, either." J.T. wasn't sure what he thought could be classified as romantic, but that wasn't it. Neither was hot Latin dancing.

"Did you read *Wuthering Heights*? What did you think of Heathcliff?" she asked.

"I only read that because I had to in high school. But let's just say two words about Heathcliff—*restraining order*."

Tansey slapped his leg. "That's exactly what I thought. He's like a stalker, and everyone I say that to acts like I'm nuts. They think he's so deep and tragic. I just think he's a creepy jerk."

"Exactly. I always thought the same thing."

And J.T. also thought he was in some serious trouble.

THREE hours later, Brenda and Jay were making out in the front seat.

Tansey picked at the remnants of her turkey sandwich and tried not to look at them, their arms tangled around each other, faces mashed together. Nothing could block out the sound though, of their eager gasps and smacking lips.

She crammed turkey in her mouth and tried not to be grossed out—or worse, jealous. "It seems like I've been eating nonstop since we stepped in the car. But it's so hard to just sit here and do nothing."

Though she hadn't been doing nothing. She'd been talking to J.T. the entire time and was now thoroughly confused. He was a total hottie, who looked like all her previous no-good boyfriends, yet there was so much more to J.T. than good looks, and they actually shared a lot of the same tastes.

On the one hand, it was great that she had someone interesting she could chat with and pass the time. On the other hand, it made her question all her assumptions about men, dating, and identifying cheaters by their looks.

"I guess that's why Brenda and Jay found something else to do."

We could do that. More than anything Tansey wanted to do that with J.T., even more so now that they'd been talking and found out they had so much in common. But she wasn't supposed to be looking for a boyfriend, not now when she had a lot of work in front of her to finish her degree. Not when she didn't think she could take the pain of one more rejection, one more betrayal.

Which was what it really boiled down to—her heart and self-esteem were still dented from Bill. She couldn't handle going through that again.

But something, an annoying little voice that was probably hormonally activated, kept insisting J.T. wouldn't be another guy like Bill.

"Do you like your job, J.T.?"

"Yeah, I do. I like working with my hands."

Of course he did. Tansey tried not to whimper.

"And I like owning the business with my dad, being our own bosses. My dad's been going through a tough time since my stepmother left him, and it's nice to be around, to keep an eye on him, you know?"

What she knew was that if he kept revealing the one hundred and one ways he was a great guy, she was going to have a hard time resisting the urge to cross to his side of the seat.

"That's nice. It must feel good to be close to your dad. My dad and I get along and we love each other, but there's no real understanding there." Her father tried, but Tansey thought she just bewildered him most of the time. "Now my mom, she understood me. But she died when I was in college the first time. That's why I dropped out."

And it was silly, ridiculous, that after seven years, suddenly tears were forming in her eyes and her voice wobbled. But then J.T.'s hand was in hers, and he was giving a comforting squeeze.

"My mom died, too. When I was six. I still miss her."

Tansey turned to J.T. Squeezed his hand back. "I'm sorry," she whispered.

Then as they stared into each other's eyes in the dimming light of the backseat of the Expedition, she heard the sound of Brenda's bra being unsnapped in the front seat.

SIX

TANSEY spit in the sink and tried not to touch anything. "Can you just say that again for me, please? I don't think I heard you correctly."

Her ears must be clogged, her brain foggy from spending the night dozing in and out of sleep curled up against the back door of the SUV. They'd been in the car eighteen hours and counting.

"I'm going out with J.T.'s father tonight on a date," Emily said, all perky smiles and artlessly tousled blond hair.

That's what she'd thought Emily had said. "How did that happen? And how old is he?"

"When I came to see you last night, John had just brought J.T. some coffee. So we got to talking, and we chatted for a half an hour. I thought he was really interesting and sweet, so I asked him out. I'm not really sure how old he is."

Just like that. Emily had just asked out a man probably twice her age after just having gone out with a twenty-two-year-old. Emily was clearly much better at the whole *joie de vivre* thing than she was.

Tansey was falling for J. T. Kowalski with all the force of Niagara Falls on high. Yet was she doing anything about it? No, she was chatting and laughing and sticking to her stupid notion that dating equaled pain. No wonder she was a twenty-eight-year-old malcontent. She was too afraid to do anything about it.

She was afraid of change. Of being hurt. Of failure.

Emily would have leapt over the seat and latched on to J.T., taking advantage of the situation just like Jay had with Brenda. Of course, Jay had fallen out of his seat trying to take a nosedive into Brenda's cleavage and had been kicked out of the car.

Tansey moisturized her face in the mall bathroom mirror, moving quickly so she didn't exceed her ten-minute time limit. "Well, have fun. Which is better than me. I want J.T. so bad I swear my hands are shaking."

"So go for it." Emily checked her lipstick and blew herself a kiss in the mirror.

"That's not the plan, remember?"

"So who says it has to be a long-term thing? Just sleep with him and get him out of your system." She grinned. "Just wait until you're out of the car though."

"You don't think that would look good on camera?" Tansey asked ruefully. She opened her foundation, slapping it on vigorously, hoping to move herself beyond transparent into only ghostlike pale.

"Just a tiny bit tacky. By the way, you're winning in the online poll at the radio station's website. Thirty-four percent of voters want you to win."

"They're voting on us?" Tansey was mortified yet oddly gratified that she was winning. Running her brush through her hair so fast she could hear the crackle of static electricity, she groaned. "For a minute, I actually forgot that there are people on the other end, watching what that camera records. All the time. God, I probably drooled in my sleep."

"Twenty-five grand is worth a little drool."

"*If* I win." Jay's falling over had been a bit of luck, but J.T. and Brenda didn't look at all ready to go anywhere.

"If you don't win, you can always take J.T. as a consolation prize." Emily moved her eyebrows up and down.

WHEN she got back to the car—with thirty seconds to spare—J.T. was still sleeping, his head tucked in between the seat and the window. Tansey slid into her seat carefully and pulled the car door shut with a soft snick.

J.T. looked younger, restless, his lips moving in his sleep, and Tansey had the sudden ridiculous urge to reach over and smooth his hair off his forehead—to touch him, stroke over his skin, tangle her fingers in his hair. Kiss him.

"He is pretty damn cute, isn't he?" Brenda asked from the front seat, her mouth around a Danish.

Tansey cleared her throat, embarrassed to have been caught gawking. "So Brenda, can I ask you something?"

"Sure."

It was none of her business, but she was dying to know. "What was that thing between you and Jay last night? Clearly you couldn't stand each other."

Brenda just shrugged, wiping her fingers with blue air-brushed nails on her napkin. "Just boredom, really. And opposites do attract sexually. Look at you and J.T. You're both about to spontaneously combust. I don't know why you don't just go for it."

want to disappoint or upset Tansey, God knew he really needed the money.

Tansey laughed. "So, where do you see yourself in a few years, J.T.? Have you reached that, 'yeah, I'm done' spot yet?"

Hardly. "Where I see myself is simple. I want to save the family business, build it back up so it's even stronger than it was when my dad settled with my stepmother. And while I'm doing that, I want to start a family."

Maybe that would scare the hell out of her, but he needed to say it. Here, while the backseat was warm and toasty and intimate, and Tansey was looking and acting beautiful, like a woman he could fall for, he needed to remind himself that he couldn't settle. He wanted a wife, children, a home.

Not a brief burst of passion.

But Tansey didn't recoil. She just looked thoughtful. "I can see that, when I look at you. Stable. Reliable. The kind of guy who comes home when he says he will and throws the kids up in the air."

That's the way he saw himself as well, and that she agreed made him lean closer to her, his fingers interlacing with hers. "What about you, Tansey? Teaching school, I can see that. Anything else?"

This was where she said she wanted to buy a nice car, go to Cancun, join a gym.

Tugging a necklace out of her cleavage, Tansey played with the tiny cross. "My mother gave me this when I was baptized. It's really too small for me to still be wearing it, but somehow I feel like it keeps her close to me."

Her wistful expression touched him. He stroked his thumb across her hand. "I understand that. I have a stuffed dog my mom gave me and I wouldn't part with that thing for a million bucks." It was packed away in a box, either. It was in his closet on the shelf, wher

"Because we're opposites. There wouldn't be any future in it." Not that she really believed they were opposites anymore.

"So? Just enjoy the moment."

It seemed like that was Emily's mantra, too. But the problem was, Tansey had been avoiding dealing with the future for seven years, and damn it, the future was now. She had to deal with it sooner or later, and J.T. couldn't be part of that.

She stole a glance at him.

Or could he?

She almost groaned. God, she was driving herself crazy.

"Did you enjoy your moment with Jay?" Tansey was struggling with that a little.

"Sure. And if he calls me, he does. And if he doesn't, no sweat. It doesn't mean anything."

And right then Tansey knew exactly why she wasn't attacking J.T. She knew why in eight years, she'd only had two boyfriends, and why no matter how attracted she was to J.T., she couldn't just have a hot fling.

She didn't do sex without emotion. She put her heart into her relationships, and she didn't have the ability to separate the physical from the emotional. Didn't want to. If Tansey made out with a guy, she damn well expected him to call her.

As of yet, J.T. was a wild card. She wasn't sure what his reaction would be, and she wasn't sure he could ever fit into the life plans she so desperately wanted to focus on.

And she was starting to think lack of sleep was getting to her.

A knock on Brenda's door had her opening it. "Hey. What?"

It was Brenda's sister, who had been there several times bringing supplies to Brenda and reporting on Brenda's three-year-old daughter, who she was watching.

"It's Mariah. She's sick."

"What's the matter with her?" Brenda sat up straighter.

"It's another ear infection—high fever, she woke up screaming this morning. Mom's taking her to the doctor now."

Without hesitation, Brenda pushed her sister back and climbed out of the car. "That's the sixth ear infection since October."

"Brenda! You can't leave the car!"

"Screw it. Mariah needs me." And Brenda walked away without a glance back.

J.T. had woken up when Brenda's sister had knocked on the car window. He saw the way she just abandoned twenty-five grand to comfort her kid, and he knew that although Brenda wasn't exactly his type, that was the kind of mother he wanted for his own children.

Would what's-her-name in the card store be like that?

Would Tansey? He turned and saw her watching Brenda's receding form thoughtfully.

"Wow," she said. "Never judge a book by its cover."

"Do you think she was crazy to walk away?" He needed to know. If Tansey was on a different page about this, he thought he would have a much easier time resisting her allure.

The look she gave him was incredulous. "No. I think what she did was the right thing. Your children should come first." Then she narrowed her eyes. "Why? What do you think?"

"I agree with you." He was slouched in the corner still, but their legs were touching. He wanted to touch her everywhere. He wanted to stop pretending he wasn't attracted to her. He wanted to get out of this car and ask her out for a real date.

But he was stuck in the car, and he found her vehemence on behalf of children very, very sexy.

"What will you do with the money, Tansey, if you win?"

"Well, I think I told you I'm going back to college, right?"

He nodded as she twirled her hair around her finger.

"I wanted to be a teacher. The need for good teachers in urban areas is overwhelming. A lot of teachers want the suburban jobs because they think it's safer and it pays better, but I want to teach kids who really need me. Kids who need someone who believes in them."

J.T. figured this pleasant, floating-in-maple-syrup feeling was a sure bet he was gone. Tansey was sweet and intelligent and beautiful, and he had fallen hard for her.

"I think that sounds like something you'd be really good at. Believing in them."

"Thank you, J.T." She smiled, a little dimple appearing in her alabaster cheek. "So that's what I need the money for. So I don't go into debt I can't afford to ever repay. What about you?"

J.T. sat up, stretching his arms, shifting himself closer to her. "My dad paid a large settlement to my stepmother in their divorce, and our business is floundering. It needs a jolt of cash, or it's probably going to fold."

It hurt to say that, but it was true. "My dad built this business from the ground up, and he's devoted twenty-five years to it. I can't just let it disappear without a fight."

"Wow. That's tough. You have a very legitimate need, too." She flipped her hair over her shoulder. "I'm almost not sure who I think should win."

He wasn't either.

"Maybe Brenda should have won," he said with a grin, because it made him uneasy to realize that they were locked in competition with each other now. That one of them would walk away with twenty-five grand and the other with nothing.

One of them would have to cave eventually, and although he didn't could catch a glimpse of the ear every day when he pulled out clean clothes.

"I want to be a mom like my mother was. I want to be there for my kids, to listen, to love, to play, to hold them. I'm not sure if I can measure up though."

J.T. squeezed her hand. Brushed her dark hair back off her face. And decided he could most definitely fall in love with her. Probably any minute now. "Tansey, you don't have anything to worry about."

SEVEN

TANSEY woke up from napping with her head in J.T.'s crotch.

Not completely facedown, but close enough. Her cheek was on his fly, and her lips rested on his hard inner thigh. Denim swam in front of her eyes, and her hand clung to his knee.

She stiffened. *Hello*. What exactly had she been dreaming about?

J.T.'s hand stroked her hair, and she couldn't stop a sigh from escaping.

But she forced herself to lift her head, which wasn't easy to do given her position, and realized things were harder behind his zipper than should be strictly necessary for sedentary activities.

"God, J.T., I'm sorry. Did I fall on you while I was sleeping?" Tansey tried to get up, suddenly aware that her legs and butt needed to stay on her side of the car. It made trying to sit up without grasping his legs damn near impossible.

"I don't mind. Really."

He eased her head back down, and Tansey let it drop gratefully. She'd been getting a crick in her neck. But at least now she was on her back, the base of her skull resting in his lap, enough distance away from the erection zone to make her feel comfortable.

She covered her mouth over a yawn and looked up at him. "What time is it?"

"I have no idea. I think it's dinnertime given the light traffic walking around the mall, but I've sort of lost all sense of reality."

Tansey was grateful that the radio station had the courtesy to rope off the area immediately around the SUV so they weren't subjected to teenagers pounding on the windows. There was a guard on watch, monitoring the cameras and their bio breaks and allowing only people they had authorized to come over and speak to them.

She must have fallen asleep after she and J.T. had discussed every movie they'd ever seen, ran through entire years of their childhood, and debated the merits of cats versus dogs.

If she had to be stuck in a car for twenty-seven hours with anyone, she was so damn glad it was him. She was also pretty sure that in that same amount of time, she had just about fallen in love with J.T.

Which was probably insane. But she rationalized that they had talked for hours and hours and hours. They were sharing close quarters, and not once had J.T. gotten on her nerves. That had to at least be some serious *like*.

Maybe all engaged couples should be forced to live in the backseat of a Ford Expedition for a weekend before they got married. It might lower the divorce rate by keeping a lot of couples from getting married in the first place.

"You hungry?" she asked, staring up at his chin, which was starting to become stubbly with wheat-colored whiskers.

"Not for food."

Hoh, boy. She knew that tone and that deep, penetrating look.

Tansey's heart kicked up a notch at the predatory look on his face. "What do you mean?"

"I mean, I'm thinking of pulling a Jay and Brenda."

His legs shifted, and she swore she could felt heat radiating from beneath his jeans, scorching her brain until she couldn't think of a single thing to say besides, "Okay."

"I've been thinking about this since you walked up to me yesterday."

She could understand that. So had she.

J.T. leaned over, his fingers in her hair, urging her head up to meet him.

The passenger side door opened, and a whoosh of warm air and mall noise rushed in. "Tansey, it's Emily. What do you want for dinner?"

Tansey dropped her head back down in disappointment. She loved Emily, but she was going to kill her.

"Oops. Sorry." Emily seemed to realize what she had interrupted. "Should I come back later?"

"Yes," J.T. said on a growl, before his hand suddenly jerked in Tansey's hair, yanking on her roots and bringing tears to her eyes.

"Oww, J.T., ease up." Tansey glanced up at him and saw that his jaw had dropped. He wasn't looking at her, but at Emily.

She glanced behind her, going cross-eyed from her position lying on his lap, and realized that J.T.'s father was standing with Emily. They looked awfully comfortable with each other.

"Are you holding hands?" J.T. asked in an outraged voice.

"Oh, I guess so." Emily laughed and held up their clasped hands. "You know, we were supposed to go out tonight and then somehow neither of us wanted to wait and we wound up spending the whole day together. We just stopped by to feed you guys before we head out to dinner and dancing."

"Dancing?" J.T. couldn't have sounded more horrified if Emily had suggested they were going up on the top of the SUV to have wild sex for cash.

J.T.'s father just nodded with a complacent smile. With his tall good looks, blond hair, and easy manners, he reminded Tansey a lot of J.T. When J.T. wasn't hyperventilating like he was now.

"I think we'll pass on dinner," Tansey said, sitting up and reluctantly abandoning J.T.'s lap. "But thanks, guys. Have fun."

"Oh, we will!" Emily smiled and hauled off J.T.'s dad.

"What the hell was that all about?"

J.T. had told her how worried he was about his father and how he felt like his father wasn't dealing with his divorce well. "It looks like your dad is recovering from whatever happened between him and your stepmother."

He snorted. "I guess so, Jesus." He rubbed his eyes. "I wanted him to move on, stop feeling so down about things, but I didn't mean for him to start running around with a girl half his age. If she thinks he has money, you'd better set the record straight."

Tansey was insulted on Emily's behalf. "Emily is one of the kindest, most generous people I know. She is not a gold digger."

"So what could she possibly see in my father?"

"Maybe you're judging a book by its cover again. Maybe she thinks he's interesting, nice, attractive. Sort of how I feel about you."

"Really?" His disgusted tone gave way to an intrigued one.

"Oh, yeah. You hadn't noticed?"

"I was hoping." J.T. stripped off his flannel shirt, giving Tansey a mouthwatering view of his biceps.

She wanted to squeeze them. Lick them. Him. Everywhere. Her breath hitched. "What are you doing?"

"Taking off my shirt. I'm hot."

That he was. Tansey swallowed. "What time does the mall close?"

"Nine."

She glanced at her watch. "Only three more hours. Then we'll be alone."

"With the cameras."

Tansey almost groaned. Damn the cameras to hell and back on a broomstick. God.

But if they turned J.T.'s back to the camera, he would block her and at least they could do *something* to finally touch each other, taste each other, without anyone seeing.

Without leaving their respective seats.

Her life was a mass of cruel ironies.

J.T. bought condoms at the mall drug store on his bio break.

What the hell he thought he was going to be able to do with those in the backseat of a car on camera with a security guard wandering around was a mystery, but it made him feel better to have them resting in his pocket.

Like they were a promise, that sooner or later, no matter how torturous the wait, he was going to get his hands on Tansey Reynolds. And he was going to explore every inch of her pale flesh and dip his tongue into all her private places and send them both reeling into ecstasy.

In the meantime, the wait was hell.

He stretched his arms over his head before he had to get back in the car. He was stiff from all that sitting around, and his ass was going numb. But it was worth it. Not for the money, which he didn't quite believe could ever be his. But for the opportunity to meet Tansey, to spend this time together.

It was like speed dating. He'd been with her for thirty hours straight, and he felt like he knew her better than some women he'd dated for six months. Forced captivity created intimacy, he guessed.

Steve strolled across the mall atrium with two coffees in his hands and handed one to J.T. "Last break for the night. The mall's closing, and I'm out of here."

"Thanks, man." Steve had been a good guy, bringing J.T. a clean shirt, deodorant, and a toothbrush, along with a couple of meals. "I owe you."

"Yeah, how about you take me out and buy me a beer when you collect your twenty-five grand?" Steve dug his keys out of his front pocket. "Oh, and by the way, how is it that your dad managed to snag the cute blond friend? Shouldn't I have had first rights to flirt with her, considering I'm your best friend?"

J.T. wanted to close his eyes and gag at the thought of his father out dancing with Emily. "I have no idea what's up with that . . . I thought my dad was still missing my stepmom, but I guess not. I hope Emily doesn't hurt his feelings or anything. He's not exactly dating savvy."

"He's doing all right if he hooked up with a woman half his age." Steve shook his head. "Damn, it's not fair. I'm having a hard enough time finding a woman to go out with—I don't need your dad overlapping into my potential dates. He should stick to his own demographic."

"I agree." Sort of. J.T. figured two consenting adults could really do whatever they wanted, but geez, did it have to be his dad? Emily was younger than J.T. by a couple years, and that was just too close for comfort.

"Maybe I should take your dad's strategy and go for a much younger woman." Steve frowned. "No wait, that won't work. She'd wind up being like fifteen. Which is illegal and disgusting."

J.T. laughed. "Get the hell out of here. You can't possibly be jealous of my father."

"Oh, but I am. I really, really am." Steve started backing up. "No girlfriend for six months makes a guy pretty desperate, if you know what I mean."

Didn't he know it. J.T. patted his pocket to make sure the condoms were still in place and headed back toward the car.

"Oh, by the way. Don't let that whole nickname thing on the website bother you."

"What?" J.T. stopped walking. Tansey had told him there were polls on the radio station website on who should win and he was losing, but he didn't know anything about a nickname.

Steve gave a cough into his hand, one that sounded suspiciously like a laugh. "Well, you know, anyone can go to the website and see you in the car. No audio, right, but you can see anything. The station's not doing it in real time, I guess because that would be boring. But you can click on the highlights. And they've got one of you reading *Cosmo* up there. So the DJs have been calling you *Cosmo*."

Nice. "I wasn't reading it. I was looking at the pictures."

With a snort, Steve gave him a wave. "Whatever. See you tomorrow, man. If you're still in the car."

"Oh, I will be." He wasn't going anywhere. Between the allure of twenty-five grand and spending time with Tansey, he definitely wasn't going anywhere.

"You know, if you're smart, you'll butter up Tansey. Maybe she'll just give the win to you."

The very thought repulsed J.T. "That's a really shitty idea. I would never do that to her." He wouldn't do that to anyone, let alone a woman he was pretty damn sure he was falling in love with. "And you're an asshole to suggest it."

Steve held out his hand, eyebrow raised. "All right, man, chill. I was just kidding, anyway."

J.T. was only somewhat mollified. "You'd better be."

But Steve only laughed. "Oh, man, you've got it bad. For your sake, you'd better hope one of you gives up soon or you're going to embarrass yourself. Have a wet dream on camera."

"Because we're opposites. There wouldn't be any future in it." Not that she really believed they were opposites anymore.

"So? Just enjoy the moment."

It seemed like that was Emily's mantra, too. But the problem was, Tansey had been avoiding dealing with the future for seven years, and damn it, the future was now. She had to deal with it sooner or later, and J.T. couldn't be part of that.

She stole a glance at him.

Or could he?

She almost groaned. God, she was driving herself crazy.

"Did you enjoy your moment with Jay?" Tansey was struggling with that a little.

"Sure. And if he calls me, he does. And if he doesn't, no sweat. It doesn't mean anything."

And right then Tansey knew exactly why she wasn't attacking J.T. She knew why in eight years, she'd only had two boyfriends, and why no matter how attracted she was to J.T., she couldn't just have a hot fling.

She didn't do sex without emotion. She put her heart into her relationships, and she didn't have the ability to separate the physical from the emotional. Didn't want to. If Tansey made out with a guy, she damn well expected him to call her.

As of yet, J.T. was a wild card. She wasn't sure what his reaction would be, and she wasn't sure he could ever fit into the life plans she so desperately wanted to focus on.

And she was starting to think lack of sleep was getting to her.

A knock on Brenda's door had her opening it. "Hey. What?"

It was Brenda's sister, who had been there several times bringing supplies to Brenda and reporting on Brenda's three-year-old daughter, who she was watching.

"It's Mariah. She's sick."

"What's the matter with her?" Brenda sat up straighter.

"It's another ear infection—high fever, she woke up screaming this morning. Mom's taking her to the doctor now."

Without hesitation, Brenda pushed her sister back and climbed out of the car. "That's the sixth ear infection since October."

"Brenda! You can't leave the car!"

"Screw it. Mariah needs me." And Brenda walked away without a glance back.

J.T. had woken up when Brenda's sister had knocked on the car window. He saw the way she just abandoned twenty-five grand to comfort her kid, and he knew that although Brenda wasn't exactly his type, that was the kind of mother he wanted for his own children.

Would what's-her-name in the card store be like that?

Would Tansey? He turned and saw her watching Brenda's receding form thoughtfully.

"Wow," she said. "Never judge a book by its cover."

"Do you think she was crazy to walk away?" He needed to know. If Tansey was on a different page about this, he thought he would have a much easier time resisting her allure.

The look she gave him was incredulous. "No. I think what she did was the right thing. Your children should come first." Then she narrowed her eyes. "Why? What do you think?"

"I agree with you." He was slouched in the corner still, but their legs were touching. He wanted to touch her everywhere. He wanted to stop pretending he wasn't attracted to her. He wanted to get out of this car and ask her out for a real date.

But he was stuck in the car, and he found her vehemence on behalf of children very, very sexy.

"What will you do with the money, Tansey, if you win?"

"Well, I think I told you I'm going back to college, right?"

He nodded as she twirled her hair around her finger.

"I wanted to be a teacher. The need for good teachers in urban areas is overwhelming. A lot of teachers want the suburban jobs because they think it's safer and it pays better, but I want to teach kids who really need me. Kids who need someone who believes in them."

J.T. figured this pleasant, floating-in-maple-syrup feeling was a sure bet he was gone. Tansey was sweet and intelligent and beautiful, and he had fallen hard for her.

"I think that sounds like something you'd be really good at. Believing in them."

"Thank you, J.T." She smiled, a little dimple appearing in her alabaster cheek. "So that's what I need the money for. So I don't go into debt I can't afford to ever repay. What about you?"

J.T. sat up, stretching his arms, shifting himself closer to her. "My dad paid a large settlement to my stepmother in their divorce, and our business is floundering. It needs a jolt of cash, or it's probably going to fold."

It hurt to say that, but it was true. "My dad built this business from the ground up, and he's devoted twenty-five years to it. I can't just let it disappear without a fight."

"Wow. That's tough. You have a very legitimate need, too." She flipped her hair over her shoulder. "I'm almost not sure who I think should win."

He wasn't either.

"Maybe Brenda should have won," he said with a grin, because it made him uneasy to realize that they were locked in competition with each other now. That one of them would walk away with twenty-five grand and the other with nothing.

One of them would have to cave eventually, and although he didn't want to disappoint or upset Tansey, God knew he really needed the money.

Tansey laughed. "So, where do you see yourself in a few years, J.T.? Have you reached that, 'yeah, I'm done' spot yet?"

Hardly. "Where I see myself is simple. I want to save the family business, build it back up so it's even stronger than it was when my dad settled with my stepmother. And while I'm doing that, I want to start a family."

Maybe that would scare the hell out of her, but he needed to say it. Here, while the backseat was warm and toasty and intimate, and Tansey was looking and acting beautiful, like a woman he could fall for, he needed to remind himself that he couldn't settle. He wanted a wife, children, a home.

Not a brief burst of passion.

But Tansey didn't recoil. She just looked thoughtful. "I can see that, when I look at you. Stable. Reliable. The kind of guy who comes home when he says he will and throws the kids up in the air."

That's the way he saw himself as well, and that she agreed made him lean closer to her, his fingers interlacing with hers. "What about you, Tansey? Teaching school, I can see that. Anything else?"

This was where she said she wanted to buy a nice car, go to Cancun, join a gym.

Tugging a necklace out of her cleavage, Tansey played with the tiny cross. "My mother gave me this when I was baptized. It's really too small for me to still be wearing it, but somehow I feel like it keeps her close to me."

Her wistful expression touched him. He stroked his thumb across her hand. "I understand that. I have a stuffed dog my mom gave me, and I wouldn't part with that thing for a million bucks." It wasn't packed away in a box, either. It was in his closet on the shelf, where he could catch a glimpse of the ear every day when he pulled out clean clothes.

"I want to be a mom like my mother was. I want to be there for my kids, to listen, to love, to play, to hold them. I'm not sure if I can measure up though."

J.T. squeezed her hand. Brushed her dark hair back off her face. And decided he could most definitely fall in love with her. Probably any minute now. "Tansey, you don't have anything to worry about."

SEVEN

TANSEY woke up from napping with her head in J.T.'s crotch.

Not completely facedown, but close enough. Her cheek was on his fly, and her lips rested on his hard inner thigh. Denim swam in front of her eyes, and her hand clung to his knee.

She stiffened. *Hello*. What exactly had she been dreaming about?

J.T.'s hand stroked her hair, and she couldn't stop a sigh from escaping.

But she forced herself to lift her head, which wasn't easy to do given her position, and realized things were harder behind his zipper than should be strictly necessary for sedentary activities.

"God, J.T., I'm sorry. Did I fall on you while I was sleeping?" Tansey tried to get up, suddenly aware that her legs and butt needed to stay on her side of the car. It made trying to sit up without grasping his legs damn near impossible.

"I don't mind. Really."

He eased her head back down, and Tansey let it drop gratefully. She'd been getting a crick in her neck. But at least now she was on her back, the base of her skull resting in his lap, enough distance away from the erection zone to make her feel comfortable.

She covered her mouth over a yawn and looked up at him. "What time is it?"

"I have no idea. I think it's dinnertime given the light traffic walking around the mall, but I've sort of lost all sense of reality."

Tansey was grateful that the radio station had the courtesy to rope off the area immediately around the SUV so they weren't subjected to teenagers pounding on the windows. There was a guard on watch, monitoring the cameras and their bio breaks and allowing only people they had authorized to come over and speak to them.

She must have fallen asleep after she and J.T. had discussed every movie they'd ever seen, ran through entire years of their childhood, and debated the merits of cats versus dogs.

If she had to be stuck in a car for twenty-seven hours with anyone, she was so damn glad it was him. She was also pretty sure that in that same amount of time, she had just about fallen in love with J.T.

Which was probably insane. But she rationalized that they had talked for hours and hours and hours. They were sharing close quarters, and not once had J.T. gotten on her nerves. That had to at least be some serious *like*.

Maybe all engaged couples should be forced to live in the backseat of a Ford Expedition for a weekend before they got married. It might lower the divorce rate by keeping a lot of couples from getting married in the first place.

"You hungry?" she asked, staring up at his chin, which was starting to become stubbly with wheat-colored whiskers.

"Not for food."

Hoh, boy. She knew that tone and that deep, penetrating look.

Tansey's heart kicked up a notch at the predatory look on his face. "What do you mean?"

"I mean, I'm thinking of pulling a Jay and Brenda."

His legs shifted, and she swore she could felt heat radiating from beneath his jeans, scorching her brain until she couldn't think of a single thing to say besides, "Okay."

"I've been thinking about this since you walked up to me yesterday."

She could understand that. So had she.

J.T. leaned over, his fingers in her hair, urging her head up to meet him.

The passenger side door opened, and a whoosh of warm air and mall noise rushed in. "Tansey, it's Emily. What do you want for dinner?"

Tansey dropped her head back down in disappointment. She loved Emily, but she was going to kill her.

"Oops. Sorry." Emily seemed to realize what she had interrupted. "Should I come back later?"

"Yes," J.T. said on a growl, before his hand suddenly jerked in Tansey's hair, yanking on her roots and bringing tears to her eyes.

"Oww, J.T., ease up." Tansey glanced up at him and saw that his jaw had dropped. He wasn't looking at her, but at Emily.

She glanced behind her, going cross-eyed from her position lying on his lap, and realized that J.T.'s father was standing with Emily. They looked awfully comfortable with each other.

"Are you holding hands?" J.T. asked in an outraged voice.

"Oh, I guess so." Emily laughed and held up their clasped hands. "You know, we were supposed to go out tonight and then somehow neither of us wanted to wait and we wound up spending the whole day together. We just stopped by to feed you guys before we head out to dinner and dancing."

"Dancing?" J.T. couldn't have sounded more horrified if Emily had suggested they were going up on the top of the SUV to have wild sex for cash.

J.T.'s father just nodded with a complacent smile. With his tall good looks, blond hair, and easy manners, he reminded Tansey a lot of J.T. When J.T. wasn't hyperventilating like he was now.

"I think we'll pass on dinner," Tansey said, sitting up and reluctantly abandoning J.T.'s lap. "But thanks, guys. Have fun."

"Oh, we will!" Emily smiled and hauled off J.T.'s dad.

"What the hell was that all about?"

J.T. had told her how worried he was about his father and how he felt like his father wasn't dealing with his divorce well. "It looks like your dad is recovering from whatever happened between him and your stepmother."

He snorted. "I guess so, Jesus." He rubbed his eyes. "I wanted him to move on, stop feeling so down about things, but I didn't mean for him to start running around with a girl half his age. If she thinks he has money, you'd better set the record straight."

Tansey was insulted on Emily's behalf. "Emily is one of the kindest, most generous people I know. She is not a gold digger."

"So what could she possibly see in my father?"

"Maybe you're judging a book by its cover again. Maybe she thinks he's interesting, nice, attractive. Sort of how I feel about you."

"Really?" His disgusted tone gave way to an intrigued one.

"Oh, yeah. You hadn't noticed?"

"I was hoping." J.T. stripped off his flannel shirt, giving Tansey a mouthwatering view of his biceps.

She wanted to squeeze them. Lick them. Him. Everywhere. Her breath hitched. "What are you doing?"

"Taking off my shirt. I'm hot."

That he was. Tansey swallowed. "What time does the mall close?"

"Nine."

She glanced at her watch. "Only three more hours. Then we'll be alone."

"With the cameras."

Tansey almost groaned. Damn the cameras to hell and back on a broomstick. God.

But if they turned J.T.'s back to the camera, he would block her and at least they could do *something* to finally touch each other, taste each other, without anyone seeing.

Without leaving their respective seats.

Her life was a mass of cruel ironies.

J.T. bought condoms at the mall drug store on his bio break.

What the hell he thought he was going to be able to do with those in the backseat of a car on camera with a security guard wandering around was a mystery, but it made him feel better to have them resting in his pocket.

Like they were a promise, that sooner or later, no matter how torturous the wait, he was going to get his hands on Tansey Reynolds. And he was going to explore every inch of her pale flesh and dip his tongue into all her private places and send them both reeling into ecstasy.

In the meantime, the wait was hell.

He stretched his arms over his head before he had to get back in the car. He was stiff from all that sitting around, and his ass was going numb. But it was worth it. Not for the money, which he didn't quite believe could ever be his. But for the opportunity to meet Tansey, to spend this time together.

It was like speed dating. He'd been with her for thirty hours straight, and he felt like he knew her better than some women he'd dated for six months. Forced captivity created intimacy, he guessed.

Steve strolled across the mall atrium with two coffees in his hands and handed one to J.T. "Last break for the night. The mall's closing, and I'm out of here."

"Thanks, man." Steve had been a good guy, bringing J.T. a clean shirt, deodorant, and a toothbrush, along with a couple of meals. "I owe you."

"Yeah, how about you take me out and buy me a beer when you collect your twenty-five grand?" Steve dug his keys out of his front pocket. "Oh, and by the way, how is it that your dad managed to snag the cute blond friend? Shouldn't I have had first rights to flirt with her, considering I'm your best friend?"

J.T. wanted to close his eyes and gag at the thought of his father out dancing with Emily. "I have no idea what's up with that . . . I thought my dad was still missing my stepmom, but I guess not. I hope Emily doesn't hurt his feelings or anything. He's not exactly dating savvy."

"He's doing all right if he hooked up with a woman half his age." Steve shook his head. "Damn, it's not fair. I'm having a hard enough time finding a woman to go out with—I don't need your dad overlapping into my potential dates. He should stick to his own demographic."

"I agree." Sort of. J.T. figured two consenting adults could really do whatever they wanted, but geez, did it have to be his dad? Emily was younger than J.T. by a couple years, and that was just too close for comfort.

"Maybe I should take your dad's strategy and go for a much younger woman." Steve frowned. "No wait, that won't work. She'd wind up being like fifteen. Which is illegal and disgusting."

J.T. laughed. "Get the hell out of here. You can't possibly be jealous of my father."

"Oh, but I am. I really, really am." Steve started backing up. "No girlfriend for six months makes a guy pretty desperate, if you know what I mean."

Didn't he know it. J.T. patted his pocket to make sure the condoms were still in place and headed back toward the car.

"Oh, by the way. Don't let that whole nickname thing on the website bother you."

"What?" J.T. stopped walking. Tansey had told him there were polls on the radio station website on who should win and he was losing, but he didn't know anything about a nickname.

Steve gave a cough into his hand, one that sounded suspiciously like a laugh. "Well, you know, anyone can go to the website and see you in the car. No audio, right, but you can see anything. The station's not doing it in real time, I guess because that would be boring. But you can click on the highlights. And they've got one of you reading *Cosmo* up there. So the DJs have been calling you *Cosmo*."

Nice. "I wasn't reading it. I was looking at the pictures."

With a snort, Steve gave him a wave. "Whatever. See you tomorrow, man. If you're still in the car."

"Oh, I will be." He wasn't going anywhere. Between the allure of twenty-five grand and spending time with Tansey, he definitely wasn't going anywhere.

"You know, if you're smart, you'll butter up Tansey. Maybe she'll just give the win to you."

The very thought repulsed J.T. "That's a really shitty idea. I would never do that to her." He wouldn't do that to anyone, let alone a woman he was pretty damn sure he was falling in love with. "And you're an asshole to suggest it."

Steve held out his hand, eyebrow raised. "All right, man, chill. I was just kidding, anyway."

J.T. was only somewhat mollified. "You'd better be."

But Steve only laughed. "Oh, man, you've got it bad. For your sake, you'd better hope one of you gives up soon or you're going to embarrass yourself. Have a wet dream on camera."

There was an image. Not that he would. But then again, he was really edgy. Annoyed, he started walking away. "Go home, Steve. Worry about your own dreams."

He continued to hear Steve's obnoxious chortling until he got in the SUV and slammed the door.

"You just made it." Tansey said, curled up in the corner, as she looked at her silver watch. "One minute left on your break."

Great. Steve had almost caused him to lose the stupid contest by babbling about nicknames and dreams. "That was close."

Yawning, she gave him a sleepy, catlike smile. She was wearing jeans and a turtleneck sweater, and when she dropped her chin, she let the collar cover up to her bottom lip. "We're going to die in this car, aren't we? We'll be eighty years old, metastasizing into living statues, our legs no longer able to straighten."

"I think at that point, they'd probably just give us both a car." J.T. tried to shift around and get comfortable, but it was impossible. His body was stiff everywhere, and his knee popped when he tried to put his leg over it. "And then it would be an antique, worth even more."

She gave a soft laugh. "I can't stay awake. I feel like I do in the morning before I've had my coffee."

"Go to sleep." He touched her hair, brushed it off her face. "You can lean on me if you want to."

"Okay." She didn't even try to demur, but snuggled right up next to him, her eyes already fluttering shut. Her fingers wrapped around his arm, and her cheek settled against his shoulder. "Tell me a story, J.T."

It hit him then, her words knocking him out like a sucker punch, that he really did feel something deep and wonderful and promising for Tansey. It was exhilarating, honest, and scary as hell. Forcing himself to take deep, even breaths to loosen the sudden tension coiling in his body, he thought a minute. "I don't know any stories."

"Sure you do." Her words slurred a little as she drifted closer toward sleep. "Tell me the story of the princess who had black hair with red streaks."

He was probably going to embarrass the hell out of himself, but J.T. complied. "Okay, once upon a time there was a princess with black hair that had mysterious red streaks in it, a royal stamp for all the kingdom to see. She was untouchable to all the commoners, except for one daring, dashing carpenter who was making repairs on the castle. He fell for her and followed the princess around until she allowed him the privilege of being her love slave."

"Ooohh, I like the sound of this. What happened then?"

J.T. was hoping they'd find out soon. "She favored him with her glorious attentions until she got tired of him and then she sent him back to the village with a broken heart."

She made a soft raspberry sound with her tongue. "That's not a very happy ending."

"Do you believe in happy endings, Tansey?" His arm felt good around her, and he barely brushed his lips back and forth over her hair, tickling his flesh.

"I try not to, because they always seem to let me down. I don't want to, but the truth is . . . yes. I believe in happy endings."

As her breathing evened out and she drifted into true sleep, J.T. wondered if maybe together, they could write one.

EIGHT

"J.T.? Are you awake?" Tansey swallowed the lump in her throat and tried to move her neck. She was pretty sure she was paralyzed. Or at least suffering vertebrae damage. So on the up side, if she didn't win the twenty-five grand, she could still sue the radio station for severe spinal trauma.

She'd been lying awake staring at the back of the headrest in front of her for a few minutes, thinking that the mall was an incredibly creepy place to be in the middle of the night. There were soft security lights casting a feeble glow toward the car, and the skylight in the atrium gave some moonlight, but it was still dark.

Still empty. Still horror-movie-worthy.

"Yeah, I'm awake."

Thank God. It was just too weird to be alone.

There was supposed to be a guard right outside the car, but she couldn't see him. Nor did she see any sign of mall security. If it wasn't for the stupid flipping camera, its red light blinking at her, she would be out of the car and jogging around the fountain.

"Does anyone know we're still here? Have we fallen into some kind of snuff video where masked men are going to come out and start torturing us?" The very thought—which she didn't really believe, but it did seem possible—made her shiver.

"Damn, I hope not." His words were amused, and even in the dim light, she could see his lips turning up.

"Isn't it weird being here in the dark? I shouldn't have fallen asleep at nine o'clock. Now I can't sleep and it's the middle of the night. How many hours until the mall opens?" Even her own voice sounded too loud. Tansey switched to a whisper. "Don't you have a watch? I can't see mine in the dark."

"No. It's impractical to wear a watch when I'm working."

Not knowing how long she had to sit there before it was light made her feel a bit antsy. Anxious. Hysterical. "I think I have to get out of this car or I'm going to scream."

J.T. reached out and took her hand, stroking it calmly.

"Aren't you going crazy yet?" she asked him in disbelief. "It's so *dark*."

Embarrassed by her whininess, she was about to apologize, but he didn't give her time.

"I was thinking the dark could actually be helpful."

Ooohh, she knew that tone. It was the one he had used during the screen test. It was flirtatious, sexy.

"For what? Usually the only thing to do in the dark is sleep." Her fear was receding, replaced by intrigue. What exactly could they do in this SUV with the camera still running?

She didn't think she'd be embarrassed to be caught snogging on camera, but anything beyond that was a little too voyeuristic for her. She liked sex, but she was a traditionalist. No splits on the headboard for her, thank you very much. And always one-on-one with no chance of exposure.

"I can think of way better things to do in the dark besides sleep." He tugged her hand. "Meet me halfway, and I'll show you."

Here it was. The big moment. The Kiss. Tansey was glad it was dark, because she was pretty sure she was blushing like a thirteen-year-old. Of course, nowadays thirteen-year-olds wore hoochie tops and called boys on their cell phones. But when she was thirteen and Kevin Brown had put the moves on her, she had blushed.

Like she was now. Damn, it was taking forever for his lips to get to hers.

But it was worth it when they did.

They sort of collided together in a sigh of relief, their mouths not mashing but not brushing, either. It was a nice, smooth sliding of lips over lips, hands reaching out and touching, faces tilting toward each other.

Oh, yeah. J.T. tasted like sleep and toothpaste, and he was hot, his chin scratchy, tongue already making its way into her open mouth. Everything inside her exploded in a kind of desperate wave of desire, yanking a moan from her mouth.

"I've thought about doing this a hundred times," he whispered, his big hands finding their way into her hair. "Would it be crazy to say that I want to see you again when this whole thing is over? That I think you're really amazing?"

He could say that all he wanted. It sounded just fabulous. "It's not crazy at all . . ." Tansey moved her hands across his chest, enjoying the way his muscles twitched at her touch. "I feel the same way. I really like you, J.T."

They moved into another kiss, and this one went deeper, hotter, until Tansey was stretching, stretching, trying to get closer to him without leaving her seat, her breasts aching and her body zinging with want.

Their labored breathing filled the car, and J.T. broke away to pull off his flannel shirt. He tossed it over the headrest of the driver's seat, partially blocking the camera.

"I got hot and took off my shirt. I didn't realize I was blocking the camera." He winked.

Oh, it was so tempting. But mind over body, she could do it. She could resist. "It's not all the way blocked. And we shouldn't, or they'll disqualify us. Neither one of us will win."

The horror. Enduring nearly two days of this for nothing. "We have to stay in our seats."

Even if it killed them.

J.T. just looked at her for a minute, his shoulders tense, his fingers still entangled in her hair. "Okay," he said very slowly.

Then he reached out and cupped her breast right as his lips moved over hers. "I can still do this without leaving my seat."

And he stroked his fingers over her nipple. They both moaned, faces pressed together.

Tansey started groping for J.T.'s chest, figuring fair was fair. She had been dying to dig her nails into all that studly muscle, and she gave in to the urge. Their kisses accelerated from soft and curious, to desperate, wet. Every brush of his fingers sent her squirming, and Tansey leaned farther and farther, her feet pressed against the floor to stabilize herself.

"I want you, I want you," J.T. murmured in a little chant as he moved down her neck, yanking at the material of her sweater.

Why the hell had she worn a turtleneck? He was going to suffocate in all that cable-knit. A quick glance toward the camera had her calculating that she was visible only from the waist down, the part the contest coordinators needed to see still in the seat. The rest was blocked from view.

So she didn't exactly put up a fight when a frustrated J.T. abandoned the neck of the sweater and went up the bottom with his hand.

In fact, when he unpopped her front-loading bra and his bare skin hit hers, she gave up on the whispering and cried, "Yes! That feels so good."

Normally she would be embarrassed, but since her brain had ceased to function and she was operating solely on the basis of sensation, it never occurred to her. And when J.T. bent over and plucked her nipple with his lips, she gave another enthusiastic shout-out.

"Come here," he whispered, sounding like he was in pain. "They'll never know you left your seat. God, I have to touch you, all of you."

"They'll know," she moaned, forcing her brain to turn back on. Think college, think future, think . . . oh, my, yummy. A hand had slipped down between her thighs, and it wasn't hers.

Jerking back completely to her seat, she took deep, battered breaths and wiped her shiny lips. The camera could see her side of the car. The camera couldn't see the middle. The camera could see J.T.'s side of the car.

Which basically meant she was in a forty-thousand-dollar torture chamber.

But suddenly she had an idea. It seemed brilliant. But her powers of reasoning were compromised by the tight ache between her thighs, so it seemed she should run it past J.T.

"Only one of us can win the car or the cash."

"Yeah?" He was giving her a "who gives a shit, let's get naked" kind of look.

"So . . . if one of us just gave up, or say, moved into the other person's seat, one of us would still win. But we could split the cash and not have to spend who knows how long in this car."

"That's true." He spread his legs like he needed more space.

Which even in the dim light, she could tell he did. That was one impressive erection.

Rubbing his chin, he added, "And I would actually feel better about it that way. We both deserve some money, we both deserve to win."

"Yeah, and as soon as one of us moves out of their seat, the other wins, and we can both get out of the car." And go do it.

It was only eight minutes to her apartment. She had it clocked down to the second for those mornings when she just couldn't get her ass out of bed. They could be at her place and naked in eight and a half minutes.

"So you don't mind only getting half of the cash, J.T.?"

He shrugged. "More than twelve grand is better than what I had two days ago, which was nothing. I can do a lot with twelve grand. How about you?"

Considering the sum total of her checking account was about a hundred bucks, she figured it would work for her.

"Oh, yeah. I can pay my credit card bills and still have enough for a whole year at Cleveland State."

J.T. smiled and ran his finger through her hair, wrapping the strand around and around. "You, me, and twenty-five grand. We're going places, baby."

"Are we?" Tansey asked, a bit of flirt in her voice. "Because I wasn't go to date until I got my degree. I was going to be celibate and concentrate on school."

"You trying to break my heart?" He had a half smile, and his voice was low, sexy, and serious. "We've got a start on something good here. I'll respect your time studying. I'll support you."

She could read the sincerity in his voice. Part of her balked, the image of Bill's naked butt rising over Terri Baumbecker still fresh in her mind. But the other part, the one who had heard J.T. talk about his parents, his hopes and dreams, his little stuffed teddy bear, knew he was different. He was one of the good guys.

And he was skilled with his hands. What more could a woman want?

"You'll be like a cheerleader?" She grinned. "Rub my neck when I've had a long night studying?"

"Absolutely. But I'm not shaking any pom-poms."

"I'd like to see what we've got going here, too." She pulled his finger out of her hair and bit the tip. "And celibacy is overrated."

J.T. felt the jolt of her tongue everywhere as she trailed it over his finger, slicking him up before sucking it into her mouth. "Amen to that."

He wanted Tansey. In his life, with her bright smile and quirky outlook on things. He wanted to make love to her. He wanted a future with her.

"So who leaves their seat? You or me?" He actually wanted Tansey to be the one to move. Somewhere at about their twenty-ninth hour together, she had told him about the schmuck boyfriends who had cheated on her. He knew she needed to learn to trust him and that it wouldn't be easy. He'd be the one to move if she couldn't, but he would love to see her trust him with something as important as the money.

She dropped his finger, her expression a little wary. "You won't stiff me, will you?"

If she only knew how stiff he was. "No, I swear to you, I won't." J.T. cupped the side of her cheek and kissed her.

He meant it to be a short kiss, to reassure her. A sweet, sincere kiss.

It spiraled quickly right down into the gutter, and he was going in with tongue and groping her chest before he was even aware of what he was doing. He had zero self-control when it came to her.

Might it never change.

"Oh, damn," she murmured, her head lolling back away from him.

J.T. kissed her neck, rolling down the thick sweater. He couldn't get to her skin, and he was pawing his way through all the fabric, trying to lean, his left hip numb from the straining position. He tried to kiss her neck and wound up with a fuzz ball in his mouth. It wasn't very satisfying.

"That's it." Tansey pushed him back so forcefully he slammed into the head rest.

Stunned, he was about to ask what was wrong when she grabbed his shoulder and hurtled herself at him. With a sort of leap she landed on his lap in a slap of denim, their arms entangling and her chin cracking his nose.

While his eyes watered, he grabbed her ass to prevent her from sliding to the floor. It was then he realized what a really fabulous ass Tansey had. Firm and curvy, and it was resting right on his thighs, cupped by his hands. And the fact that her knees were spread on either side of his hips was an added bonus.

Plus he had full contact with her breasts.

Tansey grabbed his shoulders and stared down at him. "Nothing's happening." She gave a cautious glance around. "I thought the second I got out of my seat an alarm would go off or something. Or flashing lights on your side to show you're the winner. But nothing is happening."

Something was happening all right. He lifted his hips and bumped between her thighs. "That's a good thing. It gives us a few more minutes alone."

"That's nice," she said, her eyes fluttering shut. Then she reared back. "The camera."

He wasn't feeling much like worrying about it, but Tansey was really uncomfortable with it. Which sucked. Plain and simple. There was a warm, willing, and probably wet woman draped across him, and he couldn't do a damn thing about it.

But he had just won twelve thousand, five hundred dollars.

At the moment, it didn't seem like a fair trade.

NINE

THERE was a little bit of red tape. When the guard returned from strolling around the mall, Tansey and J.T. had both gotten out of the car. She hadn't been able to stand one more second in there—both claustrophobia and severe horniness were testing her sanity.

The guard had called in the powers that be, and the tapes had been reviewed, which was a really embarrassing fifteen minutes as she watched bits and pieces of herself straining toward J.T. You could never see either of their faces when they were kissing on camera, but it was really obvious that's what they were doing.

Then when she ripped the T-shirt down and jumped into J.T.'s lap, rubbing against him like a cat, one of the male staff members watching actually said, "Whoa. Look out."

Tansey shifted back and forth in her socks, having forgotten her shoes in the car. This was a wee bit humiliating. J.T. squeezed her hand and nudged her with his shoulder.

"It's no big deal," he whispered. "We didn't do anything."

The tape was rewound and replayed *four* times to be sure no rules had been broken. The last time they pushed play and she made like a flying squirrel across the backseat onto J.T.'s lap, she suspected the crew was watching for entertainment value, not for any verification of any so-called rules.

"Did J.T. win or not?" she finally snapped. She was tired, hungry, horny. Not necessarily in that order.

"Looks like it to me," one guy dressed in khakis and a plaid shirt said. "Susan?"

"I'll verify that," Susan said. "Okay, get the morning show here. We have interviews to do! Start editing that video footage." She smiled at J.T. "Congratulations, you just won yourself a car or twenty-five thousand dollars. Which one do you want?"

"The cash, please." J.T. grinned. "Thank you. God, this is unbelievable."

He turned and Tansey laughed when he lifted her a foot off the ground. "We did it, Tansey! Show me the money, honey!"

The thought of all that money, the thought of what she had discovered with J.T., made her giddy. The room blurred a little, and she gripped his shoulders for balance. "Thank you," she murmured, giving him a little kiss.

In the end, the money wasn't really the important thing. It was that she had become reacquainted with confidence and knew beyond a shadow of a doubt that she would finish her degree, do what she really wanted to with her life. If things worked out with J.T. long term, it would be because she had learned to trust herself and not be afraid of failure.

Her mom would want that for her.

With a laugh, she slid back down to the floor. "Oh my gosh, I have to call Emily! I owe her a really nice dinner or something for being so awesome during this."

She grabbed her messenger bag off the floor and dialed Emily on her cell phone, not thinking that it was only seven in the morning. When Emily answered on the fifth ring, she sounded like she'd been ripped out of a sound sleep.

"Em, J.T. won the car contest, but we're splitting the money!" she blurted. "Can you believe it? I have twelve thousand bucks!" And possibly the love of her life, but she'd tell that one to Emily a little later, when the love wasn't standing next to her.

"What?" The sleepiness in Emily's voice disappeared. "He's splitting it with you? Oh, that's so sweet! That's awesome, Tansey." There was a rustling sound, and Emily murmured, "John, wake up. J.T. won the contest."

Oh, my. Tansey darted a quick glance at J.T. and blushed.

"What?" J.T. asked, his eyebrow shooting up.

"Umm . . ."

"Tansey, put J.T. on the phone. John wants to talk to him."

"Hang on." Tansey cleared her throat and shoved the phone at J.T. "Your dad wants to talk to you."

"My dad?" He looked puzzled. "But you were just talking to Emily . . . *oh*." As understanding dawned, his lip curled up.

J.T. stared at the phone in horror before taking it. He really didn't want to know that his father was having sex. Truly. And there was something really unjust about his dad getting lucky last night when he was still straining against his jeans.

"Dad?" He clung to the hope that another man would answer.

"You won the car?"

Damn, it really was his father's voice.

"Yep, but I took the cash and split it with Tansey."

"That was the right thing to do, John Tyler. I'm proud of you. And you spend that money however you want—don't think you have to dump it into the business."

J.T. frowned. "But I want to."

There was some rustling like his father was sitting up in bed—which made him want to vomit. "Listen. I know you've been worried about me, and I appreciate that. But things happen in life and then you get through them. I'm getting through this. You need to worry about you, not me. Do what you want with the money—what's best for your future."

"My future is working with you." He wasn't being stubborn. It was just the way he had always wanted it to be. What he hoped to pass down to his own child—a family business that worked because family supported each other. "And later on, Dad, you can explain to me what exactly your relationship with Emily is."

"Not that it's any of your business, but sometimes a chance for a little bit of happiness comes along in a way you didn't expect. And you can worry over it, ignore it, decide it's wrong for you. Or you can just enjoy it, you know what I mean?"

If J.T. hadn't been forced to live with Tansey for forty hours straight in close quarters, it's possible he would have ignored her and any sort of happiness he could find with her. He would have ignored her flirtatious smile, and that would have been a damn shame. "Yeah, I know exactly what you mean."

J.T. winced then and rubbed his forehead. "And I can't believe I'm going to suggest this, but how about the four of us go out to dinner tonight—mine and Tansey's treat."

"Great idea. Now Emily is making faces at me that she wants to talk to Tansey again."

* * *

TANSEY took back the phone and patted J.T.'s arm. He looked so stoic yet nauseous. Like her brother Eric always had when their mother would slam on the brakes on road trips.

"Can you guys make it to dinner, Em? I heard J.T. ask his dad."

"Sure." Emily's voice dropped to a very low whisper. "John just went to the bathroom."

And she needed to know these things because . . . ?

"And I had to talk to you Tansey because Oh. My. God. I am in love. You're my best friend, and so I have to tell you first. This is the man I'm going to marry."

Tansey was startled. Emily was known to be impulsive, but she wasn't a kook. She never got quickly attached to lovers, nor had she ever been known to profess an interest in love or marriage. Emily was more live-for-the-moment than live-together-forever.

"I know that sounds lunatic insane, but oh, Tansey, I just can't describe it. My mom always said you just know when you meet the right one, and I always thought that was a little silly. I like to have fun, I believe in happily ever after, but I just wasn't looking for that right now. Then wham . . . there it was." Emily gave a beatific sigh.

There it was. Tansey glanced over at J.T., who had headed for Starbucks to get them some coffee. He was on his way back with a cup in each hand, dangling down by his thighs. His jeans were sinking low from excessive wear, and he was smiling.

Wham. There it was.

"I'm with you, Em. I think I've met the man I could marry, too." She was in love with J.T. She really was.

"Tansey, then I'll be your mother-in-law!" Emily broke out laughing.

Tansey giggled with her. "At least then I'd know what to get you for a Christmas present. I'll call you later, you nut." No sense getting the marriage ahead of the wedding. Or weddings.

"What's so funny?" J.T. handed her the coffee while taking the phone from her and dropping it in her bag. He also gave her a mind-melting, knee-shaking kiss.

Well, the honeymoon aspects of marriage she could see investigating right now. "Nothing." She gave in to temptation and put her free hand on his butt. The crew wasn't looking. They were bustling around looking busy but not doing anything as far as she could tell. "Now take me home and seduce me. I promise I won't throw myself in front of a train afterward like Anna Karenina."

"That's comforting. And I promise not to stalk you."

Tansey laughed. "Then I guess we both come out of this a winner."

J.T. dusted a kiss across her forehead. "Absolutely. Now let's go back to your place, and I'll show you my tools."

"Ooh, private demonstration. Sounds good." Tansey reached for her bag and her car keys.

Sayonara celibacy.

It was time to do some ball bouncing.

The Naked Truth About Guys

ALESIA HOLLIDAY

To Cindy Hwang, for inviting me to the naked guy party. You're the best! To Paola Soto, for your fabulous help with *Nice Girls Finish First* and your lovely name.

And to Manda Clarke, for the two-hour drive with fortune cookies. You rock!

AS SEEN IN THE *SEATTLE TIMES*:

***THE NAKED TRUTH ABOUT GUYS*, BY COLUMNIST C. J. MURPHY**

Marriage and Herring, or Other Smelly Fish

When you bring up marriage (because it will *always* be you who brings it up), a Guy will say: "I'm just not ready to make that kind of commitment."

In human speak, this means: "Are you OUT of your MIND? I'm living the free, happy, single life [Note: A Guy will think this even if he's living in his mother's basement], and the LAST thing I want is to tie myself down to a healthy, secure, monogamous relationship. Because at ANY TIME, a busload of hot Swedish bikini models might drive by and say, 'Hey, YOU! The guy with the ring on his finger! We were going to take you on our Bus of Unrestrained Sexual Urges and oil you up like a sexy little herring of lust. But we see that you're married. Too bad; your loss!"

(Except, maybe, they might say it in Swedish.)

This kind of thinking is rampant in the typical Guy mind.

What "I'm just not ready to make that kind of commitment" does NOT mean includes the following:

1. *"If you make yourself over completely until you're a carbon copy of me and pretend to enjoy sports, keg parties, and Hooters, I'll marry you,"* OR
2. *"If you give up your friends, your hobbies, and your life to sit around by the phone waiting for me to call, I'll marry you,"* OR
3. *"If you make me jealous by dating my best friend, I'll marry you."*

So STOP THE MADNESS!! Reclaim your self-esteem. If your Guy says he's not the marrying kind, believe him. Then kick him to the curb. Remember that old saying about fish in the sea? (And we're not talking oily herring . . .)

Until next time, remember: *Guys! Can't live with 'em, can't attack them with your new corkscrew.*

ONE

"C.J., you've got another marriage proposal. Looks like maybe two or three of them, if this envelope with somebody's unwashed socks sticking out are any clue. What does that make, fourteen this month?" My editor strode into the tiny closet that served as my office with a whole pile of envelopes and a couple of boxes.

I felt my lips curl. "Socks? *Yuck*. And some idiot thinks I'll marry him after that? And it was only nine before today, so don't exaggerate." Slouching back in my totally-not-ergonomic desk chair, I scanned my desk for an inch of free space. *Bingo!* I lifted my shabby running shoe (and the foot inside of it) from its resting place on top of the pile of old magazines I like to call "research material" and crossed it over my right foot, which had pride of place on top of my college *Webster's*.

(It helps my status in the office if I at least pretend to look like a real reporter instead of what I really am: somebody who makes fun of herself, other people, and the human condition for a living. Or as my brilliant agent Steve calls me: a humor columnist. He ought to know, I guess. He just got me a sweet syndication deal.)

I grinned, as the boss dumped the pile of mail in the middle of my desk, on top of my feet. "Just put that anywhere, Donny."

Donald Donaldson, managing editor of the *Times* for the past twenty-two years, aimed one of his most menacing snarls at me—even the tips of his spiky white hair were trembling in annoyance. "Don't call me Donny. Donny is for toddlers or Osmonds. It's Boss or Mr. Donaldson to the likes of you, Murphy."

I laughed and swung my feet down to the floor, scattering envelopes everywhere. "Oh, right. Doing your 'Spidey's boss' impersonation, again, Boss? If you'd schedule these fits of grouchiness in advance, I'd be able to work up a more convincing intimidated cower. Plus, since when are you the mail dude?"

He grumbled again, but I could see the edges of his lips twitching. He was just an old softy at heart, but I seemed to be one of the few people at the paper who realized it. When you grow up as the lone female in a house with a cop for a dad and five older brothers, it takes a lot to intimidate you. Mr. Donaldson didn't even come close.

"Curiosity. The socks got me," he said. He turned and stalked back out of the office, then stopped at the door. "C.J., 'sexy little herring of lust'? Your mind must be a very scary place."

I stuck my tongue out at his departing back and then started sorting through the mail, playing my daily game of "try to separate the *positive* (good job; yeah, I agree; my guy is just like that, too) from the *negative* (you suck; you are a sexist pig; you must be a man-hating lesbian) from the *screwball* (my birthday is the same month as yours, so we should plan a joint birthday party; will you marry me?) from the *downright creepy* (you must be my soulmate; I'm writing from prison and you sound like my type; my girlfriend took your advice, so she left me, and now I'm going to hack off your arm)."

Sadly, these are all actual examples from real letters. That last category gets copied to the Seattle PD and a file I call the "open in case of my disappearance" file.

When you write a weekly newspaper column, you tend to attract attention. When you write a column called "The Naked Truth About Guys," you attract a *lot* of attention.

Not all of it good.

As I half-heartedly dug around in a drawer for my letter opener, shoving last year's Buckeye football schedule, a flyer for Wok and Bowl (our traditional twice-a-week lunch hangout), and several dried-up pens out of my way, I heard one of my favorite voices.

"Hey, gorgeous. I hear you're getting married a few more times." Bill Curran, the best sportswriter on the West Coast (and one seriously cute guy), stood in my doorway, grinning. "I bet it was the lust tadpole thing."

I closed my eyes and moaned. "If you're going to mock me, at least get it right. It was herring. Lust *herring.*"

"Yeah, but most of those guys have probably got more of a tadpole, if you know what I mean," he said, measuring out what looked like about two inches between his outstretched index fingers.

I tried to look stern, but I couldn't help cracking up. "Right. Is that two inches a personal best, or more like an aspiration for you, Cheese Head?"

(Bill was born and raised in Wisconsin, and the rest of us tried never to let him forget it. He had the blue-eyed, blond-haired, corn-fed farm-boy look to him, too, but we already called Margaret down in obits Farm Girl, so you see the problem.)

He winced. "Ouch! Kick a man right in the gonads, why don't you? That's what I love about you, Murphy. You're one of the guys."

He shoved his hands in his pockets and left, whistling, while I dropped my head on my arms on top of my latest batch of mail.

Great. The story of my entire love life. *Just one of the guys.*

★ ★ ★

"QUIT moping, already, you big baby. I hear I'm ahead in the marriage proposal pool—I bet seventeen this month. Did you get two or three today, *chica?*"

My beautiful and annoyingly tall and thin best friend, Paola Rossini, stood by my desk. I could never figure out how she can sneak around so quietly in three-inch heels. I raised my head and glared at her. "I don't know. I can't bring myself to open it yet. And you're Italian; you don't call people *chica.* You call them . . . something Italian. Anyway, what kind of best friend bets against me in the office pool?"

She shook her head of perfect, shiny black hair and smiled. "It's not betting *against* you; it's betting . . . *near* you. Come on, I'll buy you lunch. I want to show you my new car."

I considered refusing, but the way to my heart was definitely through my (loudly growling) stomach.

Plus, I may break down and ask her for help, thinks desperate me.

But, I don't want *help,* thinks too-proud me.

"Yeah, but I need help," I muttered, stuffing my nondescript mud-brown curls under a nondescript mud-brown ball cap. I stood up and glanced down at the old T-shirt I wore over my faded blue jeans. *Brown again.* I sighed and rushed to catch up with Paola, eyeing her perfect little red suit, perfectly accessorized, in her usual . . . *perfect* . . . way.

Maybe just a little bit of help . . .

I TOOK a deep breath, inhaling the spicy aromas of my favorite restaurant as my favorite server brought our food. "Szechuan chicken, C.J. You need to branch out and at least try the Szechuan beef, sometime," Lin said, as she placed my lunch on the black-lacquered tabletop.

I laughed. "Maybe next time. Thanks, Lin."

She grinned. "No problem. Loved that column on men and commitment."

After Lin walked away, Paola unwrapped her chopsticks and stole a chunk of sesame beef from Bill's plate.

"Hey!" he protested. "Why don't you ever order the beef yourself, instead of stealing mine?"

"Yours tastes better. Why are you the only man who doesn't give me exactly what I want?" she replied, doing a fake eyelash bat.

He rolled his eyes. "Yeah. Like that Mercedes in the parking lot? What did you have to do to earn that?"

I gasped, a little, but it didn't faze Paola at all. "I took Lulu to Fashion Week with me in New York and pointed her to clothes that actually suit her. Her hubby was so happy, he gave me the car. It's just a lease; I have to give it back in three years."

The hubby she so casually referred to owned half the Mercedes dealerships on the West Coast; his wife Lulu was known for spending vast quantities of his money on truly hideous clothes. No wonder he was so happy with Paola. For a woman who never, ever had sex ("not till I'm in a serious relationship"), rich men always seemed to give her expensive presents.

I smacked Bill on the hand as he reached for the last potsticker and snagged it for myself. "How come I never get sweet deals like that? I'd be glad to take some rich guy's wife shopping. Or . . . what did you do that last time? Pet-sit for the champion shit zoos? I can do that," I said.

Paola shuddered, delicately, and then wiped her mouth carefully. "Shih Tzus, C.J. Not shit zoos. And I simply have a talent for being in the right place at the right time." She aimed a sweeping look at me from ball cap on down. "Also, dressed in the right clothes."

Waving a hand through the air, she continued. "Do you think your . . . *clothes* . . . would inspire confidence in someone? You dress like a . . . like a . . ."

Bill interrupted. "She dresses like a reporter. Not everybody is a fashionista like you, Paola."

I stared at Bill, surprised that he even knew the word. "*Fashionista,* Bill? You'll lose access to the locker rooms if the Mariners or the Seahawks ever find out you know the word *fashionista.*"

Paola brushed imaginary crumbs off of her white silk blouse. "Speaking of fashion, let's talk about that makeover, C.J." She moved her plate out of the way, more than two-thirds of her meal uneaten, and leaned forward. "Are you ready for me to make you over into a star?"

Bill glanced up midway through shoveling a huge bite of spring roll into his mouth. "Um, waaggg erten?"

"Manners, Bill. Manners." Paola rolled her eyes.

Bill swallowed hastily and took a drink of water. "What are you talking about? Why would you want to make her over? She's fine like she is. Not everybody wants to be an overdressed princess, Rossini."

I knew we were in trouble at the word *overdressed* and tried to ward off the battle.

Too late.

"Princess? *Every* woman is a princess, you Neanderthal. And how dare you call me overdressed? Just because you prefer to look like you rolled in to work off of a three-day bender doesn't mean you can mock those of us who take pride in our appearance. *Fashion* is not a dirty word."

Bill aimed a disbelieving glance at me. "Are you really buying into this crap? You're one of the guys. If you start prancing around in spike heels, it'll throw off the whole working dynamic of the newsroom."

"Well, I . . ."

"Working dynamic?" Paola spat out. "Aren't those big words for a sports hound? The day we need your input into fashion is the day I quit my job to . . . to . . . work at some job that makes me wear a polyester uniform."

The word polyester stunned us into silence. But she went even further.

"With a *nametag*."

Nobody could top the idea of Paola wearing a nametag on a polyester uniform, so we selected our fortune cookies in silence. Bill crunched his cookie in half, pulled out the fortune, and read it aloud, a tradition on our lunches. "Change your thoughts and you change your world."

Paola sighed, but read hers, too, willing to let the fashion debate drop temporarily. "Coming together is a beginning; keeping together is progress; working together is success."

I grinned. "These are always the same. Nothing specific, always vague and wisdom-y. Nobody ever gets bad news in a fortune cookie."

I snapped my cookie in half, pulled out the slip of paper, and then read it. "See, greatness and fame. Ha! 'Greatness and fame will . . .' um, *what*?" Staring at the fortune, I wondered if stress was killing the brain cells that worked my optic nerve.

Paola reached over and plucked it out of my hand. "What, already? Greatness and fame *what*?" She studied the fortune and did a classic double take, blinking owlishly, then read aloud slowly. "Greatness and fame will pass you by, and you will lead a life of bleak despair."

Bill rolled his eyes. "Very funny."

"No, really. Read it," she said, shoving the fortune toward him. He picked it up and read it, and his face did the same funny kind of thing Paola's had. "No shit. This is freaky. I thought these things had to be positive; there's some kind of fortune cookie rule or something, isn't there?"

We all stared at each other, spooked, for a second and then I laughed it off, in spite of a weird squicky feeling down my spine that Grandpa would have called a goose walking over my grave. "Remember when you were a kid you used to joke about fortunes that said, 'Help! I'm trapped in a Chinese fortune cookie factory'? Guess somebody really *is* trapped and forgot her daily Prozac."

We shoved back our chairs, and I tossed the crumpled fortune on the table. "I'm guessing I don't need a fashion makeover for a life of bleak despair, Paola, but thanks anyway." I laughed again, but it sounded shaky even to me. I'm not very superstitious, but I don't go out of my way to walk under ladders carrying a black cat, for example.

Bill slung a friendly arm over my shoulders as we walked out. "No, you don't need made over. You're perfect just the way you are."

TWO

"WHY is Aaron Judson sending you his socks, C.J.?" Bill gave me a funny look, shaking the box he'd snagged off my desk. "What did you do this time?"

I gave him my best innocent look, which was easy because I didn't have a clue what he was talking about. "I don't know. Aaron Judson, the *Mariners's* Aaron Judson? The best shortstop since A-Rod? The Savior of Seattle?"

Bill looked at me, surprised, and then he nodded. "Oh, yeah. You and your five brothers grew up at the ball park. I sometimes forget you're not a girl. Paola wouldn't know a shortstop from a shortcut."

I grabbed my box out of his hands and glared at him. "Get out of my office, and get your hands off of my socks."

"But, what did I—"

"Out!" I pointed to the door and started tapping my foot.

"Fine. Whatever. But I want to know about those socks." He ambled out the door, and I strode over and slammed it behind him. Well, actually I shut it quietly, but I felt like slamming it. If one more person told me I wasn't a girl, I was taking Paola up on her idea of doing a Pygmalion on me.

It's not like Hugh will ever notice me the way I look now.

I tossed my ball cap in the corner and flopped down in my chair with my box of socks and read the label. Yep, the return addy was Aaron Judson, care of the Mariners's home office; I'd spent enough time at Safeco Field to recognize the address.

Ripping off the tape, I pulled the flaps of the box open. A letter-size envelope rested on top of the mate to the sock that had been peeking out from the edge of the box. They looked clean, and I didn't smell *eau de* stinky feet, so I cautiously pulled the envelope out and opened it. It was from Aaron Judson, all right, or somebody who had the handwriting down cold—I recognized the distinctive signature scrawled on a single sheet of paper. It's not like my nieces and nephew hadn't coveted and collected that autograph for the past year and a half.

C.J.,

Dude, you're brilliant. Your column on why guys dig baseball rocked Seattle. Have dinner with me—I'm desperate to meet you, fall in love, and raise a dozen kids with you.

Yours forever,
Aaron Judson

Okay, this had to be a joke. "Raise a dozen kids" with me?? Famous sports stars don't write notes like this to women they've never met. Somebody in the newsroom had to be going overboard on the practical joke thing. Slow news week, probably. Plus, how old was the guy?

Twenty-two? At twenty-five, I was practically old enough to be . . . well, anyway, he was just a baby.

Not that I really believed the note was from him.

But . . . what if?

Before I could spend any quality time pondering the thought of sex with an athletic, twenty-two-year-old baseball star, my door banged open and the evil hellbitch sauntered in.

Other people call her Kaspar, but I call 'em like I see 'em.

"Did you steal the stapler out of the copy room again, C.J.? Truly, it's getting tiresome." She looked kind of like a low-rent Paris Hilton. All peroxided hair, big lips, and bony hips. Sadly, this type appealed to some guys.

Like the ones who were breathing.

"No, I don't have the stupid stapler, Kaspar. Did you try sports? And seriously, you need to cut down on the perfume. Didn't you get that memo about the chemical-free workplace?"

She sneered at me. "Puh-*leeze.* Just because you refuse to display any feminine attribute whatsoever doesn't mean the rest of are so inclined. It's no wonder no man ever wants to commit to you, as you so pathetically wrote about in your laughable excuse for a column." She swept a disdainful glance at my outfit.

(It felt so much meaner coming from her than from Paola.)

"Brown again? Were they having a special at Goodwill?"

It only took four minutes from the time she left my office for me to come up with a blistering comeback. *My time is definitely getting better.*

After a brief mental pep talk on why I needed to quit letting Kaspar get to me so much, I opened my file for next week's column and then immediately got distracted by the mystery of the socks. Who would play a practical joke like this and go to the effort to forge Aaron's name so perfectly?

I flashed on Bill, but it wasn't his style. He'd be more likely to dump a cooler of Gatorade on my head and think it was funny. Subtle and complicated jokes were *so* not him.

I picked up one of the socks with the tips of my finger and thumb and peered at it, as if it would give me a clue. Then a knock on the door startled me, and I dropped the sock on the floor. It had to be Paola. Nobody else ever knocked, but she was always afraid (hopeful?) that I'd be having sex on my desk or something.

"Come in," I called and bent over to pick up the sock. "You won't believe the practical joke somebody played on me—"

"Hey, you got my socks," drawled a voice I'd heard many, many times on the six o'clock news.

I raised my head enough to peer over my desk and stared at the very real, very tall, cute-as-a-button Aaron Judson.

Somebody is taking this joke way too far . . .

"I . . . you . . . you really sent this box? I thought somebody was playing a joke."

"No, it was really me. Where's C.J.?" he said, looking around, like I might be hiding the real C.J. somewhere.

I laughed. "I'm . . ." Suddenly I flashed on what I must look like, with hat hair and in my Goodwill clothes. "Uh, I'm not sure where she is. She's on assignment. In Africa, I think."

Africa? I'm such a moron. Nobody will believe that.

He tilted his head and looked puzzled. "Africa? Seriously? Dude, that's so cool. But is she coming back soon? I gotta meet her. I just know she's my soul mate."

My mouth fell open so hard my jaw hurt. *Soul mate? Is he kidding or just insane?* "Uh, well, I'll tell her you stopped by."

He shoved his hands in his pockets and frowned. "Sure. I guess. I was just so amped to meet her today. This sucks. But, you know, Africa. I'm sure it must be important, right? Tell her Aaron Judson stopped by, and I'll be back to collect my lucky socks and take her out to dinner."

He started to walk out but then stopped and whirled around. "Dude, you're totally busted."

I FROZE, clutching the sock of the apparent psychopath standing in front of my desk. "Busted?" I managed, in a weird, squeaky voice. "What are you talking about?"

"C.J.'s out of the office, and you're sitting at her desk opening her mail. You're totally busted for snooping."

I squeezed out a sigh of relief. "No, it's . . . I mean, I'm her . . . assistant. This is my job. I'll tell her you socked by. I mean, *stopped* by. Thanks. See you later."

He grinned but seemed to get the point. "Right. Later."

As he turned to leave again, I could see half the newsroom lined up in the hallway, staring in my office. Bill wasn't even pretending to be subtle; he shoved past everybody else until he stood in my doorway. "Aaron! How's it going, buddy? What are you doing here?"

They did the handshake, arm-punch thing and then—thank the merciful gods of humor columnists—walked away. I slumped down in my seat as far as I could, wondering if I could fit under the desk for the next five or six hours. As I released the breath I seemed to have been holding for days, I heard Aaron's voice.

"No, I can't talk about it. It's the . . . ah, Africa connection, dude."

A little moan reverberated in my throat as I buried my head in my hands. What the hell have I gotten myself into now?

"WHAT the hell have you gotten yourself into now?" My words coming out of Bill's mouth was a little creepy, but not really surprising.

"Did you give me away? And quick, shut the door and tell the gawkers to get lost," I hissed at him.

He chuckled but shut the door and then leaned back on it. "Africa? Why is *C.J.* in Africa? Writing humorous columns about elephants or something?"

"I don't—"

A knock on the door startled us both. *Oh, crud.*

"If it's him again, make him go away!" I scrambled to climb under my desk. (What's so bad about cowardice, really?)

Bill opened the door a crack. "Oh, it's you. Come on in. C.J.'s either in Africa or hiding under her desk, but I'll let her explain it."

I climbed out of the crawlspace under my desk, brushing off the knees of my jeans. "Paola, you will not believe—"

Zero for two on the Paola sightings.

It was Hugh.

(Okay, so I haven't discussed Hugh yet. Remember that moment, probably in junior high, when you first realized boys were more than an annoying joke that the world played on girls, and you dived headlong into your first crush? Remember the halo of golden light you saw around his beautiful face whenever he walked into a room? The sick squigglies in your tummy whenever you thought about him? Yep. That's Hugh. Sadly, my have-no-taste-whatsoever friends think he's a player.)

"C.J.? Why are you underneath your desk? And what about Africa?" He had just the faintest hint of a drawl and, as usual, the sound of his voice sent heat-seeking tinglies down my spinal cord to my nerve endings. The green eyes and tousled dark brown hair that curled just a touch too long to be strictly professional didn't help either.

"Um, I . . . ah . . . dropped a contact," I muttered. (Did I mention the long legs? The absolutely-flab-free-never-eats-donuts waist? Yeah. Right. Excuse me while I mop up the drool.)

He smiled at me. "You have your glasses on."

"Right," I said, shoving my glasses back up my nose. "But I wanted to put my contacts in, but I dropped them, and anyway, what do you want?"

It always went this way. I tried to be smooth around our hot new investigative reporter and wound up surly. I had all the social graces of a twelve-year-old boy. I'd grown up with five of them, so it wasn't surprising.

"Charming, as usual," Bill commented. I was *so* going to hurt him for that later.

"She's always charming," replied the Prince of Charming. "I wondered if you'd seen the new show at the Paramount?"

OH. MY. GOD. He's going to ask me out right here in front of Bill. I haven't had a date in six months, and I've had two offers in the past twenty minutes. Lightning is going to strike me down any second.

I snuck a glance up at the sky through my grimy window and then eloquently responded. "Er, you, I, ah, well—"

Hugh smiled again. Seriously, when the man smiles, a butterfly must get its wings or something. "I just thought because you're always so on top of what's going on around town, you might have a recommendation for me. I have tickets for Friday, but I don't want poor Kaspar to be bored to tears. I hate to make a bad first impression."

Kaspar?? He's not asking me out; he's asking for a recommendation for his date with the hellbitch?

I flashed back to that fortune cookie. A life of bleak despair was sounding exactly right just then.

"It's fine," I said flatly.

"Thanks, C.J. I knew I could count on you. You're one of the good guys. See you later."

After he left, Bill snapped his fingers at me. "Earth to C.J. You still haven't told me what was going on with Aaron Judson and you and

Africa. I'm not leaving until I get the scoop. I didn't rat you out, by the way, so you owe me."

I held up a hand for silence. "One of the good *guys*? Good GUYS? That's it. I have SO had it." I picked up the phone and dialed. "Paola? You win. Let the extreme makeover begin."

THREE

"YOU'VE got to be kidding. I am *so* not putting on a towel and going back in the waiting room with all those naked people." I clutched the tiny towel—really, more like a washcloth—that they'd handed me at the Spatique front desk and stared at Paola in disbelief. "And why do we have to get naked, anyway? Why can't I just get a haircut and some new shoes or something?"

Paola had spent the past week setting up a series of tortures for me, from the looks of the itinerary she'd thrust at me when I met her at the spa half an hour before. Most of it seemed to involve being naked in front of strangers—the idea of which, oddly, I'm not a big fan.

"What the hell is a sea salt scrub, anyway? I finally just last month started using sea salt in my cooking, like you told me to, instead of the box with the girl and the umbrella. Why would I want to be scrubbed with it?" I am totally suspicious of all stupid-sounding fads. Remember when the coffee enema was the big thing on the West Coast? I made fun of that for three weeks in my column. I mean, *hello,* is that really the place you want caffeinated?

"This is like the coffee enema, isn't it? Some freak made up the most ridiculous thing possible and said, 'Hey! Let's see how gullible people really are!' and now we're going to buy into it like sheep."

I hid behind the pastel pink locker door (color-coordinated to the pastel pink towels and the pastel pink walls) and pulled off my jeans, muttering, "Like salty sheep. *Baaa.*"

Paola pushed the locker door out of the way and glared at me. I noticed that her elegant silk bra and panties matched. *How do women* do *that? Do they have a separate closet with shelves to color-coordinate their underwear?*

I glanced down at my Hanes briefs (beige) and my Playtex bra (gray) and sighed. This would be easier if I had even the slightest hint of girly genes.

No such luck.

"Here's your robe, you big baby," Paola shoved a fluffy square of terrycloth at me. It was tied up in a bow with some kind of weed, and I looked at it blankly.

Paola rolled her eyes. "Just untie the raffia and put it on. It's almost time for our scrubs. And speaking of ridiculous, who would have guessed you had a great figure under those baggy clothes you always wear? You look like you're a size six, and you've been wearing what? A ten? A twelve?"

"Clothes have numbers? I always just buy the stuff with the "M" on it. I used to buy "S" but it was kind of snug on top." Okay, I was exaggerating just a teensy bit (I did know about the numbers thing), but a girl can only take so much criticism first thing in the morning.

Paola sucked in a moaning breath. "You . . . you . . . oh, I can't take any more stress before my massage. We'll discuss clothes that fit and the concept of *matching* underwear later."

I waited until she'd escaped toward the waiting room before I hurriedly shed panties and bra and put on the robe, stuffing my undies in a ball underneath my jeans in the locker (like somebody was going to snoop around in my locker to see what my underwear looked like, for Pete's sake). Clutching the towel in front of my securely belted robe like a shield, I dragged myself toward the torture chamber . . . er, pastel pink waiting room.

It was all downhill from there.

"YOU want me to *what*?" I looked at Hans in disbelief. Actually, his name wasn't Hans, but the name he'd given me didn't seem to have a single vowel in it, in spite of being several syllables long, so I was cool with thinking of him as Hans. We stood in a small room (also pink), and Hans was pointing at a gigantic baby bath tub, propped up on a pedestal.

Seriously, the thing looked like the tub I'd seen my friends use with their newborns. It was long and flat, with a rectangle of blue rubber in the middle, and a little moatlike thing all the way around it, just inside the rim. Even more ominous, a hose protruded from the wall and pointed at the baby tub, and the hose thing looked a lot like the Wash-O-Matic where I took my car every so often.

"You lie down now. I go. I go now. You lie down no robe." He pointed at me and then at the baby tub, with hands the size of roasted hams.

"I lie down no robe?" I squeaked, suddenly monosyllabic, clutching my robe even tighter and feeling my heart sink down to my churning gut.

"You lie down no robe. You keep towel. I be back." At that, he shoved the curtain at the doorway aside and tramped out of the room, his head nearly smacking the ceiling on his way out.

No way do I want to be practically naked in a car wash with Hans Ham Hand.

I scanned the room, desperate for a way out. Nothing. Not even a pastel pink air duct.

I'm screwed.

"You ready?" Hans rumbled from just beyond the curtain.

I sighed and climbed up on the oversized baby tub. Paola was *so* dead. "I ready."

Hans trundled back in the room. I measured his six-and-a-half-foot height with my eyes, wondering if I'd have a chance to escape if he tried to get fresh with my naked self. I could always yell at the top of my lungs, right?

No worries from Hans, though. Either spending his time hosing down naked women had made him immune, or else (more likely) he was more interested in the gorgeous clients like Paola than in average-looking women with fish-belly-white skin, like me. He flipped on the water and started hosing me down. Once I got over the shock of the first blast, it actually felt kind of good. Soothing, even, with the warm water streaming over my arms and legs.

I closed my eyes for a moment and heard the water shut down. Before I had a chance to think, Hans grabbed my leg. "I scrub now."

"You—*ouch*!" I tried to yank my leg away while holding my miserably inadequate towel over all important parts. But I may as well have been a fly trapped by a Norwegian wrestling spider, for all the good it did me.

"You relax. I scrub."

If "scrub" is Norwegian for "use sharp, gravel-like substance to grind six layers of skin off your body," Hans totally scrubbed.

And scrubbed.

And scrubbed.

"You not shave legs, yes?" He glared at me, as though removing leg hair was a punishable offense.

I unclenched my jaw enough to respond. "No. I mean, yes. Yes, I shaved my legs. Didn't want to have hairy legs at the spa, right?" (Insert weak laughter here.)

"No shave. Bad. Skin sensitive. Red." He glared at me again.

Seriously, I wondered if Hans was a former Death Squad ringleader from some unpronounceable country, currently in the Witness Protection Program. The man looked like he could snap my neck easier than I could bust open a fortune cookie.

"You flip."

I snapped out of my pain-induced trance. "What?"

"You flip over, now. Hold towel." He held up another, drier, towel behind me, probably to block the sight of my offending red skin from his view.

Too dazed to protest, I grabbed the sodden towel covering me and flipped over. Or, actually, more like *creaked* my way over, with little grunting noises escaping from me as I did, and trying really hard not to roll clear off the table.

This girly stuff is rough. Paola has gotta be tougher than she looks.

After he'd scoured the appropriate amounts of skin off of the backs of my legs, arms, and, well, my back, he hosed me off again and then grabbed a bucket from a ledge and lifted a spatula dripping with goo out of it.

"What is *that*?" If it's wax, I'm *so* out of here. No way is Hans waxing anything on me.

"Is oil. I oil now." He slathered the warm oil on my legs, and I finally relaxed. Now *this* felt good. Sinfully good, even. If I could have skipped all that scrubbing stuff and gone straight for oiling, I would have called the whole thing a rousing success. After more oiling and more hosing off, Hans finally pronounced me done.

"You done. I go."

Before I could summon the energy to say anything (although *thank you* seemed a bit over the top, considering), he was gone, and I was left alone with my bright red limbs and sodden towel. I looked around for a basket or hamper but didn't find one, so I finally just left the towel on the table and shrugged back into my robe.

Is it time to go home yet?

"IT was three days ago. Quit whining, already," Paola said, as she swiped the last potsticker before Bill's fork reached it. Wok and Bowl was crowded with lunchtime regulars, and we hadn't seen much of Lin.

"I'm telling you, Bill, it was total hell. You would not believe the torture she put me through. First, I had to go through the car wash. He HOSED me."

Bill cracked up and possibly snorted Sprite up his nose. "Did he have a really *big* hose?"

My cheeks heated up. "You know what I mean."

"Yes, he does know what you mean. You've been complaining about it throughout our entire lunch. Didn't you think that perhaps the pain of underarm waxing was a subject best left for a time when we're not eating?" Paola pushed the tray of fortune cookies at me. "You go first this time, because you got that weird one last time. Gloom and despair or something?"

I'd forgotten. But now that she mentioned it . . . " 'A life of bleak despair.' Which does describe my day with Hans pretty well—"

"C.J.!!" Both Bill and Paola shouted it at the same time. *Oops. Maybe I am going on a bit much . . .*

I started to reach for the fortune cookie nearest me but then stopped, my hand hovering over the tray. Okay, I'm not superstitious, but still. I picked up the cookie nearest Bill and then held it in my hand, unopened, while they selected theirs.

Bill crunched his open first. " 'A welcome stranger will come into your life.' Hey, maybe Judson will come up with those box seats he promised. Speaking of which, are you back from Africa yet?" He snickered (quite rudely, I felt).

"Maybe in a day or so, after the shopping trip," I muttered.

Paola brightened. "Shopping is still on? I thought after all your complaining that you were going to cancel on me." She delicately snapped off the end of her cookie and then pulled out the slip of paper. " 'Great fame will shine upon you through all of your days.' Hmmm. That sounds about right."

Bill rolled his eyes. "Ego, much? How about you, Africa girl?"

I studied the cookie. Hey, the last time had to be a fluke, right? I cracked it open and read my fortune. "No way. No freaking way."

Bill and Paola stared at me. "No freaking way what? Did you get another weird one?"

I looked at them, a teensy bit frazzed, but still smiling. "Um, you're not going to believe this one: 'You will go on a long ocean voyage—' "

"That's normal," Paola broke in.

I fixed her with my death-ray glare and continued. " '—and the ship will sink, carrying you to a hideous, watery grave.' "

Bill snatched the fortune out of my hand. "No way. That's . . . *watery grave.* Okay, that's bizarre. We need to find out where these fortunes are coming from. I'll call Lin."

I shook my head. "No, let's not bother Lin. She and her mom are fighting again, didn't you notice when we came in? It's no big deal. Seriously. Let's just go. I'm supposed to turn in my column today, and I'm way behind."

Just to be safe, I tore up the nasty fortune before we left.

AS SEEN IN THE *SEATTLE TIMES:*

***THE NAKED TRUTH ABOUT GUYS,* BY COLUMNIST C. J. MURPHY**

Sports as Religion

A Guy may not be able to remember your birthday or your mother's name, even after you've been dating for six or seven years★ [★see: "Guys as Commitmentphobes"], but he remembers every stat of every player currently active in the NFL, NBA, and the European soccer league.

Plus all the stats for players who retired twenty years ago, and even those for players who are, in fact, dead.

This is nothing personal; it's just how the Guy brain works. In every official medical pie chart of Guy brains, as designed by actual brain doctors, you will see a breakdown like this:

- *25% Completely useless trivia, like the fact that Popeye said "Open, Sez Me" instead of "Open Sesame" in a cartoon he once watched twenty years ago;*
- *18% Job-related stuff, like which VP at his office has the best handicap and should be schmoozed up before the annual company golf scramble;*
- *53% Arcane sports stats, like how many times his favorite pitcher scratches his crotch before throwing a curve ball; and, finally:*
- *4% Relationship issues. But before you get excited, this includes every relationship he's ever had, including the biggies, like with his dog Sparky back in sixth grade. Therefore, the actual percentage of a Guy brain that is focused on you and your relationship at any given time is approximately .0001.*

Until next time, remember: *Guys! At least they're good for the sports questions in Trivial Pursuit.*

FOUR

"YOU are so totally a size six. No, you can*not* have a size twelve. What is wrong with you?" Paola was getting kind of screechy if you asked me.

I stared at myself in the mirror of the tiny dressing room (luckily for my sanity, it was *not* pastel pink). *Holy shit, I've got boobs.* "Try growing up with five brothers who took turns wearing your training bras on their heads while they made fun of you, and see how you turn out," I muttered.

For about the seven-thousandth time in my life, I wondered how differently I'd have turned out if Mom had lived through childbirth. *I might not be forced to go through this utter humiliation, for one thing.*

"Well? Get out here and show me already," Paola yelled.

"Paola, you don't have to yell. You're three inches away from me. And there's no way I'm ever, *ever* wearing this dress in public. It's . . . it's indecent." I tried to pull the silky red fabric down over my thighs, which, unfortunately, deepened the cleavage until I felt like a wannabe stripper. "Were you out of your mind when you picked this dress? Where am I going to wear it? To a football game at UW with Dad? My ass will freeze to the bleachers."

Paola snickered. "Ladies don't swear, sweets. And I'm sure Aaron will keep you warm. Move over, I'm coming in."

Sadly, the padlock was missing from my dressing room door. (I'm sure one should have been there.) I jumped back and out of the way of the door, which narrowly missed my nose. Paola shoved her way in, closed the door behind her, and then looked me up and down, eyes widening. "Holy shit!"

" 'Ladies don't swear,' " I said sourly. "And leave Aaron out of this. He's too young to even look at a dress like this. This is an R-rated dress, minimum. I'm *so* not buying it."

Paola did the twirly finger thing, which I took to mean she wanted to see me from the back, so I reluctantly turned. (Only to show her how ridiculous the dress looked on me; it had nothing to do with the look of approval in her eyes.)

"Oh, C.J., you have to have this dress. I'll buy it for you—for an early Christmas present, if you're short of cash—but you MUST have this dress. It's killer on you. The red plays up the highlights in your hair."

I narrowed my eyes. "What highlights in my hair? I don't have highlights in my hair."

She gave me the "who, me?" innocent face. "Didn't I mention? We have an appointment at three with Jean-Claude for cut and color. You'll adore him. He has a razor-cut technique that is to DIE for."

"Paola, isn't 'to die for' like, so last year? You need to update your expressions, if you're going to stay on top of your trendsetter image."

I wiggled around a bit but couldn't figure out how to reach the as-symetrical zipper. "Help me out of this dress, will you? I'm sort of trapped."

"That's the point," she said, flashing me her most evil grin. "Then you'll need a hot guy to help you out of it. If Hugh's going to be a weenie, you should take Aaron out to play."

After she unzipped the dress, I sighed and shrugged my way out of it. "Out to *play* is about right. Can you still arrange play dates for twenty-two-year-olds? He's very young, and I don't just mean in years. I mean, honestly. 'Dude, C.J.'s my soul mate??' "

"I think it's romantic. Hey! Your underwear and bra match!" (She was way too excited about the simple set of blue panties and bra I'd picked up at Target on sale for nine ninety-nine. I think the woman needs to get a life, to be honest.)

I pulled on my old jeans and (in deference to Paola) the red sweater she'd made me buy at . . . at . . . at some shop or other. I'd totally lost track by then, in the haze of frenzied clothes-trying-on, clothes-buying, and credit-card destruction. The instant the sweater swallowed my head, I heard the door bang shut.

"Paola? Get back here!" I shoved my head through and looked around. The dress had vanished. I was going to be forced to DO something about that woman.

I shoved on my shoes, grabbed my backpack, and ran for the cashier's. *Too late*. She was signing the credit card slip and then the clerk handed over a lovely, wrapped package just about the size of the Dreaded Dress of Doom.

Oh, well. If the columnist thing doesn't work out, I'm all outfitted for my new career as a hooker.

THE phone on my desk buzzed. *Who would be calling me at eight o'clock at night?* I'd stayed late to make up for the lunch that had metamorphosized into two hours of shopping and another three at the hair place. In spite of myself, I had to admit I looked totally hot in the new 'do and the little green dress Paola'd picked out that showed up the auburn hightlights in my newly short hair. I almost looked—okay don't laugh, but—*glamourous.*

Metamorphosis was exactly the right word, come to think of it. I felt like the caterpillar that turned into a butterfly. Except, you know, a butterfly with a tendency to trip over her own uncomfortable shoes.

From comfortable, confident woman to an idiot who trips over her own kitten heels. (And for future reference, why is it called a kitten heel? Do cats wear high-heeled shoes? Were actual cat *parts* involved in the manufacture of the shoes? And how gross is it that I'm even thinking this?)

I glared at the offending felines, er, *shoes*, which crouched in the corner where I'd thrown them earlier, and answered the phone. "C. J. Murphy. What?"

(Okay, there's nothing in my job description mandating phone skills, as you may have guessed.)

"C.J.? *C.J.!!* Dude!! I finally caught you. Didn't your assistant tell you I stopped by?"

I groaned and then took a deep breath. "Hello? Who is this?" (As if I didn't know.)

"It's Aaron, dude! The love of your life waiting to happen. What's shaking?"

"Oh, Aaron. Aaron Judson?" I asked politely, still stalling.

"Right! Did you get my lucky socks?" From the excitement in his voice, you'd have thought he was on the phone with Lindsay Lohan.

"Socks? You sent me your . . . socks? Ah. Interesting. No, I did not receive them. My assistant isn't very efficient, though. They may be lost in the piles and piles of mail I have to wade through. Just back from Africa, you know."

That should fend him off. Busy, busy woman here.

"Africa; that's right! Did you have fun? Where did you go?"

Crap. You'd think I would have prepared for this question. "Um, you know. Safari and whatnot."

He laughed. "That covers a wide range. Did you go to Masai Mara? The Serengeti? Or maybe Victoria Falls? I lived in Africa for the first twelve years of my life, after I was about six months old."

Figures. I have to lie to the only Africa-phile in the entire National League.

That's what you get for lying, my conscience said.

Two lies cancel each other out, my inner bad girl said.

Either way, I'm in trouble.

"So about those socks. Was there something you needed? Did you mistakenly think I'm running a laundry service?" I put a teensy bit of bite in my voice. Must discourage Junior.

"What? No! Of course not. I sent you clean socks. It was kind of to make a point about how much you mean to me. Those are my lucky socks, after all." He sounded sweet and bashful and—let's face it—adorable, and suddenly I couldn't tease him any more.

"Oh, right. The socks. I think I do remember seeing those. So what's up?"

"I read your column every week!"

"You and half the prison population of the West Coast, evidently," I muttered.

"What?"

"Nothing. You read my column. Okay, thanks. And . . . ?"

"It's like you're totally speaking to me. I mean, those columns are so spanking. You're the best!"

Spanking is apparently a good thing, even outside of the S&M community. Who knew?

"Thank you. I'm so glad you enjoy them. Best of luck with the season and all that. If there's nothing else . . ." I twirled the phone cord around my fingers, absently wondering if he still had the six-pack abs I'd seen in some promotional picture or other. How do you even get definition like that? It's gotta be painful.

"—Friday?" His voice interrupted the beginnings of a delicious fantasy about caramel syrup running over the hills and valleys of those abs. My face turned bright red, which probably clashed with my new highlights.

"I'm sorry, Aaron, I didn't quite catch that. What about Friday?"

"No problem. I'm sure you're mondo busy writing important stuff and all. And it's A.J. I mean, my close friends call me A.J. Which is totally karma, dude. You're C.J. and I'm A.J. It's, like, cosmic."

I closed my eyes, wondering if darkness and focused concentration would help me understand what the heck he was talking about. "What's cosmic? And what about Friday? No, on second thought, let's forget cosmic and go straight to Friday. What's up?"

"Will you have dinner with me Friday?"

I stared at the phone and then ran a hand through my newly designer hair. I had the hair, I had the clothes. I'd even been waxed from eyebrows to toes. Why the hell not?

(I can think of about a billion reasons why the hell not.)

Sucking in a deep breath, I agreed before I could talk myself out of it. "Yes. Sounds fun. What time, and what should I wear?"

There was a pause. "Dude, how should I know? I've never seen inside your closet."

(Is banging the phone against my head going to make this better in any way or just increase the pain quotient?)

"I meant, are we going someplace casual or dressy?"

He laughed. "Oh, gotcha. For a minute there, I was like, *woooooo*; she's tripping. But yeah, I got ya. Wear something dressy but, you know, kind of waterproof. Oops, gotta go. I'll see you Friday."

"But—"

Click.

Dressy but waterproof??? What does *that* mean? Are we going on a dinner cruise in a leaky ship? And what about the little details like what *time* Friday? Or where he's going to pick me up???

Sighing loudly, and trying not to think about *watery graves*, I hung up the phone. "It'll all work out somehow. After all, it's cosmic, dude."

"What's cosmic? And . . . *wow*. Who are you, and what have you done with C.J.?"

(You know that deer-in-the-headlights expression everybody talks about? I just figured out exactly how it feels when you're the deer.)

I stared up at Hugh, framed in the doorway of my office. He wore a black sweater and jeans instead of his usual suit, and he looked a little scruffy, with the shadow of a beard.

He looked a little less sophisticated city reporter and a little more . . . dangerous bad boy.

(As someone who has never, ever dated a bad boy, let me confess here to a certain fascination with the species.)

"Hey, there," he said, smiling. "You look fabulous, but I'm guessing the trip to an actual hair salon robbed you of the power of speech?"

Uh-oh. He said *fabulous*. He's gay. I'm out of luck in the romance department. "Fabulous?"

He laughed and walked into my office and then eased his long body down into my chair. "Yeah, I know. Straight men don't say fabulous. But I couldn't think of a better word. You're . . . you're actually *gorgeous*."

(The tone of shock in his voice wasn't doing much for the old ego, you understand.)

He sent an exaggerated leer my way. "You're hot. Where have you been hiding? I know—trapped under all those brown clothes."

I couldn't help it. I had to smile. "Yes, it was an evil right-wing conspiracy. They forced me to hide in plain sight to fool my enemies, and how better to do it than with brown camouflage?"

"Of course. I've heard about those conspiracies. The ultimate goal is to force all beautiful women underground to live in caves and farm turnips," he said.

"Can you farm turnips in caves? Don't they need sunlight or something?" (I'm *so* not a farm girl; can you tell? Hey! Did he just call me beautiful?)

He stood up. "Speaking of turnips, I'm starving. Want to grab something to eat?"

Oops. More deer headlights. What would Bambi do in a situation like this?

"Uh, well, I could eat," I said casually, if you call my pulse racing, my heart pounding a zillion beats per second, and my skin tingling casual.

"Let's go. I can bore you with the story of the dead ends I chased down all day, and you can explain why Aaron Judson is sending you his socks," he said, holding out his hand to me.

(Let me repeat that part: HOLDING OUT HIS HAND TO ME.)

I stood up and made a big deal out of collecting my backpack and some papers so I could brush by his outstretched hand with my arms full. He grinned, like he was totally on to me, but I could never live it down if I had sweaty palms or something. "Sure, let's go. Although I don't think even Aaron Judson himself can explain the motivation behind the socks. Something about soul mates and dinner Friday that's going to be both classy and waterproof," I said, rolling my eyes.

Oh, crap. Did I say that out loud??

"Classy and waterproof? Dinner's on me, if you can explain that one." Hugh outmaneuvered me on the full hands technique by taking my backpack to carry. He's not only so gorgeous he's a god among men, but he's chivalrous, too. If ever I were going to turn into a sweaty-palm type of girl, *that* would have been the moment. Instead, I tossed what I hoped was a sexy come-hither look back at him over my shoulder.

Naturally, that's when I ran into my door.

Looking back, I should have gone with the sweaty palms.

FIVE

“I **SURE** know how to show a girl a good time, don’t I?” Hugh said, smiling at me from across the table at Wendy’s. “How’s your head?”

I grinned, in spite of feeling like a total moron. “It’s fine. No worries. Black eyes are the hot new fashion accessory for the fabulously clutzy, didn’t you know? And anyway, at least you’re unpredictable. The Paramount one week and Wendy’s the next.”

Oh, *crud*. I can’t believe I said that. Now he’ll think I’ve been obsessing over the date he had with the hellbitch.

(Not that I was. I hardly even remembered it. *Really*.)

He snagged another one of my fries.

“Hey! And let’s not forget—too cheap to buy your *own* fries.”

“I’m wounded,” he said, putting his hand over his heart. “I bought yours—I even told them to biggie-size, in honor of your new haircut.”

(He had, actually. Right before he asked the ancient man just behind us in line if I didn’t look a great deal like Audrey Hepburn.)

"*Weeelll* . . . I guess you can share my fries. After all, I don't get compared to Audrey every day. Or is this your standard Mr. Smooth kind of line? Did you compare Kaspar to Paris Hilton?"

Ouch! Must quit fixating on his date with Kaspar.

He leaned forward and raised one eyebrow in a quizzical sort of way. (The man even has gorgeous eyebrows, I tell you.) "Speaking of our colleagues, how long have you and Bill been dating?"

I stared at him in shock, my grilled chicken sandwich halfway to my mouth. "What? Me and *Bill*? I mean, Bill and *me*? Are you nuts? That would be like dating one of my brothers. Yuck."

He gave me an odd look, sort of happy and sharklike at the same time. Not in a, say, *lawyer* shark sort of way, but more like an "I want to put my teeth on you" kind of way.

The tinglies shot through my neurons again, and something down low in my stomach tightened up.

I think it was indigestion.

Or, you know, maybe not.

"That's good to know, C.J. Just for future reference. Anyway, what does C.J. stand for? Nobody will tell me, and I've been working at the paper for nearly six months."

I slurped up the last of my Frosty. (Paola would have been appalled. She'd told me I should only eat dainty food, in a delicate way, on all dates. This was after she'd watched in horrified and not-so-quiet dismay while I chowed down on a hot dog with everything at a baseball game this summer. There was, evidently, mustard drippage.)

Being Pygmalioned is hungry business.

"Right. C.J. Well, I'd tell you, but then I'd have to kill you. And where would we be without our hotshot investigative reporter? Donny would be ticked, and—"

"Donny? Mr. Donaldson lets you call him *Donny*?" he interrupted. "Are you his long-lost granddaughter or something?" He had shock all over his face. Also, I noticed, a little ketchup. I leaned forward to wipe it off his lip with a napkin and then whatever I'd been about to reply got swallowed up in the heat shooting through my body when he gently grasped my wrist.

"I—" I said.

"You—" he said.

"More Diet Coke?" the cheerful table attendant asked, shattering the moment.

After we no-thanked the woman and watched her shuttle off to save the rest of the room from dry mouth, Hugh looked at me again. "So you and Curran don't have a thing. Looks like I've wasted five months," he said softly, releasing my wrist.

(Question of the day: Is it possible to fall in love at Wendy's? I mean, totally over-the-top, rip-my-clothes-off-right-here-on-the-table kind of love? Or is it just a thermal reaction caused by too many hot sauce packets in my chili?)

Either way, I'm in trouble.

He looked at his watch. "I have to stop by the city council meeting and ambush the mayor, or we'd continue this fascinating conversation about who you're not dating right this minute." He flashed a darkly predatory grin my way, and my panties suddenly felt a little damp. "But be warned. We *will* continue this conversation."

I stood up on knees suddenly gone weak and rolled my eyes. "I don't let guys tell me what I will or will not do. Even hotshot reporters who look like . . . er, who look like trouble." No need to confess the naked truth—or anything about tinglies or panties. (Even matching ones.)

Suddenly I realized I was acting exactly like every bimbo he'd bagged in the past five months. *Ooooooh, Hugh. Let me fall down and open my thighs, Hugh.* Naturally, my annoying self-respect chose that exact moment to kick in.

Damn. No thigh-opening for me, tonight. Poor C.J.

"I don't think so. I've been writing for the paper for almost three years, and I'm not going to be the butt of jokes for dating the new office Romeo." I stalked over to the wastebasket and dumped the rest of my fries. Time to start watching my weight, anyway, if I'm going to keep buying slinky clothes.

He must have snuck up behind me, because when I turned around he was standing six inches away. He touched a finger under my chin and gently tugged until I was looking up at him. "No? You'd rather be the butt of the office pool on marriage proposals?"

I moved my head away from his hand and laughed. "That's just silliness. Becoming another notch on your . . . *laptop* . . . isn't."

He followed me out the door in silence. As we reached his car, he finally responded. "C.J., I can see how you might think that about me. The thing is, though . . . it's all . . ."

"It's all *what*?" I asked, scanning his face for clues to whatever he was trying to tell me. He looked puzzled, frustrated, and a little bit determined, all at once. (It made me want to kiss him, but then again, so many things do.)

Hugh seemed to come to some decision, because suddenly he stepped back away from me after he opened my car door. He grinned and walked around to his side of the car. As we shut the doors and buckled our seat belts, he smiled again. "Here's the thing. I really like you. No 'moves,' no charm, and definitely no 'notches' on my laptop or anything else. Do you think we could start small—maybe with a real dinner?"

There are times in life when you know you're making a decision that may irrevocably change the course of your entire life, in a catastrophic, cataclysmic, and utterly unforeseeable way.

This wasn't one of them.

It was just *dinner*.

Denial, much?

As he drove me back to work to pick up my car, we chatted about everything and nothing, and somehow, by the time we reached my car, I'd agreed to dinner. (We both conveniently avoided discussing the fact that I was having dinner with A.J. the same weekend.)

After he parked the car, I grabbed the door handle and then glanced at him, suddenly feeling like I was back in junior high. *Will he kiss me? Does my breath smell like onions? Will he ask me to the prom?*

Well, maybe not that last one.

"Okay, so Saturday for the no-notches-on-laptops dinner?" I asked.

"Yes." He paused and flashed another of those temperature-raising grins at me. "Although, in the spirit of total journalistic honesty, you really need to quit saying the word *lap* while you sit there looking so beautiful. I'm trying to keep this conversation PG-rated, and you're not helping. Green is my new favorite color."

Then, before I could open the door, he leaned over and kissed me. It was a warm, friendly kiss. Firm but gentle. (No tongue, even.)

But then it changed, and he . . . *wasn't.* Warm or friendly. More like hot and demanding, which was okay because I was demanding right back. My fingers clenched on his arms, and I heard a tiny noise like humming—*moaning?*—and it was coming from my throat.

He pulled away and looked at me, eyes widening, and said my name. Just "C.J." Then he put his hand in my hair and pulled me back to him, and his mouth took mine with heat and pressure. I felt his tongue touch the seam of my lips, I opened to him, and he moved his head to an angle, his hand tightening in my hair. The temperature exploded, the heat in my belly shot out to my fingertips, and I wanted to climb on his lap.

Lap.

Laptop.

Notches.

Earth to C.J. This is your self-respect calling!

I pulled my face away from his, almost gasping. "Damn self-respect."

He looked dazed. "What?"

My face flamed. No way did I want to explain my internal monologuing to a semi-normal person. It was bad enough Paola and Bill knew I did it.

"Um . . . *health inspect.* I need to research the health inspector. You should council the city mayor. I mean, see the city and the council's mayor. I mean . . . oh, the hell with it."

I grabbed his face in between my hands and pulled him back for one more sear-the-pants-off-a-man kiss. (Did I mention I'm a five-star kisser? And I may have finally met my match. This man could kiss in the Olympics.)

Then I jumped out of the car before my newfound resolve to take it slow could vanish or my new bra and panties could spontaneously disappear. "Gotta go. Saturday. See you. Then. Ah, bye." Then I walked over to my car and climbed in, resisting the urge to bang my head against the steering wheel.

At least until after I'd waved and watched him drive off.

Research the health inspector? I'm such a moron.

I touched my swollen lips with the tips of my fingers. *Yes, but a well-kissed moron. I give it a 9.8, with high hopes for a perfect ten in the future.*

As I pulled out of the parking lot, all I could think was, *Paola is never going to believe this.*

SIX

"I DON'T *believe* this. You had a date with Hugh last night and you didn't call me? What kind of friend are you?" Paola stared at me, mouth hanging open in shock. Unfortunately, Paola is so beautiful—even with her mouth hanging open—that I had to shove through all the guys in the coffee shop who were staring at her. Except . . . some of them seemed to be staring . . . at *me*?

No way.

But . . . I snuck a quick glance around. Oh, wow!

"Paola," I whispered when I caught up to her. "Check out that guy in the green shirt over by the display of cappuccino makers. He's staring at my ass!"

She glanced at him. "Pervert."

"No, you don't get it. I haven't had a guy look at my ass in years! Even construction workers go out of their *way* to avoid looking at my ass. There might be something to this makeover thing."

She looked up at me and laughed. "Okay, sit down already, and stop showing off your traffic-stopping derriere. And just for the record, that's the blue skirt I had to force you to buy. Anyway, I want to hear about this date. With *details*."

I sat down and put my latte on the table. "It wasn't actually a date, really. It was just two coworkers grabbing something to eat after work."

She looked skeptical. "Right. Except this is the coworker about whom you've lusted for the past five months. And if it's all so casual, why didn't you call me last night?"

Heat shot up in my face. "Um, well, I didn't get home till around one in the morning."

"Ah HA! I knew it. Spill," she commanded, leaning forward.

"What? Oh. No. Not like that," I said, shaking my head. "He had to go to the city council meeting. I was trying to finish my column, which is total shit, and I worked at it for a couple hours and finally gave up when I realized it was midnight and all I had was a first line."

I took a slug of latte. "Which was a sucky first line, by the way."

She rolled her eyes. "Nobody cares about your first lines, you dolt. Tell me about HUGH."

Suddenly, the napkin looked fascinating to me. I focused on tearing it to tiny shreds (which is impossible to do while maintaining eye contact with way-too-perceptive best friends). "Nothing. I mean, I know he's a Romeo and a shark and all that other stuff. I'm not going to be a notch—"

My face flamed red, as I remembered where the laptop notch conversation had led me the night before. "Er . . ."

"Ah HA!" She pounced, as I'd known she would. "I recognize that red face. That is the red-face-of-C.J.-hiding-something. You had SEX with HUGH!"

"Shut UP!" I whipped my head back and forth, scanning for possible coworkers. "I did *not* have sex with Hugh. There was kissing. Well, one kiss. Maybe two. That's all."

She narrowed her eyes. "I know you, *chica.* You don't turn fire-engine red over one kiss. What happened?"

Giving up, I looked up at her and grinned. "He's an Olympic contender."

She shrieked. "No! Not Hugh the smarmy serial dater? You know better than that! What are you possibly going to get out of a relationship with a man like that? He even asked *me* out once."

(I hadn't known that. From the way my stomach felt a little sick, I kinda wished I still didn't. So what does that make *me*? The leftover meatloaf of potential dates?)

"It's not a relationship, already. It was one meal. At Wendy's, even. And, well, I guess there's dinner this weekend . . ."

"You're going out to dinner with him, too?" She covered her eyes with her hand, shaking her head. "Have I taught you nothing?"

I smiled wryly. "Apparently not, because I'm going out with *him* Saturday, after I go out with Mr. Aaron 'call me A.J.' Judson Friday. Can you believe it? I'm in a dating Sahara for six months, and now it's a dating smorgasboard. Not to mix bad metaphors or anything."

Finally, for the first time in my life, I'd done it. I'd rendered Paola Rossini totally speechless. She gaped at me in disbelief, and I started laughing. "You may want to close your mouth, Paola. The beached fish look is *so* last year."

She closed her mouth with an almost audible snap and stood up. "Fine. TWO dates in TWO nights. We are going to have to take extreme measures, no matter how painful it is for you."

I climbed out of my chair, feeling a nearly palpable wave of dread creeping up my spine. "You don't mean . . ."

"Yes." She fixed her beady fashionista eyes on me. "We're going shopping."

Aaaaaarrrghhhh!

BACK in my office, I stared at the remains of my seventy-fifth attempt to write the week's column. It kept starting out as a logical and sane discussion of the modern Guy's obsession with tools but turning into a diatribe against the instrument of torture known as the high-heeled shoe. I stuck my tongue out at the current weapons of doom, aka stiletto-heeled boots that Paola had decided were a great idea.

Speaking of Paola, the evil sadist popped her head in my office. "What time are we leaving for shopping?"

I glared at her. "I'm sick of shopping. Sick of shoes. Sick. Of. Fashion."

She kicked the door shut behind her. "C.J.! Don't ever, EVER insult fashion!"

Balling up my latest pitiful attempt at a column, I tossed the wadded sheets of paper in the general direction of the wastebasket that overflowed in the corner, a silent testament to my idiocy. (I'd resorted to writing in longhand—a sure sign of desperation.)

"What is that?" She strode over and picked up the paper. "Since when do you have this much of a problem writing your column? What's your topic this week?"

I sighed. "That's just it. I can't seem to focus. Ever since you turned me into a *girl,* I don't have the same focus. I wanted to write about freaking men and their freaking obsession with their freaking tools, but somehow I wind up writing about freaking shoes. It's ridiculous."

I moaned and put my head in my hands. "I actually spent ten minutes picking out my underwear this morning. Can you believe it? Ten freaking minutes!"

Paola grinned at me. "I'm just guessing here, but are you having a 'freaking' problem?"

I shot a glare at her. "Don't laugh at me. This is *your* fault. I have twelve different bottles of crap on my bathroom counter. *Twelve.* I don't even know what half of them are for. Does exfoliant have something to do with hair follicles? I used it after I shampooed, and my hair looked hideous."

Paola was trying (fairly unsuccessfully, I might add) to keep from cracking up, but something about exfoliation must have rocketed her over the edge. She clutched the arms of the chair, howling.

If ever I'd wanted to hire Hans Ham Hands to torture somebody to death with sea salt, *that* was the moment.

"It's not funny," I said, growling at her. "I'm having an identity crisis. Who am I? Am I C.J. the normal person or C.J the girly girl? And why does a skirt and makeup change my entire personality, anyway? Why does my new hairdo make Ricky down in classifieds start stammering and stuttering like I'm some sort of . . . some sort of *girl*?"

It took some effort, but Paola sobered up enough to answer me. "It's not the skirt or the makeup or the hairdo. It's the fact that you're beautiful, but you've been hiding it under brown clothes and shaggy hair and your 'I'm just one of the guys' attitude."

She stood up, brushing imaginary dust off her skirt. "It's like finding a pearl in a bowl full of rocks. They're just all in shock."

"Thanks a lot. I'm a *rock*, now?" I grinned at her, but she didn't rise to the bait. She walked to the door and then turned around and delivered her parting zinger. "Being a girl doesn't preclude being a person."

I sighed. Person, girl, whatever. Is metamorphosis really a good thing?

AS SEEN IN THE *SEATTLE TIMES:*

***THE NAKED TRUTH ABOUT GUYS,* BY COLUMNIST C. J. MURPHY**

The Drawer

In the great scope of relationship milestones, the moment when a Guy offers you a drawer at his place is huge. To you, it may be simple common sense: You've been spending more nights at his house than at your own, to the point where your plants are dead and there's a layer of dust a half-inch thick over the contents of your refrigerator. It just makes sense that you should have somewhere to keep a few things at his place so you don't have to keep running home to restock the overnight bag, right?

Wrong.

In the Guy mind, The Drawer is a terrifying encroachment into his personal space. To understand this concept, we must return to the original Guy, whose idea of fun was to grab a club and chase after a big animal like, say, a dinosaur or a wooly mammoth. [Note: Complaints about prehistoric timeline issues should be directed to Donald Donaldson, Official Complaint Dept., c/o the paper.]

So there they are, the hominids, running around clubbing away on giant animals and generally celebrating the joy of life and their delight in the fact that deodorant had not yet been invented. Then one of the females of the tribe came out of the cave to ask a simple question, like "How long until you actually CATCH one of those animals? The pot has been boiling since the Jurassic Age."

This would enrage the preverbal males so much, they would all rush at the woman, forcing her back into the cave, where she would discuss the disadvantages of mates with low foreheads with her fellow females.

The men, appeased by her retreat, would march around puffing out their chests and inventing fun things to do, like armpit farting.

Today's Guy no longer stalks and hunts the wooly mammoth. [Historical fact: The wooly mammoths all became extinct when they died of boredom waiting for Early Guy to finally catch one of them.] Instead, he picks up Chinese takeout and almost never chases his woman into a cave. But he still has a huge need for personal space, and the fact that you want an ACTUAL DRAWER in his ACTUAL APARTMENT has terrifying ramifications, in his allegedly evolved mind:

- *If I give her a drawer, she will probably want space in the closet.*
- *If I give her space in the closet, she's gonna want space in the bathroom for girl stuff.*
- *If the guys come over and find icky feminine products in the bathroom, I'm toast.*
- *If I give her all this space for clothes, she won't have any reason to go home. EVER. I'll have to give her a KEY. And forget about those Swedish bikini models!*

Therefore, in a state of abject panic, the Guy will shout at you about "How can you be so demanding?" and "Why is it always about you?" and "I really just need some space," when you only asked for a six-by-twelve-inch box of wood in which to keep a spare pair of panties.

Then you will break up, never quite understanding what happened, and the Guy will march around, puffing out his chest and making farting noises with his armpits.

Until next time, remember: *Guys! Won't give you a drawer; can't hunt wooly mammoths worth a darn.*

SEVEN

"**DUDE,** that's what you're wearing?"

Holding my door open for the pride of Seattle baseball, it occurred to me that maybe he'd been raised by wolves. Hippie wolves. "I'm fine, thank you. Yes, it is a new dress. Thank you for asking. It's great to finally meet you in person, too," I said, eyes narrowed.

He at least had the decency to look a little embarrassed. "Sorry, C.J. It's wonderful to meet you! But you can't wear that—it's a dress! And, like, *wow!* It's a seriously hot dress!" He bounded in the apartment and walked around me, staring at me in open-mouthed admiration.

(Okay, it felt kind of great; I admit it. I was wearing the simple Ann Klein black cocktail dress with Nine West heels—for the "dressy" part—with my new Burberry raincoat standing by for the "waterproof" part. It *was* hot. *I* was hot. I'd finally achieved hotness. *Hee hee hee.*)

A.J. slung an arm around my shoulders and pushed my door closed with his other hand, since I'd been frozen in place in contemplation of my own hotness. "Vain, vain, vain," I muttered, suddenly worried about turning into a clone of the hellbitch.

Suddenly he pulled away from me and peered into my eyes. "You look a lot like your assistant. Is she your sister or something?"

Oops. How could I have forgotten about this little problem?

I forced out a brittle laugh. "Oh, people say that all the time. She just quit, by the way, to, er, move to Africa."

"Oh, wow. That's, um, what were we talking about?" asked A.J., stepping closer to me. He stared down at me, and I felt his breath on my hair. "C.J., we don't have to go out. We could . . . stay in and order pizza. You're . . . I . . ."

I looked up at him, and the desire in his eyes made me catch my breath. Nobody ever looked at me like that; at least, not for long. "I guess—"

Then he kissed me. It was warm and gentle, and he was totally a world-champ kisser. Clearly the man knew his technique. It was . . .

Nice.

Damn.

He pulled away, breathing deeply. I'm guessing it was more than just *nice* for him. "C.J., I—"

I twisted slightly and moved out from under his arm. "Right. Thanks. I mean, we should get going, right? What do I need to wear, if this isn't right?"

"You . . . ah, right. Wear. You should wear jeans and boots, like me, and bring a rain jacket. But nothing you don't mind getting dirty. *Really* dirty."

Midway to the bedroom, I stopped dead, again flashing on the "watery grave" fortune. "Um, really dirty? What exactly *are* we doing?"

"PAINTBALL? We're fighting a *paintball* battle?" I looked around at the group of guys—mostly A.J.'s teammates—and their wives and girlfriends surrounding me in the dimly lit parking lot. "Are you insane? This is your idea of a Friday night date?"

My personal shortstop grinned at me. "It rocks. You'll love it! Your dad and brothers told me you're into sports. What better way to show you I'm your destiny? Bet nobody else takes you out to play paintball."

I gaped at him. "You—you *what?* You talked to my dad and brothers? When did you do that?"

(I decided to ignore the "I'm your destiny" part of the conversation.)

"I called them yesterday to find out what you might like. You're not exactly hard to find. I only had to call about twenty-two . . . no, twenty-four Murphys before I found your family." He sort of bounced up and down like a puppy waiting for a liver snap.

Does that make me the liver snap?

"You ready?" He grabbed my arm and pulled me forward into the waiting crowd and started introducing me as "C.J., my destiny."

It got worse from there.

"SHOOT him, shoot him, SHOOT HIM!" I dove for cover, shouting myself hoarse. About ten minutes into the game, I'd discovered my inner Rambo. By the half-hour mark, I had three confirmed "kills" to my credit. I also smelled like I hadn't bathed in a month.

Our battleground was two acres of forest. Think trees, trees, and more trees. We crawled through mud, jumped over bushes, and generally acted like idiots.

It was a blast.

A.J. turned, too late. The electrical engineer from the computer firm shot him in the leg. "Owwww!" A.J. yelled, falling to the ground, clutching his thigh. "Damn, damn, damn. That really HURTS!!"

(This is a little-known fact about paintballs: They hurt like crazy when they explode on any part of your body. The rest of our team, who'd clearly done this before, were all wearing padding. We, sadly, were not.)

I dove toward my fallen comrade, er . . . date. "Are you okay? Do you need help?"

He smiled up at me, reaching up as if to hug me. "C.J.! My darling angel of mercy. I—"

I pushed his hands away. "Dude, I'm not hit yet. Don't slow me down. Hey, Max! Cover me! I'm going in!" I rolled away from A.J., who watched me in stunned disbelief.

"You're not going to leave me, are you? You're my date! You're my destiny!" he called after me.

I ignored him and yelled at the weenie engineer aiming at me. "I'm your worst nightmare. Go ahead. Make my day!"

" 'GO ahead. Make my day'?" My brother Jerry asked me the next morning on the phone. "What the heck was that?"

I tucked the phone between my ear and shoulder, wincing at my sore and aching ribs. "What can I say? I was channeling my inner Dirty Harry."

"Right. You have to channel Dirty Harry when you're dating the hottest shortstop in the country. Are you ever going to act like a girl?"

I slammed my fridge door shut and glared at my collection of sports trivia refrigerator magnets. "I *am* acting like a girl. You have no idea. I have three different kinds of moisturizer. I have high heels. I even own a pair of *pantyhose*," I said, darkly.

He laughed. "I'd pay money to see that. *You* in pantyhose? You're gonna have a tough time playing racquetball in pantyhose and high heels."

"Life is not all about racquetball."

"*Your* life is. Racquetball and softball and hiking and skiing. Why are you suddenly going all princess on us?" If he'd sounded sarcastic, or amused, or anything but honestly perplexed, I probably would have hung up on him. But because I was pretty perplexed myself, I sighed.

"I don't know. Every guy I've dated in the past three years has broken up with me with the 'you're such a good buddy' line. Two of them sent me their wedding invitations within six months of dumping me."

"But—"

I held up a hand, even though he wasn't there to see it. "I know, I know. I'm not waiting for a marriage proposal. I'm only twenty-five years old. But a relationship that lasts longer than three or four months would be nice for a change."

It was Jerry's turn to sigh. "I know, sis. But if you change what's real about yourself to start dating a guy, you're stuck with somebody who's in love with somebody who's not even you."

Once I figured out the tangled skein of that sentence, I had to smile. "When did you get so wise?"

"I've always been the smartest one in the family. The sooner you admit it, the better your life will be. Speaking of life being better, is Aaron Judson coming to lunch today? Dad promised him barbecue."

I glared at the phone. "You and Dad can butt out of my love life, thank you very much. Quit inviting my dates to family dinners."

Jerry laughed again. "Hell, it had nothing to do with him being your date. If Lebron James, Lance Armstrong, or Tiger Woods call the house, we'll invite them to dinner, too."

With a family like this, I'll probably be eighty years old before I get a real boyfriend.

EIGHT

"**AARON,** it's great to meet you! I'm John. C.J.'s really moving up in the world. You wouldn't believe some of the losers she's gone out with in the past few years." The Giant Mouth of Destruction, also known as my brother, grabbed A.J.'s hand and pumped it enthusiastically.

I punched John in the arm. Hard. Back in the house where we grew up, all our bad childhood habits came rushing to the surface. If somebody tried to give me a wedgie, I was *so* out of there.

"Ouch! That woman has a mean right hook. You should watch out for her," John said, rubbing his arm and giving me the evil eye.

A.J. caught me up in a big hug and planted a huge, smacking kiss on my mouth. "Not C.J. She's my darling Pookie Bear."

I winced and looked at John over A.J.'s shoulder. The expression of shock on his face mirrored my own, I was pretty sure.

Pookie Bear? Oh, no. That is so not happening.

"Um, A.J.? If you call me Pookie Bear again, I'm going to have to hurt you."

He squeezed me even tighter. "Awww. You're so cute. Do you see why she's my destiny, John?"

I clenched my eyes shut, horrified at the prospect of the unmerciful torture I'd have to endure from my brothers for weeks to come. "Pookie Bear" and "my destiny" pretty much gave them enough ammo to last for the next five years.

Ducking under his arm, I escaped off toward the kitchen. "Well, I have potato salad to make. Feel free to mingle amongst yourselves." I walked off as fast as I could, nearly running, and then rounded the corner to the kitchen and skidded to a stop.

"Okay, you evil traitor. What the heck were you thinking?" I pinned Dad with a death glare, not even pausing to do my usual scan of his unchanged-since-the-seventies kitchen. (Orange wallpaper. Seriously.)

Dad backed away, eyes wildly scanning the room for a method of escape. "I don't know what you're talking about. What was I thinking about what? By the way, I really need to get out to the grill. Coals to heat, meat to grill, you know."

I moved to the side, blocking his exit. "Nice try, Bucko. Since when do you invite men to the Saturday lunch for me?"

Dad grinned, totally unrepentant. (He thinks the white hair and twinkly blue eyes thing softens me up. Sadly, it does.) "Honey. Sweetie. *Pookie Bear.* I just want you to be happy."

I stalked toward him, trying really hard not to smile. "Eavesdropping, too, I see."

He feinted left and then made a break right. "Hey, if you're going to date sports stars, I'm going to be nice to them. That's just the kind of dad I am."

I sighed and looked for the potato peeler as he dashed out to the yard.

Is it too much to ask that I could be an orphan for just one day?

"HERE'S the potato salad, everybody," I announced, finally walking out of the kitchen where I'd been lurking, um . . . hiding, er . . . *working hard* for the past half an hour. "I guess we're ready to . . . *Hugh*?"

Hugh looked up from where he was sitting on the couch with my brother Jack and aimed one of his slow, dangerous smiles my way. "I heard a rumor you were here, somewhere."

What the heck is he *doing here?* I caught sight of Bill out of the corner of my eye, arguing with Paola on the deck. *If Bill brought Hugh, he is* so *dead.*

Hugh stood up and walked over to me. "Your brother was just telling me all about your *boyfriend,* Aaron." He reached up and touched my cheek with his finger. "Is your boyfriend going to appreciate our date tonight?"

The touch of his finger on my cheek sent a shock wave through my body that almost stopped my breath in my throat. I stared up at him, unable to speak. A smile quirked the corner of his mouth. "Are we still on, Audrey? I have very definite plans for you tonight."

Why, why, why, why? Why does the nice, sweet, boy-next-door sports star (who probably makes a zillion dollars per year) do nothing for me, and yet the office Lothario zaps every nerve I've ever had—and a few I never even knew about?

A.J. and the boys picked that moment to walk in from the yard, sweaty from playing football, and I backed away from Hugh, still speechless. He smiled at me again—a smile that made promises I wasn't sure he could keep.

Promises I wasn't sure I wanted him to keep.

Getting involved with Hugh is a bad, bad idea.

A.J. evidently agreed. He walked over to me and slung his arm over my shoulder, measuring Hugh with his eyes. "Dude. I'm guessing you're not another brother. Are you Paola's date?"

Hugh smiled at him, but the smile didn't reach his eyes. "No. I work with Bill and C.J. Bill brought me after our racquetball game. And you are . . . ?"

The level of testosterone shot up about a thousand percent in the room, and I sighed and stepped between them. "A.J., meet Hugh. Hugh, meet A.J. Now, if you need to have a pissing contest, please step outside. Dad just had the carpets cleaned."

Paola, who'd stepped inside at some point, sputtered into a coughing fit. "The burgers are done, everybody. Please come out and fix your plates and rescue me from Bill, before I'm forced to kill him."

Saved by the fashionista. I sent a psychic major thank-you to Paola and headed for the door with my stupid bowl of potato salad.

It's going to be a long, long afternoon. But tonight . . .

I tried (and failed miserably) to suppress a thrill of excitement from thinking of my date with Hugh that evening.

I'm in so much trouble.

Jerry caught up with me at the door and took the potato salad from me. He leaned in close to my ear and spoke quietly. "You're in so much trouble."

"Yeah. I *got* that."

I WANDERED around my tiny apartment, my head aching miserably from playing referee all afternoon. A.J. had stalked around Hugh like a dog scenting a rival; my brothers clamored for A.J.'s attention and (except for Jerry) spent a lot of time trying to discourage Hugh from ever coming within a five-mile radius of me. Then first one, then another, then another of my brothers—and finally even my dad—had cornered me at some point.

"But Hugh doesn't have season tickets to the Mariners' games; why would you date him*? Think of us, for once!"*

(Like I hadn't spent my entire life thinking of nothing but my five brothers. This is why my first attempt to be a girl ends up with me trying to play paintball in stilettos.)

But on the other hand, do I really want to date the laptop notcher?

The doorbell rang. Notcher or not, Hugh was here. Sucking in a deep breath and, hopefully, a lung or two full of courage, I smoothed down the skirt of the slinky red dress Paola had bought for me.

If I'm going down, I'm going down in some serious flames.

I opened the door and pasted a smile on my face. "Hello, Hugh. You're right on time."

Right on time and, oh, holy Armani. He wore a pair of black pants and a matching sweater that clung to the lines of his body in a way that I'd often fantasized about doing. I felt my mouth go as dry as the time I'd slid into third base with it hanging wide open. My headache had magically vanished, too.

His answering smile faded slowly, as his gaze swept down my body and back to my face. "If I'd had any idea you'd be wearing that dress, I'd have been here hours ago. C.J., you're beautiful." His voice sounded husky and a little unsure; there was no evidence of the smoothly sophisticated hotshot reporter whom I knew and . . . well . . . *lusted* over.

Pulling the door open wider, I motioned him in, fighting the dryness in my mouth to respond. "Come in for a second while I find my new purse. My old backpack won't go with the dress."

He caught my arm as I reached for the door and then pushed it closed behind him with his foot. As I looked up at him, startled, he pulled me in closer to his body. "I can't help it, C.J. You have no idea how long I've waited to do this. I've been going nuts all weekend wondering what you were doing with that stupid ballplayer."

As I opened my mouth to respond, he leaned his head down and murmured, "Shhh," against my mouth and then kissed me. Unlike A.J.'s kiss, this one wasn't *nice* at all. It was all heat and demand and *oh, yes, yum,* finally, *my toes are tingling* goodness.

Hugh pulled back from me, and we stared at each other, vying for title of "most shocked expression." A kiss from a guy you barely know at all—and what you *do* know about him isn't good—isn't supposed to blast off through your hormones like a NASA rocket through the atmosphere.

But it did. I tried to talk, but weird, stammering noises came out of my mouth. Oddly enough, considering his laptop-notcher rep, he was making the same noises.

Hmmm. This was interesting. Even as my brain was imploding, part of it was wondering why Mr. Smooth was acting all . . . NOT smooth. So I decided to ask. Naturally, it came out as a study in sheer elegance and grace: "You . . . wow. Um, my family wants me to date A.J."

(You see what I mean about the grace?)

Hugh bent his head back down to mine and nibbled kisses up the side of my neck. "Then let them date him," he murmured.

It seemed like a good solution at the time.

NINE

"WHAT do you mean, you like him better? You can't like smarmy Hugh better than sweet, adorable, 'you're my destiny' Aaron!" Paola sounded outraged. Or shocked. Or both. Luckily, she was out at Nordstrom's for a trunk show and calling on her cell, so I didn't have to face her in person. I'd spent most of the morning mooning over those first hot kisses with Hugh, and then the terrific fajitas we'd had at Rosalita's, and even over how much of a gentleman he'd been to not try to rip off my clothes.

Damn gentlemen.

Unfortunately, that didn't hold true for my boss. I winced when my office door crashed open. "I'll call you later, Paola," I whispered and then hung up quickly. I'd wondered how fast Donny'd be by to rake my uncreative body over the coals, thanks to the uninspired essay I'd finally tried to pass off as my weekly column.

"What the hell is this? Men and tools as an analogy for women and high-heeled shoes? What the *hell*, I repeat, is this girly crap? Did getting your hair cut do a mental Samson on you?"

You've got to be impressed by Biblical references to weakness at eight-thirty in the morning.

I squirmed a little in my chair. "I know, I know. I'm sorry, Donny, er . . . Mr. Donaldson. It *is* crap. I was desperate to get something—anything—out before I went nuts looking at the page."

He glowered at me. "Right. Instead, you send it to me so *I* can go nuts looking at the page. May I remind you that I'm your boss? It's in my contract that I don't have to read crap. Not now; not ever."

He crushed the offending pages in his hand and tossed them down on my desk. "This is utter garbage. You know I like your voice, C.J. I fought for you when the board said your stuff was lighthearted fluff. But you're going to lose your core readership if you lose the focus of your column."

I forced my gaze up at him when I really wanted to stare at the floor in shame. Donny's version of "I'm disappointed in you" was deadly. "I'm sorry. I'm so sorry. It's just that I'm so confused about the nature of the man/woman thing, and being 'one of the guys' versus being a girlfriend, and—" I broke off, finally catching the stare of abject horror he was aiming at me.

"I don't want to hear about your *issues*. Damn sensitivity training. The column is crap. Fix it."

"I will. I'll fix it. I'm sorry. I just—"

He snorted. "I don't want to hear apologies. Apologies are for wussies. Just fix it. Have it on my desk by five." He turned and stomped his way out of the room, banging the door shut behind him.

If I'd been more of a girlie girl, that's the point where I would have cried.

* * *

THREE hours later, the column still wasn't working. I felt like I was sucking all humor out of the ozone layer just by touching fingers to keyboard. My phone rang, and I jumped to answer it. Even telemarketers selling vinyl siding had to be better than this torture.

"Hey, gorgeous." The heat that shot up through my face was an instant Hugh-O-Meter. "Are you free for lunch?"

After our date Saturday night, when we'd closed down the restaurant, just talking about everything and anything, I wanted to say yes so badly it hurt. But I looked at my unfinished column, and I just couldn't do it. I sighed. "I can't. My column still isn't working, and Donny already . . . er, mentioned that he needs it by five. I really need to work through lunch. How about a raincheck?"

He chuckled, and the smooth warmth of it curled around me. This is how drug addicts go down, I bet. They know it's bad for them, but they just want it so badly. Like a craving. That's how I felt about Hugh's kisses, after trying out a few Saturday.

Okay, maybe more like a few *dozen.* But he was a gentleman and didn't even try to get in my pants, which—maybe, just maybe—means that his Mr. Smooth rep is a teensy bit overinflated.

Or maybe he doesn't think I'm sexy.

"C.J.? Are you there?"

"Yes, just having a momentary brain fade . . . um, I mean, mentally working through my column. Very busy, you know." I shuffled papers near the phone, trying to sound busy.

I could hear the smile in his voice. "Right. I hear much paper shuffling. Okay, then, forget lunch. I've been invited—kinda last-minute—to a charity thing at the Seattle Opera Friday. Some new coloratura named Brianna Higgins is being showcased, among others. Would you like to go with me? It's a black-tie deal, I'll warn you in advance."

"I don't have a black tie," I muttered.

"That's okay. I'll wear the black tie, and you can wear some incredibly sexy little dress like that red one you wore Saturday. In fact, why don't you wear that dress on every date we have, ever? The image of you in it is permanently burned into my brain," he said, his voice husky.

Epiphany: Now I understand the appeal of phone sex.

"Um, well, fine. Yes. I'd love to come. I mean, not *come*, but go. With you. Opera, right? What's not to love? A bunch of fat ladies singing. Who needs football tickets when you can have opera?" I was babbling, and I knew it, but I was terrified my sex-obsessed brain would force my traitorous mouth to ask what color underwear he had on or something.

Cravings, I tell you. Cravings.

"I'll pick you up at seven."

I hung up the phone, smiling like a fool, and then glanced at my computer screen. Suddenly, I knew exactly what to write. But first I had to call Paola about a dress . . .

AS SEEN IN THE *SEATTLE TIMES:*

***THE NAKED TRUTH ABOUT GUYS,* BY COLUMNIST C. J. MURPHY**

Tools and Opera

Part of a Guy's genetic code involves a little squiggle, buried deep in the DNA, that commands any Guy over the age of five to develop an enduring, uncontrollable obsession with his . . . tools.

From his first trip with Dad to the hardware store, a Guy becomes mesmerized with the sight, sound, and smell of any large item that can hammer, pound, or saw. This obsession reaches a whole new level when he gets a little older and discovers the rapture of power tools.

Being women, we try to take our Guys' minds off of tools for a little while each month, to introduce them to other things in life. Like culture. Chick flicks. Even ballet and opera.

This never works. Most Guys would rather undergo unanesthetized surgery than sit through an entire ballet or any movie involving "girlie stuff" or "weep-fests."

I have a suggestion for all cultural venues: If you'd try to write an opera on a subject that really interests Guys, your ticket sales would quadruple in a matter of days.

The Car Chase Ballet? The Exploding Building Symphony? The Power Tool Opera, anyone? Where's Handel when you need him? Being a Guy himself, he probably would have totally loved the idea.

Until next time, remember: *Guys! Can't force them to enjoy culture, can't get them out of the power sander aisle.*

TEN

TWO solid hours of being ignored by Seattle's beautiful people. Was I having fun or what?

Pretty much *or what.*

Scanning the glittering room for the elusive Hugh, for the three-hundredth or so time, I wondered again why I'd ever thought I'd fit in at a charity ball for the rich bigwigs at, of all things, the Seattle Opera. The closest I'd ever been to opera before was my own personal DVD of *The Phantom of the Opera* with hottie Gerard Butler.

(Hey! *That's* who Hugh reminds me of—no wonder I put up with a lot. If he'd only get a cape, I'd be toast.)

I'd met the featured singer, Brianna, and she was super-nice (and gorgeous). She'd introduced me to her boyfriend, Jamie (think a young Brad Pitt; also gorgeous) and her friends Kirby and Banning (also gorgeous—are you seeing the theme here?). They were all very nice, but I'd felt like yesterday's lunch compared to their casual elegance. Even in the admittedly fab silver sheath dress Paola'd found somewhere—and don't think I wasn't a little self-conscious about the thigh-to-floor slit up the side or the nearly backless part—I felt like a little girl playing dress-up.

It didn't help that slimeball Hugh had pretty much abandoned me the minute we walked in the door, in favor of networking with what looked like every mover and shaker in the city.

But I *want a little moving and shaking,* mourned the part of my brain that had demanded I clean the apartment and buy condoms, "just in case." All of a sudden, I'd had enough. I'm not the wallflower type, but I was so intimidated I'd been lurking by the dessert table, like an idiot, when I'd gotten cornered by the most boring man in the history of the world. Mr. Pompous Airbag (possibly not his real name) had spent the past twenty minutes telling me about his stock portfolio's ups and downs. I hadn't even stabbed him with my dessert fork yet, either.

As my mind wandered, yet again, I realized that at least A.J.'d had the decency to take me someplace fun and stick with me. Well, until that man had shot him in the thigh and killed him, but you can't trump death by paintball when you're still on the field.

I wonder what A.J. is doing this weekend, since I didn't return any of his fifteen or so phone calls.

Again with the enough already. *You're having a miserable time, alone and abandoned, and you're daydreaming about another guy you don't even like in a romantic way while you're on a so-called date with Hugh. That's pretty much a wake-up call that even nongirlie girls can understand.*

Okay. That was it. I murmured something to Mr. Pompous and made my escape. Setting my glass down on a passing waiter's tray, I tightened my grip on my tiny clutch purse and started threading my way through the crowd to the door.

Just as I made it to the door, a hand caught my arm. I looked down.

It was Hugh's hand. "C.J.? Where are you going? The ladies' room is the other way."

I shook his hand off my arm, ignoring the tingling radiating out from where he'd touched me. "I don't need the bathroom, but thanks so much for pointing it out. In fact, thanks so much for condescending to actually talk to me for the first time all night. Run out of bigwigs to suck up to?"

An expression that looked a lot like hurt crossed with shame flickered in his eyes and then the look I'd come to think of as the Mr. Smooth Hugh Mask replaced it.

I'd come to hate that damn Hugh Mask.

Actually, I wasn't too fond of the man himself at that very minute.

I hadn't stopped my march toward the exit; he matched his step to mine. "I'm sorry; I didn't realize you'd feel that way. You've lived here all of your life. I guess I just figured you'd know lots of people to talk with, and I didn't want to horn in on all of your friendships and relationships."

I stopped dead and gawked at him in disbelief. "You thought I'd know all *these* people? These rich, opera people? My dad is a cop, Hugh. I write a newspaper column. This is not exactly my kind of crowd. Thank you so *much* for rescuing me from that pompous windbag, too."

A couple dressed in clothes that probably cost more than my annual salary stood nearby, clearing listening to our conversation. I stuck my tongue out at them and started stalking toward the exit again.

Mature, right?

Hugh chuckled. "I've wanted to do that to several people all night long. You've got guts."

"Right. Guts. Is this the 'be charming and witty' portion of the evening? 'Cause I've gotta tell you, it's too little, too late. But I'll be glad to recommend another place you can take the hellbitch. Goodbye." I shoved the door open and stepped outside, taking a deep breath and wondering why I hadn't called for a cab before I made my grand exit.

Hugh stepped outside right behind me and put his hand on the small of my back. "No, thank you. I don't want any recommendations for any dates with anybody else. Although at some point I do want to explore why my date with Kaspar bothers you so much. But what I want right now is to take you home and explain something that I should have told you a long time ago."

He raked his other hand through his hair and made an impatient noise. "If I hadn't been so damned worried about fitting in, or so intimidated by you, we wouldn't be having this misunderstanding now."

Intimidated? By me?

The thought of Mr. Smooth being intimidated by me stunned me into acquiescence, and I allowed myself to be guided to his car in silence.

This ought to be good.

On the way to my apartment, I clenched my jaw together to keep from blurting out anything stupid before he had a chance to explain. He started to speak several times, but it kept coming out in false starts. Then he'd be silent again for a few minutes. (This is evidently a good way to torture humor columnists, in case you're wondering. I was lathered up into a frenzy of curiosity and impatience by the time we reached my place.)

There was no way he was getting away from me without explaining all that stammering and stuttering, so I dragged him up to my apartment, conveniently forgetting that I'd vowed never to see him again less than an hour before. I pulled him inside, flicked on the light switch, and slammed the door behind him.

"Okay. Spill it." I kicked off my shoes, folded my arms across my chest, and waited. Strategically, this was a bad move. It put me a couple more inches shorter than Hugh, so I had to tilt my head to look up at him. The glint of amusement in his eyes melted into pure heat, and he stepped closer to me and reached out to run a fingertip down the length of my arm. "C.J., I—oh, to hell with it. I need to tell you something, but I need this even more."

I saw it coming. I could have escaped. But part of me wanted—no, *needed*—to feel all that heat pressed up against me again. So I unfolded *my* arms and stepped into his. He made a little humming noise in his throat and leaned down to kiss me, but I was tired of letting him lead. I reached up and pulled his head down to mine and—this time—I kissed him.

I kissed him with all the heat and craving and unrequited lust of the past five months rolled up in it.

I kissed him with all the pain and fury of my "I don't want to date you—you're one of the guys" history whirling around in my head and heart.

I kissed him, and he shuddered against me. *Finally, finally*. I smiled a tiny smile at him and tried on a flirty look, but I think it came out just how it felt inside me—*wicked and oh, so good*. "So Hugh. Do you see me as just one of the guys, too?"

His mouth fell open. "One of the guys? One of the *guys*? Are you nuts? You're the sexiest woman I've ever known, even when you're wearing your turnip-farming clothes." He pulled me against him and then slid his hands down to my butt and pulled me, even tighter, into the hardness of his body. "Does that feel like a reaction to one of the guys?"

I laughed, giddy, glorying in his reaction to me. "Well. Um. 'Don't ask, don't tell'?"

He made a weird growly sort of noise in his throat and leaned down and picked me up. "Oh, I have a lot of telling to do. And you're going to listen. But right now, I'd really, really appreciate it if you'd point me to your bedroom. I have a deep-seated need to do the caveman thing. Now, C.J. *Please*."

I might have played with him for a bit longer, but that husky *please* touched me in a way that all the smooth charm in the world never could have done. I reached up to touch his mouth with my fingertips and sighed. "I'm *so* not Scarlett O'Hara, but the 'sweep me off my feet' move just won you points." I pointed down the hall with the hand not clutching his shoulders and then, because I couldn't help it, I gently bit his neck.

He groaned again and started down the hall. "I love that dress, C.J., but it's coming off. *Now.*"

And so it did.

"WHAT is that horrible noise?" I raised my head and gazed blearily around my room. Hugh hadn't let me fall asleep until after three (not that I'm complaining), and the room was still dark. The hideous buzzing noise shrilled its electronic annoyance through the room. I elbowed Hugh, who hadn't even moved. "Wake up. Is that for you? Phone or something?"

He opened one eye, startled awake, and then opened the other and a slow, lazy smile spread over his face. There was a lot of satisfied and a little bit of smug in that smile.

After the seventh or eighth orgasm (breaking my previous record for most orgasms in an entire week), I'd quit counting, so I guess he deserved to look a little smug. I grinned back, not in the least shy or embarrassed like I usually was after the first time with a guy.

But all this mutual admiration wasn't solving the problem. "Hugh. The buzzer? Is that you?"

He blinked, suddenly awake. "Oh. Yeah. Yeah, that's my pager. The D.C. connection must have broken. I have to make a call. You don't mind, do you?"

He sat up and jumped out of bed, heading for his pants, which were, to the best of my memory, somewhere in the kitchen, along with my bra. (Don't ask.)

I admired the sight of his very adorable butt walking away from me so much that I almost didn't notice he'd jumped out of bed without waiting for my answer to the "do you mind" question.

Almost.

The buzzing stopped and then I heard his voice on the phone. "What time? Is there a direct flight? Is Senator Vauxhall involved? The evidence is clear?"

Suddenly I wasn't sleepy anymore. Hugh had told me he was hot on the case of financial mismanagement of Washington's state teacher pension plans by the senator's brother. Breaking the story would be an enormous scoop for him.

I sat up and drew the sheet around me as he came running back in the bedroom. He came straight for me, pants already on, pulling on his shirt as he walked. "This is it! I've got him now. I have to leave for D.C. right now. There's a flight in two hours. I ought to just have enough time to make it through airport security, if I break all speed limits going to the airport."

He pulled me halfway up off the bed into a huge hug. "This is it! This is my big break! You're my good luck!"

He kissed me with one of those big, smacking kisses and started to pull away, but I grabbed his head and pulled him back for a real, live, honest-to-goodness sizzler of a kiss. He looked a little dazed when I pulled away. "If I'm your good luck, I deserve a real kiss, at least," I said.

He laughed and hugged me again. "You deserve a lot more than that, but I really have to go, in spite of what that kiss just did to me." He gestured down to where the evidence of his arousal tented out the front of his tuxedo pants.

Speaking of tuxedo pants . . . "You're going to wear your tux on the plane?"

"I always carry a bag in my car. Never know when you might have to leave on a story with no time to pack. I'll change on the plane or at the airport in D.C."

He was shoving his feet into his shoes as he talked. Then he straightened and headed for the door. "I have to run, but I'll call you when I get to D.C."

I was already snuggling back down into my pillow with its warm scent of Hugh's cologne. "Wait for a reasonable hour, okay? I'm thinking I'm going to need to sleep in. You wore me out."

He stopped at the doorway and flashed me another of those all-male grins. "Same goes. And count on me doing it again, as soon as I get back, okay?"

Then the smile faded from his face and he turned and crossed back to the bed. "C.J.? We still need to talk. There's something I need to . . . about that damn book . . . Will you promise me one thing? Will you promise not to go out with that baseball jerk until we do? I'm discovering I'm a guy who wants an exclusive. At least with you."

He smoothed my bangs out of my eyes and stared at me with an almost tangible need in his eyes. I swallowed, feeling a strange warmth spread out from the direction of my heart. "I . . . sure. No problem. But . . . you, too, okay? I don't share." I tried to grin, but the intensity of his gaze left me unable to utter one of my usual tension-busting wisecracks.

He pressed a soft kiss to my lips. "No problem. You don't have a thing to worry about."

And then he was gone.

ELEVEN

THREE *days later . . .*

"What do you mean, he hasn't called? He has a cell phone, doesn't he? He's in D.C., not in some third-world country with no cell service, right? He's scum. All men are scum. Forget him and go out with poor Aaron. The man sent you another dozen roses just this morning." Paola's voice was shrill with indignation on my behalf, which was nice, considering I was way past indignation, annoyance, and even anger, and back to hopeless despair.

I'd really thought our night together meant something to Hugh, but clearly he was either a good actor or a great liar, and I was only another notch on the infamous laptop. "Oh, it's even worse than that. Not only has he not called me, he called the hellbitch. She took enormous pleasure this morning in telling me that they'd had a long, *looooong* chat last night. You were right. He's a player. I've been played.

This is even worse than the 'buddy' thing. I'd really thought we had something after . . ."

My voice trailed off as a fresh wave of pain spiked through me at the thought of our night together. I shoved my plate of uneaten moo goo gai pan to the side. Somehow, I didn't have much of an appetite.

Bill snagged the last eggroll and glared at Paola. "I'm a little sick of the 'all men are scum' routine, Paola. You just pick the scummy men for some reason. The ones who only want you for your looks. And sheesh, if you're going to date somebody, C.J., why not date the guy who can get you box seats at the Mariners' games? Plus he took you to play paintball. He likes you for who you really are, not as some stupid dress-up doll."

Paola glared right back at him. "What other kind of men are there besides scummy ones? The men who are interested in my personality? My *soul*? Ha! Men are all shallow and superficial. I will never, ever be content until I find a man willing to make the Grand Gesture for me—a man who values me more than his male pride, more than his stupid ego."

I dropped my head in my hands. "There is no such man. Except my brothers. Well, no, maybe only one of them. You're right. Men *are* scum. And for your information—*both* of you—I don't date by committee. Leave me alone about Aaron Judson, already."

Bill slammed his cup down on the table. "Hello? *Man* right here. When have I ever been scummy to either of you?"

Paola waved a hand in dismissal. "You don't count. You're not really a man; you're just a buddy."

He shoved his chair back from the table and stood up. "I am most definitely a man, Paola. You just don't see me that way. But that's going to change," he said, his voice dangerously low. Then he threw money down on the table and stalked out of the restaurant as we gaped at him in surprise.

Well, Paola gaped at him in surprise. The way the two of them always bickered, I'd kind of been wondering if Bill had a thing for Paola. It was looking like he did. There was no way *that* was going to work out.

Of course, I'm pretty much batting zero on relationship success, so I guess my predictions on the subject are worth exactly zilch. Zero. Nada, even.

Paola crushed a fortune cookie with her fist. "That man! Can you believe the way he talks to me? He's the only man I've ever met who can make me so . . . so . . . furious!" She picked up the sliver of paper and read aloud: " 'Wise men learn more from fools than fools learn from the wise.' "

She snorted. "Well, I guess that means I have to learn something from Bill, because I've never met a bigger fool."

I sighed, too worn out even to pursue the subject. (Did I mention I haven't been sleeping, either?) Paola selected a fortune cookie and handed it to me. "Here you are. I picked it out, so you won't have to worry about your fortune cookie curse."

I shook my head. "No way. I have enough bad luck without opening another evil fortune cookie. Forget it."

She laughed. "There's no way it will happen again, *chica*. Here, I'll read it for you." She snapped it open and pulled out the fortune. I pressed my hands over my ears and started humming, loudly, and closed my eyes.

When I stopped humming to take a breath, I heard nothing, so I opened one eye. The look of dismay on Paola's face snapped my other eye open. "What? What is it this time? I'll meet a tall dark stranger who will crush my heart? Been there, done that."

She crumpled up the fortune. "No, it was fine. Something about a life of luck and love. Let's go."

I held out my hand. "Let me see it."

"No."

"*Now*."

"No."

I grabbed her hand, pried her fingers open, and then snatched the fortune. I *needed* to see it after all that. I smoothed out the paper and read: " 'You will inherit a fortune, then waste every penny and become a hooker with a crack habit.' "

What the hell?

I met Paola's horrified gaze. "This is whacked. No way can this keep happening and happening. Plus, isn't this bad for business? We *so* are going to talk to Lin about this."

I stood up, grabbing my check, looked around for her, and then stalked over to the cash register and smacked my hand down on the bell. "Lin!"

She came out from behind the kitchen door, swiping at her eyes. The trackmarks of tears were clearly visible on her face, but she tried to paste on a bright smile. It came out more like a grimace. The angry words swelling up in my throat died in transit. "Lin? Are you okay?"

She nodded, swallowing hard. "Yes. Fine. Just a disagreement between two cultures. How are you? How was lunch?"

It was the perfect opening to tell her about the cookies of death, but I couldn't look at her red and swollen eyes and blather on about cookies. "Everything was fine. You let me know if you want to talk, okay? You have my number at the office, right?"

She nodded, blinking like she was trying to suppress a fresh wave of tears. "Thanks, C.J. You're one of the good guys."

I sighed. Yep, that's my biggest problem. I'm one of the *guys*.

ANOTHER *day later . . .*

My phone rang, startling me out of a black funk. Sometime after my chat with Kaspar, I'd finally quit jumping every time it rang, hoping pitifully that Hugh was finally calling me, after the gang that had kidnapped him and held him captive far from any telephones had let him go.

Pathetic, huh?

I picked up the phone. "C. J. Murphy."

"Finally! Didn't you get any of my messages? Or my roses? Or the carnations or violets or orchids?" Aaron still sounded like a puppy, but a *sad* puppy. It occurred to me that I'd been treating him kind of like Hugh had treated me, and I wasn't very proud of myself.

"I'm sorry. I've been so busy this week, but anyway, that's no excuse. I should have called. I'm really sorry. How are you?"

He sounded a little mollified, but he still had a hurt tone to his voice. "I'm okay. Hurt my elbow a little and have to go see the PT, but fine. Missing you, though. How can you be my destiny when we never see each other? I talk to your dad more than I talk to you."

I'm going to have to hurt my dad. Nothing fatal, just a black eye or something.

Suppressing my violent tendencies, I sighed. "I'm sorry. I don't know what else to say. It's been a sucky week. Speaking of which, there's something I need to tell you. We really need to talk." I couldn't string him along when I didn't feel anything for him beyond friendship. That's not how you treat a friend.

"We *do* need to talk! That's what I've been telling you! I have reservations for us to go whitewater rafting for the weekend down at Truckee River, near Lake Tahoe! It's going to be totally awesome! You'll love it! Plus, all my buds are going and my brother, too, so you can meet the whole gang. They're gonna totally love you, like I do."

"I—*love* me? Aaron, you can't love me. You just *met* me. Aren't you exaggerating a teensy bit?" *Finally somebody uses the "L" word with me, and it's a mental teenager with delusions of "destinyhood." No wonder I'm going to end up as a hooker with a crack habit.*

"C.J., sometimes you just know. I'm almost twenty-three years old; I'm not a kid anymore. I know what I want, and you're it. I knew you were my destiny just from reading your columns." He sounded so sure of himself, so certain. I wondered when the last time was I'd been so certain of anything.

The sound of cheering from the newsroom broke into my mental wanderings, and I looked up to see Hugh walking through the desks. I'd heard from Bill that Hugh'd cracked the pension scandal wide open, and the powers that be were already talking major journalistic awards. Everybody was pounding him on the back and high-fiving him.

Figures. The evil geniuses always win.

I realized two things simultaneously: Aaron was still talking, but I hadn't heard a word he'd said for the past several minutes, plus Hugh was heading straight down the hall for my office.

Crap.

"C.J.? Are you there? Do you want to go with me? I got you your own room, so it's no pressure to do the deed already, if that's freaking you out," Aaron said.

"What? Um, no, I'm not freaked out . . . It's—"

Just then, the hellbitch stepped into the hallway, directly in front of Hugh. She clutched at his arm with her slut-red nails, and he stopped to talk to her. Of *course* he stopped to talk to her. He probably hadn't been coming to see me at all. I wasn't only pathetic, I was pathetic warmed over. *I AM chopped liver.*

"Aaron, tell me more about the weekend," I said into the phone, self-disgust firming my voice and my resolve.

As he began to describe the wonders of rafting down class-three rapids, I snuck another look at Hugh and Kaspar. Except she was gone, and he was almost to the doorway of my office. Another step and he walked right in and shut the door behind him.

Wow. That takes a lot of freaking nerve.

"Excuse me for a moment, *Aaron*," I said into the phone, putting all the sultry into my voice I could muster. Then I tilted my head and gave Hugh my best freeze-your-balls off glare. "Is there something I can help you with?"

He looked exhausted; his face was pale, and he had dark circles under his eyes. I ruthlessly shoved down the glimmer of sympathy I started to feel and waited for his response.

"Help me? Can you *help* me? Is that all you have to say?" he said, his voice rising in apparent disbelief. He looked pissed off, too, which didn't help with the fury sweeping through me. After what he'd put me through, *he* had the nerve to be angry with *me*?

Before I could even think about it, the rage took over and I heard myself saying something I hadn't planned to say. "Aaron? Honey? I'd love to go away with you for the weekend. I'll call you later to set up the details. Thanks! Bye."

I hung the phone up with a decisive click and then looked up at Hugh again. "I'm sorry. You were saying?"

He simply stood there, hands hanging loosely at his sides, shoulders slumped—the very picture of dejection. The man was an Academy Award–worthy actor, that was for sure.

He didn't say anything. Just stood there for a minute. Then he shoved his hands in his pockets and said, "How could you do that? I haven't even been gone for a week. Do your promises mean so little to you?"

I slammed my chair back and stood up. "How dare you talk to me about promises? You slept with me, got up out of my bed in the middle of the night, and then never called me once. But of course you had time to call the hellbitch and have a looong, loving chat with *her*."

I slammed my fist down on the top of my desk. "I repeat, how *dare* you talk to *me* about promises?"

He opened and shut his mouth a couple of times, confusion evident in his lovely, er, evil green eyes. "What? What are you talking about? I didn't—I only talked to Kaspar—"

"I don't want to hear any more of your lies. Everybody warned me that you were a player, but I thought I saw something beyond your Mr. Smooth image when we were together. But it was *all* a lie, and I was just another notch on your laptop, wasn't I? Just get out of my office."

He started to speak, but I held up a hand to silence him. "Just get out, Hugh. I'd be an even bigger fool if I let you play me again."

He whirled around and yanked open my office door but then stopped. "For the record, I didn't call Kaspar. I called *you*. But you were out, and the receptionist forwarded me to Kaspar, for whatever damned reason. The entire extent of our phone call was to ask her to tell you that I'd flown off without my cell phone charger, so my phone was dead and I couldn't call you from the stakeout, but I'd be standing by a pay phone at eleven o'clock every night for you to call me. I gave her the number and made her repeat it back to me twice."

He swiped a hand through his hair. "I waited by that phone for you every night for nearly twenty minutes. But you never called. And now I get back, desperate to see you and hold you and find out what happened, and you're making plans for a romantic weekend with another man."

It was my turn to stutter. "But I—she never—"

It was his turn to hold up a hand for silence. "Forget it. You've told me over and over again that you'll never trust me, and I'm tired of being pathetic. I've been following you around at a distance for five months and you never noticed me. Now that you have, you don't want me."

I shot from anguish to anger pretty fast. "Five months? You mean the five months you pretended you thought I was dating Bill, so you could go out with every glamourbot in town? I'm not a glamourbot, Hugh, in spite of Paola's best efforts to fix me up. I'm not somebody who's comfortable in high heels at a society gala. I'm the girl who likes to go to ball games and hang out with my friends."

He stared at me for a long moment, sadness and resignation in his eyes. "C.J., I—"

"Forget it," I said wearily. "Forget it. We don't work, okay? Let's just leave it at that."

He started to speak again but then just nodded and left my office, quietly closing my door behind him. I sucked in a deep breath and then put my head down on my arms and cried.

I guess I had some girlie genes, after all.

I'D finally quit sobbing and was scrubbing makeup off my face with a wad of tissues when I heard a quiet knock on my door. "It's Paola. Are you up for lunch?"

She opened the door and peeked in, her eyes widening in shock when she caught sight of my swollen face. (I'm not a delicate crier, either. There's nose blowing and eye swelling.)

She rushed in and came around the side of my desk to hug me. "What happened? Are you okay? Did that slimeball Hugh come in and upset you? I'll string him up by his puny little nuts, the prick."

I couldn't help it, I had to laugh. "Paola! You never use bad language! I can't believe you said *nuts*. Or the 'P' word."

She sniffed. "I'll do more than say it. I'll break every bone in his smarmy body for him. And a few of Kaspar's, too."

I smiled again, touched by the warmth of a truly good friendship. What are friends for, if not to wreak bone-crushing destruction on your enemies?

Grinning at the fury radiating from Paola's designer-clad, size-zero body, I stood up, tossing the tissues in the trash. "It's okay. Turns out maybe he did try to call me. *If* I can even believe him. I don't know what to believe any more; I just don't want to go through another week like this. Maybe I'll stick to being one of the guys for a few more years."

She frowned at me. "We're not back to that, are we? What about Aaron?"

I sighed and glanced at the phone. "Right. Aaron. I have to call him and back out of going away for the weekend and give him the 'let's just be friends' talk. I hope he forgives me, at least for my dad's sake."

Paola put her arm around me. "Let's go to a long lunch and drink margaritas and talk about all of this."

I shook my head. "No, let's drink green tea. We need to go back to the Wok and Bowl and make sure Lin is okay. Plus, I want to get to the bottom of the fortune cookie issue. I could use something to distract me, anyway."

As we walked out of the newsroom, we didn't see Hugh anywhere in sight. Bill stood up when he caught sight of us. "Ready for lunch?"

Paola tossed her head. "Not with *you*. We've had enough of scummy men. This is a girls-only lunch."

Bill just stood there, looking confused and a little upset, as Paola dragged me past him. I turned and mouthed "I'm sorry" over my shoulder at him, but he shook his head and turned away.

Great. Another apology to add to my ever-expanding list. Honestly, though, I just couldn't worry about it right then, what with my heart still down around my kneecaps and all.

Maybe later. Much later.

TWELVE

I INHALED the aromas of teriyaki chicken and Szechuan beef, suddenly a little bit hungry in spite of my emotional turmoil. Funny how turmoil is always so much more . . . *turmoilier* . . . than you expect it to be. The first thing we saw, though, was Lin and her mother yelling at each other in what was, I'm guessing, Chinese.

When they saw us, Lin's mouth abruptly snapped shut and she tried to shush her mother, but the tiny woman quivered in rage and pointed straight at me. She yelled, if possible, even louder than she had before. I didn't need to speak Chinese to understand that, somehow, she was mad at me.

Never one to get in the middle of family fights, even my own family's, I hesitated just inside the doorway, shooting a questioning look at Paola. "Should we leave?" I whispered.

She shrugged, looking as confused as I felt. Mrs. Liu decided the point for us by stomping over to me, grabbing my arm, and then stabbing a finger in my chest and yelling right in my face. I still didn't understand a word, but it didn't sound good.

Lin rushed over and tried to drag her mom off of me, but it wasn't working. Lin yelled, her mother yelled, and I stood there like a frozen idiot, trying not to start crying again. Finally, Paola broke in by yelling at the top of her lungs. "SHUT. UP. NOW! What the HELL is going on here?"

Stunned, because they'd never heard delicate Paola so much as raise her voice before, both Lius stopped shouting in mid-shriek. We all looked at Paola in disbelief, and I took the opportunity to snatch my arm back from Lin's distraught mother.

Paola modulated her voice back down to her normal purr, but with a little bite to it. "Will someone please tell me what in the NAME of GOD is going on here? Why is your mother yelling? And WHY, while we're at it, is C.J. getting evil fortune cookies of death every time we eat here lately?"

Lin aimed a scowl at her mom, who stood there and smirked at us. "Mom? Did you mess with their fortunes? You know that's bad karma, not to mention seriously bad for business. Leave C.J. alone, already."

Her mother glared right back at her, switching into flawless English. "You don't tell me what to do. You were going to marry a perfect Chinese gentleman until that horrible girl told you not to. This is all her fault. Your marriage is ruined. I am ruined. Our entire family is dishonored, and it is all the fault of that stupid . . . *reporter.*"

If the word *reporter* had ever sounded exactly like *Unholy Demon from Hell,* that was the moment. I gaped at all of them, utterly in shock. Because, for *this* turmoil, I didn't have a freaking clue what they were talking about.

"It's not C.J.'s fault, Mama. I told you a hundred times. Just because I mentioned something she said in one of her columns about independence and not being a doormat for a guy doesn't mean it's her fault I called off the wedding to Paul."

She grabbed her mother's hands, her eyes pleading for understanding. "I don't love him, Mama. I want to *love* the man I eventually marry. Can't you understand that?"

Her mother snorted and yanked her hands away. "Love. What is that? Marriage is about security and family honor, not love. You never used to have these foolish notions. This is all *her* fault," she repeated, pointing at me again.

I finally found my voice. "I'm so sorry you feel that way. I never would have done anything to hurt your family, Mrs. Liu. But you must understand that Lin has to be true to herself . . ."

Even as Mrs. Liu ranted and raved at me, and poor Lin kept apologizing for the cookies, which her mother had apparently doctored to put some sort of evil voodoo hex on me, the sounds of their voices faded as my brain took over.

My admittedly slow brain.

True to herself . . .

That's what I'd needed to hear all along. *I* needed to be true to *myself*. I needed to find a man who could love me for who I am, not for the person I could pretend to be.

Hot on the heels of this epiphany, I reached a decision. I flashed the warmest smile I could muster at Lin and Mrs. Liu. "I'm so sorry. Really, I am. I hope you can resolve this. Mrs. Liu, you have a terrific daughter who is trying really hard to help you understand her decision. I hope you can love her as much as she loves you and find your way to acceptance. But I have to go."

I turned and practically ran out of the restaurant, leaving all three of them standing there gaping at me. I'd explain to Paola later. But just then I had some major true-to-myself-ing to do.

* * *

ALMOST as soon as I'd said hello, Aaron and I both spoke at once.

"We need to talk," I said.

"We need to talk," he said.

We both started laughing, and we both sounded nervous. Before I could wonder about *that,* I jumped in. "Me first. Here's the deal . . ."

As I told him about my feelings and about how I couldn't go away with him for the weekend, there was total silence on his end of the line. Finally, I finished up. "So I'm really, really sorry, but we can still be great friends, if that's okay with you, A.J."

I waited, holding my breath for him to respond. It was pretty awful to break up over the phone with a man who called you his destiny, but I couldn't stand for him to have the wrong idea for a minute longer. Plus, I hadn't wanted him to make any more plans for our now-cancelled weekend away.

There was a long silence. I drew in a deep breath and was trying to find another way to explain—to let him down easy—when he spoke up. "Um, C.J.?"

"Yes?"

"Dude, if that's the way you want it, fine. Can I still come for barbecue Saturday? I have an X-box deathmatch scheduled with your brothers."

The breath I'd been holding whooshed out with a wave of relieved laughter. "So what you're saying is that I'm not breaking your heart or anything, destiny aside?"

He chuckled. "Yeah, I got kinda carried away with that destiny thing, didn't I? Anyway, what I wanted to tell you was that I met this cute physical therapist today, and if you don't mind, I thought I'd ask her out to dinner Friday."

I smiled, totally relieved (even though I'll admit a teensy part of me was miffed that he'd gotten over me so easily). "Of course I don't mind. We're great friends, remember? How about you bring her with you when you come over Saturday, so we can *all* get to know her? Be prepared for my brothers to tease you unmercifully, now that you're practically part of the family, though."

"I'd love that. I always wanted brothers and sisters. Hey! You can be like the older sister I never had!"

"Watch it with that 'older' stuff, buddy, or I'll put you in a headlock and tickle you," I said in my best stern voice.

He just laughed. "C.J.? Dude? I'm totally glad I sent you my socks."

"So am I, Aaron. So am I."

OKAY, one down, one to go. I squared my shoulders and headed out to find Hugh. But when I walked out of my office, the hallway was blocked by Paola yelling at Bill. "Get out of my way! I will NOT apologize for calling you scum. You can forget it!" Then she let loose with a long string of what sounded like some seriously evil swearing in Italian.

It was my day for multilingual profanity education, apparently.

Bill smiled at her, but it wasn't a smile I'd seen from him ever before. Easy-going, amiable Bill had vanished, replaced by a man who looked very determined and a little bit dangerous. He put his hands on her shoulders and looked in her eyes.

By now, everybody in the newsroom was gathered around, staring at them.

"Paola. Shut. Up," Bill said quietly, yet somehow with enough force to be heard over her diatribe. She stopped in mid-word, shocked into silence, and stared up at him, eyes widening.

He caught her hand and dragged her into the middle of the newsroom, with all the rest of us crowding them like paparazzi surrounding

Brad Pitt. When he reached the large open space between the sports and news departments, he skidded to a stop, still clutching her hand. Then he put one hand on her shoulder and stared into her eyes. "You want a Grand Gesture, Paola? Well, you've got one. I'm hereby declaring, in front of everyone I've worked with for the past ten years, that I am in love with you."

A lot of gasping and a smattering of applause followed his announcement, but Paola gaped up at him in silence, so he went on.

"I love everything about you. Your personality that sparkles like diamonds on fast-forward, your sense of humor, your generosity to your friends, and even—yes—your soul that glows like a firebrand. I love you, Paola. So get used to it."

This time, the wave of applause nearly deafened me. But I wasn't clapping. I hadn't heard Paola's reaction to any of this yet. I watched them, concerned.

Evidently Bill realized the same thing, because he stood there staring at her, eyes wary and pleading all at once. "Paola? Honey? Do you have *any* feelings for me, or am I a total moron?"

She tossed her head and yanked her arms out of his grasp. *Oh, no.* My heart sank for him and (let's be honest) for the strain this was going to put on our friendships. I strained to hear her response.

She finally spoke, voice ringing out loud and clear. "Yes, you are a complete and *utter* moron." He fell back a step, and his whole body did a kind of slump. She shoved at his chest with one hand and continued. "All I can say is . . . is . . . what *took* you so long?" With that, she grabbed his head and pulled him into a major-league, out-of-the-ballpark kind of kiss.

This time, the applause rang out even louder, and I was clapping like crazy. I didn't even realize I was crying until I felt the tears running down my face. I was so happy for my friends.

I *was*.

But I wanted the chance to be happy for me, too. I caught sight of Hugh, leaning against the wall across the room, arms folded, one eyebrow raised sardonically. Guess he wasn't in the mood for happily ever after.

Well, that's too damn bad.

I stalked across the room, stopping to hug Bill and Paola on the way, and then shouldering my way through the crowd of my colleagues hanging around chatting and laughing. Donny would have a fit if he could see this, I thought, and then I saw him standing by the copy machine, clapping as loudly as anybody.

The old softie.

I marched right up to Hugh, grabbed him by the arm, and then dragged him into the nearest room and closed the door. Unfortunately, it was the supply closet. I kicked a ream of paper out of the way and turned to face him.

"Here's the deal. *This* is who I am. Like I said before, I'm the person who likes to go hiking and to ball games and just hang out. I'm not glamorous or fancy or, by any stretch of the imagination, a bimbo. I'm sorry I didn't trust you. I should have known better than to believe anything Kaspar said to me, and I can see how that hurt you. If you'd like to try again, I'd like that."

The flow of words rushing out of me slowed, then stopped, as I realized he hadn't changed his expression. He coldly stared at me. Unbending. Unmoved.

Fine. At least I tried. I took a deep breath and tried not to cry. "I guess I'm too late. I guess I'm not the kind of woman anybody will ever make a Grand Gesture for. Well. Whatever. All I have to say is that it's *your* loss. The real me is a great person, and I'm really crazy about you and . . . well . . . and that's it, I guess. Good-bye."

I shoved past him and out the door and then I ran out of the newsroom. All I wanted to do was go home, shut my door, take my phone off the hook, and wallow in a little healthy self-pity. Assuming I could make it to my car without bursting into tears.

Or at least into the elevator. Might want to start with more achievable goals.

I made it, too. Clear up till the elevator doors closed behind me.

Then I was toast. Soggy, girlie toast.

AS SEEN IN THE *SEATTLE TIMES*:

***THE NAKED TRUTH ABOUT WOMEN,* BY GUEST COLUMNIST HUGH LEONARD**

The Grand Gesture

I've come to realize that women have a need for something they like to call the Grand Gesture. The capital letters are deliberate—you can almost hear them when a Woman utters the phrase with all due reverence.

This means your average, normal guy is history. We have a hard enough time with normal gestures (no capital letters required). I've heard my brother tell my sister-in-law, on more than one occasion, "Of course I love you! I changed the oil in your car, didn't I?"

This, as those of you who are wincing while reading already know, does NOT count as a Grand Gesture. In fact, it may be grounds for divorce in some states.

So because I've been a total fool for the past five months, and especially for the past five days, I want to take a stand here with my own Grand Gesture:

I, Hugh Leonard, hotshot investigative reporter, am a fake. Yep, that's right. All that charm, all that sophistication, all those smooth moves: total fraud.

I grew up in a little town called Buttesville (Butte rhymes with *cute,* but go ahead with the jokes already, I've heard them all), Indiana, and I got all my *smooth* out of a book. Every move I've made since I got this job was straight out of Dr. Phil Snakey's book, *Schmooze Your Way to Success.* Like chapter three: *Date, but never sleep with, a succession of beautiful women to give the appearance of being irresistible.*

Ha. Irresistible. All I've managed to do is make the one woman I've cared anything about in the past five years hate me. Her name is C.J. Murphy, and she's usually in this space, making you laugh with her trademarked brand of honest humor about the craziness of relationships between men and women. Today, with a little help from a friend, I've hijacked her space to make my own personal Grand Gesture.

So if you're reading this, C.J., here goes:

I'M NUTS ABOUT YOU. Forget charming and smooth and all that shallow stuff. Your eyes don't sparkle like sapphires, and your lips aren't like rubies. But your eyes *do* sparkle with humor, intelligence, and warmth. And your lips are soft and wonderful, and the words that come out of them are some of the funniest and most thoughtful I've ever heard.

THIS is my Grand Gesture. I hope it's enough.

Until next time, remember: *C.J. Murphy! She's perfect just the way she is!**

[*Unapologetic footnote: And she's mine, so back off, Judson.]

THIRTEEN

MY phone rang as I threaded my way through the various cardboard boxes in my living room. I kicked the one labeled *yard sale* out of the way and leaned over the one marked *Goodwill* to grab the phone, grinning at the piles of clothes, shoes, and other assorted mishmash I'd sorted through in a frenzy since waking up drained yet oddly refreshed from last night's sobbing spree.

Life was looking up—I was kicking all uncomfortable shoes to the curb, all before lunchtime.

"Hello, yard sales are us, can I help you?"

"C.J.? What are you talking about? Did you see it? Did you SEE it?" Paola's normally cultured tones were a bit shrieky. (I seem to have that effect on her.)

"Slow down. Have I seen what? And how's Bill? I'm assuming he's there with you," I said with a sly grin.

"He's . . . shut *up*, Bill. Yes, already, your Grand Gesture was way grander than his," she muttered, clearly talking to the man in question. I could hear him in the background, going on and on about something . . . *paper?*

"Paola? What's up?" I asked, absently sorting through a pile of magazines on the table. May as well declutter the whole apartment, right?

"Did you read the paper yet? Obviously you haven't, or you wouldn't be so calm. Or is he there?" She sounded totally jazzed out of her mind, but I still didn't have a clue what she was talking about.

"What about the paper? Is *who* here?" I walked over to the door to retrieve the paper, which should still be right outside my door, if the hairy guy in 2G hadn't stolen it again. I unlocked the three locks (with a cop dad, you're gonna have a lot of locks) and pulled the door open, not expecting in the least the sight of Hugh standing in front of my door, hand raised as if to knock, my newspaper tucked under his arm, and a bag of what smelled deliciously like Chinese food in his other hand.

"Hugh?" I said, sort of gasping, and backed into my apartment a step. "What are you doing here? Why do you have my paper?"

Paola shrieked in my ear again. "He's there, Bill. He's there! C.J., don't hang up the phone. We want to hear this."

I held the phone away from my ear and stared at it, wondering if falling in love had made my best friend lose her mind completely. Hugh took advantage of my momentary distraction to gently nudge me farther inside my apartment and follow me in, closing the door behind him. He looked a little awkward and a little embarrassed but not at all smooth. The Hugh Mask was nowhere to be seen. He reached over and took the phone out of my unresisting hand and listened for a minute, grinning. "Paola. I thought that might be you. C.J. will have to call you back. Yes. Yes. Yes. No. Okay. Later."

He clicked off the phone and put it down on my end table, stepping even closer to my stunned self. "This seems like it would be a good time to read the paper," he said, handing it to me. I glanced down at the paper, opened to my column.

Except, it *wasn't*. Wasn't *my* column. I shot a look at him and then looked back down at the page. "Guest columnist Hugh Leonard? What the hell is going on?"

He smiled again, but the smile was shaky around the edges, like he was terrified of what might happen next. (Or else maybe he had some weird cardboard box phobia.) He walked over to my tiny kitchen table, put down the bag of food, and then shoved a hand through his hair. I'd come to recognize the gesture as one of intense discomfort on his part.

Which, in a mean way, made me a teensy bit gleeful. It wasn't like he hadn't caused me a little *discomfort* myself lately. I managed to swallow the evil snicker bubbling up in my throat and sat down on my ancient rocking chair to read.

He never said a word in the few moments it took me to get to the end, not even when I laughed a little at the footnote. I looked up at him, and I could feel my eyes glistening with the beginnings of tears.

(Once you start this girlie stuff, it's hard to stop.)

"Hugh? Really? I'm perfect just the way I am?"

He crossed to my chair and knelt down beside me, lips quirked in a hopeful half-smile. "You are. Every part of you. Even in your turnip-farming clothes. Hell, especially in those, because I don't have to freak out about every man in a five-mile radius staring at you in your brown clothes." He laughed and put his hands on mine where they rested on the arms of the chair. "So what do you say? Is it a grand enough gesture for you? Can you forgive me?"

I practically launched myself out of the chair into his arms, knocking him backward so we ended up in a tangled heap on the floor. When I could quit laughing, I raised my head and looked down at him. "It's plenty grand enough. And I'll forgive you, if you'll forgive me."

* * *

IT was nearly an hour and a half later before, while searching for our clothes, we decided we'd forgiven each other enough times that we could eat the lunch he'd brought. We laughed and talked about everything and nothing and fed each other bits of food with our chopsticks, and just generally were sickeningly gooey. I laughed so hard when he told me how Donny had reacted to Hugh's plea for help with the column, I almost fell off the couch. "No! He kicked you out of his office?"

Hugh laughed and popped another bit of Szechuan shrimp into my mouth. "He was on a tear, muttering something about *damn kids* and *Grand Gestures* and *journalism going all to hell*. I thought I was dead in the water. Then, not thirty minutes later, his secretary called me asking where the heck my column was." He shook his head, smiling. "That old goat has a soft spot for you, that's for sure."

I grinned. "It's my charming nature."

The phone rang again, for about the fifteenth time since Hugh had hung up on Paola. I reached for it, sighing. "I've got to answer this, or she'll send out the SWAT team, you know."

"No problem. I'll open your fortune cookie for you," he said, snapping one in two.

"Nooo!" I tried to grab for it, but I was too late. He was already reading. The logical part of me knew that, because the food was from a different restaurant than Wok and Bowl, the cookie would be fine. But the superstitious part of me didn't want to chance it on such a perfect morning.

The phone kept ringing. I clicked it on. "Paola, hold on."

Hugh had a funny look on his face. "This is weird."

No, not again, not again, not again, not today. No. No. No.

I took a deep breath. "What is weird?"

He flashed that sexy grin at me and read my fortune out loud. " 'Trust yourself and anything you do will be right.' I've never seen a fortune be more appropriate, have you?"

I relaxed back against the couch and started laughing like a loon. "Nope. I never have."

Truth or Dare

DONNA KAUFFMAN

ONE

ALICE in Wonderland had nothing on Bailey Madison. No way could her fellow klutzy blonde have felt more out of place after falling down the rabbit hole than Bailey did at that very moment. She stared in awe as the limo passed through the medieval-style, piled stone gateway to billionaire Franklin Dent's Carmel by the Sea estate.

She'd been a staff writer for two television soaps, helping to create fantasy worlds where it was supposed to be perfectly normal for one small town to have multiple murders, secret babies, amnesia victims, reincarnations, and closets full of skeletons—sometimes literally. The gothic manse spreading out before her looked like it could have quite plausibly housed every one of those outlandish secrets and then some. But this was no fabricated television set. This was real.

"Surreal is more like it," she murmured beneath her breath. Bailey supposed being a billionaire could do that to a person. But honestly, the place looked like the set for some bizarre new reality television show.

And now that she thought about it, her reasons for being here did pretty much fit the format. Except even the most warped reality television producer couldn't have come up with this premise: Former soap opera writer moves onto eccentric billionaire's creepy estate—alone!—to ghostwrite his autobiography.

Bailey gazed out at the fat, stacked-stone pillars that lined the long drive, each one topped with a uniquely designed, whimsical gargoyle. Well, if you considered various fanged beasts with googly eyes and huge spiked collars to be whimsical. She wondered if anyone had mentioned to Franklin Dent that the "ghost" part of the term "ghostwriter" wasn't to be taken literally.

You lobbied hard for this. You deserve this break. You're the best person for the job.

Somehow the oft-repeated mantra that had held her in good stead during those nerve-wracking weeks while she'd waited to hear if she'd been chosen wasn't giving her quite the same confidence boost now as it had then. For three grueling months after she heard Franklin Dent was shopping his unwritten memoirs around the New York publishing houses, looking for a contract and a ghostwriter, she'd endured what amounted to one long continuous audition.

It had been a lengthy and, frankly, at times insane screening process, consisting of repeated interviews with Dent's various assistants, who'd asked her all kinds of wacky, off-the-wall questions. What were her feelings on the ivory trade in Africa? Had she ever jumped off a cliff, with or without a parasail? Did she still have all her original teeth? Ultimately, she'd been convinced that not being invited to meet Dent personally at any point in the interview process was a sure sign he'd picked someone else.

So imagine her shock when she'd received notice three days ago from Dent himself, who was in some godforsaken village in Botswana, or somewhere like that, halfway around the world. Okay, so geography wasn't her strong suit. That's why they made atlases. She'd made a point of Googling information on the ivory trade situation, though. As for cliff diving, surely it didn't really matter if she had actually done it or not. In addition to a positively morbid fear of heights, she saw no reason for any sane person to jump off of a perfectly stable cliff.

Being hired anyway should have relieved her of worrying about all that, except she'd ended up getting the job for an entirely different reason. Not that that should have come as any real surprise to her. No way had Bailey aced her interview. Because, honestly, how did you even pretend to lie about things like, "Have you ever eaten international delicacies that would be considered undesirable to the American palate?" Examples given included beetles, snakes, and pigs' brains. Ch-yeah, right. What did they think this was, anyway? An audition for *Fear Factor*?

What did surprise her, however, was that he'd apparently chosen her exclusively based on the fact that she'd ghostwritten the book for the famous, long-running soap *Love in Eden Gulf*. Written supposedly by a beloved character from the show, aging novelist Susan Lovering, the book covered every twist and turn of the decades-long series. It was an enormous project that had taken Bailey many long months to complete. Turns out Dent was a rabid fan of the show and thought of the book as his *Eden Gulf* bible.

It was a shame there hadn't been more viewers who shared his opinion. The book had, by any measure, been a spectacular flop. Of course, it wasn't her fault the network had cancelled the thirty-four-year-old soap the same week the book had hit the stands, thereby enraging the show's zealously dedicated fans who saw the book as nothing more than a cheap way to capitalize on their heartbreak. Bailey was certain the producers had planned the cancellation all along but had failed to mention that little tidbit to her.

When it had backfired on them about as badly as it could have, with fans flocking to the Internet, raging on bulletin boards and blogs alike, and mass boycotting the book . . . it wasn't the producers who watched their dreams go down in flames. So much for her big break, her big opportunity to finally gain entrée into the world of publishing so when she finished writing her great American novel—okay, so it was more like a middle-class America novel—she'd have editors lined up, salivating over the chance to publish her. Yeah. That hadn't exactly panned out for her. Funny thing, but publishers weren't all that excited about taking you on when your one and only release sank so low, so fast, that even Amazon didn't bother ranking it.

But now her karma had come full circle. That only happened to deserving people, right? When the very book that had almost destroyed her career single-handedly had been the reason for her biggest break yet, that had to be a good sign. Dent had said, through his chain of assistants anyway, that anyone who could encapsulate thirty-four years' worth of hidden babies, amnesia victims, and alien abductions into a coherent, four-hundred-page novel was definitely the person best suited to write his life story. "So there ya go," she murmured beneath her breath, pressing her hands against her jumpy stomach. "This was meant to be."

She wished she sounded even remotely convincing.

As the mansion loomed closer, it was hard to believe she'd been standing in her Brooklyn second-story walk-up just this morning, packing pretty much everything she owned for her open-ended stay here.

"Alternate universe, for sure, Alice," Bailey muttered, staring out at yet another spike-collared gargoyle. She clutched the backpack that held her laptop, the latest printout of her book in progress, and the thick stack of paper comprising every detail she'd uncovered about Franklin Dent—yes, indeedy, Google was a wonderful thing—to her chest as the limo finally rolled into a huge circular drive. So much had already been written about the man and his amazing exploits, both in the business world and, more frequently, in his adventurous personal life. But those were all surface articles, written from an exterior—and often awed—viewpoint.

Her job would be to treat this story the same way she had *Eden Gulf.* Straight-faced, with complete sincerity, as if over-the-top soap plotting made perfect rational sense and was completely plausible. To do that here, she would have to step inside Dent's head and tell his story the way only the man who lived it could tell it. That meant she'd have to write it as if she'd lived it. She couldn't be awed, by him or his story.

"Yeah, sure, piece of cake. Or piece of beetle, as the case may be," she said, and then let out a shaky exhale of breath as she peered out at the soaring stone and marble edifice. The mansion front came complete with massive pillars and heavy wooden double doors so big and wide they could have easily afforded entrance to a full team of horses—and whatever carriage they were pulling. Knowing what she did about Dent, she wouldn't be the least surprised if that very thing had happened at one point or another.

The driver—a tall, Middle Eastern gent complete with turban, not to mention wearing a uniform that sported an even better cut than her prized rack-sale Dior original—opened her door and quietly motioned her to exit, stage left. Gathering all her belongings, Bailey silently wished she'd worn that black suit. Because of the long traveling day, she'd opted for her black DKNY trouser and jacket combo, matched with her wrinkle-resistant Claiborne tank top. Hot pink, of course—her confidence color.

As she tilted her head back and squinted up at the three-story central section of the sprawling gothic mansion, the sun blinded her before she could take in the full extent of its glory. Blinking the white spots from her eyes, she thought it would take a hell of a lot more than a power color to make her feel less than completely intimidated. So she took a moment to breathe deeply, regain her internal balance—or just find it in the first place—and make at least a semblance of an effort to look like the cool, calm, and most importantly, competent professional Franklin Dent had hired her to be.

Just then, with a shuddering groan, the massive front doors swung open, moving with such surprising speed she was startled into stumbling back a step—which wouldn't have been a problem had she been at least two steps from the curb—which, of course, Rabbit Hole Alice Incarnate that she was, she wasn't.

To make matters worse—often not possible in these types of situations, which she found herself in with alarming regularity—she tripped over the dangling straps of her backpack, sending her arms flailing, thereby launching the rest of her possessions into the air.

The driver—bless his quick-thinking heart—opted to make the diving catch for her backpack, which he managed to secure with the graceful skill of someone who had extremely disciplined control of his body.

Bailey didn't have extreme discipline, or any kind of discipline for that matter. In fact, when it came to body control, she had anti-discipline. Hence, her landing wasn't nearly as graceful. And there she sat, in a lovely, ever-so-unprofessional sprawl in Franklin Dent's gutter. It was as if karma, having given, was now making sure she knew it could be taken away again at any time.

As the entire wad of printed Google pages entailing a lifetime worth of Franklin Dent's trials and trevails wafted down through the breezy summer air and landed on and about her wrinkled, sprawled body, she thought this time her embarrassment couldn't possibly get any worse. *Wrong again, young grasshopper,* she thought, as a dark shadow fell across her body.

And it wasn't the driver, who was to her right, deftly snagging pages out of the air. No, no. She couldn't be that lucky. She scraped at the hair on her forehead, making a mental note that never again would she let Lars talk her into getting "fringy bangs." Blinking hard at the spiky, prickling ends, every one of which were stabbing at her eyes, making them water, surely smearing her mascara, she finally managed to squint upward. The sun created a golden halo around the figure, casting his face in darkness.

Her stomach knotted up. This was about the very last way she'd ever dreamed of first meeting her new boss. Her billionaire boss. The same boss who was giving her the opportunity of a lifetime. And she couldn't make it past "Hello" without doing something mortifying.

It was only when he leaned forward and extended his hand, completely and mercifully blocking the sun from her eyes, that she realized it wasn't Franklin Dent at all.

No. No. It was far worse.

Her mouth dropped open in shock. Karma was indeed a bitch after all. Just who had she murdered in a previous life to deserve such treatment in this one?

Stunned momentarily speechless, she absently wondered if perhaps she'd struck her head as she'd fallen. Because if she was presently suffering from a severe concussion, that might explain the hallucination that was surely standing in front of her, offering his assistance.

As if she'd take anything he offered, hallucination or not. He'd taken enough away from her to last her a lifetime.

"Noah?" she finally choked out. "Noah Morrissey?" She immediately pulled back when he leaned lower. At least this time her self-preservation instincts kicked in where he was concerned. Where had they been six months ago, huh? "What in the hell are you doing here?"

And then the smile shifted to a grin. That grin. His grin. There was only one man walking the planet who had a grin like that. A grin that made her pulse race and, well, she refused to discuss the other bodily reactions it triggered. She was mortified and confused enough at the moment, thanks.

He reached down and took her hand without waiting for an invitation. It was exactly the same way he'd gotten her naked, if she recalled. Which she did, of course, with unfortunate clarity and detail. On numerous occasions, in fact.

"Apparently I'm rescuing you," he said, in that deep, way-too-sexy voice she remembered all too well . . . and had never quite gotten around to forgetting. "Again."

TWO

"**RESCUE?** Me? I beg your pardon!"

Noah forgot how cute Bailey was when she was blustering. "Only seconds after seeing me again and you're already begging me? Honestly, I'm flattered."

He thought her eyebrows were going to lift straight off her forehead. "You were insufferable in Los Angeles, and you're insufferable now. Thank God I had the good sense to let things end between us when I did."

Noah debated for all of three seconds whether he should let her have that little lie as a sop to her ego. But the Bailey Madison he knew wouldn't appreciate being pandered to. "Which is exactly why I didn't call. I knew that was what you wanted, and I was merely acceding to your wishes."

Her gaze narrowed. "You think you're oh-so-clever."

He grinned. "You used to think so. Remember how much you liked it when I did that thing with my hands where—"

Her mouth dropped open and then immediately snapped shut. "You really have no shame at all, do you?" Her hand flew up, palm out. "Don't answer that." Suddenly all business, even though that becoming flush still colored her cheeks, she smoothed her hair, ran her free hand over her suit, and stepped around him. "I don't know what you're doing here, but I don't have time to swap insults with you."

The driver moved forward at that moment and handed her the neatly stacked papers he'd recovered and then helped slide the strap of her backpack over her shoulder. "Thank you," she said with the kind of exaggerated politeness intended to make it clear she didn't hold Noah in near the same esteem she did her driver.

Perversely, it just made his smile widen. He'd known when he'd lobbied for this job that she wasn't going to be happy to see him again. But that didn't mean he wasn't looking forward to the challenge of breaking down whatever well-deserved barrier she'd erected between them. Just because their brief, albeit tempestuous, relationship hadn't worked out in the long run, didn't mean they couldn't enjoy a reunion of sorts. Besides, Noah was nothing if not motivated by challenges. It was why he'd pursued Franklin Dent with such single-minded determination.

He watched Bailey Madison walk into Dent's home, although it was more of a march really—shoulders square, chin high, stride confident. And a big splotch of street grime smeared across her fanny. If anyone could pull that off with aplomb, it would be, well, Charlize Theron. But Bailey Madison was giving it a pretty good go. Chuckling, he shook his head and followed her inside. And he caught himself wondering why he hadn't pursued her with that same kind of single-minded determination.

Because you don't pursue anyone like that, he reminded himself. Besides, even if he did want to see the same person for a long-term period of time, which he didn't, she was all wrong for him anyway. His focus was global. He was motivated to tell real stories about real people, spotlight the vast variety in the human condition, and by doing so, make the people who watched his documentaries realize just how closely linked every human being was with another, no matter how seemingly different. Bailey, on the other hand, wrote soap operas, creating a fantasy of the human condition that had nothing to do with the real world.

Noah was aggressive, confident in his goals, and he moved toward them with unwavering certainty. Bailey was determined, but too accepting of her limitations. She wanted to be a novelist, to write the kind of contemporary fiction that entertained and enlightened, which was a worthy goal, except, to his knowledge, she'd never actually done anything about it.

He jumped into life with both feet. He was daring and bold, excited by the new and different. Bailey was . . . well, a klutz, quite frankly. She stumbled through life, somehow managing to stay upright more often than not, but there was no sense of command or control.

It was a wonder they'd hooked up at all, really.

His gaze drifted to her fanny again, only this time he wasn't thinking about the grime. So okay, maybe that part wasn't all that hard to figure out. They'd certainly had chemistry where it mattered. So she wasn't the most graceful or elegant of women, and yes, he'd had to coax her a little to relax enough to enjoy a wider sexual variety than lights-out-missionary-position. But it had been worth the effort. She wasn't the most secure person about her body, or her appeal, but she was game. He'd give her that. She'd get that look in her eye, nervously chewing the edge of her lip as she mentally geared herself up to step outside her comfort zone and tackle whatever it was he was pushing her to do—even though she knew, more likely than not, it was going to be a spectacular disaster.

He grinned. Yeah, that had been pretty damn captivating, actually.

Too bad they were so wrong for each other in every other way.

So lost in his thoughts, he almost ran right into the back of her when she stopped abruptly in the center of the massive, open foyer.

"Wow," she whispered as she looked around, tipping her head back to stare all the way to the domed ceiling two stories up.

He silently agreed with her. He'd arrived the day before and had stood just where she was now, several times now, in fact, and he still had that same sense of awe she was feeling right now.

"Is it me, or do those look a lot like Michelangelo's panels in the Sistine Chapel?" she asked, her voice hushed.

"Exact copy, I understand. It's pretty amazing, isn't it?" Noah's career had led him to be the invited guest in a wide variety of homes, from hovels to palaces. He'd thought himself somewhat immune to being awed at this point. Nothing surprised him much anymore, mostly because he'd learned to enter a new project with as little a predetermined opinion as possible. But this—well, it was hard not to be taken somewhat aback by the sheer audacity of it all.

Bailey turned in a slow circle, still looking up at the walls and the dome. "Understatement of the century. I'm not sure there is a word to adequately describe this."

"You're gonna have to come up with a bunch of them, I imagine, before this is all over. Hope you packed a thesaurus."

She paused and crooked her head toward him. "What does that mean?"

He lifted a shoulder and shifted his attention back to the curved walls that were studded with the very unique combination of gaudily framed paintings, tribal artifacts, and stuffed and mounted heads of an array of dead critters, some of which he'd never seen before. "Just that if you're going to adequately describe the man's life story, I would imagine you're going to need a whole lot of descriptive words you might never have needed before."

"What do you know about it?" She folded her arms, both wary and irritated. It was an arresting combination, really. It made her eyes flash really green. "Why are you even here?"

He copied her pose, folding his arms. "For the same reason you are."

"This is a solo project. Mr. Dent was adamant about that. No one said a word to me about it being a collaborative effort. And you're not a writer."

He merely raised an eyebrow to that.

"You write action-adventure movies for a living."

Blockbuster scripts, each and every one, he could have pointed out. And he mostly only did those to fund the documentaries. But why quibble?

She waved her hand. "This—"

"Is a real-life action-adventure story," he finished for her.

He saw the light dawn in her eyes. "No. Tell me you are not here to make his life into a movie."

"I could. But I'd be lying."

"Wouldn't be the first time," she muttered.

"I never lied to you."

She just rolled her eyes.

"I—"

She stopped him with a raised hand. "More lame excuses I don't need."

"I don't make excuses. Lame or otherwise," he said, affronted when he knew he had no right to be. So he hadn't ended their relationship as cleanly as he should have. He wasn't in the habit of explaining himself to anyone, nor was he planning to start. She'd known he was a rolling stone when they hooked up. So why it was all his fault if he'd rolled on without, you know, exactly warning her ahead of time, he had no idea. She would have kicked him out sooner than later anyway. He'd just made it easier for both of them.

And that sounded a whole lot like an excuse—a fairly lame one at that.

"Well, maybe you should start making a few," she told him. "Maybe if you had to come up with excuses for your behavior, you'd think twice about some of the decisions you make."

"You're a very contrary woman, you know that?"

She shot him a patently false smile. "Yay me."

Before he could come up with a snappy rejoinder, Dent's majordomo entered the foyer. Seeing as his reunion with Bailey wasn't exactly going quite as well as he'd have imagined, he was happier to see the dour Spaniard than he should have been, particularly since the old guy didn't seem to have any real affection for him. "Hey there, Costas." He refrained from asking him how it was hanging, just to see how pinched his expression could get, but it took considerable restraint.

The glorified butler merely stared in his direction for a prolonged moment of silence and then glanced toward Bailey. And the most amazing transformation happened. Costas smiled. His teeth were perfect and gleaming, especially the two that were capped in gold.

He sketched a slight yet elegant bow. "Ms. Madison, we are happy to make your arrival," he said, the words heavily accented. "Mr. Dent has requested that I show you to your rooms and that you take some time to refresh yourself after your long journey."

He was bemused by Costas's deference to Bailey. He'd been barely civil to Noah. Okay, so maybe Noah was a bit put out by the brush-off, but come on, what was wrong with him anyway? People of all ages usually gravitated to him. Must be a gender bias thing was all he could think. Costas was from a particularly paternalistic part of the world. Or perhaps he just liked the ladies. He'd have to warn Bailey about that.

The majordomo's expression smoothed as he shifted to include them both in his gaze. "Mr. Dent will be joining you for dinner this evening. Precisely at six. Dress is informal. You'll be alerted fifteen minutes prior." He looked to Bailey, and his craggy face softened again. "My name is Costas. If you'd like an advance wake-up call, you've only to ask."

Bailey's smile was ready and easy. "That's sweet of you, Costas, but I should be fine."

He glanced at Noah, dour once again. "I trust you can find your rooms without assistance?"

He'd asked with utmost politeness, but Noah heard the undertone and knew the probable reason for it. The Spaniard had discovered Noah wandering the house the previous evening, snooping around basically, and had been quite frosty about it. True to his claim, Noah made no excuses then, and he'd be damned if he would now.

He'd stipulated in his agreement with Dent that to properly document his life, he had to have full access. Dent hadn't exactly given him carte blanche, but Noah was used to pushing boundaries when it suited him. Familiarizing himself with Dent's personal space was only the beginning of the boundaries he planned to push. Costas was going to get his starched shorts in quite a bunch before this was all over.

"I can take care of myself," was all Noah said.

The Spaniard nodded tightly and then turned his beaming smile once again on Bailey. "Your bags have already been taken up. Right this way. I'll show you to your rooms." He motioned to the wide staircase that wound down from the open second story above. It was an exemplary creation of both elegance and craftsmanship. Made entirely of mahogany, both steps and railing, it was laid with an exquisite runner of Oriental carpet and brass fittings on each riser. The carpeting alone had to have set Dent back a pretty penny, much less the hand-carved mahogany railing. But then, from his wanderings the previous evening, Noah knew this was only one of many such elaborate details.

In every room he'd seen so far—and really, even with the dozen or so he'd been in already, he'd still barely begun—it was clear that Dent paid a great deal of attention to every element, no matter how seemingly inconsequential. Every room was filled with the same kind of craftmanship and exquisite, if eclectic, pieces. It would take repeated trips to every room to really take it all in, something he'd already begun planning. All those details, both ornate and simple, spoke to the man Dent was. Or one facet of who he was anyway.

Noah watched as Bailey followed Costas up the stairs without so much as a backward glance in his direction. He wondered what she would make of this giant mausoleum of a mansion, each room like its own period museum. What would he see through her eyes that he might not see through his own?

And why in the hell was he even thinking like that? She was here to ghostwrite the man's autobiography. He was here to film a documentary about Dent's life. Both of them would try to tell a story that would convey to the readers and viewers who this complex man really was, what made him tick, what made him so successful, what it was about him that so captured the world's attention. But they'd approach it their own way, with their own vision.

He felt the familiar rush of adrenaline he always got when embarking on a new story. Let Bailey put to paper the myriad black and white facts that typically compiled a biography. Noah would be the one to truly tell Dent's story, to reveal the real man behind the fortune, in the rich, colorful, exciting detail that only a visual medium such as film could create. He didn't need Bailey's insight for that.

Well, he had a few hours before dinner. No point in wasting them standing around. He glanced down at his faded jeans, beat-up Nikes, and the short-sleeve-over-long-sleeve T-shirt combo he'd donned earlier today. Costas had said the evening meal would be informal, hadn't he? No point in meeting Dent as anything other than himself. Besides, people expected movie industry professionals to be a tad eccentric. Dent, of all people, would understand. Likely it was only the butler who would get wound tight.

Noah grinned and abruptly turned and left the foyer, heading not up the stairs to his own set of rooms, but down the center hallway that ran beneath the stairs, all the way to the back of the main section of the house. He knew the kitchens were back there. That seemed as good a place to start as any.

THREE

BAILEY debated staying under the drenching shower heads—all four of them!—a bit longer, but she didn't want to meet Franklin looking like a prune. Her plan for a quick, invigorating shower had turned into an almost hour-long soak. Every muscle she had was relaxed to the point of complete inertia. The massive down-filled four-poster bed she'd all but drooled over upon first seeing her bedroom was calling her name big time. She could quite easily sink into it and drift off for a few hours. Days. Weeks.

A little late to be contemplating that now. Maybe she should have grabbed a few winks instead of spending her time in her rooms—yes, rooms, as in plural, as in more square footage than her entire apartment back in Brooklyn—going over all her notes on her biography subject. She'd sorted through and rearranged all her Google papers, reviewing for the umpteenth time the basic facts of his entire life.

Noah would probably smirk if he knew how obsessively she'd researched Dent. God, she still couldn't believe he was here. She hadn't heard a single word about Franklin Dent simultaneously filming a documentary about his life. And of all the people on the planet, he had to pick Noah. This was her big break, dammit. She could be civil and polite—when Franklin was around anyway. Beyond that she simply wouldn't let Noah get to her.

Because, look how well that had turned out last time.

She resolutely turned her thoughts to the more important matter at hand: What was she going to wear to dinner? Costas said informal. Of course, Franklin's idea of informal was probably a cocktail dress instead of floor length. If that was the case, she was woefully unprepared. She had her Dior suit, sure, but that was pretty much the extent of her socialite wardrobe. She was a soap writer for God's sake. As long as they stayed locked up in their slave quarters long enough to produce a complete script, with minimal complaining about the insane number of rewrites and inhumane have-no-life hours, they could work in the nude for all the producers cared.

Ha! Not anymore. She hugged herself and spun around, only to find herself grinning at her reflection in the floor-to-ceiling mirrors that lined the entire wall. Well, my God, that was a bit too much, wasn't it? Who wanted to see every inch of themselves like that? She yanked another towel off the heated rack and quickly wrapped it around herself, still grinning despite the momentary horror.

"Eat your heart out, network execs," she crowed, allowing herself a moment to wallow in the smug feeling of satisfaction she had every right to savor. Her life was finally on an upswing. Instead of dreaming about what she'd wanted, she'd taken action. And it had paid off! Okay, so writing someone else's life story wasn't exactly her dream. But getting this job would allow her to pursue her real goal: becoming a published fiction novelist. When the Dent biography was delivered, surely that would finally afford her some face time with a New York editor or two. They'd forget all about the *Eden Gulf* book.

She wasted a minute wondering what Noah was going to wear, but as he'd probably already met Franklin, he'd already made his first impression. It bugged her a little that Noah and Franklin had already met. She'd assumed coming in that she'd be competing for his attention with all the myriad details a billionaire spent his day attending to. She hadn't anticipated competing for his time and attention with another writer. Certainly not Noah Morrissey. Who, despite her personal opinion, could be quite charming and amusing when he set his mind to it.

After all, he'd gotten her naked within hours of meeting her, hadn't he? A pattern he'd shamelessly repeated for most of the several months they'd gone out with each other. Well, "out" wasn't entirely an appropriate term, as they were more often in than out. In and naked. God, he was good in bed.

"Enough!" She was about to meet Franklin Dent for the first time. The absolutely very last thing she should be thinking about was Noah's sexual prowess.

And yet she caught herself sighing. She turned her attention back to her wardrobe dilemma while squeezing the water out of her hair with another of Franklin's impossibly thick towels. He really had been that good.

Well, one thing was certain, she thought, looking again around the Italian marble bathroom that could easily house her living room and kitchen with room to spare, a girl could quickly get spoiled, living like this. The least she could do was look good for their first meeting. "Dior it is."

Lotion, where was her lotion? That was the one thing she sprung for when it came to makeup. Okay, so it had been a two-for-one sale at Macy's. And so what if there wasn't anyone in her life at the moment to enjoy her slavish devotion to keeping her skin soft? It was a little ritual she performed for herself. Her traitorous thoughts shifted to that afternoon when Noah had walked in on her smoothing lotion on her legs . . . and had slipped the bottle from her hands and taken over the job himself.

She sighed. "I really have to stop thinking about him." Then she remembered her lotion was in the bag she'd taken on the plane. Still squeezing the water from her hair, she left the bathroom and padded through the bedroom to the living room. Whereas the living area was inlaid wood floors topped with Oriental carpeting and filled with antiques, fringed lamps, and massive, heavily framed landscapes, the bedroom was all girl, an homage to Victorian lace and delicate antiques.

As she'd followed Costas to her rooms earlier, she'd wondered about the rather decadent, over-the-top style Franklin had used when decorating. But the bedroom was curious for another reason. Thus far, though eclectic, what she'd seen of the house had been done in a decidedly masculine tone. So to say she'd been surprised by her ultra-feminine room was an understatement. And it made her all the more curious to see more of the house and learn more about the real man behind the hype.

She spied her backpack on the antique desk by the double doors leading to the main hallway and quickly fished out the lotion. It felt chilly out here, so she turned around to head back to the steam-filled bedroom—only to scream and throw the bottle up in the air.

"Jesus!" She clutched the towel she was wrapped in to her chest with one hand and the towel on her head with the other. "What the hell are you doing in here?"

Noah leaned back on the settee he'd made himself at home on and spread his arms along the inlaid wood back. That insouciant smile that came so easily to him curved his lips—lips she'd been doing her damnedest to forget since the morning he'd taken off six months ago, leaving her naked and, okay, pretty happily exhausted in bed. Not that he hadn't left her naked and in the same exact state the morning before that . . . and the morning before that. But he'd always shown up again. At some point. She didn't think this quite qualified.

"Need some help with that?"

She shot him the "you wish" glare of death and then bent down to pick up the lotion bottle. Thank God it hadn't spilled. Not the way to make a good first impression, ruining a Persian rug that likely cost more than her entire apartment building at home. As she picked up the bottle, her towel began to slip, and with her other hand on the towel still wrapped around her hair, something had to give. So she tossed the bottle in the general direction of Noah's midsection and then grabbed at both towels as she wobbled to a stand.

"Hey, watch out—*oof*."

She glanced up in time to see that she'd misjudged her aim, by oh, about six inches or so. She tried not to laugh as he yanked the bottle up just before it hit him between the legs. "Good save," was all she said. Okay, so maybe she smirked. A little. But really, he deserved worse for barging in here uninvited and scaring the crap out of her.

She tried mightily to gather some shred of dignity as she stared him down. "I hate to be redundant. I seem to be asking this of you a lot lately. But what the hell are you doing here?"

"I'm in the suite across the hall. I thought we'd go down to dinner together. I knocked, but you didn't answer. I poked my head in, in case you'd fallen asleep or something, and I heard the shower."

"So you figured you'd just make yourself at home? Remind me to start locking my door." Another thought occurred to her. She looked past him into the bedroom where she'd stacked her laptop and piles of notes by the bed, but her view was blocked. Dammit. He wouldn't have gone in there and snooped around, would he? Was that the real reason he'd come in her rooms?

Then another thought came to her. "You write as well as direct your own documentaries, right?"

If he was surprised by the sudden shift to a new topic, he didn't let it show. He stood up and leaned across the coffee table to hand her the bottle of lotion. "Yes. Scripts, both fiction and non, are all mine."

She let go of the towel on her head long enough to take the lotion and then tucked it under her arm and backed up a step. *Stay in control. Don't let him fluster you. You're a cool, competent professional.*

So what if she was hyper-aware of the huge, oversized, overstuffed bed right in the next room? And so what if all that stood between her being modestly covered and bare-assed naked was a ridiculously plush bath towel? She could handle this with aplomb and dignity. She owed herself that much.

She cocked her head, her expression serious. "How did you get this job anyway? I didn't know Dent was going to make a documentary."

"Neither did he until I suggested it to him."

Her gaze narrowed. "And when, exactly, did you do that?"

His grin was unrepentant. "Right after I read the blurb in the trades saying you'd gotten the job ghostwriting his autobiography."

Her mouth dropped open and then snapped shut. Of all the nerve. And to just baldly admit it like that, too! "Did you use your connection to me to get in the door with Dent?"

His smile turned just a hair pitying. "I have one or two credits of my own, you know."

She did know. Not about his documentaries so much. He'd been working on a movie script during the time they'd dated, and they'd never quite gotten around to talking about his other work. But everyone who was anyone in the industry knew the name Noah Morrissey. Three of his action-adventure scripts had been made into blockbuster movies. So he wasn't hurting for work, if he wanted it. He was hot and in demand.

In more ways than one, she happened to know personally. Geesh. She really had to stop going there. Stop mentally undressing him out of that T-shirt and—"You're wearing that to dinner?" she blurted.

He looked down at himself and then back to her with an artless shrug. "Sure. Why not? Informal is the dress code."

"Well, there's informal and then there's street bum."

"Street bum?" He held out his arms. "I bathed, no holes, and I even used deoderant."

"I'd clap, but I don't seem to have a free hand at the moment."

"More's the pity."

She frowned. "Okay, we need to set some ground rules." He had that twinkle in his eye. Well, he almost always did. But she acknowledged she had a weak spot for it—see, she had grown and changed since he'd left—so she was being smart and mature and doing what was obvious to anyone with two eyes in their head had to be done.

She moved toward the double doors leading to the hallway. "Rule Number One: No uninvited entry into each other's living quarters."

"Don't go making rules for me now."

She turned to face him. "Fine. No uninvited entry into *my* living quarters. If you're worried about my well-being, have Costas come check on me. Rule Number Two: There will be no resurrection of any previous interactions between the two of us that were . . . physical in nature."

He laughed. "You mean no sex?"

She sniffed. "If you want to put it crudely." The wobbling towel on her head probably detracted slightly from her attempt at poise and decorum, but she was certain he got the point. He'd probably come here thinking she'd be a convenient, easy bed partner while he worked on this project. And to be fair, given the nature of the bulk of their previous relationship, she could, possibly, maybe, see where he might get that grossly misinformed impression. Best to make certain he realized, in no uncertain language, that she was not now, nor would she ever be, interested in having sex with him again. At least not that she'd ever tell him about.

He tilted his head slightly. "Do you plan to write your great fiction novel in the same style you're talking to me now? Because it might be a wee bit inaccessible to the reader. Why don't you just speak plainly?"

Her jaw tightened, and she flung open one of the two doors. Well, after yanking on one handle and discovering it was locked, she flung open the other one, but there was no mistaking her intent. "Fine. How is this for plain? Get out."

To make her point, she thrust one arm, finger pointed, in the general direction of the hall. Much too late, she realized it was the hand holding up her towel—or the hand that had been holding up her towel. The very same hand also clutching the pump bottle, which, when she'd pointed her finger, had depressed said pump, ejecting a long stream of coconut-papaya-aloe-vitamin-E hydrating lotion across the hall, where it landed with a splat on the matching set of double doors across from hers.

She stood, frozen, not to mention naked, staring at the creamy glob as it oozed down the mahogany paneled door. To punctuate the moment, the leaning tower of turban on her head chose that moment to lose its battle with gravity. It slid completely sideways and off, dumping wet, stringy hair onto her face. Yes, yes, the moment was now complete.

"Nice trajectory," Noah said, winking at her as he slid past her through the door. "At least now when I wander back to my rooms in the middle of the night in the dark, I can find my doors by feel."

She peered through sodden ropes of hair and watched as he scraped off a glob, sniffed it, and then hummed with appreciation. "You know, I always loved the smell of this stuff."

Before she could reply with something suitably scathing—granted it would have been hard bordering impossible given her current state—

he robbed her of that pleasure and ducked into his rooms, shutting the lotion-smeared door behind him.

Jaw clenched in both anger and complete mortification, she stepped back into her own rooms and barely, just barely, refrained from slamming her door. She was an adult, after all. She could be mature about this.

She scooped up the towels, pushed her hair from her face, and took a deep, steadying breath. Then she stuck her tongue out at the door.

She was going to have to do something about this situation. This massive mansion simply wasn't going to be big enough for the both of them.

FOUR

NOAH paced the length of the study he'd been guided to by one of the house staff upon descending the grand staircase thirty minutes earlier. He'd refused the offer of a before-dinner drink, but as the pendulum on the gargantuan grandfather clock in the corner continued to swing back and forth, with neither Dent or Bailey making an appearance, he was beginning to rethink that decision. It was already a quarter past. Where were they?

He'd come down early in hopes of spending a few moments alone with the man before it became a cozy little threesome. Not that Bailey Madison was the kind of woman who made an entrance. Unless she was tripping over something, anyway. Femme fatale she was not. Fatale, maybe. She didn't command the attention of a room. She was more the secondary character type. The best friend, the girl one step to the side of the main action. Not the beauty queen, but the cute girl next door, a little gawky, yet endearingly awkward. The one who would gladly listen to the buddy of her gorgeous best friend's date as he droned on all night long, all so gorgeous best friend could dance the night away and make out in dark corners.

She was the one who laughed at all the right intervals and had that way about her that generally made a person feel like they were the most interesting person in the room. Yeah, that was Bailey's secret weapon.

Not that it would work on a man like Dent.

Even if it had, to some degree, worked on Noah. Briefly, anyway. He'd come to his senses soon enough, hadn't he? Writing was the only thing they had in common, and even that couldn't be more polar opposite. She wrote about alien baby abductions, for God's sake. If Dent hadn't been a closet freak for that wacky soap she'd ghosted the book for, she would never have gotten this gig.

So where was she anyway?

Surely she wasn't hiding in her room because of that little hallway incident. It wasn't like he hadn't seen her naked before. Although he had to admit it hadn't exactly bothered him to have his memory banks jogged a little. He caught himself sniffing his hands again and abruptly dropped them back to his sides. So he'd rubbed in the lotion. Isn't that what you're supposed to do with body lotion?

It was a proven fact that scent was the strongest trigger for repressed memories, so it wasn't exactly his fault he'd spent some time in his suite remembering a whole lot more about his time with Bailey Madison than he otherwise would have.

Not that he'd actively repressed those memories. It wasn't like their time together had been bad. Not at all. In fact, it had been pretty damn good, for what it was. Which was a short, intense affair between two physically compatible people. They just weren't long-haul material.

Okay, so maybe it was Noah who wasn't long-haul material. But he'd never pretended otherwise. Bailey had "committed relationship girl" all but tattooed on her forehead.

He raked his hand through his hair, paced back the other way, caught a whiff of that scent again, and sighed. Where did Dent hide the booze anyway? There was no obvious bar in the room nor tray full of decanters. A cold beer would be very well received at the moment. Maybe he should ring for Costas and ask the old man for a Bud. Picturing the Spaniard's facial tic twitching into high gear entertained him for a few moments.

Then his thoughts drifted right back to Bailey. Laughing Bailey. Angry Bailey. Naked, fresh-from-the-shower Bailey.

Enough with that already. They'd be cooped up here for weeks. He'd best get a grip now. She wanted nothing to do with him and, though the challenge was tempting, the last thing he needed was trouble. And Bailey Madison was quickly proving she was going to be nothing but. Why complicate matters?

He paced to the other end of the room, barely paying attention to the clutter of antique clocks that lined the walls and mantles, also filling various small tables and several glass-fronted shelving units scattered about the oblong room. He'd been in here before and had already mentally catalogued the place, making notes on lighting and what angles he'd shoot if he used this room during the filming.

He glanced at the small handheld digital movie camera he'd brought down with him and put on a small side table. He'd already filmed this room and shot some preliminary blocking footage of the other rooms he'd been in. He planned to shoot most, if not all, of their time together. A great deal of that footage would be for his private notes, helping him to outline the documentary itself, which would be a more staged production once he had a handle on how he wanted to tell the man's story. But clips, bits and pieces of the candid filming, would very likely be cut into the film as well. It was a combination that had always worked well for him in the past, and he saw no reason to change his approach this time.

He knew Dent was an avid photographer himself, though he'd been surprised to see no proof whatsoever in any of the rooms he'd been in so far. Artifacts from Dent's many world travels filled the place almost to bursting, but there were no framed prints capturing any of it, with or without Dent himself in the photograph. He was hoping to access some of Dent's films of his more daring escapades, as the man had had many of them recorded and used in various marketing campaigns for his vast and varied business empire.

Flamboyant Virgin Atlantic billionaire, the recently knighted Sir Richard Branson, had nothing on Franklin Dent when it came to pimping himself out for the sake of furthering the cause of his own financial interests. Noah saw nothing wrong with that approach, and apparently neither did the global business community, as Dent's net worth continued to soar with each new project he launched. Noah's pacing intensified. He was really excited about this project. It was the perfect blend of his two biggest passions: action-adventure movies, and telling the story of any man as everyman.

In both cases, telling Dent's story was going to be one of the biggest challenges of his career. He wondered how Bailey was going to approach his life story. Whatever angle she decided on, he wasn't going to veer from his own vision. She'd have to deal with that. The documentary was separate from the book, not a film version of same. He wasn't going to work around her; she would have to work around him.

Just then, laughter floated into the room, growing louder as the double paneled doors opened and Dent and Bailey entered, arm in arm. Dent's head was thrown back as he laughed at something Bailey must have said, because she was grinning and looking quite pleased with herself. And since when did she own a dress? Well, it was a suit, but it was tailored to fit and obviously designer couture.

Not that he should know stuff like that; he was about as nonmetrosexual as a heterosexual guy could be. But he'd done a documentary several years back on Parvii, an up-and-coming designer from India who was forging his way into the European and American fashion industry. So although Noah wasn't ready to audition for *Queer Eye* anytime soon, he had done his usual amount of exhaustive research on the subject. Still, it made about as much sense that he knew she was wearing Dior as it did that she was actually wearing Dior. A fashion maven Bailey was not. She was jeans, pullovers, and the occasional eclectic accessory, circa Carrie Bradshaw. So okay, maybe he'd spent too much of their time together taking off her jeans and pullovers. If he'd taken her out more, maybe this wouldn't be such a surprise.

Noah had the camera in his hand and aimed at them without even thinking about it. Of course, the magnetic draw was supposed to be Dent. The man was every bit as dynamic as he was reputed to be. At seventy-one, he could easily pass for a man a decade or so younger. He wasn't big in stature, an inch or two shy of the six-foot mark, and not broad of build, though tennis player lean and fit. He was tanned, his face weather-worn, with deep crinkles fanning from the corners of his pale blue eyes and bracketing his broad mouth. His hair was silver and receding, but Dent kept it buzzed almost to the scalp. It enhanced his general hale heartiness. But more than his appearance was the energy that emanated from him. He exuded a vitality so vibrant, so electric, it was almost tangible and instantly drew every eye to him the moment he entered a room.

Had anyone asked Noah at that moment, he'd have immediately agreed that Dent quite naturally owned his role as the subject matter of Noah's work and was, of course, the exclusive focus of his attention. Bailey was merely in the frame as an accessory to Dent, the secondary character providing the byplay off of which Dent would act and react. What was important was what it revealed about the man. Bailey was merely a foil.

Which did nothing to explain why Noah couldn't take his eyes—or his camera—off her.

So much for Bailey's inability to make an entrance, huh? As much as Noah wished he could convince himself that it was merely Dent's charismatic aura spilling over onto her, he knew better. The camera never lied.

Dammit.

Dent finally stopped laughing long enough to notice Noah. He waved his hand dismissively toward the camera. "There will be plenty of time for that tiresome thing. For now, I would like us all to spend the evening getting to know one another." He motioned to the grouping of furniture in the center of the oblong room facing the fieldstone fireplace. There were two heavy, studded, leather couches, framed by two equally weighty leather-bound arm chairs. "Have a seat, and I'll ring for drinks."

Bailey passed by Noah just then as she made her way to the couch. He'd never get that scent out his head now. "Drinks, definitely," he murmured and shifted past her so he could extend his hand to Dent. "A pleasure to finally meet you." He caught the look of surprise on Bailey's face. So she hadn't been trying to gain standing by making first contact. Best he stayed on his toes anyway. Especially if she had any more outfits like that one hanging in her closet upstairs.

Dent's handshake was firm and confident. "Pleasure is mine. I've enjoyed your work, both big market and small. The documentary you did on the water management irrigation system they set up in China's Sichuan province was in part what inspired me to expand my enterprise in that direction."

Noah smiled, pleasantly surprised. "Thank you. It was a tricky one to shoot."

"Having traveled there extensively, I can well imagine." Dent grinned then. "Of course, I expect it's your experience with some of your other more mainstream film projects that might hold you in better stead here."

Noah wasn't entirely certain he was joking. "If I wrote your life like an action-adventure screenplay, the studios wouldn't buy it. Too outlandish and unbelievable, they'd say."

"Yes, truth can be stranger than fiction." Dent laughed, and Noah relaxed a little.

He knew Dent had been attracted to both avenues of his professional career, but he'd hoped the emphasis would be on his documentary experience. Noah both wrote and directed them, whereas his action-adventure scripts were produced and directed by others.

As if he reading his mind, Dent said, "Well, now you'll get your chance."

Noah played dumb, hoping he was wrong. "To?"

"Write and direct the action-adventure film of a lifetime."

"Yes, well, this will be a little different in that—"

"Yes, yes, of course." Dent nudged Noah toward one of the wingback chairs. For all that Noah easily had a half a foot in height on the man, he was sitting a moment later.

"It must be frustrating to hand your story over to someone else's interpretation. You're a director; doesn't it bother you to relinquish control of your work?"

Noah wasn't entirely certain how to answer that one. The truth was, he didn't really mind. He'd never give away one of his documentaries to be filmed by someone else. But the action-adventure screenplays . . . those were fun, paid the bills, and allowed him to indulge himself in the selfish endeavor of making small films that would play mostly at film festivals and to perhaps a handful of paying customers.

Dent leaned forward, his blue eyes gleaming. The energy emanating off the man was truly palpable. "You can't tell me you haven't felt the desire to step behind the camera on the set of a major motion picture. Use that big-studio budget to bring your ideas—which are quite fantastical themselves, I must say—to life before your very eyes?"

Was he envisioning this documentary as some kind of blockbuster movie people would rush to see at the local cineplex? How exactly should Noah break it to him that, even as a man of his wealth, fame, and stature, it was unlikely his life story would ever see anything close to mass distribution? He'd probably fire Noah on the spot and bring in some hack who'd be thrilled to do whatever Dent wanted him to. Or make him believe anything was possible anyway. Noah couldn't do that.

Bailey spoke up before Noah could. "I don't think Noah feels the same sense of ownership over his fictional work as he does with his real-life stories." She smiled. "He's kind of opposite of me in that respect."

Dent sat back and looked from Bailey to Noah. "I'm sorry, where are my manners. You two have met already, yes?"

Noah caught Bailey's gaze on purpose and smiled, enjoying the rather pink glow that came to her cheeks. "Yes. We've known each other for some time."

Dent wasn't slow, but his smile was. "Ah, I see. Will there be an issue with either of you working so closely on our dual projects?"

Bailey shut out Noah and turned her full attention to Dent. "Not at all. Noah and I are professionals first and foremost." She shot him a quick glance. "I'm sure we'll have no problem respecting each other's work ethic."

Dent clapped his hands together. "Most excellent." He glanced between them. "I must admit, I adore tension. People tend to pay better attention."

Noah and Bailey exchanged another brief glance, but neither dared to ask for clarification. Noah recalled Dent's fixation on that soap opera Bailey had written for and stifled a sigh. So the man enjoyed high drama. Well, he was going to be disappointed. He'd be damned if he turned this cavernous gothic mansion into some kind of personal reality show for the rich. Not that he supposed Dent had thought of any such thing, but there was definitely a new spark in the older man's eyes as he looked at the two of them. Better to get his mind back to the matter at hand—which was his own amazing life, not the love lives of his two biographers.

Again, he was cut off before he could speak, this time by Dent.

"Before we adjourn to the lovely dinner my chef has prepared for us, I want to welcome both of you and thank you for giving up a chunk of your life to document my own." He pressed his hands to his knees, stood, and then waited for them to follow his lead. "I assure you, your sacrifice will be one worth having made. When this is all said and done, I will have my life story in print and on film." His smile shifted from the beneficent to the wee bit mischievous. "And you both will leave here wealthier in pocket and in experience. I might go so far as to say the experience of a lifetime." He winked. "But there will be plenty of time to detail our first adventure after dinner."

He waved them both ahead him toward another set of double doors. As Bailey passed Noah, she whispered, "What is he talking about?"

"Damned if I know." He bumped elbows with her. "But knowing Dent's appetite for adventure, it sounds like it could be quite interesting."

"Yeah," she said, her skin losing a little of its pink glow. "Quite."

FIVE

BAILEY wisely put her wineglass back on the dining room table and thanked God she hadn't been mid-sip when Franklin had made his little announcement, or it would have been spew city. She tried for her very best confident smile. Okay, so that was totally out of the question. Something slightly less than abject terror was her best bet.

"I'm sorry," she said, thinking, *Laugh casually, no worries, smile brightly.* Unfortunately, the smile was forced and the laugh came out sounding more like a death gurgle. "But I thought you just said you wanted us to go skydiving with you. You meant that we'll watch you dive, right?" She continued talking, mentally willing Franklin to agree with her. "Great idea! Give us a firsthand feel for some of the things you do for fun. Noah could get some film footage on it as well." She knew better than to look to Noah for help on this. Like as not, he was very amused by the whole idea.

Franklin leaned forward, his elbows propped on either side of his fourteen-carat-gold-trimmed china dinner plate. The table settings were unreal: a decadent hodgepodge of whisper-thin bone china dinner plates; hand-thrown heavy salad bowls; colored blown glass goblets; flatware in a variety of patterns; and two linen napkins, one white, one a boldly colorful Asian print. Central on the miles long, hand-carved, walnut medieval-style table was a monstrous crystal bowl filled to overflowing with gorgeous blooms of every variety. No stems, just the blooms, all tossed in, along with bright green, perfectly shaped leaves, as if in some wild mixed floral salad. It was quite different, but truly stunning.

"I expect you to jump with me," he said, his gleaming smile splitting his deeply tanned face. "Bailey, you need to feel that sense of exhilaration if you're going to capture me properly. And Noah, film footage in the air would certainly be more appealing than watching some tiny speck descend through the sky from a distance."

Bailey reflexively gulped down the rest of her wine before she'd even realized it. She carefully put the goblet on the table and pushed it away—far, far away—although self-medicating sounded like an excellent plan at the moment. If she stayed totally sloshed, she might actually allow them to throw her out of the open cargo door. Which is what it was going to take. Because, stone cold sober or falling down drunk, there was no way was she jumping voluntarily out of a perfectly good plane.

"I'll need slightly different gear," Noah said.

I'll need slightly different gear, too, Bailey thought. *Like all new DNA.*

Franklin waved a hand. "Whatever you need, just tell me and I'll make sure you have it. No worries there."

If only you could do the same for me, oh great and powerful Oz.

"Excellent," Noah replied. "I've jumped before, but it's been a while." He looked to Bailey, that twinkle of mischief sparking in his eyes. "Have you ever been skydiving?"

They hadn't dated all that long, so Noah didn't know everything about her. But after their one disastrous attempt at fixing the loose iron railing on her miniscule, third-story balcony, he was quite well aware of her fear of heights. "Never got around to trying it, I'm afraid," she said, all bravado and derring-do. It was clear Noah was enjoying himself immensely, and at least partially at her expense. It was also clear he wanted to be top dog in their joint endeavor here.

Well, just because he had more experience in filming documentaries than she had writing biographies didn't mean she wasn't as confident of her abilities as he was of his. So what if she wasn't a pro at jumping out of airplanes—perfectly good, nonmalfunctioning airplanes? That merely meant she was sane. It didn't mean she wasn't a pro at writing. And after all, that's what she'd been hired to do here. Not defy death. So she let Noah have his smug little moment of superiority. She was quite confident that she and Franklin would work very well together, thank you very much.

Just as soon as she made it clear to him that she was staying in the damn plane.

Franklin dabbed at the corners of his mouth with his napkin and then laid it across his plate. "I'm afraid I have a phone meeting I must take. But please enjoy dessert and coffee. I have quite the selection, if you're so inclined." He pushed back his chair and stood. "I'll have Raj come out and tell you all about them. I'll see you both bright and early in the morning. We're off at seven; breakfast will be ready by six."

And just like that, he was gone.

Noah tossed his napkin on his plate. "He's something, isn't he?" He sighed and leaned back in his chair. "That meal was fantastic."

Bailey looked at him, eyes narrowed, wondering what angle he was playing now. There was always an angle with Noah. "Yes, it was," she said, opting to continue the banal, after-dinner chat, at least until he played his hand. "If he keeps feeding us like this, I'm going to need a whole new wardrobe."

Noah chuckled. "I don't know, sounds like this is going to be a hands-on work experience. Something tells me we're going to need all the sustenance we can muster."

Bailey tried not to, but she swallowed reflexively anyway. And that wonderful meal rumbled a little bit in her belly. Noah was a great observer. It was one of the few things they had in common.

He cocked his head. "Something the matter?"

She just rolled her eyes. "Franklin isn't here, so we don't have to pretend to be civil. You know damn well I can't jump out of that airplane."

"You know," he said, in lieu of a direct response, "I wouldn't be surprised if he doesn't already know everything there is to know about us."

"What?"

Noah leaned forward and nudged her wine glass toward her. "Have a sip. You're looking awfully pale."

She ignored the gesture . . . and the wine. "What do you mean you think he knows all about us? After the interview process, he knows more about me than my own mother does."

"I didn't mean us as individuals. I meant us as a couple. Dent doesn't strike me as the sort to invite guests for an extended stay, much less hire them to tell his life's story, without doing some serious background research."

"You think he knows we used to date? I got the impression it was a surprise to him that we even knew each other."

"I think he knows what kind of jockey shorts I prefer."

"You don't prefer any kind of jockey shorts," she replied without thinking.

Noah just grinned.

She rolled her eyes. "You're hopeless," she said, but she couldn't deny the accompanying visual that memory had brought with it, of Noah in all his commando glory . . . Maybe she was the one who was hopeless.

"It doesn't really matter what he knows of our past anyway. It's over now. We're just here to do a job. We're both professionals."

"If you say so." He lifted a hand when she huffed. "Okay, okay. So what are you going to do about the jumping from the plane thing?"

"I'll just tell him I can't. Honestly, I don't really see the need to reenact all the stunts he's done in his life. The man is a hard-core adrenaline junkie. My idea of an extreme stunt is driving into the city during rush hour."

"Hey, that requires a certain level of fearlessness." Before she could respond, he went on. "I hate to say it, but I do think Dent has a point about this. If you're really going to get inside his head and write his life story as if he were the one telling it, it would have to be a bonus to have felt something of what he's felt when he takes chances like that."

She shook her head. "It's a flawed plan. He leaps off a cliff and probably feels nothing but a mad rush of exhilaration. Me, on the other hand . . . Well, first off, you'd have to shove me off the cliff, after prying my fingers from the ankles I'm clinging to, as I sob and beg you not to make me do this. After that, the only thing I'd be worried about was having clean underwear on, so when they scraped my mangled dead body from the base of said cliff, at least I won't have the added embarrassing little detail of dying with ratty drawers on in my obituary."

Noah laughed. "Don't be such a drama queen. People jump out of planes all the time, and almost all of them live to jump again."

She felt her skin grow a bit clammy. "My point exactly. *Almost all.* It's not a percentage game I'm willing to play. All I'm trying to say is that me jumping won't inform me about how he feels. I'll only know how I felt. Abject terror followed by a very loud, long scream."

"I'm sure Dent would let you jump in tandem with an instructor or something. Just close your eyes and fall. I think you'll be surprised at how big a rush it is. Most people want to go again before they even land."

"Your 'most people' would likely be those without an irrational fear of heights. Or death."

"You said the word, not me. *Irrational.* You got in an airplane to fly all the way out here, and that didn't bother you."

"Just the takeoff and landing. The rest of the time I pretend I'm on a train."

He laughed and shook his head. "Well, be that as it may, you still do it."

"Yeah, but the key word there is fly *on* the plane. Not leap *from* the plane."

Noah folded his arms. "So you think you can just tell Dent no? I'm not sure many people actually get away with that."

Bailey sighed and leaned back in her chair. "He won't have a choice. Even if I was willing, I'm not just going to get over my fear of heights. And I don't think leaping into thin air at ten thousand feet is the kind of baby step I would likely need to take if I was at all interested in getting over my phobia. Which I'm not. Honestly, I could have a heart attack or something."

"I repeat, then what are you going to do? Let me go up there with him while you sit back here? You'll very likely be packing your bags while Dent flies in your replacement."

"He spent months selecting his ghostwriter. I don't think he's going to fire me over—"

"You haven't written a word yet. If he was ever going to switch hitters, now would be the time. And as tests go, I would imagine this isn't going to be the only one."

"Gee, Noah, you're so supportive. Selfless, really."

"I'm just being honest. Logical."

She sighed. "I know." *That's what I'm afraid of.* She might be able to get out of one adrenaline rush adventure, but what were the chances she'd get out of the rest of them without pissing off Dent? But then she tried to visualize herself standing on the edge of an open cargo door at ten thousand feet, and her stomach threatened to return dinner on her. "I guess I'll have to take my chances."

Noah's face lit up. "Atta girl!"

"Atta girl?" She snorted a laugh. "Who says 'atta girl'? Shall I fetch something for you next?"

"Yeah, Raj with the coffee."

"I was kidding. And you read me all wrong anyway. I didn't mean take my chances jumping, I meant take my chances with Dent and staying in the plane."

"If he gets you up there—"

She shuddered a little. "Unless one of you drags me through the open door, I'm not leaving the plane until it's back on the ground. I don't succumb to peer pressure. But the least I can do is go up there with him. I can talk to him about what attracts him to the sport and what it feels like, and you'll have footage I can watch for visual description."

Raj entered just then with a sterling-silver tray bearing two rows of tiny espresso-size cups, each filled with what looked like coffee. "A selection for you to sample."

"Excellent," Noah said, reaching for one as soon as Raj set it between them.

Bailey took a sip of the cup closest to her and tried not to make a face as the very bitter brew hit her tongue.

"Try another one, Goldilocks."

She just arched her brow at him, but, of course, the third one was just right. Noah grinned when she grudgingly told Raj she'd like that one—it was really too good—and as soon as he turned his back, she stuck her tongue out at Noah. He just laughed and toasted her with his mini mug.

"So," he asked, "do you really think being in the plane is going to be enough?"

"Don't underestimate my powers of persuasion. I'm sure I can make him see that my jumping isn't actually necessary."

SIX

BAILEY stood in the open door of the plane with a death grip on either side of the frame. Noah knew he should be filming Dent, but he couldn't seem to stop aiming the camera at her.

"Franklin," Bailey said, shouting to be heard over the roaring noise of the open cargo door. "Honestly, I don't think I—"

"Nonsense," Dent reassured her, waving his hand dismissively. He held onto the wall strap and edged closer to her and the instructor she was harnessed to. "Matt will see you safely down." He thumped the instructor enthusiastically on the back. "Next time you'll solo."

"Next time?"

Noah hadn't thought her face could be any whiter. He'd been wrong.

Dent grinned in the face of her abject terror. "You'll thank me for this, dear." Then he gave the signal to the instructor and backed up.

Bailey's gaze swung wildly from Dent to Noah. It was the first time she'd deigned to make eye contact with him since boarding Dent's private plane an hour ago. But whatever pride she had left vanished now in the face of her sheer terror, and it was clear she was beseeching him to do something, anything, to help her out.

Up to this point, he'd been mildly amused when all of Bailey's calculating, well-reasoned arguments about why she shouldn't jump had fallen on deaf ears. He'd stayed out of it—not that she'd have asked for his help anyway—but privately he'd been in agreement with Dent. If she was going to write the man's life story from his point of view, it wouldn't hurt for her to experience at least a sliver of what Dent had. And skydiving was quite tame considering the variety of life experiences he had to choose from. She should be thankful Dent hadn't wanted her to trek across Antarctica or dine with headhunters in New Guinea.

Besides, what better way to get over her fear of heights than to face down the monster under her bed right here and now? Sure it was scary, but once she was out there, flying through the air, she'd see that it wasn't going to kill her, that nothing bad was going to happen. Shoot, she'd probably be back up in this plane begging them to let her jump again.

But in the instant her gaze had connected with his just now, he'd realized that this wasn't just some moderate exercise in mind over matter for her. Unfortunately, he'd waited a split second too long to make up his mind to step in. Just as his hand faltered and he began to lower the camera, the instructor pushed them out the door and tucked her into his body as they went free-falling through space.

Instinctively his hand came right back up, film rolling. But the unearthly scream that echoed up through the air, filling the inside of the plane, also filled the inside of his head. And he knew it would be a very, very long time before that echo died out.

Dent turned and clapped his hands, smiling. "Okay then, shall we?"

Noah realized on the one hand that Dent's life experiences had probably inured him to a great many things, jading him to certain elements of humanity, but even he was surprised by the man's apparent complete lack of sympathy or concern for Bailey. And yet, what was there to say? Except, "Sure, ready when you are."

Both of them being experienced, they were jumping without any instructor aid but as close together as possible, so Noah could film as much of Dent's descent as he could. He adjusted the camera scope attached to his harness as well as the one attached to his head gear and then gave Dent a thumbs-up. He would go out first, get situated, and then hopefully capture Dent from the initial jump all the way to the ground.

He looked for Bailey's chute, but the position of the plane as it circled the landing spot momentarily blocked his view. Of course she was going to be okay, but still . . . he shivered just a little as that scream echoed in his mind again. Blocking that out as best he could—he had a job to do here after all—he braced himself in the open door and relished the punch of adrenaline that rushed through him.

With a quick glance back at Dent, who gave him a thumbs-up, he pushed through the door . . . and went sailing weightlessly through the air. He had very little time to get himself situated, adjust the lenses attached to various parts of his gear, and get ready to film as much of Dent's jump as he could. So what in the hell was he doing, scanning the horizon for Bailey's chute? Like there was any chance she wasn't perfectly fine. She was strapped to an instructor for God's sake.

As it was, he missed Dent's initial leap from the plane, but he got his act together, and by the time they reached ground, he knew he had some good footage. He saw Bailey's instructor about a hundred yards away on the dusty, dirt-brown desert floor they'd jumped into. He was busy dragging both their chutes into a smaller heap, but there was no sign of Bailey. Framing his eyes to block the sun, he scanned the surroundings. There was the fully decked out white service van with a dish and tracking cam mounted on top—Dent had ground filming done as well during the whole thing—and a sleek black limousine parked just beyond it.

Aha. Noah grinned. She was probably in there, downing everything in Dent's liquor cabinet to numb the terror she'd just survived. He motioned to Dent, who was crossing to the van to talk to the driver and jerked his head toward the limo. Dent gave him a thumbs-up, so Noah got out of his harness and handed it to a waiting attendant—working for a billionaire really did have its perks—and headed off to find Bailey.

She was in the far corner of the limo's rear seat, dry-eyed and empty handed, staring blankly out of the window. She didn't so much as blink when he got in across from her and closed the door.

Her face was dirt-streaked from the swirling dust on the desert floor, much as he imagined his own was. But there were no tear stains, no bitten-off nails, nothing to indicate outwardly that she'd just experienced something quite harrowing. Maybe he'd underestimated her after all. Although it didn't appear she was in any hurry to do it all over again, she'd apparently survived her demon-facing ordeal rather handily.

Except she wasn't speaking to him. Hell, she wouldn't even look at him. Probably embarrassed by that shriek of death she'd let out when they'd left the plane.

Noah waited another moment, but she didn't even bother turning her head. So he reached into the limo's mini-fridge and pulled out two bottles of water. He offered her one, which she didn't even bother to acknowledge, so he tossed it in the seat next to her. "You know, I might have screamed, too, the first time I jumped," he said.

"Bully for you," she said, the words a flat monotone.

"It must feel good, knowing you conquered your fear."

Her jaw tightened then, and there might have been a slight facial tic somewhere around her temple area, but otherwise she remained outwardly unmoved by his comment. "Just peachy."

Noah leaned back and stretched out his legs. "Oh, come on, I know it was high-handed of Dent to put you out there like that, but you have to admit it all worked out fine in the end. And you will have a greater appreciation for the feel of that adrenaline rush, having experienced it yourself. You have to agree he was right about this."

"Right."

Never had a single word been uttered so unconvincingly.

Noah sighed. "So what's the problem?"

She slowly shifted her gaze so it was directed right at him. It was only then he saw the stark emptiness there. She hadn't been just scared up there; she'd been completely traumatized. So much so she'd withdrawn into some kind of shell. "I'm fine," she said flatly, when it would have been clear to a blind man that she was anything but.

"Bailey—"

"Shut up, Noah," she said, then shifted her gaze back out of the window. He had to resist the urge to rub his arms, the sudden chill was so arctic.

"I just want to say . . ." He stopped, not sure exactly what he wanted to say. Well, that wasn't true. He'd been about to apologize. For not stepping in and telling Dent to take a hike. For not being there for her when she needed him. Which, of course, was ridiculous. He was here to film a documentary, not baby-sit his former girlfriend. She was a grown woman; she didn't have to leap out of that plane. He wasn't here to run interference for her with Dent, either. "If you can't handle this, maybe you should consider leaving now."

She stiffened slightly, which, considering how rigidly still she was holding herself, knees and ankles pressed together, arms wrapped around her waist, was saying something. "Go to hell, Morrissey."

If she'd wondered why they weren't together any longer, certainly she wondered no longer. His intentions had been good, then and now. But as usual, when he'd opened his mouth, he'd said exactly the wrong thing. This is why he left without saying good-bye. It only made things worse. Before he could say or do anything else—and really, hadn't he done enough already?—the limo door opened and in climbed Dent.

"Well," he said, clasping his hands together after he settled in, "wasn't that fantastic?" For a man of relative slight stature, he filled the interior space of the limo to bursting with his energy and enthusiasm. His face was split in a wide, beaming smile, and his eyes were gleaming with exhilaration.

Out of the corner of his eye, Noah saw Bailey make the Herculean effort required to pull herself together and force a smile. Only he knew how much that likely had cost her at the moment. Before he could question the intelligence of once again trying to do the right thing where Bailey was concerned, he jumped in before Dent could focus his avid attentions on her. "I think I got some great footage up there. When will I have access to what they shot on the ground?"

As hoped, Dent shifted his attention immediately to Noah. "By early evening, easily." He crossed his legs and settled back as the limo began to move. "I should set some ground rules for your footage."

Noah was instantly wary. He had his own rules about the film he shot, but better to hear Dent out before jumping in with them. "Which are?"

"Due to my schedule, I won't always have time to sit through everything we film, but know that I would if I could. I'm a stickler for details and though managing an empire requires smart delegation of duty, when it's important to me—and make no mistake, nothing could be more personal to me at this moment than this project of mine—I tend to take a direct hand in seeing it done to my exact specifications."

Noah hadn't missed the very proprietary "project of mine" part of his little speech. And although he'd worked with investment partners before, and certainly worked hard to establish close relationships to his focal subjects, along with any and everyone he needed to work with to gain the kind of personal access his documentaries required, there was never any doubt in anyone's mind whose project it ultimately was. A Morrissey production meant just that. And although he'd known this was an entirely different sort of collaboration he'd gotten himself into, he wasn't going to simply hand over his work to someone else to splice together at their whim.

"I am also very particular about my work," he said carefully. "I think when you see what I put together, you'll be very happy."

Dent merely smiled. "I'm sure I will. Because, schedule demands or not, I will be overseeing every frame. Those you keep, and as many of those you cut as possible. I will expect to have dailies, as I believe they're called, prepared for me as best as possible. We'll be devising a story board of sorts of my life, and we'll go over my thoughts on exactly what I want represented and how." His smile remained, but the light in his eyes flattened a little. "Make no mistake; I respect your work, but this is my life. Nothing is finished until I say it's finished."

Noah struggled to maintain an even tone. Sure, Dent made it sound like it would still be a partnership, but Noah knew from dealing with investors over the years what the real message being delivered here today was all about. And just after he quietly explained that he financed his own documentaries—and often did—before allowing anyone else to interfere with his vision of the work, he would make Franklin Dent understand that he could trust him to bring this biography to life in a way that would fully honor Dent's wishes . . . while keeping him firmly out of the director's chair. "Mr. Dent, I fully respect your care and concern, but I need you to understand how I work. You hired me because—"

A shrill, chirping noise interrupted them, and Dent pulled a cell phone from a jacket pocket. "Must take this. Enjoy the ride. We'll finish this little chat back at the house." With that he flipped open the phone, took out his Blackberry, and began conducting a rapid-fire conversation with one of his many assistants.

Frustrated by his inability to finish their discussion now, Noah knew he had no choice but to sit back and wait Dent out. Tuning out the older man's conversation, Noah glanced at Bailey, only to find that her attention was once again directed toward the window. This time, however, the tiniest of smiles quirked the corner of her mouth.

So glad you find my rescue attempt amusing, he thought, wondering again why he'd bothered. Fine, then. He settled back and sipped at his water. Next time she was on her own.

SEVEN

BAILEY turned on the water in the shower full force and then went back to her bedroom to grab something to change into. She stared at the empty suitcases lining the back of her spacious walk-in closet, and briefly fantasized about grabbing the next flight back to New York. Or maybe the next train. It was a good fantasy, except she wasn't a quitter. If she was, she'd have never gotten on Dent's stupid plane in the first place.

But she *had* gotten on the plane, leading her to do the single most insane thing she'd ever let herself get talked into. She still couldn't really believe she'd actually strapped on a parachute and—She stopped the mental replay right there, as lunch threatened to come back up. Putting her hand over her stomach, she sank down on the edge of her bed. Peer pressure sucked. So did paycheck pressure. And once-in-a-lifetime-career-opportunity pressure.

She'd put up a pretty good fight against the first two . . . but when it came down to losing this chance, she'd caved.

So okay, the fact that the jump instructor had been drop-dead cute with an Aussie accent to match might have swayed her a teeny tiny bit. It had gotten her to take the jump class anyway. Even then she'd told herself she wouldn't actually do it. Right up to the point that she was bodily strapped to Drop Dead Cute Aussie she was still telling herself she wasn't going through with this. She was too busy wondering if the jump suit made her ass look big and would DDCA think she was still viable date material if she screamed like a banshee all the way to the ground. She should have paid more attention to the Drop Dead part.

It really wasn't until that instant right before they left the plane that she realized the only person who didn't think she was going to go through with it was her. Small oversight on her part. Then they left the plane and it was too late. She still preferred to think about it as leaving. Exiting stage left. As if they'd merely been passing through any old open doorway. Describing it as leaping out or jumping off had all kinds of death connotations she still couldn't handle.

She'd survived, sure. With several less layers of stomach lining and at least a few years less remaining on her life span. Performing one death-defying stunt in her lifetime had officially put her over her strict limit of none. She had a zero-tolerance policy for risking life and limb. After today, she still thought that was an excellent policy. So there would be no repeats, no do-overs. God forbid Franklin had some other crazy idea all lined up. She groaned and flopped back on the bed. Because of course he did.

Given Franklin's complete cluelessness to her total lack of enthusiasm for playing *Survivor: Biographer!* she was well aware today's little stunt wasn't going to be the only one.

She closed her eyes and thought about everything else Franklin was handing to her. "Good-paying gig, lap-of-luxury digs, chef on call, free time to work on your book," she said out loud, wanting to sound like the Voice of Reason. She opened her eyes and stared at the gaudily ornate white and gold Rococo ceiling. *Yeah,* she thought, *and to keep it, all you have to do is be willing to laugh in the face of death on a routine basis.*

As it turned out, she didn't have that kind of a sense of humor.

"Talk about making a deal with the devil."

"And here I thought the only devil in your life was me."

She swiveled her head toward the open bedroom door. "For God's sake! What part of 'knock first' don't you understand?"

Noah folded his arms. "The door was open. I called out, but with Niagara Falls running in there," he motioned toward the bathroom with his chin, "I guess you didn't hear me."

She didn't think she'd left the doors to the hall open, but what the hell did it matter? Clearly Noah had no intention of respecting her privacy. She shifted her gaze back to the ceiling. "If you came in here to continue gloating about how much more in tune you are with Dent than I am, please know, and I say this with utmost sincerity and sensitivity, that I could give a flying f—"

"That's not why I came in here."

She clenched her jaw. "Good. Because last time I checked, this wasn't some twisted game show and neither one of us has to get voted off the island. I know you don't want me here, but it's not like I'm competing for your job."

"I never said that."

She rolled her head to one side, eyeing him warily. "You didn't have to. And the feeling is mutual, by the way, so don't worry about hurting my feelings." *As if he would,* she thought. "You stay out of my way; I'll stay out of yours." She rolled to her side and propped her head on one hand. "Which means staying the hell out of my room unless invited." She hoped the look she gave him made it quite clear a certain part of the earth's core would have to freeze over before that invite would be proffered.

Noah, being Noah, just smiled, crossed the room, and sat on the edge of her bed.

With a sigh of exasperation, she immediately went to roll off the other side. The bathroom door had a lock, and she wanted—no, needed, dammit—the escape and restorative power of a nice, hot shower.

Noah blocked her escape with an easy hold on her forearm. "Don't go running off, Goldilocks. My intentions are actually good and kind and noble."

He'd said it so seriously she cracked up laughing. "Yeah, right."

He nodded to the edge of the bed, a silent request that she sit back down.

She pulled free and crossed both arms in front of her. Just seeing Noah sitting on her bed—any bed—brought back a host of visuals she definitely didn't need to be revisiting at the moment. Like she didn't have enough sensory overload to deal with after today. "I'll remain standing, thanks."

He grinned. "What, afraid you'll cave to my charm and good looks all over again?"

She gave him her best "as if" look, but he seemed more convinced of her resistance to him than she did at the moment. He laughed as if he couldn't imagine such a thing happening, either. Somehow she ended up being insulted anyway. Classic Noah.

"Go ahead, say whatever it is you feel you have to say. Even Dent's hot water tanks have to bottom out at some point, and I'd really like a shower."

Noah stood and tugged at his shirt. "Well, if you insist."

She swatted at his hand before thinking better of it. "Very funny."

He snagged her wrist, more gently this time, and tugged her a step closer. His smile faded, but the sincerity stayed in his eyes. "I just wanted to say that I'm sorry for what Dent put you through today. I know it was no picnic for you, but you pulled it out."

"Exactly when were you overcome with this oh-so-noble sentiment?" she shot back, more than a little disconcerted by his apparent sincerity. "Would that be when you were grinning like a loon as they strapped me into my harness? Or perhaps when you were filming my entire nervous breakdown? Because, honestly, I was so touched at how you stepped in on my behalf and told Dent to take a flying leap, not me."

The corner of Noah's mouth quirked. "You said you didn't want me rescuing you any more."

She spluttered. "I wasn't expecting a rescue, thank you very much. But would it have killed you to support my side of the argument? Oh, wait, that's right, you thought it was a good idea. Well, bully for you."

"Actually, right there at the end, before you jumped—"

"Was pushed, you mean."

"I did think about stepping in. You looked to me, and when I saw your face . . ." He just gave her a half shrug. "I'm sorry. I should have done something. That scream." He shuddered a little. "But even then I thought maybe once you were out, you'd realize how thrilling it was and overcome the fear."

She was going to pull her arm away again, really she was. But then he started stroking the inside of her wrist with his thumb, and somehow she was talking instead of leaving. "I know he means well, Noah, but honestly, I don't need to do this crazy stuff to write about the man's life. In the interviews I have on file, he's quite capable of describing even the wildest events in his life with such colorful detail, he makes you feel like you were there. And that is, after all, my only real job here. To write his story in such a way as to engage the reader's imagination, make them feel the excitement, the danger, as if they were there. Dent is so good at the details, he could probably write his own damn autobiography."

"Why don't you suggest it? Solve your problems all the way around."

"Not exactly. I'd be out of a job. And I don't have the savings account to take a sabbatical to write a novel. I need this job. Obviously. It's the perfect setup for me right now. All I'm saying is it wouldn't hurt for him to hear your point of view on this."

"Are you suggesting he respects me more than you? Because I'm not entirely certain of that."

She just snorted.

"I'm serious. Were you not paying attention when he escorted you in to dinner the other night? He looked like a man completely besotted."

"Right. Please."

"Okay, maybe besotted is too strong. Charmed, for sure. In fact, I was a little jealous."

She was surprised by the comment. "You? Jealous of a man showing me attention? Why on earth would you be jealous?"

"Jealous that you'd so easily staked your claim. I'd come downstairs early in the hopes of getting some time with Dent first, and then the two of you waltz in, all laughing and chummy."

She felt like an idiot. Of course it was professional jealousy. Noah Morrissey was incapable of feeling any other kind. At least that was the sop she fed her ego. "Well, after today, you must be feeling much, much better. You and Dent had your manly bonding moment." *While I puked my guts up ten seconds after my feet were safely back on earth.* So much for any chance with the hot Aussie instructor. Somehow she doubted he appreciated her not at least waiting until they'd unhooked harnesses before getting sick. Yeah, that was a surefire way to make a man want you. Barf all over his shoes.

Noah tugged a little on her arm, making her look at him. "You know what I think? I think you can do this, crazy stunts and all. You wanted it badly enough to jump out of that plane today."

She was surprised once again, and it must have shown on her face.

"What?" he said with a short laugh. "You think I'm that big of a bastard that my saying something nice strikes you so odd?"

She shook her head. "Not that. I just . . . well, for the short time we were together, you used to tease me about my work, about my phobias, about, well, everything."

"Affectionately rib a little. There is a difference."

"Right." She tugged at her arm; he held on tight.

He actually looked a bit offended. "It was affectionate. I wasn't picking on you."

"Please. I might have been stupid enough to think you actually felt something for me, or at the very least respected me enough to say good-bye—which you made clear wasn't the case when you took off without so much as a Post-it note. But it was clear that you didn't really respect my work."

"Then why the hell were you with me?"

"The sex was great," she shot back, which was absolutely the truth. And not even close to the whole story. But she'd be damned if she'd give him that.

"So if I was just a good lay, then why all this pent up anger?"

"Meaning since I was obviously the same for you, I should just shrug off the fact that you disappeared off the face of the earth and just thank my lucky stars I had it good while it lasted? I should just shrug off your complete and utter selfishness and pretend like that was okay? Because you know what, Noah, even people having casual sex—though I think you'll at least agree there was nothing casual about the way we had sex—are decent enough to say good-bye when they're no longer interested in continuing."

She yanked her arm free then, and before he could say anything, she strode to the bathroom door. She really, really, didn't want to hear him confirm that was all she'd been to him. She knew it, of course, but she didn't need to hear him say it. "I'm taking a shower. I'll see you downstairs later for dinner. You know the way out." She glanced over her shoulder. "After all, you've never had a problem with leaving."

EIGHT

NOAH stood there and watched her close the door. Heard the lock click into place. And wished she hadn't been right.

He was good at leaving. Too good, probably. What he sucked at was saying good-bye, so he avoided it whenever possible. Besides, his rationale was that he always kept things light, kept the relationship as physical as possible, and then when it was time to go . . . he went. At best, the woman in question would be relieved, not wanting a serious relationship either, and maybe have a few fond memories to store away. At worst she'd be pissed, which meant she'd gotten emotionally involved, and then it was just as well she was angry, right? An angry woman wasn't a clingy, needy, chase-after-him woman.

At the moment, however, staring at the closed door between him and Bailey, he wasn't going through his usual pattern, which was either being thankful she'd fallen into the angry-woman-scorned category—clean break, no future messiness—or contemplating renewing old ties, which meant picturing her naked beneath the multiple, drenching rain shower heads and working on just how hard it was going to be to talk his way in there. Okay, so maybe he was picturing that last part just a little. But mostly he was thinking about what she'd said.

And the realization that although she fell squarely into the first category of past girlfriends . . . he wasn't all that willing to leave her there.

"I need my head examined," he muttered and then finally turned to leave. Talking his way back into Bailey's good graces, or her bed, was the last thing either of them needed. Because the truth was, he might be experiencing a momentary twinge of conscience, but he knew himself pretty well. It wouldn't last. He'd already pissed her off once; better to leave her ill opinion of him intact rather than reinforce it by encouraging history to repeat itself.

As he turned to leave the room, his gaze fell on her closed laptop and the spiral notebook and stuffed three-ring binder stacked on top of it. He knew he had absolutely no business whatsoever poking through her things, but he was nothing if not a curious bastard—and hell, she'd already condemned him and thrown away the key, so what did he have to lose? He had no intentions of doing more than glancing at her notes, her preliminary research, which is what that had to be, considering they'd barely begun working directly with Dent. He was just curious, that was all. No harm, no foul.

He flipped open the spiral notebook and skimmed over the page of scrawled notes. His lips quirked at the corners. Her handwriting was worse than his, and that was saying something. He couldn't really make anything out except—"Who the hell is Daisy?" He mentally reviewed his own research, but he already knew that no woman named Daisy figured anywhere into Dent's life. Unless Bailey knew something he didn't. He flipped the first page over and immediately zeroed in on another name: Trent. "What the hell?" Then he laughed as he realized what he'd stumbled on. These weren't Bailey's notes on Dent; these were her notes on her great American novel. "Daisy and Trent, huh?" he murmured. So much for making a great literary statement. Sounded more like she was writing for another soap opera.

He flipped through a few more pages, but the notes were truly illegible and probably only meant something to Bailey anyway. Character details or plot points. He flipped the notebook shut, smiling and shaking his head. He turned to go, and his sleeve caught on the spiral binding and pulled both the notebook and the binder to the floor, scattering pages across the rug. "Shit."

He knelt and scooped the papers into a pile, praying Bailey didn't pop out of the bathroom until he got everything back in order. "Yeah, right." She wasn't the most organized woman in the world. He knew, he'd been in her apartment. Clutter was the order of the day.

She wasn't a slob or anything, but she did have a lot of stuff. Brightly colored, overstuffed furniture had been squeezed into her little walk-up, all of it in different patterns. Plants were everywhere—hanging, sitting, stalking, taking over. Bookshelves were crammed into corners and wedged between furniture, all full to bursting. And knick knacks, God but the woman loved her dust-catchers. Any available surface had some kind of kitschy collection on it. Bailey was apparently biologically incapable of passing up a flea market.

So she probably wouldn't notice if the pages he was stuffing back into the binder weren't precisely in the same order they'd been. They looked like a lot of print-outs from websites—probably research or something. When he went to tuck the pages into the inside front cover pocket, he noticed that the pages clamped into the rings of the binder were different. Typed, double-spaced, these didn't look like notes so much as a . . . "Manuscript." He grinned. "Ah, the adventures of Daisy and Trent, no doubt." He shouldn't read it. The pages were all marked with red pen, notes jotted in margins, lines slashed out. It was obviously an early rough draft. But there was that curiosity thing again. And scanning a page or two wouldn't hurt anything. It wasn't like he was reading her private journal or diary. Even he would draw the line there. Probably.

Forty-five minutes later he was roused from his deep engrossment in the lives of Daisy and Trent when Bailey came back into the bedroom and found him leaning back against the side of her bed, legs bent, the binder open across his lap.

"What in the hell do you think you're doing? And why do you keep making me ask that?"

He'd been startled, but he kept his composure. In fact, he didn't even look up. "Reading. Do you mind?"

She snorted in disbelief. It should have been very unbecoming. It wasn't. Yet another reason not to look up and take in the rest of what he could already see in his peripheral vision. Given that his emotions were all over the place at the moment, thanks in large part to the creative talents of the woman standing over him, once again in nothing more than a towel and damp skin, it would be really unwise of him to give her even a shred more of an edge at the moment. Even if she wasn't aware she had the edge in the first place. Defense was always his best offense. "Why haven't you put more time into this?"

He knew she was all set to let loose on him with a tirade about him invading her privacy and worse, just as he knew his question was calculated to derail that tirade, or at least postpone it a little. But it wasn't until he'd put it out there that he realized he really wanted to know the answer.

"None of your damn business," she shot back. "Give that to me."

Okay, so much for derailing the tirade. He marked his place in the manuscript and looked up at her. "I'd tell you I'm sorry I snooped, but at the moment, that would be a lie. When I saw your stack of notebooks, I didn't intend to do more than glance at your notes." He shrugged and tried for a guileless smile. She didn't appear to buy it any-more than he did. "I'm curious by nature, what can I say?"

"You're completely incorrigible by nature, and you have absolutely no shame."

"That, too," he easily agreed. "But it gets me where I want to be."

She just huffed with increased impatience. It really shouldn't turn him on like that. But it did.

"I can't imagine why any of my research on Dent would be of interest to you. I imagine you have ten times the notes I do. You're a seasoned biographer, and you already have a clear idea of how you want to approach your documentary." She clutched her towel more tightly and a wary, somewhat vulnerable look flashed across her face. "Or were you simply amusing yourself at my expense?"

He shook his head, knowing this was no time tease her, affectionately or otherwise. He'd definitely done the wrong thing by leaving her the way he did, but he wasn't bastard enough to poke at her where she was most vulnerable. "I was curious. In the simplest form, that was my sole motivation for opening that first notebook. I thought it was your notes on Dent. I was curious what approach you were going to take, nothing more." What he didn't add was that he now realized it wasn't Bailey's approach to telling Dent's story that had intrigued him—it was the woman herself. "I had no idea it was your novel in progress."

"But when you figured that out, you didn't exactly put it away."

His smile shifted to a genuine one. "What can I say? You had me on page one. I wasn't even aware of how lost in it I was until you walked in here just now. You're a gifted storyteller, Bailey."

She opened her mouth but then shut it again, apparently that taken aback by his praise.

"Is it that leaving you like I did was so bad you can't believe I'm capable of being sincere? Or is it that leaving you like I did was so bad you can't trust me enough to believe I could be sincere?"

He didn't realize how important her answer was until he'd put the question out there. And for the first time he truly questioned his actions in regard to relationships. Of course he knew it would have been more politically correct to go through the whole painful good-bye process, but he'd done that a few times and no one really seemed to prosper in that situation. The idea it provided some kind of closure was a myth.

But sitting here now, staring at Bailey and those wounded eyes of hers, he was confronted with the thought that maybe his actions when ending a relationship hadn't been so altruistic after all. Maybe it was more self-serving . . . and worse.

"Why didn't you say good-bye to me, Noah?" she asked quietly. "Explain that to me and then maybe I'll be able to give you your answer."

A dozen different throwaway comments rushed right to the tip of his tongue, automatic and easy because that's how he'd normally have handled such a situation. She was demanding more than that. And maybe it was time he demanded more from himself, too. "I hate saying good-bye." It was a simple answer, but it was as honest as he could be.

"You didn't seem to hate leaving, so why should going through that motion be so hard?"

He let his head tilt back on the bed. "You know, that's a good question. I guess the psychobabble answer would be to blame it on my childhood. I moved around a lot growing up, Army brat. Saw a lot of the world. But it meant constantly making friends and constantly—"

"Saying good-bye."

He didn't look at her. There wasn't any pity in her voice, but it was soft with understanding. And he didn't really deserve softness from her. "It got old," he said, hardening his tone a little. It wouldn't serve either of them to pretend like things could be different between them. "So I stopped doing it."

"How nice for you," she said dryly.

He smiled a little at that. "Most of the time, it doesn't seem to be a problem."

"I find that hard to believe, but then how would you know, because you're already gone?"

She had a point. "I guess I typically date women who don't mind the easy-come-easy-go type."

She let out a little laugh, and he rolled his head a bit so he could look at her. Big mistake. Her eyes were dancing a little, even as she quashed the smile. "What?"

"Nothing," she said. "Bad pun averted."

He thought back over what he'd said and then grinned. "Yeah. Good call." He kept staring at her, and both of their expressions softened.

"So," she said at length, suddenly busy adjusting the fit of her towel. "Is that how you saw me?"

"No," he answered, instantly and honestly. He owed her that much. "You were different." Yes, Bailey had definitely been different from the norm. Far from the more cosmopolitan, self-absorbed women he dated, she had this kind of vulnerability about her that would normally send him running in the opposite direction. Needy women were dangerous, and he was definitely no white knight.

And yet, he realized, he had deluded himself into thinking he could be hers. At least for a while. Maybe it was because she was so self-deprecating and accepting of her flaws that it had simply been amusing to him to cast himself in that role. Looking at her now, he had to face up to the lies he'd told himself . . . and the reality that maybe, just maybe, all his preconceived ideas about the negatives associated with forming long-term relationships were wrong. Very wrong.

But how in the hell could he tell her that now? She'd laugh in his face. And he'd deserve it and then some. He looked away, and his gaze fell to the manuscript in his lap. Better to stick with what he did know how to finish. "This really is good, Bailey."

He could see she was torn between feeling flattered by his praise . . . and the need to yank her baby out of his hands and toss him out of her room. She didn't trust him with something that was so precious to her. And God knows, she had every right to feel that way. She'd trusted him with something far more precious six months ago, and look what he'd done with that.

"You say that like you're surprised," she said, voice harder, walls firmly back in place.

"I guess I am," he confessed. "But in a good way."

She snorted. "Right. Thanks for proving I was right all along."

"About?"

"That you never respected what I did for a living. In your lofty estimation, writing for soaps was, at best, merely a way to earn a paycheck while I pursued the more worthy goal of writing a novel. And obviously, you didn't really believe a soap hack had it in her to write anything of substance." She glanced at the manuscript in his lap with a look that bordered on desperation. Regardless of his praise, it was clear she hated that he had access to her work like this. To another piece of her.

His grip tightened instinctively on the pages. It was the only part of her he could still hold on to. "I know you have a very low opinion of me, and I realize it might be well deserved." He ignored her arched brow at his use of the word *might* and pushed on. "But I never believed that. I never once said anything like that to you. I wouldn't have. I'd be quite the hypocrite then, wouldn't I? A guy who writes action-adventure scripts for a living?"

"Which," she pointed out, "you do mainly to support your more 'worthy' projects."

"Boy, I really did a fine job of screwing this up, didn't I?" He said it more to himself than her. "Is that what you think of me? That in addition to being a rat bastard who doesn't say good-bye, that I'm also some kind of film or literary snob? It's a wonder you ever agreed to that first date. Much less the second."

"Even snobs can be great in bed."

He ducked his chin. They both knew that only one of them had been in it for the sex. And it hadn't been Bailey. But he let her have her pride. "Point taken. But I'm not a snob."

She shrugged. "How would I know? You never gave me any access to those parts of you."

He looked up. "That's crazy. We talked shop all the time."

"You talked about the big-budget script you were working on, about how it was going to fund your next documentary, and it was clear you assumed I felt the same about my work as staff soap hack, that it was just a means to an end. You never once talked to me about the work that was really important to you."

"First off, you're wrong. The action-adventure screenplays are important to me, and not just as a means of income. Sure, I get more passionate about my documentary work, but both are important to me, just in very different ways."

"Again, how would I know? You kept things between us pretty superficial. Well, physical anyway." She lifted a hand when he went to argue. "I'm not casting blame. It wasn't like I put up a huge fight." She paused for a moment and then apparently decided against finishing.

"What?" he asked. "What were you about to say?" He smiled briefly. "Might as well at this point."

She looked at him, really looked at him, and then sank down on the side of the bed and sighed. "I didn't push to get more from you, because I guess I thought we'd have more time. Time to get to those parts. You know, once the heat finally dialed down a little." Now she smiled briefly, a little wistful, a lot resigned.

He didn't know which part made him feel worse. "I'm sorry," he said, never more sincere. Her wary look of surprise didn't do much to boost his self-esteem.

"For?"

"The way I treated you. The way I left." He lifted a shoulder and then scooted up so he could sit next to her on the bed. She didn't look at him at first, so he bumped her shoulder gently with his, sent her a sideways smile, and bumped her shoulder again until she cracked a smile of her own.

"What?" she asked, a delightful shade of pink creeping across her cheeks.

"I am sorry, Bailey."

Her smile faltered, and she looked at him more directly. "I am, too."

"You deserved better. Still do."

The moment between them grew, the tension spiked. It took remarkable willpower to keep from closing the distance between their lips and kissing her. But if he was truly going to take something from all this, learn something about himself and be a better man in the future, the future had to start now.

He broke eye contact first and motioned to the manuscript in his lap. "This is good work. I'm not denigrating the work you do for the soaps. I understand that need, that outlet, better than you think I do. And I'm not talking about money here, you know that. But this is good stuff. You're passionate about this, and it shows in every line."

"Thank you," she said quietly. "That . . . well, that means a lot to me."

"Thank you," he said, and meant it. "Although I don't know why my opinion should matter to you," he added dryly. "I certainly don't deserve that much credit where you're concerned. But I'm glad you got this job with Dent so you can get the time and financial peace of mind to finish this." He tapped the pages. "I bet it'll sell whether you have the Dent biography publishing credit or not."

Her lips quirked. It was clear he was making her uncomfortable with his sincerity and praise, and it didn't surprise him that she would deflect it with humor. It was one of the things that had drawn him to her that night they'd first met at that Screen Actor's Guild Awards after-party.

He'd heard her laugh, wandered through the throngs until he found her, listened to her for a while, and knew damn well she wasn't his type, as she was way too sincere, too down-to-earth. But he'd found himself drawn in anyway. He'd only meant to talk to her, and they had, but he'd quickly shifted to his usual Plan A when it came to socializing with someone he was interested in. He seduced her. Of course she was quite happy to let him, but now he wondered why he'd been so quick to shift gears. Why he hadn't taken her at face value, explored getting to know her in the true sense, the relationship sense.

Well, he knew why. Seduction, keeping things light, that was his comfort zone. She was easy to talk to . . . almost too easy. Before he knew it he'd be lowering walls, getting emotionally involved. When he'd left her bed the following morning, he'd had no intentions of seeing her again. But he had. They'd had several months of one-night stands. At least that's how he kept trying to think of them. When the big-budget film he'd been working on at the time called him to the set to do some rewrites, he'd used it as his escape hatch.

Looking at her now . . . he wondered just how big a mistake that had been. Perhaps one he'd regret the rest of his life.

"If you want out of this deal with Dent, and financing is an issue, well—just tell me. I'll help you out however I can."

She laughed.

"What?" he said.

"Noah Morrissey, sensitive, caring male?"

He laughed then, too. "Yeah, I know. The idea is laughable, isn't it? But, ah . . ." Now it was his turn to let the words trail away.

"What?"

When he didn't respond right away, she bumped his shoulder and sent him a sideways smile. "What have you got to lose?"

He was beginning to wonder about that. Of course, he'd already lost her, but—He shook that thought right out of his head. He'd help her; he owed her that much and besides, he just wanted to. But he'd be damned if he'd risk hurting her again. She nudged him again and he sighed. "You make me wish I was a better person, Bailey." When she laughed, he wasn't surprised, but this time he grew more serious, suddenly wanting, needing, to make her understand. "I mean I want to help you. Not to be confused with saving you," he added with a little smile, enjoying her quick roll of the eyes. "I know I screwed up with you. Badly. Even when I was there, I wasn't there in the ways I should have been. And I know you don't trust me, and you have every right not to. I suck at relationships, of which you have clear proof. But I'm a good supporter of things I believe in. And I believe in this," he said, squeezing her manuscript. "And I believe in you. So in whatever way I can be there to help with this, I'm offering to help."

She surprised him with a knowing smile. Gripping her towel with one hand, she finally took the manuscript away from him with the other.

He reluctantly let it go. He wanted to finish it, but he knew someday he would get the chance. He'd be able to walk into any bookstore and buy his very own copy.

"You know what the biggest shame is?" she asked him.

"What?"

"If you absolutely believe in your capacity to support something you believe in—"

"I do."

"Then why don't you believe in having a real relationship? Support that?"

Nailed. "Good question. Maybe I don't know how."

"How did you learn to write screenplays? How did you learn to write, direct, and produce documentaries?" She didn't let him answer. "You just did, because you wanted to. If you want something badly enough, Noah, you just figure it out. You, of all people, know that."

"Maybe I've never wanted that badly enough."

"Then that's a real shame." She shook her head, got off the bed, and then went to her dresser and stacked her manuscript on top of her other binders. "I need to dress for dinner. I can handle Franklin. But I appreciate the offer."

He was being dismissed. A part of him was relieved that she was letting him off the hook. The surprising thing, as he got up and left the room . . . was how small a part of him that was.

NINE

"BOTSWANA?" That was it, she wasn't drinking any more wine with dinner. At this rate, Franklin's casual announcements were going to be the death of her. And his pristine white linen tablecloth wouldn't fare too well either. With exaggerated care, she set down her wine glass and looked across the dinner table. Considering the day's events, it took considerable willpower to form even the barest sincere smile, but she gave it her best effort. It wasn't like Franklin could see her nails digging into her thighs or hear her stomach slowly turning to lead. "As in, the one in South Africa?"

"Why, of course. Is there another?" He laughed and then leaned back and favored both of his guests with a broad smile. "I have to go to Kenya on business, and I thought it would be the perfect opportunity to share with you both another passion of mine." He was all but vibrating with intensity. It was a wonder the table didn't shake with the force of it.

"What would that be?"

"Big game hunting!" he proclaimed, clapping his hands together.

Bailey felt an instant desire to throw up. Dear God. When he'd said Africa, she'd thought it would be a trip intended to give them some insight into one of his many philanthropic ventures. She'd barely had time to envision herself in full khakis and cute leather hiking boots, trekking out into the African bush, visiting small tribal villages where she would embrace small children and see firsthand how his financial help had brought them water or education or something equally fulfilling.

But no. No, no. They were going to go out into the bush country all right, but it was so they could get up close and personal with very large wild animals. The kind that would look at her in her cute hiking boots and think, *Scooby snack*. Then the rest of what he'd said sunk in and her throat closed over. "Um," she started and then cleared her throat when all that came out was a small squeak.

"Yes, dear?" Franklin asked, using the term of endearment as only a man from his generation still could and get away with it without it seeming like it was a form of sexual harassment.

It still made her grit her teeth. Hopefully he'd take that as a smile.

"You do have your passport?" he asked, frowning slightly. "I'm certain you were told—"

"Yes, I brought it with me." As instructed by his assistants well beforehand—which had been a good thing, as she'd had to apply for one. She remembered standing in the post office, daydreaming about flying off to London for the opening of a new play, or going to one of the many charitable galas Franklin so often attended. Somehow not one of those daydreams involved her pointing a big rifle at exotic creatures with large fangs and questionable endangered status.

"You said hunting," she began, pasting a hopeful, upbeat, look-at-me-I'm-such-a-good-sport-I-leaped-from-a-plane-for-you smile. "In Africa, the animals are all on preserves or something, right? To protect them? So when you say hunting, you mean like a safari, where you ride around and take pictures of the animals. Right?"

He favored her with a look that people reserve for the adored, but somewhat dotty members of the family. "Much of the area is secured with reserves and the like, yes, but big game hunting is still an economy boon. I have many friends there with private property. Don't worry—it's fully legal where we'll be hunting."

Ah, the perks of being filthy rich. You could kill all the animals you wanted if you had enough money. Lucky her.

"Of course, feel free to bring your camera. You'll want a record of your first trophy kill. And Noah will be capturing it all on film as well." He turned to Noah, who had been quieter than usual during dinner. "Don't worry, though, we'll make certain you get your go at a big one."

Noah smiled briefly but didn't do more than nod.

Bailey had kept her attention on Franklin during dinner and off of Noah. She wasn't entirely sure what had happened back in her room earlier, but he'd obviously not been himself. She wondered how he felt about shooting animals. Of course, he had the handy excuse of being behind the camera. It wouldn't be as hard for him to bow out of this particular activity. Lucky him.

But whatever he might be thinking, he wasn't sharing it. He was being all enigmatic and removed. Not that she'd expected him to leap to her defense after she'd all but told him to back off and let her handle things herself. But sitting here now, she wondered why she'd been so hasty to reject his offer.

No, no, she couldn't go there again. The minute she let herself even think about giving him so much as a toehold in her life, she was just asking for trouble. She didn't need to get tangled up with Noah Morrissey again. What she needed was a way to handle Franklin Dent, to make him see her side of things. Noah would see she didn't need him or anybody running interference for her.

"We'll have a grand time," Franklin was saying, still favoring her with that same affectionate I-know-you'll-like-this-even-if-you-don't smile.

Right. Like he'd known what was best for her earlier today. Not. As far as Bailey was concerned, she'd have to be dotty and then some to even consider going on this trip. She'd never so much as touched a gun! Mostly because, you know, they could kill someone. The only way she could ever bring herself to shoot anything was if it was going to shoot her first. And even then she'd have to let someone else deal with the aftermath. No way was she even going to look at something she'd just been forced to shoot, much less pose for photographs with the grisly thing. She'd be too busy hyperventilating or throwing up.

Of all the things she'd prepared herself for Franklin to throw at them, she could have guessed all day and into next week and not come up with anything this bad. She'd really been praying that after the plane jump, he'd surely pick something completely different, something glamorous and fun, to juxtapose against the adrenaline junkie side of him. A fashion show opening would have been nice. In Paris. Or Monaco. She wasn't picky. Really.

And if either Franklin or Noah thought she was okay with riding along and watching them shoot poor, defenseless animals in their own backyard, they were so very, very wrong. All she had to do was find a way to explain her position to Franklin without jeopardizing her job.

It took more willpower than it should have to keep from looking over at Noah. Why she thought she'd be able to draw strength and support from that corner she had no idea. And yet, something about his steady demeanor, his strength of conviction about things—even the things she didn't like—still called to her. He might not always handle things the way she'd have liked, but at least he was consistent. And therefore, in some wacky way, reliable. Which only proved she was a total idiot.

He was probably sitting there quite smug and amused, waiting to see how she'd pull this off. He knew she was a giant marshmallow. She'd been known to tear up over a marginally poignant television commercial. No way was she going to hunt down lions and tigers and bears, oh my . . . and then shoot at them. And considering her aptitude for being a klutz, she'd just as likely shoot one of them by accident.

Wait!

She sat up a little straighter and folded her hands on the edge of the table. So what if her nails were still making tiny indentations on the backs of her knuckles? "Franklin, I think this sounds like an amazing trip, but you need to know, I'm somewhat of a klutz." She tried for one of those self-deprecating quasi-ditzy laughs. "You probably shouldn't entrust me with a firearm. No one would be safe." She smiled as sincerely as she was able. "In fact, if we can find some time to sit down and go over my outline, I could start framing out the book while you and Noah—"

"We'll have plenty of time to talk on the flight over. We're taking my private jet, so you'll be quite comfortable. And don't worry, dear, I'll personally oversee your handling of the firearms. You'll be quite the marksman by the time we're through—trust me." He shoved his chair back and stood. "Now, I have some business to attend to that will tie me up the rest of the evening. Please enjoy dessert, which will be out shortly."

He smiled at them both, and if Bailey wasn't mistaken, it appeared to be a bit of a knowing one. What, did he honestly think she and Noah had resumed their previous relationship or something? Even more disconcerting was the realization that if he did, the idea seemed to amuse more than upset him.

"I'll see you both in the morning, first thing," he said, clasping his hands together. "We'll go over the itinerary at breakfast. Seven sharp. We depart at eight." His smile widened, and there was no mistaking now what he was assuming as he looked at them both. "Enjoy your evening." Then he left.

Silence fell as Bailey's face heated in abject embarrassment. She'd been nothing but the consummate professional, dammit. At least around Franklin, anyway. Okay, so maybe that scream she'd let out earlier today hadn't exactly shown her as calm, cool, and poised. But as she'd been plummeting toward certain death at the time, honestly, he really couldn't hold that against her. So it was annoying, not to mention frustrating, seeing as she'd done such a good job of keeping Noah at arm's length—he was the only one crossing boundaries here, not her!—to have it assumed she couldn't be under the same roof with the man for more than twenty-four hours without leaping back into bed with him. That Franklin seemed to get some kind of kick out of that just made it that much more mortifying.

One of the house servants came in bearing a silver tray with a huge tureen and serving spoon. He sat it between them, arranged new dishes and silverware in front of them, and then left as quietly as he'd arrived. The silence continued for another excruciating minute, but neither made a move to serve themselves any dessert. Bailey wondered if he'd picked up on Franklin's obvious assumption about the two of them.

"So," Noah began, "that went well."

"If you're referring to my talking Franklin out of me shooting anything, don't be so quick to be smug. I've got him right where I want him."

His mouth quirked. "Oh yeah, I could tell."

"Besides," she went on, determined not to let him get to her. Again. "Franklin does makes a good point about the flight over providing a great opportunity to work. We haven't even started work on the book. The man doesn't sit still long enough to talk for any productive length of time. It's like pinning down a dragonfly." She scowled when he merely smiled. "Just because I'm flying out there with you all doesn't mean I'm going to shoot anything. I'll have plenty to keep me busy while you two are out playing Great White Hunter together. You should be thrilled. I won't be around to get in your way or ruin the whole thing by inadvertently killing the driver or something."

"The only thing I'll be shooting with is my camera," Noah told her. "And I imagine Dent is not going to want to hunt by himself."

"He'll have to find someone else to buddy up with then. I'm not going along on that part of the trip."

Noah's smile grew. "Sort of like you didn't jump out of a plane today?"

She had an instant flashback, which was accompanied by an instinctive full-body shudder that made her tummy reconsider whether eating dinner was really a good thing.

To her surprise, rather than razz her further, Noah looked immediately contrite. "I'm sorry. That was out of line. You know, what you did today, considering your fear, was either the bravest thing or the stupidest thing I've ever seen."

"Gee. Thanks."

"It's just, your heart really isn't in this biography project, not the way it might need to be anyway. I know it's a fascinating challenge and you think it's going to help you get published on your own, but you don't need this to succeed in becoming published. Just finish the damn book."

She immediately leaped to her own defense, partly motivated by the fact that he'd just voiced her biggest fear. That her heart really wasn't in this project. That she was mostly here for what this project could do for her. "This is the opportunity of a lifetime. I have free room and board in an amazing mansion, with plenty of time to work on finishing my book while someone pays me to do it. Having this publishing credit will definitely give me more credibility than my writing career thus far. I don't see the downside or why you're questioning my commitment. I am certainly capable of—"

"I know you can write. I was absorbed into your book before I even realized you'd hooked me. And trust me, as a fellow storyteller who spends more time analyzing the workings of the puppet strings when he reads than enjoying the puppetshow itself, that's a huge compliment. At least for whatever that's worth from me. I'm not questioning your talent."

"Then what are you questioning exactly?"

He sighed and leaned back. "Hell if I know. You're going to do whatever you want anyway. And if you only occasionally have to leap out of airplanes and shoot wild elephants, that's just the price you pay for success, right?"

Bailey lifted her hands in the air, completely at a loss to figure out what in God's name was wrong with him. "Why do you really care about any of this? Why do you care what I do or don't do?"

He opened his mouth to retort but then shut it again.

She leaned forward to take the lid off the tureen. But when she caught his contemplative expression, she paused and grew wary. He definitely wasn't being himself. "What?" Stupid to egg him on, really. A quiet Noah was certainly better for her, but she couldn't seem to help herself.

His smile this time was a bit more wistful, and entirely unlike any smile she'd seen from him before. "I don't know why." He pushed back from the table and stood. "But for some reason, Bailey Madison, I do care. I really do."

This time around he got the exiting line. Without waiting for a response, he turned and walked out, leaving her to face a bucket-size serving of strawberry compote. And a whole lot of questions she wasn't sure she wanted the answers to.

TEN

SHE looked cute in khaki, he'd give her that. But despite the way her shorts hugged a backside he'd been paying far too much attention to since they'd taken off into the bush this morning, his focus at the moment was on the very big hunting rifle Dent was presently showing her how to use. He hoped to God everyone realized their lives were in sudden, most definite jeopardy.

He was in a second open-topped Range Rover, trundling along behind Bailey and Dent. He had all his gear, a guide, and two additional men to help him set up shots if and when necessary. He should have been thrilled with the day's adventure. It was the perfect weather, the perfect light, the perfect combination of things he loved. Filming a documentary, while living like a character in one of his action-adventure screenplays. It really didn't get any better than this.

Or it wouldn't have if he could have kept his attention on his job and away from Bailey's tense face.

He casually zoomed in with his handheld digital movie camera, intending to stop when he'd framed Dent, with Bailey merely a secondary subject. Instead, once again, he kept zooming until he was focused in on her face. She was biting her bottom lip, something he'd come to realize she did when she wasn't thrilled with her current situation but wasn't going to say anything about it.

She had no business being out here, and not just because she could possibly take out half his camera crew at any moment. She was just so clearly uncomfortable with their stated purpose for being here. He'd waited for her to make her plea, to take her stance, to tell Dent in no uncertain terms that she simply was not going on the safari with them. Perhaps there had been a conversation between the two of them he hadn't witnessed, but considering she was presently shouldering the rifle, if there had been a discussion held or stance taken, she'd lost. Miserably, if the look on her face said anything. It certainly spoke volumes to him.

Why didn't she fight harder? he thought, surprised by how angry he was with her. How frustrated he was with himself. It was a battle he knew she couldn't win on her own. *So why won't you just let me help you, dammit?*

And there it was. The moment.

That single moment in a man's life where everything changed. Who knew that, for him, that moment would come while riding across the African bush, watching seasoned guides duck and animals instinctively run for cover as Bailey shouldered her hunting rifle for the first time?

Although, he thought, clutching at his camera gear and the metal frame of the truck as his driver swerved when Bailey swung the gun in their direction as a herd of zebras topped the horizon to their left, it sort of made perfect sense that, in the context of his life, it would happen exactly like this.

"Pull alongside them," he shouted to his driver, who looked at him as if he'd lost his mind. A quick glance at Bailey, who was still trying to find a stable stance that would let her aim the gun and keep her balance, and he understood the man's anxiety. "Fine, fine, stop the truck then."

The driver shrugged and did as he asked.

Noah was off the truck and trotting toward Dent's Range Rover an instant later. "Bailey, stop!" he shouted. She swung around at the sound of his voice, rifle still shouldered.

Everyone in the hunting party hit the dirt; possibly several zebras might have as well. Noah wasn't looking at them, he was looking at Bailey. "Put down the gun. You don't have to do this."

Dent was frowning. Bailey was scowling. "What are you doing, Noah?" she said, lowering the gun. "I'm perfectly capable of—" Just then the gun barrel caught on the tarp spread across the back end of the truck. Bailey squealed, and Dent lunged for the gun. A shot rang out, and for the longest moment in his entire life, everything went silent.

Slowly everyone, including Bailey and Dent, straightened. A quick glance along the horizon showed the only casualty was a limb off of a nearby Jackalberry tree. Noah heaved a sigh of relief and closed the remaining distance to the Rover. "You didn't have to do this." He looked at Dent. "She shouldn't be doing this."

He ignored the subtle nods of relief of the drivers and guides in their party. That wasn't why he was doing this. He looked at Bailey, who was glowering at him, face flaming in embarrassment. Not exactly how he'd imagined this moment in his life going, but then with Bailey involved, and for that matter himself, why he thought it would be normal, he had no idea.

"I wasn't going to pull the trigger, Noah. I had a plan." She looked at Dent. "I'm sorry, Franklin. I can't kill a fly, much less any one of these beautiful creatures." She looked back at Noah. "I had it worked out. I just wasn't going to shoot."

He stopped next to the truck and looked up at her. "What were you going to do when he shot something?"

She flinched.

"Exactly."

"I would have figured something out," she muttered. "I don't need a keeper, Noah."

Again, he ignored the skeptical looks of the crew around them, all of whom were watching this little tableau unfold with unadulterated interest. He was going to make a complete fool out of himself anyway. He already knew that. So he didn't really care who watched. "No, you're right, you don't. But you do need someone to stand beside you, to help out when help is needed."

"And you're applying for the job?" It was clear from her incredulous expression what she thought of his qualifications.

All eyes swung toward Noah as he moved even closer, until he was less than a foot from her. "I know you don't have any reason to trust me. But I would have helped. You could have asked me."

"You're right, I don't have any reason to trust you. I'm better off taking care of myself. At least if I get it wrong, I'll only be disappointed in me."

His chest constricted a little at the wounded defiance in her eyes. "I know I hurt you. I shouldn't have left like I did. If I could go back and change things—"

"It doesn't matter. I know you're sorry you didn't handle it right, but you've already apologized and I've accepted. Move on. I have."

"Have you?"

She opened her mouth but then shut it again.

He felt the rapt attention of everyone with them drilling into his back.

"Even if I wanted to, Noah, I couldn't risk my heart again. Not to you."

His heart lifted, even as it constricted in pain. "Could it be at risk, Bailey? With me?" He should have been terrified, talking about stuff like this. And he was, but in an exhilarated, adventure-of-a-lifetime kind of way. He leaned against the truck and looked up so their gazes locked. "Because mine most definitely is. It might have taken me longer to figure out what the hell that ache was in the middle of my chest, and I might have screwed up any possibility I had to get a second chance to get it right, but I'm asking anyway. Is there a chance?"

She stared at him for the longest time. "Maybe," she said, the word barely more than a hushed whisper.

The pain eased, and his heart began to swell with hope. His lips curved. "You know, I thought we had nothing important in common, but I was so wrong. We both celebrate the fun side of life, you with your over-the-top soap plots and me with my equally over-the-top adventure ones. We both also celebrate the emotional side of life. Me with my documentaries, you with your heartfelt exploration of the human heart."

There was a collective sigh around them, but he didn't break eye contact with Bailey. His whole life was on the line here.

"We couldn't be any more well suited for one another."

"Except for one thing," she said. "You don't stay."

"I never had a reason to before."

"Noah—"

"I am bad at good-byes, Bailey. But when I said earlier that I wished I could go back and change things, it wasn't so I could say good-bye. It was so I wasn't stupid enough to leave in the first place." He lifted his arms to her and waited for what felt like ten centuries before she finally bent and let him swing her down from the truck. It should have come as no shock to anyone when the toe of her hiking boot caught on the edge of the seat, sending her pitching forward at the last second. Her arms flailed, he grabbed her hips, and they both ended up sprawled in a huge tire track rut.

Cheers and hoots rang out as the dust settled. Bailey blushed and laughed but made no effort to get up. Noah pushed her hair from her face and then noted there was still something unsettling in her eyes.

"I know I won't earn your trust back overnight," he told her quietly. "Just give me a chance. That's all I'm asking for."

She smiled then. "You've got your chance."

And Noah finally got to do what he'd been dying to do since she'd gone ass-backward into the gutter in front of Dent's mansion. He kissed Bailey Madison. Only this time he wasn't promising something as empty as a week or two of hot sex. This was the promise of a lifetime.

The crew started clapping and whistling and then when he finally lifted his head, they reached in to help them up and brush themselves off. Noah took Bailey's hand as soon as he was able and tugged her close before turning to face Dent, who had been silent up to that point. He studied the two of them and then broke into a wide grin and clapped his hands. "Well done, Morrissey. Well done."

"Thank you. But I have to tell you, she's not killing anything today. Or any other day."

Bailey tensed. "Noah—"

He squeezed her hand. "This is where the partnership part kicks in." He looked back to Dent. "And if this isn't negotiable, then this is where our partnership ends, I'm afraid. But let me tell you, you'd be making a grave mistake. There is no one more qualified to tell your life story in film than me." He tugged Bailey closer. "And there is no one who will do a better job of putting your life on paper than Bailey. She doesn't have to experience your life; she just needs to get to know you. Trust me, she's a natural-born storyteller. And you've got a hell of a story to tell. Trust her." He looked at her. "I do."

"Aw, Noah."

He smiled and tugged her closer. "How'm I doin' so far?"

"Pretty damn good."

He glanced up at Dent. "So what's it going to be?"

Dent hopped down from the truck and came to stand before them. "I admire a man of principal, Morrissey. You've earned my respect today." He looked at Bailey. "And I extend my deepest apologies if, in my enthusiasm to immerse you into my world, I've put you between the proverbial rock and hard place." He extended both of his hands, gripping one of each of theirs. His grin returned. "I think we'll make a splendid team."

Bailey squeezed Noah's hand and bumped shoulders with him. "Yeah. Me, too."

Nothing but the Truth

BEVERLY BRANDT

ONE

ON the day Madison Case's divorce became final, she asked the man who had been proclaimed her ex-husband two minutes before when it was that he had stopped loving her.

Jeff had turned and looked at her with his soft brown eyes and said, not unkindly, "To be honest, Maddie, I'm not sure I *ever* loved you."

That was one truth Maddie wished her ex had kept to himself. Nothing like learning your marriage had been one big lie right from the start.

Maddie sighed and pulled three bulging files toward her. She didn't know why she was thinking of Jeff today. Their divorce had now lasted longer than their six-and-a-half-month marriage had.

"Blame it on Valentine's Day," Maddie muttered to herself as she flipped open the top file. Or maybe it was the three proposals she was in charge of organizing this evening. She couldn't stop thinking about how pointless it all seemed, with everyone going through the motions as if there really were such a thing as true love.

Yeah, yeah. She knew that with this attitude, working as the receptionist/girl Friday at Rules of Engagement—a marriage preparatory service that helped potential spouses get their reluctant brides- and grooms-to-be to the altar—was probably not the best fit for her. She was running low on "happily ever after" these days.

Hell, who was she kidding? She came from a long line of losers at love. Her HEA supply had been low to begin with. Still, having her ex-husband admit he'd never loved her had hurt. Being married to a prominent plastic surgeon with his own reality makeover TV show had made her feel special. When he withdrew his love—and his last name—Maddie was back where she'd started from: jobless, single, and alone.

But at least she wasn't living in Podunk, Idaho, anymore.

Maddie allowed herself a half-smile at that. Yeah, she'd take sunny Naples, Florida, over her small, chicken-farming hometown any day. Not that there was anything wrong with chicken farmers. Or farmers of any sort. Or even chickens, although they weren't exactly the cuddly animals Easter commercials and Disney cartoons led one to believe.

It just wasn't the sort of life one dreamed about living.

So when Jeff breezed into town, scouting victims for the next season of *American Model*, and offered to marry her and take her away from it all, Maddie hadn't spent even a second pondering how it was that the wealthy, eligible bachelor had fallen in love with her after only two weeks. After all, she had managed to fall in love with him that quickly. Surely the same must have been true for him. Otherwise, why would he have proposed?

Six months later, Maddie had the answer to that question. Only, it was another hard truth she wished she'd never learned.

Maddie looked up when the sickeningly cheerful bells tied to the front door of Rules of Engagement jangled as the door was pushed open.

"Help!" a woman wailed as she nearly fell inside the carpeted waiting area.

Maddie jumped up from behind her desk, pushing her chair out of the way so she wouldn't trip on it. Her office was set up like a doctor's reception area, with two large sliding windows that opened up so she could talk to clients while sitting behind her desk. She hurried out of her office and into the waiting area, where a size-fourteen woman squeezed into a size-twelve outfit sat panting in one of the blue chairs flanking a low coffee table covered with magazines.

Maddie recognized the woman as Denise Clay, proposee number one in this evening's proposal-fest. Denise's fiancé-to-be, Guy Bromley, planned to swoop into the harbor on his forty-foot sailboat, pluck Denise out of the surf, and slip the ring on her finger while the Channel 2 news team assigned to cover the Valentine's Day Marry-Me Marathon filmed the event.

Denise and Guy had met a year ago down in the Caribbean, where they'd both been cruising with their now-ex-spouses. They'd joined a flotilla heading to Tortuga, swapped partners around Tortola, and then sailed off into the sunset together toward Trinidad and Tobago.

So their engagement-at-sea seemed only fitting.

Denise knew nothing about this, however. She thought tonight's event was nothing more than a costume party arranged by Rules of Engagement in honor of Valentine's Day. There *was* to be a party tonight, but it was the three surprise proposals that were the true highlight of the evening.

Maddie took a deep breath and wondered, not for the first time, why Lillian Bryson, the owner of Rules of Engagement, had trusted the most important part of tonight's festivities to her. Lillian was taking care of the last-minute details at the Gulf-front mansion where the

Rules of Engagement party was being held and had left the proposals in Maddie's care. Maddie only hoped her boss's faith in her was not misplaced.

Nervously smoothing her hands over her short black skirt, Maddie sat down next to Denise.

"What's wrong?" she asked, hoping she could fix whatever it was.

"I'm fat," Denise wailed again, and then covered her face with her hands and began sobbing.

Maddie leaned forward and awkwardly patted the woman's back. She tried to scoot her chair closer, but was hindered by the shopping bags Denise had tossed to the floor when she'd come in. Maddie spied a bright pink bag from Sassy Swimwear and cringed. Nothing could make a woman—even one who wasn't overweight—feel fatter than trying on swimsuits.

Unfortunately, Guy's instructions had been very clear. He'd first spied Denise sunning herself on the deck of a Beneteau 373 wearing nothing but a pair of sunglasses and a bikini. He wanted to re-create that special moment this evening, and it was Maddie's job to convince Denise to show up in a swimsuit, despite the fact that Denise had put on a good twenty pounds in the year since she and Guy had met.

If Denise refused, the mood would be broken and the proposal might be off.

And that would make Rules of Engagement look pretty silly on the evening news.

Maddie couldn't let that happen. She had to do something to make Denise stop crying, and because she wasn't exactly in possession of a magic wand that could instantly melt off unwanted fat, she was going to have to come up with another plan. Too bad she couldn't rush Denise over to her ex-husband's House o' Plastic Surgery for a little last-minute liposuction . . .

"Everyone feels that way after trying on swimsuits," Maddie

soothed. "Besides, you know it doesn't matter. Your life wouldn't be any happier if you suddenly shed ten pounds." That, Maddie knew, was the truth. She'd watched plenty of size two women walk into Jeff's office, as miserable with their bodies as Denise was with hers.

Denise's hiccup was muffled by her hands.

Maddie took this as a positive sign and continued. "I'll bet whatever you picked out is flattering. Would you like to show me? I promise to give you my honest opinion," she said, resisting the urge to cross her fingers behind her back. No way would she tell Denise if she thought her new swimsuit made her look like a beach ball with legs. For one, she wasn't that cruel. But she also couldn't risk Denise refusing to go along with Guy's plans.

Denise sniffled. "You'll really tell me if you think I look fat?" she asked.

Maddie nodded.

After taking a deep breath, Denise leaned over to pick up the bright pink bag. "Okay. I'll be right back," she said, and then disappeared down the hall toward the restroom.

Maddie stifled the urge to groan. Why hadn't Lillian put her in charge of the party? That, she could handle. Florist, caterers, musicians—they were easy. It was the romantically inclined who had Maddie breaking out in hives.

"What do you think?" Denise asked with a tremor in her voice.

Maddie smiled with relief. The one-piece black suit with white piping around the legs and halter-style neck was classy and slimming. She wouldn't have to lie after all. "It looks—" she began, and then paused when Denise turned around. There was something odd about the back of the suit, but Maddie couldn't quite figure out what it was. She tried squinting and turning her head, but still couldn't decide what had caught her eye. The cut itself was fine. It wasn't riding up into Denise's butt crack and did a fair job of jiggle-control as Denise walked toward her.

Still, something wasn't quite right. But because Maddie couldn't put her finger on what it was, she decided to ignore it.

"—great!" she finished, hoping Denise hadn't noticed her hesitation.

"Do you really think so?" Denise asked.

"Yes," Maddie answered, and then forced herself to gush. "It's amazing, like you've magically lost two sizes. Who's the designer? I'm going to have to get one of those for myself." Inwardly, she cringed at the fake enthusiasm in her voice. But what could she do? She needed tonight to be a success and, besides, it was just a little white lie. Who could it possibly hurt?

TWO

MADDIE was on the phone with Fantasy Carriage Rentals making final arrangements for a Cinderellalike coach being pulled by four white horses to be used in the second of this evening's proposals when her new-and-improved sister appeared outside the door to Rules of Engagement.

She sighed, knowing what was coming next.

"Just a sec," she told the woman on the other end of the line as Emily wafted into the office on a cloud of drama and expensive perfume. Before her sister could speak, Maddie held up a hand traffic-cop style and said, "I'll be done in a minute." Then she went back to her call.

"So you're sure the horses will be equipped with those poop-catcher things, right? I mean, nothing kills romance faster than the smell of fresh horse dung." Maddie had never understood the sex appeal of horses. Yeah, they were pretty animals and all that, but what was so romantic about galloping along a sandy beach, holding on to a saddle horn for dear life? And that was only if you could get the stupid horse to stop eating the beach grass and actually move. For whatever reason, horses also seemed to manage to turn a cup of water and an apple into ten pounds of waste. She remembered reading some romance novel once that had the hero and heroine going at it on the back of a horse. After guffawing loudly just thinking about the logistics of sex on a horse (did the author really think the horse would stand still while its riders had screaming, earth-shattering orgasms on its back?), she got a bad case of the giggles from mentally rewriting the book's tagline to read, "Their passion steamed like a fresh pile of dung."

Not exactly what the author had in mind, Maddie guessed.

"Yes, it's all taken care of. Rick Watson is to meet us at seven P.M. a block from the mansion on Gulf Coast Lane, and we'll take it from there," the woman from Fantasy Carriage Rentals assured her.

"And the driver knows to wait for my signal to let him know I'm there with the crew from Channel 2 news, right? We're supposed to get footage of the entire proposal."

"Got it," the woman said.

Maddie felt cheered by the other woman's confidence. Maybe this evening's Marry-Me Marathon wouldn't be the disaster Maddie had predicted it would be in her usual cynical manner. Where matters of the heart were concerned, she wasn't exactly an optimist.

She hung up the phone and turned to her sister, who had flopped her once-chubby body down onto one of the chairs in the reception area and buried her head in her French-manicured hands. Her curly, mousy-brown hair had been straightened and colored a rich chestnut that showcased her exotically shaped emerald eyes. Along with her hair, her breasts, her teeth, her lifted and tightened buttocks, her nipped-in waist, and her eyes weren't original parts, either. Emily had been born with droopy lids and plain old brown eyes, like Maddie. Cosmetic surgery couldn't change the color, of course—tinted contacts did that—but her complete overhaul had lifted her lids and reshaped the opening around her eyes.

The result was stunning. Emily had been transformed from a plain farm girl to a stunning woman over the course of a few painful months—months that had been boiled down into one shocking episode of *American Model*; shocking not just because Maddie hadn't known her sister was being made over for their season finale, but also because she herself had been unwittingly dragged into the drama during that final episode.

Guess that's what happens when the American viewing public is asked to text in their vote as to whether your husband should stay married to you or leave you for your newly beautified sister on national TV.

Maddie swallowed the humiliation she'd thought she'd conquered over the last ten months. Jeff wanted Emily. Emily wanted Jeff. And the American people wanted to see Jeff and Emily together. It was as simple as that.

Looked like their mother was right. Case women were doomed to pick the wrong man. They'd been unlucky in love for as far back as Mom could remember. Why should her daughters fare any better than the rest of the family?

Maddie had learned her lesson, all right. Relationships just made you miserable.

Case in point, her sister, who finally lifted her head and wailed, "My marriage is over!" when she heard Maddie hang up the phone.

Maddie closed her eyes and rubbed the frown lines on her forehead to make them disappear. Then she figured, why bother? As long as Emily was married to Jeff, she was still eligible for his twenty-five percent family discount.

She tried to inject some sympathy into her voice as she went over to comfort her sister, wondering if the gesture was the equivalent of emotional Botox—something that would temporarily smooth out the surface wrinkles without addressing the underlying problem.

"You always think that," she said. "What's wrong this time?"

"Jeff's acting strange. He must have suspected that I was following him this morning, because he shot through a red light at Sunshine Parkway, knowing I'd have to stop. I just spent half an hour searching the parking lots in this area for his car, but I couldn't find it."

"Don't you think it's a little odd that you're tailing your husband like some sort of amateur sleuth?" Maddie asked, finding it difficult not to voice her concern that love had turned her sister into a certifiable kook.

"I tell you, Maddie, he's acting odd lately. He hid his checkbook from me and he's started making calls in his office at home with the door shut. And locked! I checked his pockets the other night while he was in the shower, and do you know what I found?"

Emily didn't wait for Maddie to respond before continuing. "A receipt for lunch at a restaurant here on Sunshine Parkway," she said, as if that somehow proved her husband's guilt in some nefarious crime.

Maddie cleared her throat. "Um, and what does that mean?"

"He never leaves the surgery center at lunchtime," Emily wailed, dropping her head into her perfectly manicured hands again.

"I still don't understand, Em. So Jeff went out to lunch one day. Big deal." Maddie nudged her sister's shoulder with her hip as she sat down on the edge of Emily's chair. Seemed that today was her day to comfort hysterical women.

Maddie anxiously checked her watch and saw that it was almost noon. She really didn't have time for this. She had a million things left to do before the Marry-Me Marathon started at six.

"He's cheating on me. I know he is," Emily said in a voice so low Maddie had to lean down to hear her. "And it's all my fault. I cursed our relationship by flirting with him while he was still married to you,

Mad. It was wrong and I knew it, but I couldn't seem to stop myself. He was so kind to me, explaining all about the procedures he planned to do and warning me about the psychological side effects of the surgery. I couldn't help but fall in love with him. I know should have been stronger. I should have resisted. If I had, things would have worked out the way fate intended and I wouldn't have had to hurt you. This is karma. The pain I caused you is coming back to haunt me. That's why Jeff's cheating on me. Because I created a cosmic imbalance that must be righted."

Maddie sighed. "Look Em, I don't think Jeff's cheating on you. And if he were, it wouldn't be karma; it would be a serious character flaw that causes him to want someone new every six to twelve months. Whichever it is, you need to stop spying on him and confront him with your concerns. This isn't healthy for either one of you."

Emily looked up at her with her fake but beautiful green eyes full of tears. "Did I tell you I found a curious white spot in the passenger seat of his Mercedes the other day?"

Eww. "I guess I should have gotten you a crime scene investigation kit for your birthday," Maddie said, only half in jest. Em's birthday was today and, instead of a fingerprint kit, she'd wangled tickets for tonight's big engagement party out of Lillian for Jeff and Emily. It was just the sort of thing Emily loved—lavish, expensive, and very exclusive.

Emily took her birthdays very seriously. Even as an adult, she wanted big parties and lots of attention. Maddie, on the other hand, would rather get a surprise gift instead of something someone felt obligated to buy because of some arbitrary date on the calendar.

Not that anyone was giving her presents for any reason these days.

Maddie blinked back that self-pitying thought.

"That's another thing," Emily said, bringing Maddie's attention back to her sister. "This is my first birthday since Jeff and I got married. You'd think he would treat the day as something special, right?

Well, he didn't even mention my birthday this morning before he left for work. I think he forgot!"

Maddie winced. She knew how much her sister loved being fawned over on her birthday. She'd have to call Jeff after Em left and be sure he remembered. The least he could do was send some flowers to make the day special. Maddie had arranged for a cheerful bouquet to be delivered later this afternoon, but just getting flowers from her sister wouldn't be enough for Emily.

"I'm sure he didn't forget," Maddie lied. The truth was, she didn't know Jeff well enough to know if this was the type of thing he'd overlook. She hoped not, for her sister's sake. "He's probably just busy today. Aren't Fridays his day to check up on all the surgeries he performed over the past week?"

"Yes," Emily admitted, leaning down to pull a pack of tissues out of her thousand-dollar purse. She sat looking dejectedly at the Kleenex in her hand. "But I think there's more to it than that."

Maddie squeezed her eyes shut on a pang of sympathy for her little sister. It was very likely that Emily was right. If there was one thing they'd both learned growing up with Loretta Case, it was that relationships don't last.

With a shake of her head, Maddie reached down and grabbed the pack of tissues from Emily and pulled one out. Then she turned and put a hand under Emily's chin and gently wiped the tears from her sister's eyes.

"No matter what happens, Em, you'll be okay," she said softly.

Then Maddie had to wipe away her own tears when her sister took her hand in hers and whispered back, "We both will."

THREE

ALL of this emotional drama was making her hungry. Maddie's stomach grumbled as she pushed the three files to the edge of her desk so she could eat her sandwich without dripping anything on them. She didn't want to ruin her appetite by giving too much thought to the stain Emily had discovered in Jeff's car, but it *was* possible that Jeff had been eating in his Mercedes and got something on the seat. Of course, that didn't explain why the spot was in the passenger seat . . . but Maddie really didn't want to go there.

She raised her ham-and-Brie sandwich to her mouth and was about to take a bite when those damned bells tied to the front door jangled again.

"I should have locked the dang thing," she muttered under her breath as she put down her sandwich and pasted her best "no, of course you're not bothering me" look on her face.

A short woman with plain features and blond hair approached the opening above Maddie's desk. She had on a soft, coral-colored outfit and looked vaguely familiar, but Maddie couldn't place her.

"How can I help you?" Maddie asked.

"Is Lillian here?" the woman asked hesitantly, leaning back on her heels as though Maddie might suddenly reach out and slap her.

"No. I'm sorry, she's not," Maddie answered. "She'll be gone all day today. Could I make you an appointment for Monday?"

The woman looked down at her shoes. "I don't think so," she mumbled. "Monday will be too late."

Well, that sounded ominous. "Is there something I could do?" Maddie asked, doing her best to look nonthreatening so as not to scare the woman off.

When the blonde raised her head, Maddie was surprised to see that she had beautiful brown eyes that were as large and soft as a doe's. "Have you worked here long?" she asked.

"About six months. That seems long these days," Maddie answered with a smile.

"Yes, people just don't stick things out very long anymore, do they?" The woman's answering smile was kind and a bit sad.

Maddie tried not to think of her own half-year marriage. It was too depressing to know she'd gotten voted off the island, so to speak, in such a short time. Fortunately, the woman didn't seem to need any more encouragement from her. Instead, she tilted her pixielike face and asked, "Would you give me your honest opinion about something?"

Oh God, Maddie thought, holding back a sigh. *Not again.*

She rubbed her left temple. "Sure," she said.

"It's my boyfriend," the blonde confided. "He's been distant lately. He won't return my phone calls and he's acting sort of . . . secretive, I guess. Do you think he's getting ready to break up with me?"

Was there something in the water around here? Did the warm salt air rust men's abilities to bond with women in Naples? Maddie scowled.

Why did relationships have to be so painful? Was everyone cursed to have the person he or she loved not feel the same way in return?

And would she be doing this woman a favor by telling her what she really thought, or would it just make things worse?

As the silence lengthened, the blonde standing across from her seemed to crumple in on herself protectively. Before Maddie could figure out what to say, the woman nodded once, closed her eyes, and then opened them again, her posture clearly conveying her defeat.

"That's what I thought," she said in a quietly dignified tone of voice. "I should trust my instincts. Rick's avoiding me because he doesn't want the confrontation. He's hoping I'll just go away." She closed her eyes again and shook her head. "You know, it's funny. For a divorce lawyer, you'd think he'd be more comfortable with conflict."

Maddie wished there was something she could say. Lillian was always quick to point out that there were no rules in relationships, that each couple was unique in the way they progressed on the commitment continuum and in how they faced challenges. But Maddie had overheard Lillian telling more than one client that if a guy stopped calling, very often he was trying to tell her good-bye without actually saying it.

Despite the male-bashing movement she'd come to age with in the late nineties, Maddie didn't believe that men avoided confrontation because they didn't care enough to bother having that final conversation. On the contrary, she felt that they simply didn't like hurting a woman's feelings. Which was also why a guy might ask for a woman's phone number and then never call her. It was easier to reject a woman in absentia than to tell her face-to-face, "Don't bother giving me your number. I'm not into you enough to call."

And now she knew how they felt. The look on the blond woman's face was enough to make Maddie want to cry, and she wasn't even the reason for her pain.

"Maybe that's not it at all," she suggested, unable to stand the silence any longer.

"No. You're right. He's trying to end it." The woman swallowed and drew in a deep, steadying breath, and Maddie wanted to point out that *she* hadn't been the one to draw that conclusion, but she didn't. Instead, she watched the blonde walk to the door, her shoulders stooped in defeat.

At the door, the woman stopped. Before turning to Maddie, she straightened her shoulders, as if readying for battle. Her brown eyes were filled with determination as she looked back at Maddie. "Thank you for telling me the truth," she said. "I needed to hear it."

And then she was gone.

Maddie took a halfhearted bite of her sandwich and pulled her files toward her again. Could this day get any more depressing? Wasn't Valentine's Day supposed to be full of hope and the promise of romance? Instead, all it did was highlight the shortcomings of relationships—the constant worry that someone will stop loving you if you don't look like a model, that the person you love the most will betray you with someone else, that you'll be abandoned and alone, discarded and left to fend for yourself like a chick with a broken wing.

And having grown up on a chicken farm, Maddie knew what would happen to that chick if it wasn't taken away from the flock and nurtured—it would get pecked to death by the hardier, healthier chickens.

If that wasn't a metaphor for relationships, Maddie didn't know what was.

She pushed her sandwich away, her appetite completely ruined by the thought of dead chickens.

"Might as well get back to work," she said to herself as she opened the top file on her desk. First, she'd make a list of all the final details she needed to take care of for each of the three proposals this evening. Then she'd tackle each remaining item one by one.

She looked down at the file and felt her stomach clench around the little bit of lunch she'd had.

"Nooo," she howled. It couldn't be.

Maddie rubbed her eyes and looked again. There it was, in full color. A picture of the blonde who had just left, standing on the beach next to a darkly handsome man who had his arm thrown over her shoulders. Lillian asked her clients to bring in a picture of themselves with their significant others so she could visualize the couples together. This one showed Cleo Sumner and her boyfriend, Rick Watson, who had secretly planned to propose this evening after alighting from a fairytale carriage to ask for his beloved's hand in marriage.

And because Maddie hadn't told Cleo to give Rick the benefit of the doubt, she could only guess what Cleo was going to say on live TV.

A big fat *no way*.

Maddie was so screwed.

When she saw a flash of coral from across the street, she grabbed her purse from the bottom drawer of her desk and raced outside. She had to catch Cleo, had to tell her that she'd been wrong, that her boyfriend was just preoccupied right now and to give him some time. Maddie hurriedly locked the door to Rules of Engagement before turning to look for Cleo.

There she was. Two blocks down, about to go into a two-story stucco building painted the color of a school bus.

Maddie dodged the tourists who were lazily strolling down the sidewalk, intent on nothing more strenuous than lightening their pocketbooks at the various high-end clothing and art shops lining the street. She raced across the road, ignoring the startled looks from the drivers unaccustomed to pedestrians who didn't use the crosswalks.

She entered the building Cleo had walked into a few minutes before and stood in the lobby, panting. There was an insurance agency on one side of the lobby and a bank on the other. Maddie pressed her nose against the window of the bank, searching for a telltale glint of coral. When she didn't see anything, she checked out the insurance agency and was similarly disappointed.

Cleo must have gone upstairs.

Maddie didn't bother with the elevator, taking the stairs two at a time instead. There was only one business on the second floor, Maddie discovered, a family law office with the name "Watson, Seaver & Goldberg" stenciled in large black letters on the wooden front door. She pulled open the door and stood blinking in the doorway for a moment, trying to get her bearings. Directly in front of her was a woman seated behind an oak desk, wearing a headset over her thick red hair. Maddie didn't see Cleo here in the waiting area, so she craned her neck to look down the hall and gasped when she saw her prey disappearing around a corner.

She had to stop Cleo from talking to Rick Watson, but first she would have to get the receptionist to buzz her into the inner office.

"Can I help you?" the receptionist asked with a plastic smile.

"I need to see Rick Watson," Maddie said.

"I'm sorry. He's in a meeting right now."

The receptionist didn't offer an alternative, like making an appointment for later or seeing another attorney, but Maddie didn't have time to give the other woman customer service tips. "How about Mr. Goldberg? Is he free?" Maddie asked desperately.

The other woman glanced at something on her desk before nodding. "Yes. Mr. Goldberg is free. What's your name? I'll tell him you're here."

"Madison Case. Thank you," Maddie added, shifting her weight impatiently from one foot to the other while the heels of her black pumps dug into the plush carpeting.

The receptionist seemed to take forever relaying Maddie's name to the attorney and getting the okay to buzz her in, but finally Maddie heard a click as the lock to the inner office slid free.

"You can go on in," the redhead said. "Take a right and then your first left. Mr. Goldberg's office will be to your left."

Maddie nodded and yanked open the door. Cleo had gone down the hallway to the left, not the right, so Maddie pretended to follow the receptionist's directions and then hunkered down, turned around, and scuttled back the other way, ignoring the curious glances of people in the offices she passed. Once she rounded the corner where Cleo had disappeared, Maddie straightened up.

There was no sign of Cleo in the hall.

Cautiously, Maddie approached the first office on her right and peered in through the half-open blinds covering the slim window next to the closed door. The office appeared to be empty, so Maddie moved on to the next one and then the next. When she reached the end of the hall, she turned the corner and stopped. Cleo was standing in the middle of the hallway, her hand clapped over her mouth as she stared at something Maddie couldn't see.

Maddie dashed down the hall past what appeared to be a conference room with floor-to-ceiling windows separating it from the hallway. The blinds on the inside of the conference room were closed, making it impossible to see who or what might be sheltered inside.

"Cleo, what is it?" Maddie asked, worried about the pale green tinge of the blonde's skin.

Cleo didn't ask what Maddie was doing here. Instead, she seemed to be in shock, her large brown eyes open even wider than before. She waved a limp hand toward the conference room and whispered, "Rick," right before her eyes rolled back in her head and she toppled to the floor.

FOUR

MADDIE stood blinking over the fallen woman. She'd never seen anyone faint before. What was she supposed to do?

"Help," she squeaked and then realized how ineffectual she sounded.

Come on, Maddie, get a grip, she told herself. She shook her head to clear it and stepped over Cleo's body to grab the conference room door. When she pushed it open, she realized what had made Cleo faint.

Rick Watson sat at the head of the conference table, his eyes glued to the chest of the beautiful brunette sitting next to him as she casually buttoned her wildly patterned blouse over her voluptuous breasts. Cleo must have spotted the couple through a gap in the blinds.

"Help!" Maddie said loudly, making both Rick and the woman jerk their heads toward her.

Rick Watson stood up, his tanned cheeks coloring with two spots of bright pink. "What's going on?" he asked.

"Cleo fainted."

Rick pushed his chair back and hurried across the room. When he saw his girlfriend lying in the hall, he crouched down and put his face near hers. "Cleo? Are you all right?" he asked.

The blonde's eyelids fluttered when another door opened up down the hall. Maddie stood there, feeling like the supporting actor in some daytime drama as she wrung her hands and looked on helplessly.

"Maddie? What are you doing here?"

Maddie's head jerked toward the sound of the familiar voice. Her ex-husband, Dr. Jeffrey Allen Prescott, was standing just down the hall, his dark eyebrows running together to form a thick uni-brow as he frowned at her. Looked like Dr. Jeff, as he preferred to be addressed by his patients, was overdue for his Botox injection. Not that he really needed one. At forty-two, Jeff Prescott's lightly tanned skin was still unmarred by wrinkles. His dark brown hair was likewise devoid of gray, his waist still trim, and his hips still lean.

The truth was, while his physical perfection had impressed Maddie, it had also made her nervous. She always felt she couldn't quite measure up.

And apparently, *American Model*'s viewers had agreed.

Maddie grimaced and shoved that thought away. "What are you doing here?" she asked instead.

Before Jeff could answer, a shorter man with close-cropped sandy brown hair and the bluest eyes Maddie had ever seen pushed past her ex-husband and strode purposefully down the hall. She immediately recognized him as Scott Seaver, Jeff's divorce attorney.

Maddie's stomach dropped to the floor.

No.

This could only mean one thing. Emily's fears about her marriage being over were true.

Feeling a bit woozy herself, Maddie leaned back against the wall behind her and sucked in a deep breath. How could Jeff call it quits again so soon? Did he have no sense of loyalty? Or, worse, was he planning to leave Emily for the same reason he'd left her—to use their breakup as a way to boost ratings for his reality show?

Scott and Rick slowly helped the semi-conscious Cleo to her feet, with Scott waving away other offers of assistance from the curious office staff who had gathered to watch the show.

"I've got her," Rick said, and Scott let go of the blonde's arm and stepped back. Then he turned to Maddie and smiled.

"Don't you go fainting on us too," he said, his voice full of amusement.

Maddie wrapped her arms around herself and pushed away from the wall. "I'm fine," she assured him.

"Can I get you a glass of water or something? You drink Sprite, right?" Scott asked, making her blink with surprise. She hadn't expected him to remember her from the divorce, much less recall what she drank. It had been nearly a year ago now since she and Jeff had said "I don't" on the courthouse steps.

"Yes, but no. I mean, no, thank you. I'm fine," she said, feeling flustered without knowing why her ex's lawyer was having that effect on her.

"Maddie, I need to talk to you," Jeff said.

Huh. Funny. She'd forgotten all about Jeff for a moment. Now, worry for her sister came rushing back and Maddie frowned as she turned to see her brother-in-law standing a few feet away. The door to the conference room had been closed again, and Rick was leading Cleo away, presumably to his office, where he could attempt to explain away what his girlfriend had just witnessed. Maddie didn't even want to think about what this was going to mean for this evening's event.

Maybe she could find another couple to stand in for Rick and Cleo. They didn't even have to really mean it. When you boiled it down, this whole Marry-Me Marathon was just a publicity stunt for Rules of Engagement. Heck, maybe she could hire actors to play the part of the happy couple.

"You can't tell Emily about this," Jeff said urgently, grabbing her arm and squeezing it.

Maddie scowled up at him and jerked her arm out of his grasp. "Are you kidding? She's my sister. I'm not going to let her be blindsided like I was."

"This isn't the same thing," Jeff said.

"Yeah, right. Like I believe that." Maddie pursed her lips. Boy, he must really think she was stupid. She'd admit she hadn't been on her toes enough (or some might say, distrusting enough) to have read Jeff's behavior correctly during their brief marriage. She'd voiced her concerns about their lack of intimacy several times, but Jeff had assured her that nothing was wrong. And she'd been dumb enough to believe him. But that wasn't going to happen again. She had learned her lesson.

Jeff ran a hand through his hair with frustration. "Fine. Do what you want. I planned to tell her about this tonight anyway."

Maddie felt as if her ex-husband had punched her in the gut and struggled to draw in a breath. Jeff was going to ask Emily for a divorce on her birthday? How could he be so cruel?

"No," she whispered, her heart breaking all over again at the thought of what her sister was going to be put through.

"I have to," Jeff said. He sounded miserable, but Maddie knew how phony it all was. That was the purpose of his entire existence—to make things appear different from what they really were. Well, she'd had enough of his fake emotions, his need to pretend things were beautiful when, in fact, they were downright ugly.

Fury as thick and hot as the south Florida air in August welled up inside her. "What the hell is wrong with you? Why do you have this sick compulsion to ruin the lives of every woman you marry?" she asked, the words barely making it out through her clenched teeth.

But Jeff didn't give her the satisfaction of a response. Instead, he just shook his head and said, "It will all be clear by the end of tonight." Then the conference room door opened and the brunette stepped out into the hallway. She casually said good-bye to Scott Seaver and smiled at Jeff, who nodded once more to Maddie and then, with the other woman at his side, walked toward the exit.

Maddie had to clamp her hands together to stop from running after her ex-husband and wringing his neck like the emotional chicken he was.

"I'm not at liberty to discuss your ex-husband's issues with you, but I can tell you that things aren't always what they appear to be," Jeff's divorce lawyer said.

Maddie turned to find the attorney leaning against the doorjamb of his office, his arms crossed over his broad chest. He was wearing a pair of dark blue slacks and a light blue oxford shirt that had somehow managed to make it through half the day without getting wrinkled. A blue-red-and-white tie with a nautical theme was looped around his neck, and Maddie assumed his missing suit jacket was hanging somewhere in his office. She had never seen Scott Seaver in anything but a suit and tie, which was a nice change from the business casual trend that had swept the nation, leaving an ocean of rumpled khakis and polo shirts in its wake.

Maddie thought it was a shame—even the most unattractive man looked better in a crisply pressed suit.

And Scott Seaver wasn't remotely unattractive. Too bad he was in bed with the enemy, so to speak.

"I'm not going to let that man put my sister through the same hell I went through," Maddie said.

Scott at least had the decency to look chagrined, his eyes full of compassion as he pushed away from the doorway and took a step toward her. "I understand," he said. "I watched that episode of *American Model* and know it must have hurt to have your personal life exposed like that on national TV. But can you really say you were surprised? You may not remember this, but I was invited to several social functions you and Jeff also attended. You were supposed to be newlyweds, but I never once saw him touch you. Didn't that strike you as odd?"

Maddie felt the blood drain from her face and took a step backward, away from her ex's attorney.

That was a lie. Her marriage had not been a sham from the very beginning. It had been fine until, in a last-ditch effort to boost ratings, Jeff had come up with a plan to increase viewership. Clearly, he hadn't loved her enough not to sacrifice her for the good of the show when the situation became dire, but he hadn't neglected her all along. She hadn't been that desperate to be in a relationship that she'd put up with that.

Had she?

"My marriage is none of your business," Maddie barely managed to croak out.

Scott frowned and took another step toward her, reaching out one hand beseechingly. "I'm sor—"

Maddie cut him off, backing away as she saw Cleo Sumner exit her boyfriend's office and head down the hall toward the exit. "Forget it," she said with a shake of her head. "It doesn't matter. It's over."

She didn't wait to hear what Scott might say next. Instead, she bolted for the door, leaving her ex's attorney—and memories of her failed marriage—behind.

"Is everything okay?" she asked, following Cleo down the stairs and out into the sunshine.

The blonde turned and smiled at Maddie. "Everything's fine," Cleo said.

Maddie hated to bring this up, but . . . "Um, what about that scene in the conference room?" she asked. "That woman was clearly buttoning up her blouse when I walked in."

Cleo's tinkling laugh had a musical sound to it, and her eyes were bright with amusement as she answered, "She had just finished breastfeeding. Rick said she's a client of his, and he was shocked when she, as he put it, 'whipped it out,' but what could he do? He went on with their meeting and tried not to stare."

Maddie's sigh of relief was drowned out by a passing car. "That's great! I mean, not great that he was trying not to stare but . . . You know what I mean."

"Yes. I do. Listen, thanks for your advice. I really do appreciate it."

"Obviously, I should have kept my mouth shut," Maddie said, shaking her head at her own misguided attempt at advising someone else about love. Like she knew anything about the subject.

"I guess it's like Lillian says. There really are no rules that apply to every situation." Cleo nodded sagely, as if she had learned a valuable lesson from this afternoon's events. So had Maddie—stick to what you know, and leave the "Dear Abby" crap to someone who has a clue what she's talking about.

But she didn't say that to Cleo. No sense pointing out how badly her advice sucked.

Cleo turned and started off down the sidewalk, saying over her shoulder, "Thanks again. I'll see you tonight at the Valentine's Day party."

Maddie waved before taking off in the other direction. Cleo still didn't know that Rick intended to propose this evening. She thought they were simply attending a costume party dressed as Cinderella and Prince Charming. Little did she know that as he alighted from his fairytale carriage, Rick would get down on one knee and slide a glass slipper on her foot before slipping an equally impressively diamond ring on her finger.

Ah, how very romantic.

Maddie smiled to herself as she unlocked the door to Rules of Engagement, ducking out of the way when a woman carrying a baby in one of those heavy-looking carriers waddled awkwardly by on the sidewalk.

Maddie waited until the woman passed before pulling open the door and stepping inside the air-conditioned office. She was halfway to her desk when she stopped suddenly and gasped as if all the oxygen had been sucked out of the room.

She wheezed in a lungful of air and stared unseeingly into the waiting area.

"Nooooo," she wailed, trying to block the vision of her ex-husband and the brunette walking down the hallway together at the attorneys' office.

Rick Watson had told his girlfriend that the brunette was buttoning up her blouse after breast-feeding. But if that were true . . . then where was the baby?

FIVE

MADDIE didn't know what to do. How do you tell your sister that her husband's birthday present is a batch of newly inked divorce papers? Or tell a perfect stranger that her boyfriend is a liar and a cheat?

Would it be better if she just kept her mouth shut and let the situations resolve themselves?

Would her relationship with Jeff have turned out differently if someone had told her early on that they suspected he didn't love her? Hadn't she known deep down—though she hated to admit it—that something was wrong between them right from the start? And what did that say about her? Had her relationship failed because she'd gone into it for the wrong reasons?

When Jeff had proposed, she'd told herself that she loved him, but had she just been lying to herself to get the life he offered, a life that looked so perfect on the outside that Maddie had been prepared to pay any price—even marrying a man who didn't love her—to have it?

And had her sister done the same thing? Is that why Jeff was so unhappy that he was filing for divorce again so soon?

It would be so easy to point the finger at him, to blame Jeff and his fickle nature for this entire mess. But was it really all his fault? If Emily had married him for the same reasons Maddie had, then they were both to blame for the disaster that had befallen them.

Maddie sighed wearily and blew a stray curl out of her eyes.

"You have a lot to answer for, Mom," she muttered as she reached for the phone. No matter who was at fault here, she couldn't let Emily go into tonight's battle unprepared. She had to warn her sister what was coming.

She dialed Emily's cell phone number and left a brief message when she was forwarded to voicemail. No way was Maddie going to leave her sister a voicemail that her husband was going to ask her for a divorce. That would be like breaking up with someone via e-mail—very tacky.

Then, just as she hung up, her phone rang.

"Hello," she answered, wishing for a half-hour of uninterrupted peace.

"Maddie, it's Lillian. Are you okay?"

Maddie straightened her shoulders and tried to inject a cheerfulness she didn't feel into her voice. "Yes, I'm fine. How are things on your end?"

"Everything's great here. The Channel Two camera crew is already here setting up for the first proposal at six. The house looks gorgeous. The florist outdid herself, and the caterer is amazing. I'm so excited about our engagement party," Lillian gushed. "This is going to mean so much to our business."

Maddie felt her shoulders slump. Lillian Bryson always sounded so freaking cheerful. During the six months she'd worked for her, Maddie couldn't recall ever seeing Lillian down. Either her boss was a really good actor, or she had a never-ending supply of happy pills that Maddie wouldn't mind dipping into today.

Did she mention that she hated Valentine's Day?

Maddie closed her eyes and thought about the three proposals that were to occur this evening. First, Guy Bromley was going to sail up and pirate Denise Clay away on his sailboat after popping the question. Then, at 6:30, Rick Watson was scheduled to drive up in his horse-drawn carriage and slide the glass slipper on Cleo Sumner's foot. Finally, at seven, Noah Oxford would end the Marry-Me Marathon by delivering his engagement ring tied around an authentic-looking playbill to his girlfriend, an aspiring actor named Ally Adina.

It had all been choreographed down to the smallest detail. There was no room for any deviation in the schedule, and if she were to tell Cleo Sumner about the make-believe baby her boyfriend had conjured up, they had no way to fill the gap in tonight's program. Which meant the Channel 2 news team might start digging to find out what had happened, and that would only lead to bad publicity for Rules of Engagement.

Maddie had no choice but to keep Rick Watson's lie a secret . . . for this evening, at least.

After assuring Lillian that everything was under control, Maddie hung up the phone and studied her "to do" list. She went down the list, making sure everything she'd crossed off had indeed been taken care of. When she was done, she looked at her watch, surprised that she was actually on schedule. She only had one more errand to run—picking up Noah Oxford's playbills from the printer.

She had just finished congratulating herself on her superior organizational skills when the shrill ring of the telephone interrupted her again. If she were Catholic, she would have crossed herself before picking up the receiver. It didn't take a genius to realize that she had brought a curse upon herself by celebrating victory before she had crossed the finish line.

Divine intervention was the only thing that could save her now.

"Hullo?" Maddie said hesitantly into the phone.

"Is Lillian there? This is Noah Oxford."

Maddie closed her eyes and sent up a silent prayer to whatever deity might be listening. "Uh, no. She's not. This is her assistant. Can I help you?"

The man on the other end of the line let out one long breath, like a balloon that was being drained of its air by an exuberant child. "I don't have an engagement ring," he said finally, as if admitting to having strangled his own grandmother.

"What?" Maddie gasped. "You were supposed to have bought that a week ago."

"I know. I just . . . I had to wait for payday. I don't have a lot of extra cash right now and I thought . . . maybe I could do the proposal without a ring?"

Maddie closed her eyes and rubbed her aching forehead. "No. No, no, no. The ring is the most important thing. When a woman tells people she's engaged, that's the first thing they want to see." Maddie knew this from experience. Everyone had *oohed* and *aahed* over the one-carat platinum ring Jeff had given her. Even now, she refused to stop wearing it because it proved that, at least once in her life, someone had wanted her enough to marry her.

Maddie sighed and stared down at the twinkling diamond on her finger.

How freaking depressing was that? Perhaps it was time she took the thing off. She didn't need proof of her own self-worth. Maybe what she really needed was some quality time on a shrink's couch.

But enough about her.

"Do you have the money now?" she asked, cringing when she realized that her "extra" time was quickly being flushed down the drain.

"A little. How will I know what to get? I've never done this before," Noah said. He sounded as depressed as she felt.

Maddie pursed her lips in thought. She had to help. It was clear he couldn't handle this on his own. She'd just have to call the printer and see if they could stay open a little late for her. "Meet me at Gold's Jewelers on Sunshine Parkway in ten minutes. Can you do that?"

"I'll be there," Noah said determinedly.

Maddie hung up the phone and swiveled around in her chair to find the number for the printer. When the bells on the front door jangled, she seriously considered throwing herself under the desk and hiding.

"I'm sorry. I didn't mean to taunt you," she mumbled, glancing heavenward.

"Pardon me?" Scott Seaver asked as he came to a stop across from her desk. He had unbuttoned his cuffs and rolled his shirtsleeves up to his forearms, which were larger and more tanned than Maddie would have expected. But it was his bright blue eyes that mesmerized her, and it was only when he smiled and the dimples next to his mouth deepened that she realized she was staring.

She shook her head and then pushed away an errant curl that had stuck to her lip gloss. "Nothing. What can I do for you?" The occasional lapse into idiocy notwithstanding, she really did try to maintain a professional image.

"I came here to apologize," Scott said. "I didn't mean to be so hard on you earlier. I . . ." He cleared his throat and then rubbed his chin, looking uncomfortable. Then he glanced down at her with those hypnotic eyes of his, and Maddie shivered at the intensity of his gaze. "I was surprised to see you today. I had it all rehearsed, what I'd say when I talked to you again, only my speech went out of my head when I stepped out into the hall and saw you there."

Maddie felt her jaw drop open, but she couldn't seem to summon the will to close her mouth. Or to speak.

What could her ex-husband's divorce lawyer have to say to her?

Maddie was glad she was sitting down when she found out the answer to this question. She didn't think her legs would have supported her if she'd been standing.

Scott leaned forward and rested his elbows on the windowsill above her desk. She felt like a deer watching the headlights of a Ford F150 barreling toward her. She knew she should do something—blink or run or something—but the light was so hypnotic she couldn't move.

"Do you remember the black tie ball you attended with Jeff on New Year's Eve? The one at the Lowenstein's house on the Gulf?"

Maddie nodded almost imperceptibly, not wanting to break the spell he had over her.

"You were wearing a red dress that sparkled whenever you moved, and you had tiny red butterflies pinned up in your hair. You couldn't have been married more than a month or two at the most, and I remember thinking, *Who's the lucky guy who gets to watch her hair spill over her shoulders when he takes out all those pins?* I watched you standing there with a glass of champagne in your hand, looking a little lost and searching the crowd for someone. I was so tempted to walk up to you and try to make you forget that other man, but then you smiled and I just stood there, watching you watch that phony prick Jeff Prescott approach.

"And when he got to your side, I waited for him to do what I would have done—to lean down and brush his hand over the soft skin on the back of your neck and whisper in your ear to tell you how beautiful you looked that night. But that didn't happen. Know what he did instead?"

Maddie pulled her bottom lip into her mouth and shook her head, the skin at the back of her neck tingling as if Scott were actually touching her.

Scott's voice was low and menacing as he continued. "He didn't do anything. He barely even glanced at you, and I stood there and watched your smile turn as fake as the breasts your ex-husband installs at five thousand bucks a pop. And I hated that you thought so little of yourself that you settled for that. You had to know he didn't love you. He couldn't treat you like that if he did."

Blinking back tears, Maddie tried to push away the memory of that night. Somehow, she had managed to convince herself that her marriage had ended on the set of *American Model* when the viewing public decided she wasn't good enough for Jeff. She couldn't let herself believe that their relationship had been dead all along.

"I have to admit, I was happy to get Prescott's divorce case," Scott continued when Maddie remained silent. "I wanted him to set you free. He never deserved you, Maddie, and I've been waiting almost a year to ask—"

Maddie gasped and nearly fell off her chair when the phone rang.

SIX

MADDIE glanced at the clock and groaned. She was supposed to be meeting with Noah at the jeweler right now. He must be calling to ask where she was.

"I have to get this," she said.

Only, it wasn't Noah. It was the printer. They were closing in fifteen minutes. And no, they couldn't deliver the playbills on such short notice. Didn't she know it was Valentine's Day? All the extra delivery people in town were busy delivering flowers and chocolates and plush teddy bears to people other than her.

Maddie tossed the phone down and nearly howled with frustration. She wanted—no, needed—to know what Scott had waited nearly a year to ask her. But she also wanted—no, needed—to keep her job.

"I've got to go," she said, not knowing how in the world she was going to help Noah buy a ring and also be at the printer's at the same time, but knowing she had to at least try.

"Is there something I can do to help?" Scott surprised her by asking.

Maddie blinked. "Help?" she repeated dumbly as if she'd never heard the word before.

Scott smiled. "Yeah. Help. Four-letter word meaning 'to assist.' "

"Are you sure? I mean, I hate to impose . . ." But she hated even more to screw up the evening's final proposal . . .

Scott shrugged and stuck his hands into his front pockets. "What can I do?"

Maddie scribbled down the address and phone number of the print shop, which was only a few blocks from the house where the Rules of Engagement party would start in less than an hour. "Could you pick up a box of playbills here and bring them to 111 Gulf Coast Lane by six o'clock?"

"Sure," Scott said good-naturedly, and Maddie had to stop herself from throwing her arms around him in gratitude.

Instead, she stood up and grabbed her purse. She had to take care of Noah first.

Scott followed her to the door, leaning close to push it open before she could do it herself. Goose bumps tickled her skin as Scott's warmth seeped into her back and she inhaled his clean scent. Boy, did he smell good.

She paused on the sidewalk, awkwardly staring down at a blob of green gum stuck to the concrete. "Thanks for helping me out," she said, hating that she sounded like a nervous teenager. "I'll see you in half an hour or so. And, uh, feel free to stay for the party tonight. It should be fun."

Scott chuckled and reached out to put a hand under her chin, the touch of his strong fingers on her skin making her shiver. "I'm looking forward to it," he said.

Maddie stared up at him. "Me, too," she breathed. Then she swallowed and tried to sound casual when she spoke again. "By the way, what was it you were going to ask me?"

He leaned down, stopping with his lips just a whisper from hers. Maddie felt her own lips part, as if they were taking the decision to kiss him away from her, and Scott closed the gap between them. But to Maddie's disappointment, he only brushed his mouth against hers in the briefest of kisses before he lifted his head again, grinned at her, and said, "I've waited this long. Another hour won't kill me."

Then he gave Maddie a jaunty backward wave as he turned the corner and disappeared from sight.

WHEN Noah Oxford said he only had two hundred and fifty dollars to buy an engagement ring, the jeweler in the posh jewelry store quickly covered his gasp of horror with a fake cough.

Maddie pushed her fingers through her unruly brown hair and tried to make the best of it. "I'm certain we can find something nice in that price range. Simple is very chic these days," she said.

The jeweler cleared his throat. "Yes. We do have a few things that might work."

Noah, a tall, slim young man with skin the color of a thoroughbred, a dark brown afro, and green eyes that rivaled Emily's for their beauty, didn't appear comforted by their assurances. Both his hands were stuffed in the front pockets of his jeans, his elbows tucked tightly against his waist.

"Ally's not the type to get caught up in material things," he said, sounding defensive.

"I'm sure she's not," Maddie hastened to agree. She couldn't have her groom balking about his proposal now.

"We have some lovely silver rings over here," the jeweler suggested smoothly. From behind the counter, he unlocked a case and pulled out two rings—the only items in the store worth less than a grand, Maddie guessed. He put the rings on a royal blue mat and arranged them artfully.

Maddie craned her neck to look at the rings. One appeared to be a set of intertwining vines that looped over and then back on one another, and the other had some sort of flower engraved around the band.

She turned to Noah. "The vines are nice. Sort of symbolic, don't you think?"

Noah appeared to be chewing the inside of his left cheek. "Yeah," he said finally. "That could work. How much is it?"

The jeweler flipped over the tiny white tag attached to the ring. Maddie had never understood why jewelry stores couldn't use tags people could actually read. Probably worried their customers would have heart attacks from sticker shock.

"It's three hundred," the jeweler announced, as if that were a bargain.

Noah was already shaking his head. "I only have two-fifty."

The jeweler pursed his lips and flicked the price tag of the other ring over with the nail of his index finger. "This one is $229.99. With tax, that should be about right."

Maddie watched Noah's cheeks color, but she wasn't sure if he was embarrassed or angry. Poor kid. She knew from Ally's file that Noah worked full-time at a local coffee shop and probably made minimum wage. That didn't leave much extra for savings or extravagances like fancy engagement rings.

"That one's pretty, too," she said.

Noah frowned unenthusiastically. "You're sure I need a ring?" he asked.

Maddie considered the question for a moment and then nodded. She wished she could give Noah a different answer, but the truth was, everyone wanted to see the ring when a woman announced that she was engaged. The playbills Noah had requested be printed up for his aspiring actor girlfriend were nice, but that wasn't exactly the sort of thing that would impress Ally's girlfriends or family.

"All right. I'll take it," Noah said, pulling his hands from his pockets along with a wad of cash.

Maddie breathed a sigh of relief.

That was it. The last detail, taken care of. Maddie took a deep breath and mentally braced herself for the ordeal ahead. It was time, she thought. Let the Marry-Me Marathon begin.

SEVEN

THE house Lillian had commandeered for Rules of Engagement's Valentine's Day party was on the same street as the home Maddie had shared with Jeff during their brief marriage. Maddie glanced up at the faux-Mediterranean monstrosity as she drove by, though most of the view was obscured by thick green foliage planted there to keep curious onlookers at bay. As the host of *American Model*, Jeff had his share of groupies—the usual assortment of rabid fans, creepy stalkers, and hopeful contestants who prayed that free makeovers would change their lives.

The show had certainly changed Maddie's life, although the makeover had gone to her sister instead of her.

Maddie half-smiled at herself in the rearview mirror. Through the miracle of genetics, she had managed to come out of the womb with no significant defects. Yes, by today's perfection-obsessed standards, she could probably benefit from a tummy tuck (or, if one were to go about it the old-fashioned way, a few months of hard work on the Ab Lounge), but her nose wasn't too large, her eyes too small, or her thighs or butt too saggy. Emily, on the other hand, hadn't fared quite so well—maybe because she and Maddie had different fathers or perhaps because their mother had given up all hope of dating a nice man by the time she got pregnant with Em and had chosen instead to eat every Hostess snack cake unlucky enough to come within arms' reach. No matter the cause, Emily's flaws were the kind no amount of working out would fix: a weak chin, jutting overbite, a nose that leaned to the right, drooping eyelids, heavy saddlebags on her thighs, and tiny blips of breasts that only served to make her bottom half look even more misshapen.

Was it any wonder that her newly gorgeous sister felt insecure about being able to keep her husband's affections? Outwardly, she may look like a model, but inside, Emily was still the chubby girl in junior high who once had a boy tell her, "You shouldn't have turned around. You aren't so ugly from the back."

Maddie pressed down on the accelerator of her car and sped past her ex-husband's house. Maybe Emily would be better off if Jeff *did* divorce her. Maybe she could find someone who had never known the "before" Emily and wouldn't treat her as though he were doing her a favor by being with her.

Maddie wasn't certain whether Emily felt grateful for Jeff's affections or if she was simply projecting her own feelings onto her sister, but she knew she had wanted so much to believe that Jeff had loved her, because if someone like Jeff—someone handsome, successful, and popular—cared for her, then maybe she was okay after all.

And if she had been lying to herself about that, if she knew Jeff had never really loved her, then that meant she *wasn't* okay and never had been. Maddie squeezed her eyes shut as the truth of what Scott had said to her earlier jabbed at her like a dozen tiny needles.

Preoccupied, she drove through the wrought-iron gates guarding the mansion where tonight's festivities were being held. The gates had been flung open welcomingly, and the two-story, ten-thousand-square-foot home of one of Lillian's former clients beckoned.

Maddie sat in her car, looking up at the house for a long moment, coming to terms with the naked truth. She had always known Jeff hadn't loved her. Even worse, she hadn't loved him, either. When they met, she had been at a crossroads. She hadn't known what she wanted to do with her life but knew she wanted it to change. And, in all truth, she had been looking for someone to come in and rescue her from the one thing she was certain she didn't want—to remain stuck where she was. That's why she'd been so quick to say yes when Jeff proposed; not because she believed they were in love, but because she saw what she thought would be an easy way out of her old life.

Ugh. She'd been like freaking Cinderella, crying and moaning about her miserable life until Prince Charming came along to save her.

Only Emily was hardly the ugly stepsister (at least not any longer), and she'd stolen Maddie's prince right out from under her. But maybe that's what really happened after that whole "and they all lived happily ever after" bullshit was said and done. Maybe what Cinderella really needed was to stop sitting around waiting for the prince to save her and get off her ass and change her own life herself.

Maddie chuckled wryly at her reflection in the rearview mirror. "Well, come on Princess Charming, you've got three fairy-tale proposals to orchestrate tonight," she muttered to herself as she flung open her car door.

That much she could handle. The happy ending part was someone else's department.

"ARE you sure this swimsuit looks okay?" Denise Clay asked for what had to be the ninety-sixth time.

Maddie made a big show out of considering the view from all angles. Truth was, the suit looked as good as it possibly could on a fifty-three-year-old woman with a fondness for piña coladas and an aversion to exercise. She handed Denise the matching pareo to wrap around her waist.

"It's very flattering," she said.

Denise twisted around to check out her rear view and then sighed. "Why didn't I start Pilates last month when Lillian mentioned this party?"

Maddie had no answer as to why it is human nature to resist doing what we know we should do. Besides, she figured it was a rhetorical question, so she remained silent as Denise wrapped the black silky fabric around her waist and tied it in a knot at the side. To complete her outfit, her hopeful fiancé-to-be, Guy Bromley, had asked Maddie to provide Denise with a red hibiscus flower to wear in her hair. Maddie hadn't trusted that it would stay put if Denise simply tucked the stem behind her ear, so she'd asked the florist to rig it to a barrette instead.

When Maddie pulled the plastic container containing the flower out of her tote bag and handed it to Denise, the older woman smiled with a faraway look in her eyes.

"Did Guy put you up to this?" she asked.

Because the proposal was still a surprise, Maddie had to be careful not to give too much away when she answered, "Yes. When I was coordinating costumes for this evening's party and he told me he wanted you two to come as beach bums, he asked if I would get you a red hibiscus flower for your hair. I never asked why. Is there something special about it?"

Denise turned back to the mirror and carefully clipped the large flower above her right ear. "We had our first kiss under a hibiscus tree. It was funny, because we were both trying to act cool about the way we were feeling. Guy's marriage was on the rocks, and so was mine, and we'd both been so unhappy for such a long time. When we met, it was like . . . I don't know how to describe it. Neither of us was looking for someone else, not really. We both tried to resist it at first, but—" Denise stopped, her cheeks turning the same color as the flower clipped to her hair as she laughed. "Well, okay, maybe we didn't try all that hard to resist it. But we certainly weren't looking for anything long term. Even now, I don't think Guy ever wants to get married again. His ex-wife really did a number on him."

Maddie blinked innocently at the other woman and kept her mouth shut.

"Anyway," Denise continued, thankfully not paying much attention to Maddie. "We just felt this instant connection when we met. And that first time we kissed, it was like . . ."

"Magic?" Maddie supplied helpfully when Denise paused.

Denise snorted. "Panty-melting hot is what I was thinking." She shook her head and laid one hand on Maddie's shoulder. "Girl, magic is for kids. I want passion, not a pedestal."

Maddie chuckled and nodded toward the flower in Denise's hair. "It looks like that's what Guy wants, too."

Denise smiled as she fingered the flower petals. "That's enough for me," she said, with just a hint of wistfulness in her voice that told Maddie she wasn't exactly telling the whole truth.

"As long as you're clear about your expectations," Maddie said, ushering Denise out of the guest room she had used to change into her swimsuit.

"I'm only coming to Rules of Engagement to be sure I don't do anything to drive Guy away," Denise reassured her. "I don't expect him to marry me."

"Hmm," Maddie answered noncommittally.

"Where is he, by the way? He said he'd meet me here at six o'clock. I hope he's not going to be late. I feel silly enough wearing this swimsuit as part of our costume. I'd hate to be the only one waddling around in swimwear tonight."

Maddie glanced at her watch. It was 5:55. The Channel 2 camera crew was already set up out on the beach, ostensibly to film footage of the party for this evening's news. As she steered Denise toward the open doors leading to the patio and out to the beach beyond, Maddie squinted at a sailboat that was slowly approaching from the south.

Please, let that be Guy, she prayed.

"I'm sure he's on his way," Maddie said, crossing her fingers for luck. She caught Lillian's eye as she and Denise stepped out onto the patio and felt cheered by the smile and enthusiastic thumbs-up signal her boss sent her. Maddie took a deep breath and looked out to sea again. The boat was indeed approaching.

"Why don't we get you a drink while we wait for him?" Maddie suggested, waving toward the tiki hut that had been set up on the beach.

"Great idea," Denise said and made a beeline for the thatched roof.

Maddie followed at a more leisurely pace, watching the sailboat out of the corner of her eye as she plodded through the white sand in her totally inappropriate black pumps. She should have worn sandals, but she hadn't thought about her own attire this evening. It wasn't like anyone was here to see her.

She turned her head toward the Gulf and inhaled a lungful of heavy salt air. That was one thing she missed about living on the water. She loved the sound of the surf. Something about it soothed her; perhaps the constant crash of water against sand drowned out the sound of her own thoughts.

Maddie turned to find Denise halfway through a fruity rum punch.

"Want to go dip your toes in the surf?" Maddie asked, in part to get Denise away from the lure of the tiki hut, and in part to get her first fiancée-to-be in place for Guy's surprise proposal.

Denise sipped another quarter of her drink through the double straws the bartender had put in her cup. "Just a sec. I'm going to get another one of these," she said.

Maddie grimaced at Denise's back as the older woman slurped up the rest of her rum punch, but then she told herself to relax. Everything would be fine. A drink or two wouldn't be enough to get their client drunk.

"I'm ready," Denise said as she returned with another cup full of pink liquid.

They ambled down to where the waves splashed onto the shore, not far from the edge of the succulent green lawn that surrounded the mansion they were using for tonight's party.

Maddie surreptitiously watched the camera crew trailing them at a slow crawl, so as not to arouse Denise's suspicions. When they drew level with the sailboat that had finally anchored just outside the channel markers about ten feet offshore, Maddie stopped and took a deep breath. Okay. It was show time.

She heard a splash and nonchalantly sidestepped so Denise would have to turn away from the Gulf to continue facing her.

"So if you and Guy ever did get married, where would you like to go on your honeymoon?" Maddie asked as casually as she could, when she really wanted to dance from foot to foot in anticipation of what was to come.

"Alaska," Denise answered.

That surprised Maddie out of her preoccupation with listening for the sound of Guy's rowboat brushing the sandy bottom of the Gulf of Mexico. "What? I thought you and Guy were the tropical types," she said.

Denise took a sip of her drink and leaned forward, as if she were about to confess a secret. "Guy is, but I'm not. I'm from Seattle and only moved to Naples after that ill-fated bareboat cruise in the British Virgin Islands with my ex-husband. I'm only here temporarily. I like more moderate weather, and I don't think I could consider anywhere but Seattle home."

Maddie sucked her breath in through her clenched teeth. Oh, no. What if Guy and Denise hadn't talked over this issue yet? What if he proposed and she said, "I'll marry you . . . if you agree to come live with me in Washington State?"

"Does Guy know this?" she asked with a sense of dread.

"No, but—"

Both Maddie and Denise turned around when something heavy splashed into the water behind them. Denise gasped and Maddie closed her eyes, praying this wouldn't end in disaster.

Guy Bromley, a burly man in his mid-sixties with a graying beard and matching gray eyes, stood behind them, knee-deep in the Gulf. He had rolled up his khaki pant legs, and his brightly colored Aloha shirt hung untucked around his thickening waist.

Maddie knew there was nothing she could do now. It was too late. So she took Denise's drink from the other woman's nerveless fingers, stepped back so she wouldn't interfere with the camera crew, and helplessly watched from the sidelines as fate took over from here.

Guy held out his left hand and smiled.

Please, don't let them get bitten by a hungry shark, Maddie prayed.

A stunned Denise reached out and took Guy's hand, her own finger shaking.

Don't let them talk about where they're going to live, Maddie continued praying.

"Denise, when we met, I had come to believe that love and I were doomed to be like two ships passing in the night; sometimes close by, sometimes distant, but never destined to meet."

Please don't let him go overboard—no pun intended—on the nautical stuff, Maddie added. If one is going to pray, one might as well ask for everything one wants, she figured.

"But from the moment I first laid eyes on you, I knew that my curse was over. You and I, we may have charted different courses to our destination, but I see now that we're both heading toward that same guiding light."

Hey, two out of three wasn't bad, right? Maddie clutched Denise's sweating cup in her hands and wished she had a drink of her own to calm her nerves.

"And as we continue on our journey, I'd like it to be clear to you and to everyone else that this skipper has found his true lifelong first mate. Denise Clay," Guy continued, dropping down on one knee and getting soaked up to his waist, "will you marry me?"

At that, Guy held out an oyster and steadied himself as a wave crashed into his lower back, threatening to topple him over.

Maddie frowned. What the hell was he giving her an oyster for? Some symbol that his lust for her would never die, because oysters were purported to be an aphrodisiac? Maddie had never bought that one. Oysters were slimy and had made her gag the few times she'd been peer-pressured into trying one. *Yeah, nothing says sexy like the ol' gag reflex.*

Fortunately, Denise wasn't as clueless as Maddie obviously was. She pried the oyster shell apart and gasped at the pearl-and-diamond engagement ring nestled inside.

Holding tightly to the ring, she kneeled down in the water and threw her arms around Guy's neck with a delighted squeal. "Yes, Guy, I will marry you," she said as their lips met.

"How romantic," Maddie murmured and then realized that somehow Denise's pareo had come untied and was floating away with the tide. If she hadn't known how uncomfortable Denise would be without something covering her bottom half, Maddie would have just let it float away. But as it was, she had to rescue it.

Hurriedly, she toed off her shoes and set Denise's drink down in the sand as she trotted down the beach after the slip of black fabric. It was easy enough to catch because the waves washed it nearly onshore half a dozen feet from the still-embracing couple, and Maddie only had to get her feet and ankles wet as she snatched the pareo from the hungry grasp of the Gulf.

She held the dripping garment away from herself as she stood, ankle deep in the surf, and turned around. The setting sun blinded her for a moment, and she squinted against its warm rays. She blinked several times and looked down at the water to get her sight back.

At that moment, Guy and Denise stood up, both of them soaked from the waist down. Denise shifted as the sand beneath her toes disappeared in the surf and then shrieked when her new fiancé breathed in a horrified gasp, jerked the pareo out of Maddie's hands, and wrapped the black fabric around her like a shroud.

EIGHT

"YOU lied!"

Denise's accusation echoed in Maddie's head as she stood in the wet sand, gaping at the other woman's quickly retreating backside, which, fortunately, was still covered by her black wrap. It was clear Denise thought Guy had seen her without her pareo and been disgusted by the sight of her in a swimsuit.

Maddie closed her eyes and bit back a moan.

"I'm sorry," Guy said from beside her, sounding as miserable as Maddie felt.

"It's not your fault," she reassured him. It wasn't her fault either, but that didn't make her feel any better.

The camerawoman nearest the shore cleared her throat to get Maddie's attention. "Don't worry, we'll cut out that last bit," she said, sounding as though she were choking on her mirth.

"It's not funny," Maddie scolded, but the camerawoman just chuckled.

"I didn't know what else to do," Guy said as he waded onto the beach and started wringing saltwater from his pant legs.

Maddie also stepped out of the water onto the beach and grimaced when she realized her wet pantyhose acted like a magnet to the dry sand. "You did the right thing," she said. What else could he have done? She cringed at the remembered sight of Denise rising up out of the Gulf, the bottom half of her swimsuit transparent where it had been touched by the water. Who in the hell made swimsuits that were see-through when they got wet?

Probably some fancy designer who charged a thousand bucks a suit and expected the women who bought his swimwear to drape themselves artfully on lounge chairs around the pool and never actually get wet.

Too bad Denise didn't know Guy had done her a favor by covering her up. And now he had a choice: either tell her she had, in effect, just flashed everyone on the local news team and subject her to horrifying embarrassment, or continue to let her believe he thought she looked terrible in a swimsuit now that she'd put on a few extra pounds.

"I can't tell her the truth," Guy said dejectedly.

"But if you don't, she'll think you don't find her attractive," Maddie countered.

Both Guy and Maddie sighed in unison. He was caught between a painful truth and an equally hurtful lie.

"What should I do?" Guy asked.

Maddie chewed the inside of her cheek for a moment. She didn't have any answers. She was in the same situation herself with Cleo Sumner, potential bride number two in this evening's festivities. It would be easy for her to just keep her mouth shut about the nonexistent baby Rick Watson had conjured up in his tale to Cleo this afternoon. If Maddie didn't say anything, the proposal would go off without a hitch and no one need ever know that Rick had lied. But by telling Cleo the truth, would she potentially ruin a relationship that was solid, other than this one transgression? And who was she to say what had really gone on in that conference room? Wouldn't it be better to let Cleo figure out for herself that Rick was a cheating bastard?

Maddie took a deep breath and released it.

No. She knew she was just trying to convince herself to keep quiet because it was the easy thing to do. She had to tell Cleo what she suspected.

"I think you should tell her the truth," Maddie said, turning to Guy and reaching out to squeeze his arm. "She'll be mortified at first, but at least then she'll know you're not ashamed of how she looks."

Guy nodded but didn't look very happy about what he had to do. "Yeah, I guess it's always best to tell the truth. No matter how hard it might be."

Maddie glanced up at the mansion where Cleo Sumner was getting ready for her own Prince Charming to arrive in his horse-drawn carriage. And now Maddie was going to have to tell her that her fiancé-to-be had a particular talent for weaving fairy tales of his own.

Maddie swooped down and picked up her sand-encrusted shoes and the drink cup she'd discarded earlier.

She was beginning to hate this job.

"Good luck," she said, as much to herself as to Guy as they parted ways at the edge of the lawn—Maddie to go find Cleo and Guy to come clean with Denise.

Guy, looking glum, headed off into one of the mansion's many pool baths to towel off. Maddie did her best to wipe the sand off her feet and ankles before sliding her toes back into her pumps. Wearing shoes again made her feet feel gritty, hot, and uncomfortably pinched after having had their freedom in the surf for a few moments, but she could hardly run around barefoot.

So she kept her shoes on as she crossed the patio and entered the enormous kitchen of the house, which was abuzz with the caterer and his staff, who were busy refilling trays of hors d'oeuvres to pass among the guests. Maddie snatched a particularly appealing-looking tidbit off a tray as it went gliding by and popped it into her mouth.

"Mmm," she mumbled as the buttery cracker with a cheesy topping practically melted in her mouth. Too bad she couldn't hang out here in the kitchen sampling goodies all night. That sounded much more fun than what was in store for her.

Maddie straightened her shoulders as she pushed open the kitchen door and stepped into the dining room. An enormous champagne fountain dominated the center of a massive mahogany table. Mini-bouquets of red roses and white hydrangeas that had been threaded together with red-and-white ribbons were scattered across the tabletop, making it look as though dozens of brides-to-be had tossed down their bouquets as sacrifices to the champagne gods.

A glass of champagne sure would go down smooth right now. Maddie glanced longingly at the pink-tinted liquid flowing freely from the silver fountain and then jumped when someone beside her spoke.

"I need you to do me a favor," Emily hissed, her fingernails digging into Maddie's arm as she dragged her away from the champagne and into the butler's pantry at the back of the dining room.

Maddie blinked rapidly, surprised by her sister's sudden appearance. She realized at that moment that she hadn't prepared what she would say to Emily when she finally had a chance to talk to her sister. She couldn't exactly blurt out that Jeff wanted a divorce. No, she'd have to find a way to break the news gently. Maybe—

"I want you to have an affair with my husband," Emily announced boldly.

"What?" Maddie wheezed.

"I need you to even the score. My karma is out of balance. That's why things between Jeff and I are so strained, because we can't be at peace until the wrongs we've committed have been set right."

Maddie squinted at the nutjob who used to be her fairly normal sister. "You're crazy," she said, not unsympathetically. This is what relationships did to people—they made sane people go insane.

"No, I mean it," Emily said frantically, and Maddie realized that her sister was crying.

"You're serious, aren't you?" Maddie asked. Then she put her arms around Emily and held her while she sobbed into Maddie's shoulder. "Oh, honey, I'm sorry. I didn't mean to make light of the situation. I just don't think Jeff and I having an affair is the answer." Not to mention that the thought of having sex with her ex gave Maddie the creeps. He was married to her sister, for God's sake.

Maddie shuddered and smoothed Emily's soft brown hair away from her face as her sister looked up at her with watery green eyes. "You really love him, don't you?" she asked.

"Yes. So much that it's making me miserable," Emily said, and two fat tears dribbled down her cheeks and dripped onto the bare skin of her chest above her perky new breasts. She had on a skimpy halter top made entirely of sparkly sequins and held up by thin white spaghetti straps over a pair of silky white pants that clung to her liposucked rear end. Maddie thought she looked beautiful and wished that Emily's new looks would have brought her happiness instead of misery.

Why is it that people tell themselves that if only they were thinner or richer or prettier, they would finally be satisfied? It seemed that whenever someone got what they wanted, they realized it wasn't enough. Happiness had to come from inside, from living well and making good decisions, not from some reflection in the mirror or the size of one's bank account.

Here was Emily, thin and wealthy and pretty for the first time in her life. Only she was driving herself and her husband crazy with her insecurity.

"Emily, you have to stop this," Maddie said, gripping her sister's arms tightly. "You and I, we're even. You didn't take Jeff from me. He left long before that night on the show. He never loved me." Maddie closed her eyes and drew in a deep breath before continuing. "And I never loved him either. I was looking for someone to rescue me and he was convenient. That's all. In a way, you did me a favor by forcing him to make a decision. If you hadn't, we might still be together and still be unhappy. As it is, I'm starting a new life—the new life I should have pursued without waiting for someone else to do it for me," Maddie added.

Emily blinked owlishly at her and remained silent, which Maddie took as an invitation to keep talking.

"You need to stop feeling guilty and get on with your new life. If you don't, you're going to drive Jeff away by spying on him all the time and treating him like he's a criminal. If you really love him, go to him and ask for a second chance. Do it tonight, before it's too late," Maddie added, knowing she didn't have the heart to tell Em about Jeff's visit to the attorney. Maybe it wasn't too late for them. Maybe if Emily went to him and promised to lay off the James Bond routine, maybe Jeff would see that she really loved him.

When Emily started to smile, Maddie knew her job here was done. She gave her sister an encouraging squeeze and then pushed her away. "Go talk to your husband," she said.

Emily paused at the entrance of the butler's pantry and turned around. "Thank you," she whispered.

"You're welcome," Maddie mouthed back, but Emily had already gone.

Maddie leaned back against the granite countertop and wrapped her arms around her waist. She didn't know if Jeff and Emily would make it or not, but if they broke up now, at least it wouldn't be because of her. She had held on to her holier-than-thou attitude long enough, acting as though she were the innocent party in the whole *American Model* fiasco rather than what she truly was—a woman who'd married a guy for all the wrong reasons and should have had the courage to end it instead of playing the martyr for six long months.

Well, she was done doing that. It was time to embrace life, to decide what she wanted and go after it.

Maddie dropped her arms from around her waist and started for the dining room, but stopped short when Scott Seaver ambled into the pantry, blocked the doorway with his broad shoulders, and drawled, "Madison Case, are you trying to put me out of business?"

NINE

MADDIE blinked. "What do you mean?"

"I overheard what you said to your sister. That was very . . . generous of you, considering the part she played in the breakup of your marriage," Scott said.

"Oh. That." Maddie felt herself starting to blush and studied the tile under her feet. "It just didn't seem fair to let her believe that the breakup was her fault. Like you said earlier, it was obvious that Jeff didn't want me right from the start."

"Jeff Prescott is one dumb bastard," Scott said, the mild tone of his voice belying his harsh words.

Surprised, Maddie looked up to find that Scott had taken a step forward and was standing so close she could count the golden lashes rimming his blue eyes. Maddie licked her suddenly dry lips and cleared her throat as a shiver of awareness prickled her skin. She had to change the subject, now, before she forgot that she had a job to do and threw herself into Scott's strong arms. The thought of those arms wrapped around her, his fingers running down her back, his lips—

No. She was not going there.

Maddie backed up a step. "So did you have any trouble at the printer's?"

Scott chuckled as though he could tell exactly what she'd been thinking. "No, Maddie, I didn't. I left your box in the closet beneath the front stairs. It's a nice roomy closet. Would you like to see it?" He cocked his eyebrows suggestively, which made Maddie laugh.

"Maybe later," she said.

"I'll hold you to that," Scott countered and then stepped aside to let her out of the pantry.

"I'm going to be busy for the next hour, but help yourself to some champagne. And thank you for your help. I really appreciate it," Maddie said, forcing herself to walk away from Scott when what she really wanted to do was to take him up on his offer of a private tour of the mansion's closets.

Scott grinned and reached out to tuck a lock of hair behind her ear. "Don't mention it," he said, his grin widening when he noticed the goose bumps on her arms.

Maddie wanted to tell him not to get too cocky, that she'd just caught a chill from the air conditioner, but, of course, that would have been a lie. And she was tired of lying, especially to herself, so, instead, she stood on her tiptoes, pressed a kiss on Scott's surprised lips, and then stood back and said, "Can I mention that I've wanted to do that since the day my divorce was final?"

Without waiting for an answer, Maddie turned and walked out of the room, her own smile widening when she heard Scott mutter, "Hell yeah."

★ ★ ★

MADDIE squelched the butterflies in her stomach as she approached the second-floor guest room Cleo Sumner had been assigned as her dressing room. Maddie knew she was doing the right thing by coming clean with Cleo, but that didn't make the task any easier to face. How did you tell someone that the man who is about to propose to her is a lying cheat?

Maddie took a deep breath and knocked tentatively on the door, almost wishing that Cleo would refuse to answer.

Of course, she didn't.

Instead, the petite blonde pulled open the door and stood in the doorway, looking exactly like the fairy-tale princess she was dressed up to be. Her dress was a sky blue satin with twinkly rhinestone stars studding the skirt, and her hair had been curled into soft waves that floated around her creamy shoulders.

"You look gorgeous," Maddie said.

Cleo dipped her chin and smiled. "Thank you. Would you like to come in?"

Maddie hesitated for just a second. Ugh. She wished she didn't have to be the one to do this. "Um, sure," she said, reluctantly stepping over the threshold.

"Is everything all right?" Cleo asked, obviously sensing her hesitation. "It's not Rick, is it? He said he'd meet me out front at 6:30."

Maddie stopped Cleo with a hand on her arm before she could dash across the room and peek out the window. It was likely that Rick was almost at the gates of the mansion by now.

"No, everything's fine. Well. Sort of. I mean . . . could we sit down for a minute?" Maddie asked, knowing she was bungling this.

Cleo gave her a little frown and waved toward the neatly made bed.

"Go ahead. I can't sit in this dress. It would pouf up around me like a bell if I did."

So Maddie sat while Cleo rested her arms on the back of a chair, which did nothing to ease Maddie's nerves. Neither of them spoke for a long moment as Maddie tried to figure out how to say what she had come to say. Finally, the tension was so great that she just blurted out the truth.

"There was no baby," she announced.

"Pardon me?" Cleo tilted her little pixie head to one side, looking like a kitten that couldn't quite figure out how to get at those cute little goldfish in the aquarium.

"This afternoon, at Rick's office. He said that woman in the conference room had her blouse unbuttoned because she was breastfeeding. But I saw her leave, and there was no baby."

Cleo's gaze slid to the plush beige carpeting beneath their feet. Her pink mouth puckered, as if she had just tasted something sour. After a minute, she looked back up at Maddie, her big brown eyes clear.

"I suspected as much," she said quietly.

Maddie frowned. "You did?"

Cleo walked out from behind the chair, clasping and unclasping her small hands in front of her as she moved. "Yes. But in a few minutes, if I'm not mistaken, Rick Watson is going to ask me to marry him in front of everyone who matters in this city. I'm going to be Mrs. Rick Watson. That's all I've ever wanted," she said dreamily.

"And that's enough for you? Even knowing that he'll probably do something like this again?" Maddie asked with a sick feeling in the pit of her stomach.

Cleo's voice was steely when she answered, "I'd rather have part of his love than none at all."

Maddie had a difficult time not trying to convince Cleo that she was setting herself on a path to heartache. Of course, she thought, other people's mistakes were so easy to spot. Why was it so difficult to recognize your own personal quicksand pits when you were standing at the edge of them, looking down into the sucking mud with one foot on solid ground and the other poised an inch from disaster?

But she knew there was nothing she could say to Cleo that would change her mind. If someone had tried to tell Maddie her marriage to Jeff was going to end in disaster, she would have laughed them off and married him anyway. On the surface, which was all Maddie had wanted to see, Jeff was every woman's dream man. It was only once they'd scratched that surface that it became obvious that they were completely wrong for each other.

If Cleo refused to look beyond the fantasy of being married to Rick, there was nothing Maddie or anyone else could say to convince her that there was a poisoned apple in her palm.

And on the bright side, because Rick was in partnership with Scott, at least Cleo would get to know a good divorce lawyer . . .

Maddie pushed herself up off the bed, went over to the window, and pushed aside the heavy green curtains shielding the room from the cobblestone driveway below. Rick's carriage was in place, just beyond the wrought-iron gates, waiting for the signal from Maddie to make their dramatic entrance once Cleo was standing on the wide front steps at the entrance to the mansion.

Maddie squinted, trying to ascertain whether the rental company had indeed remembered the poop catchers under the rumps of the four white stallions.

Yes, they had. Everything was perfect.

Well, everything except the groom-to-be, that is.

"Okay. Are you ready?" Maddie asked, wishing her conversation with Cleo hadn't left her so dispirited. It seemed that every time she started to believe that relationships weren't completely destructive to the parties involved in them, she was presented with a mountain of evidence to the contrary.

"Let's go," Cleo said. As they approached the doorway, she smiled tentatively up at Maddie. "And don't feel sorry for me. Rick is a good person. If he's cheating on me, it's because I'm not doing a good enough job meeting his needs."

Maddie stood rooted to the spot, unable to believe what she had just heard. What? If Rick was cheating on her, it was Cleo's fault?

"I don't think so," Maddie spluttered, but Cleo was already halfway down the stairs and didn't hear her. By the time she caught up with the other woman, it was too late to say anything more. Rick had obviously seen Cleo come outside and signaled the driver to move ahead.

As the horses' hooves clattered majestically on the cobblestones, Cleo turned to Maddie and said, "Could you just let me enjoy this moment? I know married life isn't always going to be easy. But the proposal, at least, should be perfect."

Maddie sucked in her breath as she came to a halt on the steps beside Cleo, who nearly glowed with happiness as she watched the carriage approach.

"You're ruining my shot," a camerawoman behind Maddie complained, reminding her that Rick's journey down the driveway was being filmed.

Funny that everyone was blaming *her* for ruining the perfection of the moment.

Maddie crossed her arms over her chest and stepped back out of the way. Fine. Cleo was an adult. If she was willing to settle for a half-loved life, that was up to her.

And she did have to give Rick Watson credit. His proposal was certainly grand enough to convince the casual observer that he wanted his bride to feel special.

The carriage Maddie had arranged for was something right out of a fairy tale. It reminded her of the crystallized sugar Easter eggs her mother used to collect, the ones with holes in the ends so you could see through into the egg, which had been decorated like a miniature room in a fancy French castle.

The carriage was painted the same shade of blue as Cleo's dress, with white trim and gold spokes on the wheels. The horses wore matching blue hoods and had blue-and-white blankets with gold tassels thrown over their backs.

As the horses drew to a stop in front of the mansion, the carriage door swung open and even the camerawoman behind Maddie gasped. Rick Watson might be a lying, cheating bastard, but he cut a striking figure as he emerged from the carriage wearing black boots, black breeches, a crisp white shirt, and a sky blue coat with gold buttons and tails. He looked like some sort of nineteenth-century nobleman, which was exactly what he was supposed to look like, but was impressive all the same.

Maddie had to remind herself that he was the villain in this farce when he went down on one knee in front of Cleo and held out a glass slipper that Maddie knew would fit Cleo's foot perfectly. (This wasn't just a gut feeling. Rick had brought in a pair of Cleo's shoes so Maddie could give them to the manufacturer to make the mold. Rick had left nothing to chance.)

Cleo daintily held up her skirt as if she'd practiced the move a thousand times, and Rick slid the blue satin ballet slipper off her right foot. He paused, holding the glass shoe aloft while he gazed deeply into Cleo's eyes.

It was so romantic that even Maddie felt her hard little heart soften.

"Poisoned apple. Wicked Witch. Bad, bad man," she muttered under her breath.

Then Rick did something that tested Maddie's disbelief that true love really existed. The truth was that Rick Watson had cheated on his girlfriend and would most likely do so again and again until her heart was completely broken. And that truth meant that he was not to be trusted, not to be loved. Right?

So when Rick pulled the largest diamond Maddie had ever seen out of the glass slipper, put the shoe down on the steps, and said, "I don't need proof that you're the right woman for me. I already know it in my heart. Cleo Sumner, will you marry me?" Maddie began to think that maybe she didn't know much about love after all . . .

TEN

"**I THINK** things are going well, don't you?"

Maddie glanced disbelievingly at her boss, the ever-cheerful Lillian Bryson, and was tempted to say, "You must be kidding." First, there was the swimsuit fiasco with Denise, and then Maddie had watched Cleo ride off into the sunset with a charming fiend while everyone looked on and cheered. She couldn't wait to see what would happen next.

"Sure," Maddie answered with a helpless shrug.

Lillian patted her on the back. "You're doing a wonderful job, dear. Keep up the good work."

"Uh-huh." Maddie watched as Lillian spied an old friend across the room and raced over to do the hug-hug-kiss-kiss-you-look-great thing. One more proposal to go and then she could have that glass of champagne that had been calling her for the last hour. But maybe she didn't need it. She already felt numb.

"Hey. Are you all right? You look a little pale," Scott said as he came up beside her.

For such a big man, he moved awful quietly, and Maddie had to force herself not to be startled by his sudden reappearance at her side. "I'm fine. Thank you," she said, though she didn't feel fine. She felt heartsick for Cleo, who had a gaping future of unhappiness waiting for her after she said "I do."

"You don't look fine," Scott said. With a concerned look in his eyes, he led her over to a chair and pushed her into it. "Let me get you a glass of water. Stay there."

Maddie blinked at his retreating back, but she obediently remained seated until he returned with a plate full of hors d'oevres and some water. "Here, eat this," he said, pushing the plate at her. Maddie wasn't all that hungry, and there was a sit-down dinner planned for eight o'clock, once the Marry-Me Marathon was over, but she took the plate anyway and nibbled at another one of those heavenly crackers so Scott would stop worrying.

It was nice that he cared.

When she tried to stand up again, Scott stood over her. "Are you sure you're okay? You don't feel dizzy or anything?" he asked.

Maddie laughed despite herself. "Yes, Scott. I'm fine. You can let me get up now."

Scott shook his head. "Sorry, my sister just had a baby, and she spent the last nine months fainting. She had to eat every hour or—wham!—down she went. I guess I got trained to be overprotective." He held out a hand to help her up, but he didn't back away when she stood, so she ended up pressed up against the hard wall of his chest. All things considered, it wasn't a bad place to be. He was firm in all the right places, and Maddie heard his sharp intake of breath as she leaned into him, the better to judge just how firm how really was.

Oh, yeah. He was firm. Very, very firm. And Maddie was flattered.

It had been a long time since a man had responded so enthusiastically to her slightest touch.

"You want to check out that closet now?" Maddie teased, in part because she really did need to get those playbills out and move on to proposal number three, and in part because . . . well, because flirting with Scott made her feel sexy and attractive and just a little bit hopeful that happy endings might really exist.

Scott immediately grabbed her hand and began pulling her toward the front stairs without saying another word. In five seconds flat, Maddie found herself hustled into the roomy front closet, her back pressed up against the wall and her front pressed up against Scott as he claimed her lips with his.

And oh baby, did it feel good.

Her mouth opened under his, and she sucked his tongue into her mouth, filled with a sense of triumph when she heard him groan. He fisted his hands in her hair and pushed her head back, breaking their kiss so he could trail a line of moist, hot kisses down her neck. When he licked the sensitive spot just under her ear where her pulse beat, it was Maddie's turn to groan.

Scott pushed her legs apart with one knee, and Maddie reached up to put her arms around his neck, bringing them even closer. She could feel his erection through her skirt at the juncture of her thighs and was so tempted to pull off her pantyhose and get down to business that she nearly screamed with frustration when Scott put his hands on her shoulders and held her in place as he stepped back to put some distance between them.

She'd never known a man who could get her from zero to panting in under a minute.

"You're working. I know you've got a job to do. I'm sorry," he said.

Huh? "That wasn't your fault. I'm the one who teased you about the closet," Maddie protested.

"But you were just kidding, and I took advantage. I'm sorry," Scott repeated as he took another step back and awkwardly fumbled with the button on her blouse she hadn't even realized he'd unbuttoned.

Maddie raised her hands and covered his large, warm fingers with her own. She wished she could see his eyes in the darkness, wished he could see that she certainly wasn't offended by him taking her up on her offer. As a matter of fact, she felt quite the opposite. She'd forgotten what it was like to feel irresistible.

But she didn't have time to explain how she felt, so instead she said, "Scott, I wanted this at least as much as you did. And I hope this doesn't offend you, but I'd like a lot more of it. Want to meet me back here in about half an hour, when I'm finally off the clock?"

She hoped he could tell that she was smiling in the darkness, and she knew he understood when he laughed and said, "You got it. Scott and Maddie, 7:30 in the closet with the mothballs."

Maddie laughed, too, and then nearly tripped over the box of playbills Scott had brought with him from the printer as she tried to find the light.

"Here, I'll get those," Scott said. Maddie heard him pick up the box just before she yanked open the closet door and found a surprised-looking Lillian standing just outside.

"Oh. Maddie. I was just looking for you," Lillian said.

Maddie felt herself blushing all the way up to her scalp and instinctively looked down at her blouse to be sure it was buttoned up properly at the same time Scott breezed out of the closet with the box of playbills in his hands.

"We were just getting these," he said, smiling at Lillian with such innocence that Maddie herself would have been fooled into believing that nothing suspicious was afoot if she hadn't been in that closet with him just ten seconds ago.

"Well, aren't you the helpful sort," Lillian cooed. "You're just the type of man Maddie needs in her life. What did you say your name was? I'm Lillian Bryson, the owner of Rules of Engagement." Lillian stepped in front of Maddie, put her hand beneath Scott's elbow, and started leading him upstairs where the third of the evening's proposals was to take place.

Maddie trudged behind, listening to Lillian's blatant attempt at matchmaking and hoping Scott wasn't the sort to get frightened away by such things. Lillian believed her role in getting couples to the altar somehow bestowed her with an almost mystical ability to matchmake, yet in the six months Maddie had worked for her, all she'd seen was evidence of Lillian's failures. Lillian's own two sons were fond of reminiscing about the debacles that had resulted from their mother's matchmaking attempts, and Maddie feared that this didn't bode well for her future with Scott.

Well, at least maybe she'd get one night of wall-banging sex out of the deal . . .

As they neared the entrance to the media room where proposal three was to take place, Maddie decided she'd better get to work. She trotted ahead of Scott and Lillian, tried to take the box from Scott's hands, and said, "Okay, I've got it from here. I'll see you guys downstairs in about half an hour."

Scott grinned at her as he held fast to the box. "See you at 7:30. Sharp," he added, with a mischievous twinkle in his eyes.

Maddie tried to stifle her blush but feared she had failed miserably when Lillian winked at her and said, "Now, don't you two disappear after the third proposal. You wouldn't want to miss the dinner and dancing I have planned."

Great. So much for the mind-blowing sex. Maddie doubted Scott would wait around for hours just to get laid, and now Maddie couldn't leave early without Lillian making note of it.

She sighed and gave Scott a half-hearted wave as he and Lillian started back down the hall. *Probably the last I'll see of him,* she thought dejectedly.

She pushed open the heavy door to the media room with her shoulder. The chill air in the room made Maddie shiver, and she set down the box and turned to see if she could find a thermostat. It had to be sixty degrees in here.

When she didn't find a thermostat, she shrugged and kicked the box of playbills out of the way so she could survey the room. It was set up like a mini-theater, with rows of red velvet chairs stair-stepped up from the stage all the way to the door where Maddie was standing. There was a curtain at the front of the room that could be retracted to show movies on the white screen, and entire plays could be enacted on the fifteen-foot-wide stage.

Maddie figured the stage had been built for the children who lived in this mansion. She could recall as a kid putting together shows for the neighborhood parents and charging them each a dime to watch their children fumble though some dreadful dreck that either Maddie or another of the neighbor kids had written.

She snorted, remembering their laughable efforts. Still, it had been a fun way to pass the time in the days before iPods had been invented.

Of course, the kids in this place certainly owned iPods and probably didn't stage their own plays. If their ultra-rich parents wanted entertainment, they most likely sent for Brad Pitt or Julia Roberts. They certainly seemed like they could afford it.

Maddie shook her head and turned back to the box of playbills. She was supposed to put one on each seat before Noah Oxford came in to do his one-man, one-act play for his girlfriend, Ally.

She ripped the tape off the top of the box and was about to pull out one of the playbills, curious to read what was inside since Lillian had taken care of getting the content from Noah, when she heard a curious noise and paused. When she didn't hear anything, she picked up one of the playbills and started to flip it open.

Then she spun around.

She'd heard it again. A sort of snuffling sound, like a small animal sniffing for food.

"Hello?" Maddie called out, hoping to scare away whatever it was. She wasn't up to dealing with vermin this evening, not on top of everything else.

The snuffling stopped, but Maddie heard another sound, this one decidedly human.

"Go away," a woman said.

But Maddie needed this room, so, of course, she couldn't just go away. The third proposal was set to start in five minutes. Instead, she clattered down the stairs toward the stage and found a young woman sitting cross-legged behind the heavy velvet curtain, her head buried in her hands.

"Is something wrong?" Maddie asked and then felt her shoulders sag with defeat when the woman looked up at her with tear-soaked eyes. It was Ally Adina, bride-to-be number three. And to put it bluntly, she looked like she'd been backed over twice with a Mack truck.

"No. Nothing's wrong," Ally lied.

Right.

Maddie turned her back to Ally, put her palms down on the hardwood floor, and pushed herself up onto the stage. She sat there quietly for a moment, her legs swinging like a kid in a too-large chair.

After a long silence, she turned her head to find Ally watching her. Of the three Rules of Engagement clients getting engaged this evening, Ally was by far the most beautiful. She had rich dark skin and eyes so brown they were almost black. Her cheekbones were high and her long black hair was up in some elaborate style that Maddie envied.

Most days, Maddie did nothing with her hair except pat it down with a little gel and hope for the best.

And aside from being gorgeous, Ally had something more. Call it charisma or strength of character or star quality or whatever—Ally had "it."

But whatever Ally had, it didn't seem to be making her very happy, so Maddie asked again, "What's wrong?"

"You're Maddie, right? From Rules of Engagement?" Ally asked.

It didn't surprise Maddie that Ally didn't know her. The clients spent most of their time with Lillian, not with her. "Yes," she answered and then waited patiently for Ally to tell her what was going on.

She didn't have to wait long.

"Noah dumped me," Ally said.

Maddie's head jerked toward the other woman. "What?"

"He said he couldn't go through with it. Said he knew I was gonna be a star and that he wasn't good enough for me. After all the years we've been together, he thinks his bank balance is more important to me than his kindness, his strength?" Ally's voice was so clear, her emotions so true, that Maddie winced with the pain she felt just listening to the younger woman.

She also winced because she suspected that she had unwittingly played a part in this tragedy. "What happened, exactly?" she asked.

"I got here early, even though the invitation said I was to arrive at seven. I don't like to be late. Sometimes, during casting calls, they close the doors if you're not there early. No way am I going to miss out on a part due to my own laziness," Ally said.

Maddie waited to see where this was going.

"Noah was already here, pacing the stage. I thought that was odd. I mean, he told me we were supposed to watch a movie and then go to a party, but nobody else was here. So I asked him what was going on, and he said, 'I can't do this. You deserve better than me.' Then he handed me this ring and walked away." Ally held out the silver ring Maddie had helped Noah pick out earlier.

Maddie closed her eyes and sighed. What had she done?

Then she opened her eyes and faced the truth. She had told a man who loved a woman that the price of the ring was more important than anything else. That's what she'd done.

It was no wonder she had never found happiness in a relationship. How could she, when she *expected* them to be miserable and shallow and unfulfilling? As with most things in life, you get what you think you deserve. And now, her self-fulfilling prophecy had poisoned someone else's chance at happiness.

Maddie raised her hand to push her hair out of her face and realized she was still holding the playbill. She set it down on the stage and then looked down when it flopped open to the middle. Her eyes scanned the text—a plot summary of the play Noah had planned to act out this evening during his proposal.

When she finished reading, she looked up at Ally, who sat quietly crying a few feet away. Maddie knew she had to do something to fix this. Noah was ten times the man she had believed him to be, only she had convinced him he wasn't good enough simply because he had different priorities than saving for some stupid ring.

This was all her fault for underestimating the power of true love. She had gotten so caught up with the outward appearances of what people thought love should look like and in trying to make each of tonight's proposals look perfect on camera that she had forgotten what was truly important—each couple's love for one another.

Maddie picked the playbill up off the stage and hopped down with it clutched to her chest.

"Don't worry, Ally," she said as she started up the stairs. "I'm going to bring Noah back to you."

ELEVEN

AS Maddie burst out of the media room, she ran straight into the camera crew that was supposed to film the third proposal.

"I'm sorry, but there's going to be a slight delay in this last proposal," she said without admitting that the groom-to-be had run off. She only hoped Noah hadn't left yet. If he had, the delay might be indefinite.

"Guys, come quick! Dr. Prescott just grabbed the microphone and said he wants to make an announcement," a woman called from down the hall before the lead camerawoman could respond to Maddie.

Maddie's eyes narrowed. Damn. What was Jeff doing?

No. It didn't matter. She didn't have time to find out what Jeff was up to. She had a groom to catch.

But as she hurried down the stairs behind the camera crew, she heard someone murmur, "He's going to do the same thing he did with her sister—dump her on live TV."

Maddie's steps slowed as the words sank in.

It couldn't be. Surely Jeff wouldn't humiliate Emily the same way he'd done to her. He couldn't be that cruel.

Or could he?

Maddie squeezed her eyes shut against the memory of the night Jeff had asked her to come to the filming of the *American Model* season finale. He'd never invited her to the set before, and Maddie had hoped he was trying to repair their strained marriage by including her in his work.

When she had arrived on the set, Jeff's assistant took her to a special viewing area he claimed was for VIPs. Later, Maddie realized that she'd been set up—that the "special viewing area" was actually part of the show.

They had kept Emily's makeover a secret, and Maddie could still remember being stunned when a gorgeous woman walked onstage near the mid-point of the show and it was revealed that this beautiful creature was her sister. Then Emily walked to the room where Maddie was watching and the sisters embraced. It had all seemed very touching until Maddie figured out that the moment had been orchestrated in advance and that she was the only one who didn't know what was coming next.

That was the point in the show where Emily revealed her secret. She and Jeff had fallen in love, and it was up to the viewing public to decide if Maddie's husband should stay with her or leave her for her sister. Maddie had been too stunned to do anything but sit and stare in openmouthed shock.

And now, as she searched the crowd for her sister, her heart squeezed when she saw Emily looking up at Jeff with the same stunned expression on her face.

No way was she going to let her ex-husband do this again.

Maddie started forward with a low growl. She'd had it. The Case women's history of being cursed by love was just that: history. Maddie was through watching her and her sister settle for substandard relationships because they had been led to believe they shouldn't expect anything better for themselves.

Their mother was wrong. True love *did* exist. Maddie had just seen it firsthand with Noah and Ally. Her sister loved Jeff, and if he thought he was going to dump her just because she was a little neurotic and insecure . . . Well, Maddie wasn't going to let him do it.

She skirted the crowd that had gathered in the mansion's living room to hear Jeff's speech. She was going to get that mike out of his hands if it was the last thing she ever did.

"I made a huge mistake about a year ago by leaving my former wife for her sister," Jeff began.

Maddie scowled as she caught the sight of the camera crew eagerly filming this scene out of the corner of her eye. It figured that Jeff would want to announce his intention to divorce Emily in a public way. Wouldn't want to keep private matters private like any normal person would do.

Maybe his ratings were flagging again and this was just another publicity stunt to increase interest in the show.

Maddie started to push through the murmuring crowd but stopped when someone clamped a strong hand on her upper arm and hauled her back. Maddie turned to find Scott holding on to her and hissed, "Let me go."

Scott didn't relax his grip. "Hold up a minute. I think you need to hear what Jeff has to say."

"I know what he's going to say. I was there in your office this afternoon, remember? He's going to ask my sister for a divorce."

"That's the truth," Scott said and then added, "but not the whole truth."

"What do you mean?" Maddie asked, still trying in vain to tug her arm out of Scott's firm grip.

"Just listen. I promise you'll thank me when he's done."

Maddie considered stomping her foot down on Scott's instep until he leaned down and whispered, "Trust me," in her ear. She tensed for a moment and then relaxed.

Scott nodded with satisfaction, and they both turned their attention back to Maddie's ex-husband.

"It was a mistake because now my relationship is built on nothing but lies. You see, I fell in love with Emily while we were getting to know each other during the filming of *American Model*, and I should have done the right thing and divorced her sister right away. Instead, I let myself get talked into using both Emily and Maddie to boost ratings on the show. That was a huge mistake, one I will regret until the day I die. I lied to Maddie by staying married to her when I knew I loved Emily, and I lied to Emily when I told her that I would go along with whatever decision the viewers chose for me. In truth, the voting was rigged all along. I insisted that Emily had to be the winner, but for the sake of good drama, I let her believe that the choice was not mine to make. This only made her think that she wasn't good enough for me to fight for—that I would never go against what the viewers wanted—when the truth is, even if the vote had come in against her, I would have picked her anyway.

"Because of this, my marriage started off all wrong. My wife is constantly afraid that I'm cheating on her and doesn't realize that I only have eyes for her. But our relationship, one that is built on a foundation of lies and insecurity and mistrust, is hurting us both. I can't help but wonder that if it hadn't started off in such a dubious way, we might be happy.

"I feel that if we could just start over again, Emily would come to find out how much I truly love her."

At this point, Jeff held out his hand and Maddie watched tearfully as her sister allowed her husband to pull her up onto the raised dais Lillian had had set up in the cavernous living room for the band that was to play later in the evening.

When Jeff lowered himself down on one knee, Maddie stood on her tiptoes to get a better view, barely noticing that Scott's hold on her arm had become steadying rather than restricting.

"That's why I have to do this, Emily. Because I love you and want our relationship to have a fighting chance. So, Emily Prescott, will you please divorce me so that we can make a clean start?"

Maddie sniffled as Emily threw her arms around her husband's neck and kissed him. Her response was muffled as she buried her nose in Jeff's shoulder, but Maddie was able to make out a muted, "Yes, I will."

"Well?" Scott cleared his throat and said, moving his hand up to squeeze the back of her neck.

Maddie blinked back the tears that had gathered in her eyes. "You were right. Thank you for stopping me from interfering."

"It's okay. Your heart was in the right place." Scott smiled down at her and gave her another squeeze.

"Was it?" Maddie asked quietly. "I'm not so sure it was."

"How about now?" Scott's voice was serious, as if he understood that something inside her had shifted and would never be the same again.

Maddie reached up and took Scott's hand, their gazes locked as she slowly placed his palm over her heart and let it rest there for a long moment. Then she smiled up at him. "Yes. It's in the right place now," she said.

Scott opened his mouth to say something but was interrupted when Noah Oxford marched into the living room, pointed a finger at Maddie, and announced, "I'm not letting Ally go. I may not have the money right now to buy her a fancy diamond ring, but I love her, and that's all that matters."

He stood there panting, his chin stuck out belligerently as if he expected Maddie to argue.

"Good," Maddie said and handed him the playbill she hadn't realized until that moment that she was still clutching in her left hand. "Be sure you show her this. It will mean more to her than any stupid ring."

And as she held out the playbill, Maddie's own engagement ring from Jeff winked at her in the reflection from the lights overhead. She shook her head and let go of Scott's hand. She didn't need this anymore, not as a reminder that someone had once wanted her. She was okay—as a matter of fact, she was *perfect*—without it.

Maddie wiggled the ring off her finger and handed it, along with the playbill, to Noah. "Here, take this. Think of it as my wedding gift to you."

Noah looked at the ring for a long time, as if he didn't want to accept it, so Maddie pushed it into his hands and said, "Please. I'd be honored if you'd take it."

Noah's dark green eyes searched hers and must have found the answer he was looking for when he nodded abruptly. "Thank you," he said.

"You're welcome. I think Ally's still up in the media room. She'll be delighted to see you."

Noah nodded again, palmed the ring, took the playbill, and then ran up the stairs to claim his true love.

"What was that all about?" Scott asked after Noah had disappeared.

"Instead of saving for a ring, Noah put all his money into tuition for Ally at the New York School of Drama. Rather than buying the woman he loved some silly diamond, Noah funded her dreams instead."

Scott chuckled. "Yep. Sounds like true love to me."

"That's exactly what I thought," Maddie said. Then, because she had been so wrong about so many things that day, Maddie started to wonder what else she might have been mistaken about, so she turned to Scott and asked, "How well do you know your partner, Rick Watson?"

Scott raised his eyebrows questioningly. "Rick? We've known each other since high school. Why?"

"Do you remember this afternoon, when Cleo came to find him and he was in the conference room with another woman?"

"Sure. That was right after my meeting with Jeff ended. And you were there in the hallway, looking as if you'd just seen a ghost."

"Right. Well, when I opened the conference room door, the woman Rick was meeting with was buttoning up her blouse and—"

Scott's sigh was so loud that Maddie turned her head to see if anyone else had heard it. "That's my sister. She just had her first baby and can't seem to understand that the rest of the world doesn't think it's some sort of miracle that she's turned into a dairy factory. She whips those babies out whenever she feels like it."

Maddie didn't quite know how to broach the next subject, but knew she had to ask. "Um, but I saw her leave with Jeff, and there was no baby."

Scott closed his eyes and shook his head. "I know way more about this than I ever wanted to. I'm sure she was pumping. She went back to work last month—she works for your ex, that's probably why they came over to our office together—and she's trying to keep the milk coming in. She's been doing some estate planning with Rick, and it most likely cut into her regular feeding time. I guess she feels that because she's known Rick for years, he wouldn't be embarrassed by watching a one-woman La Leche League show."

Scott rolled his eyes heavenward, and Maddie felt one more nail being removed from love's coffin.

So that left only one more mystery to be solved. What was it that Scott had been waiting almost a year to ask her?

Maddie tilted her chin to look up at him, and he smiled down at her, making her heart jump. "So—" she began, but was interrupted by someone tapping her shoulder.

Maddie frowned and turned her head to find Denise Clay and Guy Bromley looking flushed and disheveled, as if they'd just made good use of the bed in the guest room that had been assigned to Denise as a changing room.

"I'm sorry about accusing you of lying to me about my swimsuit," Denise said, her cheeks pink with either embarrassment or the after-glow of good sex.

"Don't worry about it," Maddie said, more interested in what Scott had to say than in Denise's apology.

"Guy explained the whole thing. I'm just glad to know that he still finds me attractive," Denise continued.

"That I do," Guy said from behind Denise, who yelped in a suspicious manner that suggested Guy had his hands somewhere they shouldn't be.

"I'm happy for you. So then, the wedding's on?" Maddie asked, just to be sure.

"Yep. We're going to set sail for the BVI and get married down in the Caribbean on some strip of sandy beach," Guy said.

"And then for our honeymoon, we're going to Alaska," Denise added happily.

Maddie laughed. It seemed that Guy and Denise had worked everything out. So had Ally and Noah. And Emily and Jeff. And Cleo and Rick were probably okay, too, although Maddie planned to call Cleo at the first opportunity to clear up the mystery about the nonexistent baby.

Which just left Maddie and Scott . . .

Her eyes widened when Scott suddenly put one arm behind her shoulders and another under her knees and picked her up.

"What are you doing?" she squealed as he carried her through the dining room and kitchen before stepping outside onto the patio. The night air was warm, without any of the humidity that would come later in the year, and the sky was filled with hundreds of twinkling stars. From beyond the lawn, Maddie could hear the sound of the surf as it gently lapped at the sand.

Scott didn't answer until he was standing on the beach, far enough away from the mansion that they could barely hear the murmur of the crowd inside. "I've had enough interruptions," he growled into her ear, making Maddie shiver. "Your sister was heading toward us in one direction and your boss was making a beeline for us in another. I'm tired of waiting to be alone with you."

He slowly let her feet slide to the ground, and Maddie found herself swaying in the slight breeze coming in off the Gulf. It was a beautiful night, with the moonlight parting the dark water and the faint sounds of music drifting out from the party.

Scott took one of her hands in his, placed his other hand at the small of her back, and began moving to the rhythm of the music. Maddie sighed from somewhere deep in her soul as she rested her head on his chest. This felt so right, so perfect.

She didn't know how long they remained that way. It could have been just a few moments or it could have been hours before Scott finally spoke.

"You know, I had it on my calendar to call you on the one-year anniversary of your divorce," he said.

Maddie opened her eyes but didn't pull back her head to look at him. "Mmm?" was all she said.

"Yes. You see, I wanted to give you enough time to heal. I didn't want to be someone you dated on the rebound, or someone you were with to get back at your ex. I've seen enough of those relationships end up right back at my office a year or two later, when people realize they got together for all the wrong reasons."

That did make Maddie stop and look up at Scott. "How do you do it?" she asked.

"Well, I usually start like this," Scott said, lowering his mouth to her in a slow kiss that seemed as inexorable as the tide.

When he raised his head again, Maddie had almost forgotten what she had really meant. She chucked him on the arm and said, "Not *that,* silly. I meant, how do you keep your faith in 'forever' when half of marriages end in divorce?"

One corner of Scott's mouth quirked up in a smile. "The other fifty percent keeps me optimistic," he answered.

"Hmm," Maddie said, wondering if it were possible for her to change her perspective just like that. Well, why not? She'd been doing the half-empty thing all her life, and that had landed her in divorce court. Might as well stop being stubborn and give the other side a try for a while. She slid her arms back around Scott's neck and linked her fingers together. "So why were you going to call me on the one-year anniversary of my divorce?" she asked.

Scott put his arms around her waist and pulled her so close she could smell the faint trace of soap he'd used this morning. "Because I think you're really special and I wanted to ask . . ."

Maddie waited for Scott to finish. And waited. And waited.

Finally, she pulled back to look up at him and saw amusement shining out of his blue eyes as he let his arms fall from around her waist and dropped down to one knee in the sand.

Omigod, Maddie thought. He's not going to ask *that?* They barely even knew each other.

"Madison Case," Scott began. "Would you . . ."

Maddie held her breath.

". . . go out with me?" he finished.

Relieved, Maddie laughed and pushed at Scott's shoulders until he fell backward in the sand with Maddie on top of him. She rested her elbows on his chest while he grinned up at her with an unholy light in his eyes that told her he knew exactly what he'd been doing.

"Yes, Scott Seaver, I will go out with you," she said, and then paused dramatically before continuing. "On one condition."

Scott quirked one eyebrow up at her. "Yes?" he said.

"You have to promise me that as long as we're together, you'll tell the truth . . ."

Scott raised his hands to cradle her face in his solid grasp as he added, "The whole truth."

Maddie lowered her head until their foreheads were touching.

"And nothing but the truth," they said in unison.

And then, just as Maddie was about to kiss this man who had thought she was special enough to wait a year for, one who saw the worst part of relationships but still chose to believe the best was possible, he stopped her with her mouth just a breath away from his, looked deep into her eyes, and whispered, "As long as we both shall live."